THE ROAD OF LIES

A NOVEL

MARY PERRINE

A CEDAR POINT STORY

Water's Edge
Publishing, LLC

2024 Water's Edge Publishing, LLC
Copyright © 2024 by Mary Perrine
Cover Painting by Terri Carlson
Cover Design by TC Designs
Published in the United States
by Water's Edge Publishing, LLC, Cologne, MN

PRINTED IN THE UNITED STATES OF AMERICA

REVIEWS

"Mary Perrine weaves a captivating narrative that seamlessly intertwines the lives of disparate characters, each grappling with their own demons and desires. From the atmospheric small town of Cedar Point to the shadowy depths of Carson Springs, the story is expertly crafted with a richly textured world fraught with tension and intrigue."

-Demeteria Head

"The evocative depictions breathed life into the scenes, plunging me into the world of a psychopath whose life was a dangerous game of hide and seek, where deception, secrets, threats, murder, impersonation, and manipulation were her cheat codes, and her end game a twisted mission of vengeance."

-Keith Mbuya

"Perrine is a great storyteller, possessing a wonderful and creative imagination. The well-thought-out plot and lively characters are testimony to that."

-Danielle Petersen

"Perrine's dialogue and characters are vibrant and delightfully twisted, drawing the reader so deeply into the storyline that they will struggle to breathe. Readers will become ensnared in the tumultuous lives of the characters. Opposing forces of good and evil, right and wrong, and acceptance and revenge, drive each character. Their relentless search for answers will lead some to the point of no return."

-Bethany Holmes

DEDICATION

To anyone who is lost,
buy a map
and pick a beautiful place to find yourself.

THE ROAD OF
LIES

A NOVEL

MARY PERRINE

A CEDAR POINT STORY

PROLOGUE

Rebecca Hulls and Terah Dixon were rarely more than a few steps apart. Where one ended, the other began. Born the same day, they were practically joined at the hip from the minute they breathed life. Never had something so unusual transpired in the small town of Carson Springs, Wisconsin.

As different as night and day, Becca and Terah were on opposite ends of a rope, each pulling the other toward their way of thinking. Terah encouraged Becca to be a kinder, gentler person, while Becca coerced Terah into taking chances, to live outside the box of perfection, and walk along the edge of right and wrong. As friends, they needed one another. Yet, at times, they fought more like sisters. While Terah tried to tiptoe around the issues, Becca hit them straight on, driving emotional jabs into her best friend for holding back.

The girls were homeschooled following the ways of *Life Vision*, a religious sect that created their own *Life Vision* bible. Members were expected to live by every word. Even biblical scholars who studied it and questioned this interpretation were laughed at and repudiated. There was no room for analysis, explanation, or clarification unless it came directly from Andrew Godley, the founder of *Life Vision*. He assigned himself the role of God—judging and punishing those who fell short.

Becca had enormous contempt for the church and their endless list of rules and covenants. When she turned thirteen, after making her troth before the mythical Andrew Godley and

Life Visions, pledging her life to the ways of the church, she had gone home and burned her heavily altered bible. She may have been forced into submission because she was too young to make her own choices, but she was not about to let a group of men control her life.

The first page of the good book held Godley's name, not God's.

The Principles of Life Vision
The Mystical Experiences and Teachings of Andrew Godley
Authority, Obedience, Submission, and Responsibility will lead to everlasting life in heaven.

Page seven was the first time God's name was cited. There was no mention of love, peace, or even hope in this version. Women were to submit and be obedient to the elders and the males of the church. On top of that, every family was held responsible for surrendering forty percent of their income to *Life Visions* and the care of the elders—a group Andrew Godley fell into and oversaw. The remaining money was left to feed, clothe, and house their own family. There was no money for wants or desires.

While Terah was content with her little family, Becca's parents and siblings caused her significant irritation and anger. She begged her mother to leave her father and the church, but the frightened woman stood firm in her decision to follow her husband and live out the doctrine. Many times a day, Becca pushed her resentment down while searching for another way to free her mother and siblings.

The only thing she feared was retaliation from the elders. The sudden disappearance of people who had spoken against one principle or another, the unmarked graves, and the *relocation* of members not in good standing sent chills down her spine. Still, Becca pushed the boundaries.

Terah, on the other hand, was happy and unassuming, loving and accepting of everyone. Except for their hair color, the girls could have been twins: deep blue eyes, turned-up noses, and alabaster skin. But Terah was a blonde, and Becca a brunette.

Becca's constant lashing out made almost everyone steer clear of the pair, leaving them to huddle together away from the rest of the world. According to Becca, the relationship they had forged was damn near perfect in every way but one.

Rebecca Ann Hulls and Terah Marie Dixon didn't actually exist.

CHAPTER ONE

CHIEF BRIAN ENDERLY

Chief Brian Enderly raced into the Cedar Point Police Station. His heart thudded in his chest as he yanked one of the bulletproof glass doors open, nearly tearing it from the hinges. The corner of the door jammed on the uneven sidewalk and remained open.

His administrative assistant jumped at his sudden appearance, nearly dumping the chair she had climbed onto to peek out the transom window. Mauri grabbed the edge of the frame to steady herself as the chair with the missing foot wobbled beneath her.

"Are you trying to kill me?" She climbed down and pushed the chair back in line with the other two.

Brian ignored her reprimand. His head jerked from side to side as he scanned the room before leaning into his empty office and then heading down the hallway.

"Where is she?" His voice cracked like a hormonal teenager. He drew a deep breath and held it for several beats before releasing it loudly. It wasn't every day he had the opportunity to meet someone he didn't even know existed.

Mauri's eyes widened. "She wasn't outside?"

Brian scowled. "Why the hell would she be outside?"

"She said she was going to grab a photo album from her car."

Brian bolted through the still-open door. He scanned Main Street and the police lot. The lunch crowd had dissipated, and other than a handful of adults dropping off their preschoolers for the afternoon session at the Lutheran Church, the street was barren.

A lone car turned at the corner and passed in front of the station. A woman with blonde hair, not so unlike his own, made eye contact but did not slow. His shoulders fell, and a long sigh escaped. Either she had changed her mind about meeting him, or the woman passing by at that precise moment had been nothing more than a coincidence.

Mauri quietly appeared beside him. Her sudden arrival startled him.

"What the hell, Mauri?" He pressed a hand to his chest and bent forward. "You almost gave me a freakin' heart attack. What are you doing?"

Mauri snorted. "Just payin' you back, Boss." She gave the quiet street a once-over. "I take it you didn't find her."

The chief glared at her before reentering the station. He jerked the door closed behind him as he passed through, leaving his assistant on the outside. His brain hummed with thoughts, and his heart ached with frustration.

"Thanks for waiting for me, Boss," Mauri said as she joined him inside the station.

"What color was her hair? Close to mine?" He absently ran a hand through his blonde hair.

Mauri shook her head. "No. It was dark brown, close to black. But it was hard to tell because she wore this huge white floppy hat and crazy big sunglasses."

For the second time, Brian's shoulders fell. Then the woman in the older white CR-V wasn't the person who stopped in—no hat, no sunglasses, and she definitely had blonde hair.

Brian fixed his eyes on the camera in the corner of the station. Mauri followed his stare. He had meant to have it repaired for the past six months, but so little happened in Cedar Point that it always got pushed to the bottom of his to-do list.

"Maybe someone else on Main has a camera." Mauri straightened a stack of papers on her desk, returned them to a file marked *personal*, and shoved it into her bottom drawer.

"Right. And why exactly would they have a camera?" He pursed his lips and stared at her, waiting long enough to make Mauri uncomfortable. "This is Cedar Point. It's not like we're living in Minneapolis. People aren't spending that kind of money to watch Frank stumble out of the Sideline."

"What about somebody's doorbell camera?"

Brian shook his head. "Are you new here? You know as well as I do that most people don't even have a doorbell, let alone a camera."

Mauri disappeared and returned with a Diet Coke. She popped the top and handed it to him. "I guess I assumed after everything that went down two years ago, everyone would have installed them."

"Did you?"

"Yes. Mike put one in last year."

Absently, Brian upended the soda and knocked down more than half of it before retreating into his office.

"Boss, you know you're off today, right?" Mauri folded her arms and leaned her head against the frame of his office door.

His lips pressed into a tight line, and he stared toward the wall opposite his desk. "What did she say to you?" He turned his head toward her. "Exactly"

Mauri shrugged. "Who? The woman?"

"Yes, the woman. Who in the hell did you think I was talking about?"

Mauri ignored his petulance. "All she said was…"

"*Her words*. I want her words, not your interpretation."

She snorted. "Someone got up on the wrong side of the bed this morning." She took a deep breath and did her best to mimic the woman's words. "Hi, I was wondering if Chief Enderly is in."

"And?"

"Give me a minute, would you?" She growled at Brian. "Then I said, "He's off today. Can I help you?" Mauri raised a finger in the air, warning Brian not to say one word. "Oh, darn.

I was hoping to talk to him." She looked at Brian. "That was her."

"I frickin' know that. I'm not an idiot."

"Well…" Mauri hitched her shoulders upward. "So, I told her I would take her name and number, and you would call her."

Brian sat upright. "You got her number?"

Mauri twisted her hands. "No, because…"

"Remind me again why I don't fire your ass," Brian grumbled.

"You know damn well why. You couldn't do this job without me."

Brian rolled his eyes. "Right."

"When she gave me her name…"

"Then you got her name? I mean, other than Wren. What did she say? Exactly."

Mauri looked up and shook her head. "Fine. My name is Wren Brigham Enderly."

"She said it just like that? No other name?" Mauri nodded. "And…"

"I want to punch you so hard right now." Mauri glared at him. "For the record, that was me talking, not her. Now, shut up and let me finish."

Brian held his huge hands out in front of him. "Okay."

"I think I might be the chief…Brian's sister." She pointed a warning finger at Brian. "I told her I would call you and see if you were around. So, I called from your office. When I got back, I told her you were on your way. Then she said she was going out to her car to get a photo album."

"That's it? That's everything she said?"

"Yes. When she didn't come back, I climbed up on the chair to see if I could see her."

Brian's hand shook as he tipped the can upside down and finished the last of the soda. He slammed in on his desk, crushing it beneath his exceptionally large hand.

He twisted his mouth and looked at Mauri. "It's not possible. People who were nothing but a dream don't suddenly exist. This has to be a mistake. Or else someone's messing with me."

He drew a deep breath and launched the can toward the recycling bin. It bounced off the wall and landed a foot from the blue bin. "That's got to be it." He grunted and closed his eyes. "And I know who it is."

"Who? Who would be this cruel?"

"My dad, who else? The great Mack Enderly strikes again." Brian slapped a hand on his desk before standing. "As far as I'm concerned, that bastard can rot in prison. I hope he does." He picked up the can and side-armed it into the bin. "When Jane disappeared, Mack put on one hell of a show feigning he cared about me and my mother, pretending he was all reformed and this really incredible guy. Turns out, he's not only a drunk and a murderer, but he's the world's biggest asshole."

He nearly toppled Mauri as he brushed by her and headed toward the station door. "If anybody else shows up claiming to be some dead person from my past, let Porter deal with them." At the door, he spun around. "And get that damn camera fixed."

"Already called Clark."

Brian climbed into his squad car, flipped a U-turn in the middle of the street, and drove past the Sideline and the Food Mart before heading home. He didn't notice the white CR-V sitting on the street next to the park or the woman with long dark hair behind the wheel watching him.

CHAPTER TWO

BECCA HULLS

Becca watched her *brother* storm from the station, climb into his squad, and run a stop sign on his way out of town. His obvious frustration put a wicked smile on her face. Her grin widened, and her eyes narrowed. It served him right. His entire family had vanished from her life when she was just days old. There would be payback—something Brian would never see coming.

She had spent over a year thinking about referring to Brian as her brother. Did he deserve that title—for a role he had never fulfilled? Anger seized her heart, squeezing it like a ball of clay. Her chest heaved as loud puffs of air filled the car. A low growl escaped with the violent breaths.

Brian had grown up with his biological family. She had not been given that choice. It didn't matter that he had lost his mother when he was eight or that his father had been labeled the town drunk. They were blood. Becca repeatedly slammed her hands against the steering wheel. She would have given anything to have been there. Instead, she drew the short stick, and her adoptive father used it to beat her.

She eased her 2010 white CR-V down the narrow street, badly in need of repaving, slowing to a crawl in front of the oldest brick building in town. Large silver letters proclaimed it to be the Cedar Point Police Department and Jail. Unaware she had come to a complete stop, she jumped when the woman in the car behind her laid on her horn. She poked her middle finger out the window before pressing hard on the gas, racing down the last two blocks long before the increased speed limit sign announced the end of town. Her dark hair was held by an elastic band in a high ponytail that swished against her neck as she picked up speed.

It was mission time. Instead of turning around and heading back toward the lower duplex on Hanley, she followed the highway west, out of Cedar Point.

Her mind buzzed, and the right corner of her mouth slowly lifted. She had gotten the ball rolling. Now, it was time to set the pins. When she was ready, she would deliver the strike that would destroy her birth family. No one deserved it more.

As Becca neared Duluth, the harvest moon glowed orange on the hill above Skyline Drive. With a nearly empty tank, she pulled into the gas station at the edge of the city. Curious about who would be footing the bill for her gas this time, she glanced at the credit card before shoving it into the pump.

"Sandy Larson, you're the winner," she whispered. Then she howled with laughter, knowing this was as close to *winning* as the dead woman would ever get. Eyes glanced toward her. She spun around and stared at the pavement, chastising herself for drawing unwanted attention.

Her stomach growled. It had started complaining before she left Cedar Point, but she was on a mission, which meant avoiding security cameras. Finally giving in to the demands of her angry gut, she pulled on a heavy sweatshirt with large pockets, tucked her ponytail beneath her baseball cap, and went inside for something to eat.

Five minutes later, she exited the store with her arm shoved through the kangaroo pocket, covering the bulge of the five-finger discounted bag of popcorn and a glass bottle of iced tea that had already begun weeping. Why anyone would leave a couple of high school kids in charge of a gas station with constant foot traffic was beyond her. Based on his lack of concern, the boy with the pocked face and the spiked hair probably could have watched her shoplift all day and not outed her. If she were a betting woman, she would guess he and the bitchy-faced girl with the three nose rings and black studded collar robbed the store blind every shift.

Back in the car, she tore the bag open and held it between her thighs. After removing the top from the bottle, she tossed it into the backseat while she took a long swig. Iced tea dribbled down her chin, and she wiped it with the back of her hand. After fishing a flask of vodka from her backpack, Becca dumped a healthy shot into the bottle and swirled the two together before taking a pull. She felt the warmth of the second drink in her empty stomach. By the end of the bottle, her racing mind would slow.

Becca drove along London Road, searching for a shadowy hotel where no one would recognize her. In the past year, she had spent multiple weeks checking out the Twin Ports and surrounding area. The city, often referred to as the *San Francisco of the Midwest* because of its steep hills and water-edged topography, was big enough to hide in plain sight. Still, she could not take a chance of being seen.

Just before Glensheen, a haunted mansion and site of the most well-known Duluth murder, Becca pulled into a mom-and-pop motel that looked like it was nearing demolition. She could see the crane over the top of the three-story building. The shorting-out open sign flashed on and off, and the door hung from a single hinge. Several of the windows were boarded up. Obviously, they were trying to squeeze every penny out of this place before the wrecking ball landed.

Becca had driven through the lot before but had never entertained the idea of staying there. Perhaps the condition of the dumpy motel made it the perfect address to hang her hat for the night. Besides, the people from *her office* wouldn't be caught dead in a place like this. And the likelihood of cameras was virtually nil.

She read the name on the credit card she plucked from the wallet of her Coach purse, a gift Becca had helped herself to when she worked as a personal care assistant for a very wealthy woman who had only months to live. Sadly, or not, the woman had passed earlier than expected—*much earlier*. There were many things the old biddy could not take with her wherever she was headed. Someone may as well use them. Becca decided that someone should be her.

The lobby confirmed the demolition. It had been gutted. A wobbly plastic folding table with a worn sheet thrown over the top served as a makeshift front desk. There were no chairs, signage, or vending machines in the room. The faint echo of her voice unnerved her.

Becca registered under the name *Jennifer Olson*. There were hundreds of women with that name in Minnesota; she had checked. Connecting her to that card would be like searching for a needle in a haystack. Besides, she had already landed a job as Jennifer Olson, DSW—Licensed Clinical Social Worker. Actually, it was *Doctor* Jennifer Olson. If she was going to play the game, she might as well go big.

Becca cautiously walked down the narrow hallway, avoiding touching either side. The wood-paneled walls were missing most of their lights, and the few remaining ones either lacked shades or had burned-out bulbs. Due to the poor lighting, she was unable to read most of the suggestive and chilling messages that had been scribbled on the fake wood. However, if any of the messages regarding Snake, Fat Tony, or the Pin Man were even remotely true, she hoped they were a million miles away. Perhaps this hadn't been her brightest idea, but it would only be for a dozen hours, give or take. If people knew the crap she had put up with, they would understand how she could stay in this fleapit.

Clutching the handle of her suitcase, Becca stood at the entrance to her room and fought the urge to ask for her money back. She took a deep breath and forced herself inside. It wouldn't matter if they refunded her card. She would never see the money. It would be credited to the account of the woman no one even knew was dead.

It was by far the worst room she had ever stayed in. It was a *dump* with a capital D. At some point, most likely years before, water had leaked from the room above. Brown streaks ran down the pale green walls and spread across the once-white ceiling. Two of the three bulbs in the ceiling light were burned out. What was hiding in the dark?

The room was the size of a small walk-in closet. It held a twin bed and a chipped particle board nightstand with missing drawers. The comforter was torn and smelled of urine and dirty feet. Becca wasn't sure the sheets had been changed after the last guest. And it was highly possible the black crumb-looking pieces between the sheets were mouse turds. Anxious to kick off her shoes, Becca quickly changed her mind as she crossed the stained, threadbare striped carpet. Her jaw tightened at a memory of having her face pressed into a similar one when her father beat her.

Becca hoisted her suitcase onto the top of the rickety nightstand. The bedside table leaned toward the right until it rested against the filthy wall. Because it was so narrow, a third of her suitcase hovered over the bed. With little room to turn around without touching the disgusting walls, she carefully stepped backward until she reached the end of the bed. The bathroom had no door. Instead, a yellowed shower curtain had been stapled above the frame. Becca pulled the sleeve of her sweatshirt over her hands, pushed it aside, and stepped inside.

The smell made her gag. She was sure someone had peed on the sheetrock walls. That odor and the rotten egg smell that seeped up from the drains mingled into something no one should ever encounter. The orange streaks in the sink, toilet, and tub didn't help either.

Becca held her breath and hovered over the toilet, not letting any part of her touch the cracked seat. After washing her hands with watered-down soap from a capless bottle, she wiped them on the back of her jeans rather than drying them on the dirty towel that had been used by the previous guest and tossed onto the floor.

She stripped the bed and dropped the bedding into the bathtub. Because she was trying to fly under the radar, most places she stayed were bad, just not *this* bad. For that reason, she always carried clean bedding in a plastic zipper bag inside her suitcase. She unfolded a clean rubber sheet from her suitcase and laid it over the stained ticking mattress before covering it with a clean, oversized, fitted and flat sheet.

She attempted to drown out the screaming match from the room directly above her by turning on the television. The volume crackled as the picture faded in and out on the chunky, nineties CRT television. Around nine-thirty, she wadded her sweatshirt and tucked it under her head. There was no way in hell she could sleep with her head on the pillow covered with specks of dried blood.

Most likely, this was the last month, week, or even day of the hotel's existence. The parking lot was replete with potholes deep enough to bury a coffin. Had the inside of the hotel been in great shape, the lot alone would have been enough to shut them down.

The lights from London Road seeped through and around the decaying and ill-fitting curtains. Becca plumped her sweatshirt multiple times to create a makeshift pillow that wasn't rock-hard. She already had a stiff neck and a pounding headache from keeping her feet pulled tightly to her body rather than risking the possibility of touching some creature that might visit during the night.

It was well after two before her mind finally slowed, and she dozed for a few hours. By 5:30 a.m., she was up, and by six, she walked out of the hotel after dropping her keys on the counter. Yesterday, she was a brunette—today, a redhead.

After a drive up and down London Road, a bathroom break at the Visitor's Center, and a quick stop at a coffee drive-thru, Becca headed up Seven Bridges Road. She pulled into a small parking lot, scarfed down a cream cheese-slathered bagel, and guzzled a twenty-five-ounce latte in ten minutes. As the sun peeked through the trees, Becca watched the squirrels gather acorns for their winter stash. She doubted any of the woodland creatures had ever given away their child like her father had.

CHAPTER THREE

BECCA HULLS

Shortly after 8:00 a.m., Becca left the woods, turned away from the lake, and headed toward the prison. The closer she got, the more her hands shook. Her heart had gone to war with her ribcage, and she feared the return of her breakfast. It may have been the caffeine, but more likely, it was a bad case of nerves. Her anxiety was off the chart. Shortly before her destination, she pulled onto a side street and talked herself through the worst-case scenario. Minutes later, with shoulders squared and chin held high, Becca was back on the road. Several swallows of vodka had not hurt either.

Pulling up to the gate, she smiled—not the uncomfortable one that appeared in a lifetime of photos—but the professional one she had practiced in the mirror for months. The guard handed her the clipboard. Name: *Dr. Jennifer Olson, Social worker.* Purpose: *Work with Mack Enderly.* The voice inside her head told her to write: *To make my father suffer.* But she fought the urge.

Becca laughed softly to herself. Lying was easy. It was telling the truth that was difficult. Having been lied to her entire life, she no longer knew what the word *truth* meant. It was deceptively elusive: words that slipped through your fingers and changed like the seasons. The one thing Becca knew for certain was that the Enderlys had scattered lies for forty-two years, passing them off as the truth. They had pretended she never existed, but she had.

Becca read Mack's file daily, going over it with a fine-tooth comb, searching for a crumb of information she could use against him. He was the reason she had marketed herself as a top-notch social worker. It had not only landed her a job with a prestigious social services firm but one working with the Superior Correctional Institution. She was not stupid; she'd done her research. When she came on board, someone else had been assigned to her father's case. But Becca had created a workaround. *That poor dead girl.*

In his free days, Mack Enderly had been a drunk—*a mean drunk.* From everything she had read, he was a self-proclaimed selfish son of a bitch who cared about nothing except where he could get his next drink. Much of his life had been spent at the open end of a bottle, pickling his brain and other organs. Since his incarceration, he'd been sober. It was the longest stretch in his entire life that booze did not continuously run through his gullet. If he had a heart at all, it could work in Becca's favor. A *come-to-Jesus* moment may have made him want to take responsibility for the baby girl he tossed away. But she wasn't holding her breath.

The file was thick and read like a Grisham novel—chapter after chapter of the unexpected. Becca perused it while she waited for the guard to call her name.

When Brian was eight, their father chose to get behind the wheel with his son and wife in the car. That choice claimed the life of Brian's mother and unborn sibling, a baby his mother had planned to name Wren Brigham Enderly. Goosebumps rose on her arms. Becca crossed them and rubbed vigorously. The words she read were a lie. She was here, the flesh and blood of the woman who either died after her birth or went into hiding to protect herself from her abusive husband. But if her mother *had* gone into hiding, there would have been too many questions that needed answers. Why had their mother abandoned Brian, the son she supposedly adored? Why had the woman turned a newborn baby over to her drunken husband?

Did she know he would ditch her the first chance he got?

Somehow, Mack had beaten the system. He had gotten off on a technicality. The tire that had blown was part of a nationwide recall. Still, it did not stop him from drinking or driving drunk. Years later, Enderly stole two cars and killed someone else while driving with a blood alcohol level of three point eight. This time had been different. There had been no escape clause. Mack was forced to do his time.

Brian, a young officer, had testified against their father. Becca read his testimony. The most damning statement he made was that his old man had never once shown an ounce of remorse for either accident. According to the file, Brian had been the one to slam the door shut on *their* father's prison cell.

The corners of her mouth rose almost imperceptibly as she stared at the twenty-five-year-old, grainy newspaper photo of her father. Her brother had gotten his revenge. Now, it was her turn.

Becca sighed loudly as she closed the file and placed it inside her briefcase-sized purse. She checked the time on her phone. When she looked up, Joyce, the woman who had signed her in, was staring at her—or rather, at Dr. Jennifer Olson, DSW. It sent chills down Becca's spine. She pulled her sweater closed and tipped her head down, pretending to read messages on her phone. But, over the top of the thick frames of her fake reading glasses, she kept her eyes on the woman.

Since visiting hours began, the guard had called three others in. They had all arrived after her. Becca wondered what was going on. Was Mack refusing to meet with his *social worker*? Or was something more nefarious happening? Based on Joyce's deep interest in her, she feared the latter.

The woman's cold disposition, pursed lips, and hard stare made Becca rethink her plan. When Becca arrived, she confidently answered Joyce's many questions, but the longer she stood at the counter, the less assured she felt and the more certain she was the woman could see through her ruse. After stammering her explanation for her visit, she took a deep breath and found the words to explain her purpose of working with *Mr. Enderly*.

Although Mack had served only twenty-five of his sixty-year sentence, he had been targeted for an early release. Since his incarceration, he had been the model prisoner—earning a degree in journalism, working every job assigned to him to the best of his ability, and attending AA meetings. More importantly, after his help with outing Sean Hart, an attorney who wanted his wife, Jane, dead, Warden Bob Harmon pushed for his early release. Harmon saw him as being *reformed, rehabilitated, and repentant*. According to the paperwork, Bob had checked nearly every box to free Mack. A handful of outside evaluations remained, along with a dozen or more sessions for reintegration into the general population.

Becca wondered if the warden had shared any of this news with Brian. The visitor log told the story of a yet unforgiving son. Her brother had not had contact with their father in two years.

Another person entered the room. Again, Becca checked her phone. She glanced up at the desk to find Joyce still watching her. Uncrossing her legs, she shifted in her chair and turned away from Joyce's prying eyes. Her heart beat in her throat as her nerves battered her.

When Joyce inquired why Chelsea Bonner had not returned as Mr. Enderly's social worker, Becca lied, stating the young social worker had opted to leave the company. Half of what she claimed was the truth. Chelsea *had* left, just not by choice. The social worker had been rolled out on a gurney, zipped inside a body bag, after an *accidental* fall down a flight of stairs in the back staircase of the office.

While the staff mourned the death of their friend and coworker, the CEO of the company struggled to cover the woman's clients. Timing was everything. Becca gave her a few days to mourn, then made her sudden appearance with an impeccable resume and a half dozen glowing references—all with numbers that forwarded to the same burner phone tucked inside her purse. She was a dream come true, a streak of good luck in an otherwise dreadful week. Days later, she seamlessly stepped into the role Chelsea had left open. To be honest, she had no idea what a social worker did. But that didn't matter. Becca was a quick study.

When the guard finally called her name, Becca jumped. She was grateful to be out from under Joyce's judging stare.

"Purse in the bin and empty your pockets," the enormous guard barked. He pointed to the X-ray machine. "Follow the picture."

"Can you hand me my purse," Becca asked once she reached the other side.

"Ain't gonna happen," the guard said, setting it on the shelf behind him.

"But…"

The massive guard crossed his arms and spread his feet wide as he faced her. "Listen, lady. You can go in without it, or you can haul your ass back out that door. I ain't negotiating with you."

"But I'm a social worker."

"Well, la-dee-dah. I couldn't care less if you were the Queen of England." He snapped his fingers loudly. "It's a purse, not a notebook." He tilted his head and narrowed his eyes. "So, it stays with me."

Becca opened her mouth, thought better of it, and closed it again. Turning her back toward the guard, she stood in front of the door and waited to be buzzed through. The guard on the other side walked her to a table, pointed to the exact chair she was to sit in, and informed her she was not to touch the prisoner. Did the woman really think she would touch Mack Enderly, a man she had never met—at least that she remembered—a man she hated before ever hearing his voice?

As she waited for Mack's arrival, panic hammered in her chest. She drew a deep breath and let it out slowly, trying to convince herself to relax, playing the worst-case scenario for the second time in ninety minutes. If the guard or crazy Joyce rifled through her purse, they would discover a cache of credit cards and IDs belonging to a dozen people, some with Becca's picture on them, others without. She had to trust they wouldn't. At least she had been smart enough to leave her pistol tucked into the sling beneath the seat of her car.

Becca drew deep breaths, closed her eyes, and imagined their meeting. It was another technique she had been taught by a therapist she had spent time with. *Imagine the outcome you want.* It didn't help.

Several minutes later, Mack Enderly entered the room. Becca's mouth nearly dropped open. He was an older version of his son, Brian. The resemblance unnerved her. She had not seen it in the newspaper clipping, but in person, it was as clear as night and day. They both had the same sad eyes and crooked mouths. It was impossible to peel her eyes off him. This was what it was like to have someone who looked like you. Her heart skipped a beat. Did she look like either of them? Would either of them see it?

Mack sat down across from her. "Who the hell are you?" His eyebrows pressed together. "Where's that other woman I was meeting with?"

Becca swallowed hard and cleared her throat softly. *So much for reformed.* "Chelsea? She doesn't work for the company any longer." She stared into her father's eyes. "I've been assigned to your case. I'm B…" Her face grew red, and she coughed, attempting to hide her almost fatal mistake. "Dr. Jennifer Olson. I'll be helping you with your transition from prison to the outside."

Mack crossed his arms along the front edge of the table and leaned toward her. Slowly, he shook his head. "I don't know, Ms. Olson…"

Becca raised a finger. "It's actually *Dr.* Olson."

Enderly laughed. "A little high on yourself, aren't you?" The lines at the corners of his eyes deepened. "I don't know what it is, but there's something I don't like about you." Becca broke her stare, dropped her head, and studied the tattoo on his forearm.

What doesn't kill me makes me stronger. It was precisely what she needed to hear at that moment.

Becca pointed toward his arm. "I like your tattoo."

Mack pulled his sleeve down and slowly rocked his head back and forth. "I'm not sure what it is, but I'm usually pretty good at reading people—and you've got a lot of…" He held his enormous hands in front of him, palms out, and moved them in small outward circles. "I just don't trust you. I think it'd be better if we parted ways. Tell your boss I want somebody else."

Becca squared her shoulders and smiled. "That won't be necessary, Mack. May I call you Mack?"

He raised an eyebrow. "Mr. Enderly is fine," he said. "I don't expect us to be friends, *ever*."

Becca's eye twitched. It was an anger response she had dealt with since childhood. Whenever anyone upset her, her left eyelid would pulse and quiver.

"Okay, *Mr. Enderly*. Let's talk about your plans when you're released. I know your wife has passed, but do you have any children who might help you acclimate to the outside?"

Mack huffed and stared at the far wall. "Got a son." He shook his head. "But he's not an option."

"Why not?" Becca waited for him to explain to her what she already knew.

"He don't wanna see me. It doesn't matter that I've been twenty-five years sober. I burned too many bridges back then for him to forgive me." He tightened his jaw. "I can't say as I blame him."

Becca nodded. "Well, then, do you have other children?"
Mack shook his head.

"Really?" She pulled her neck back and went in for the kill. "I swear I read you had a daughter. What was her name? Oh, yes. It was something like Gwen." She looked into his eyes. "No, Wren. Yes, that's it."

Watching his face, Becca rejoiced over the nerve she had just driven a knife into. She bit the inside of her cheeks to keep from smiling.

Mack's eyes grew wide. His jaw tightened. "Who the hell told you that? Who've you been talking to?"

Becca leaned back, straightened her back, and pressed a hand to her chest. "I'm sorry, Mr. Enderly. I didn't mean to anger you. I believe I saw it in your case file."

Mack leaned close to her. "Listen to me. I don't have a daughter. *Period.* You got it?" He stood up and hollered toward the desk. "Guard!" Then he kicked his lightweight plastic chair over and headed toward the exit door.

"It seems I've struck a nerve. I'll review your file and come back tomorrow," Becca called to his back.

"Don't bother," Mack grunted as the guard escorted him from the room.

Becca grinned. It was apparent Mack Enderly was hiding the knowledge of his daughter, the child he had thrown away forty-one years ago. *Her.*

CHAPTER FOUR

BECCA HULLS

After the awkward meeting with her father, Becca spent the remainder of the day moving from one coffee shop to another. Purchasing a small coffee or soda earned her the right to hunker down in a corner for a couple of hours to review the electronic photos, clippings, and notes she had kept on the Enderly family. With each transition to a new location, she slipped on a different T-shirt and wig.

The diverse hairstyles and colors had been gifts to herself, stolen from dying women who no longer needed them. She never bothered to steal the cheap wigs with synthetic shiny hair that could be spotted a mile away. No, Becca was selective. She wanted real hair wigs, the ones that went undetected by the snoopy assholes of the world.

There had been perks to working as a personal care attendant for hospice patients. They rarely missed the things she took. And if their family came looking for something they couldn't find, typically, she wasn't the only one questioned. The homes were virtually a revolving door of PCAs, hospice workers, medical delivery people, and a dozen others with access.

Like all cars licensed in Michigan, Becca's had a single back plate. Before she left the small town of Carson Springs, Wisconsin, she had purchased it from a man whose mother had died while she was visiting him. Becca had paid cash and had

"

never filed the title. It would be easy to pass herself off as borrowing her great aunt's car. And, unless she caused an accident or committed some other horrific act on the road, the cops were not likely to stop her. She was a good driver. Still, everywhere she went, she parked as far away as possible, backing into the spot and shielding the plate from any camera view. Becca wasn't stupid. She had covered her bases. If anyone were watching, it would be nearly impossible to figure out who she was or to connect her to another blonde, brunette, or redhead who may have looked vaguely like her.

Around 3:00 p.m., she settled on a different hotel. This time, she chose comfort over obscurity. Besides, that hellhole she had stayed in the night before had left her with bed bug bites that itched like hell.

With each passing moment, Becca's confidence grew. But there was a fine line between that and cockiness. If she did not keep herself in check, her mission could destroy her rather than the family she had been a part of for about a minute and a half.

Ordering a burger the size of her face seemed like a good idea when the words came out of her mouth, but she realized her mistake just a few bites in. Becca rewrapped the remainder and pitched it to a homeless man she passed on the sidewalk outside. No one could say she didn't care about humanity. She cared about others, just not the Enderlys.

After dinner, she took a shower and crawled beneath clean sheets that smelled of bleach. She pulled up the dark green comforter, which appeared to at least have been washed sometime in the last decade. Once Becca was settled, thoughts of being cheated out of the life she deserved stirred in her. To distract herself, she scrolled through her phone, watched YouTube videos, and flipped through television channels, but her memories kept banging to be let out. Finally, she gave in.

Her earliest memories of her father were of him beating her mother with a thick yardstick. Becca was only three, but her mother had taught her to read. The red lettering on the yardstick advertised Mason's Hardware.

Daniel was one. He could barely walk, but he understood the need to hide when his father's voice blasted through the house. The children clung to one another beneath the long tablecloth that kept them out of their father's sightline. Each time the yardstick connected with her mother's bare skin, Becca wanted to scream. To remind herself to remain quiet, she pressed her hand over her mouth. She had not been on the receiving end of her father's wrath yet but knew the time was coming. Her father's patience was paper-thin. All it would take was one tiny spark to light the fire and have him turn on her. At some point, she would not move fast enough or look at him in the wrong way, and she would be standing where her mother was. So, she minded her Ps and Qs.

By four years old, she had gotten the stick, a willow switch, and her father's belt more times than she could count. She had also been the victim of his nightly visits to her bed. In the beginning, she tried to fight, but he always pinned her arms down and held them at her sides. Over time, her arms no longer moved. She imagined driving a knife into her dad as she blanked out his five-minute visits. Even after being warned not to speak about their *special time* together, Becca tried to tell her mother. "Oh, what a big imagination you have, Becca. Now, run along and play," was all she said.

At seven, Becca learned to sew. Her mother taught her to make her own clothes: dark-colored, floor-length homely tops and skirts that covered the entirety of her arms and legs, as well as the old lady underwear she wore beneath. Only her face and hands were allowed to show. She was not allowed make-up, braided hair, or fancy adornments. As the bible stated, and her father often reminded her, *beauty was to come from within.*

Before her tenth birthday, she began to develop breasts. Mortified, Becca tightly wrapped her chest with torn sheets to keep from looking womanly. Weeks after her birthday, she got her period. For three days each month, she lay in bed, moaning.

Prayer, her mother told her, was the only thing that solved everything. She prayed; she prayed harder than she ever had. It hadn't worked, at least not as she expected. She still had horrible cramps, but her father no longer visited her room in the middle of the night. For that alone, she was grateful.

Now that she had become a *woman*, she wore sturdy, nondescript brown leather shoes that often did not fit and knee-high socks. Her long hair was pulled back and held in place with a rubber band. A bow would have drawn unwanted attention. *Boys will be boys,* she was reminded almost daily. Even Daniel could not be expected to stay away from her if she didn't follow every rule.

In her teenage years, Becca had fought her brother Daniel off more than once. She began sleeping with a baseball bat and a knife. Her brother had explained away multiple black eyes, split lips, and bruises over the years.

Children continued to join their family—one right after the other. When each girl turned eight, they were assigned a younger child to care for. Once the baby was weaned from her mother, the daughter took on the role of nighttime feedings, diaper changes, and potty training. The child slept in the daughter's room until they were old enough to sleep through the night, but even then, they were on call if *their child* woke.

As the eldest, Becca was parenting her siblings. Her mother didn't have time to waste on raising children. Her job was to "go forth and multiply." And she did. Between births, her mother suffered numerous miscarriages. Becca, privy to information parents should not confide in their children, could not recall her mother not being pregnant.

At seventeen, Becca was sent to a Christian homeschool conference. It was the first time she had ever been away from her family, the first time she could be Becca Hulls, not Robert and Katherine's daughter, not the sister of Daniel, Eve, Abigail, Michael, Rachel, Leah, John, and Benjamin.

Before she boarded the bus, her mother told her the purpose of attending the conference was to find a mate, someone who shared the family's beliefs. That was the last thing Becca wanted to hear. All she wanted was to get away from her parents and to sleep all night without a *little* needing her.

The conference had been held at the Bethany Christian College in Illinois. The boys were housed in one building and the girls in another. They were only brought together under the watchful eyes of a dozen women dressed similarly to her mother.

On the second day, each girl was presented to a boy—like a gift. The only thing missing was a big pink bow. Becca and Luke had been designated partners based on a questionnaire their mothers had completed. The teens had had no input. And why would they? Under *Life Visions*, they had been taught to believe they were no one until they became adults in the church.

Becca tried to sidestep Luke daily, but that became more difficult as they were forced together repeatedly. During the social on the final night, she feigned sickness, making herself throw up a handful of times, counting the minutes until she could board the bus back home. On the last day, Luke handed her his address and his phone number. When he turned away, she crumpled it and tossed it into the nearest garbage can.

To say her parents were gravely disappointed with her inability to find a mate was an understatement. A female mouth to feed, without plans of marriage, beyond eighteen was an embarrassment. It just wasn't heard of in *Life Visions—LV* for short, *or* LOVE, as the adults called it.

As a teenager, Becca knew she was growing up in a cult. That word was not one she was familiar with, but she understood her life was religiously controlled by others. Everything but *love* was taught through the church: self-righteousness, intolerance, control, and abuse. There was a hierarchy that began with God. Next came the founder, Andrew Godley (surely a made-up name for a man who often placed himself above the Lord). Following him was the father of the family. Even sons over twelve had more say than the women. And even though God was supposed to be at the head of everything that happened in the church, Becca rarely saw His goodness in her house.

On the morning of her eighteenth birthday, the shunning began. No one looked at her or spoke a word. Her chair had been removed from the table. As far as her family was concerned, she didn't exist. With no marriage prospects, no one to take her off their hands, and no way to give them grandchildren to care for them in their old age, Becca was worthless to them, an embarrassment.

After breakfast, her bed was moved into a windowless storage closet in the unfinished basement. From that day forward, her meals were eaten in the kitchen, not in the dining room with the others. She supposed she should have felt fortunate that they fed her at all. Had it not been for the afternoon shift, prepping for the baker at Pauline's, she would have been entirely alone in a house full of people.

When she returned from work that night, a folded sheet of paper lay on her bed—a handwritten bill for room and board—one hundred dollars, payable on the first of each month for her keep. How could the parents, who claimed to love her just days ago, treat her as a boarder?

Two weeks later, unable to stand their silence one second longer, Becca walked away. Just before she closed the door, her father approached her. She thought he had changed his mind and was coming to apologize, beg her not to go. But that was not the case. He looked down and, in a hushed voice, told her he never wanted to see her again. She had disgraced the family and brought shame to God and *Life Visions*. He told her she was not a woman of God but of Satan. "You are no daughter of mine." He spat on her shoe and scraped his boot across the top of it. "As God scraped the devil from heaven, I am scraping you from my life." Then, he walked away. Her mother had been watching from the doorway of the kitchen. Her eyes brimmed with tears. Before Becca left, her mom threw the dish towel over her shoulder, nodded to her daughter, and returned to the kitchen.

Until she secured an overnight shift in a nursing home, Becca slept in her rusted-out car that barely ran. Sometimes, she grabbed a few hours of sleep in an empty bed or recliner in a resident's room. But it was never enough. For six months, that was her life. Then, suddenly, she was back home raising eight kids on government assistance. Was it karma that took her parents' lives in the accident? Or had it just been terrible timing?

When Becca left home, she broke free of the traditions her parents clung to, the ones they imposed on their children in the name of God, using whippings as punishments. Gone was the book and teachings of Andrew Godley. Her modest dresses were replaced with jeans and T-shirts, open blouses over tank tops, and shirts that hugged her thin frame. If she wasn't barefoot, she wore flip-flops, sandals, dress boots, and tennis shoes. And God forbid, she painted her toenails. Her face was accentuated with eyeshadow, mascara, blush, and lipstick. And her hair, the crowning glory of *Life Visions*, was cut into a short, chopped bob that showed off its natural curl. For the first time in her life, Becca felt normal.

As the head of the household, she was not interested in remaining part of the sect. Her beliefs had never meshed with those of *Life Visions*, but now she had no one to be accountable to. Because of that, she and her family were shunned by nearly everyone they knew. Homeschooling her siblings wasn't anything she was interested in or had time to do. Other than learning to read, the little education she received had come via a computer screen in the small schoolhouse she attended with the other kids a couple of days a week. It taught only three things: basic math, reading, and religion. There was no history, empathy, or understanding of others. And, of course, the church outlawed anything remotely scientific. The books Becca brought into the house, trying to learn about the past, science, and life outside her religion, were confiscated and destroyed.

As an adult, she made decisions based on her observations. She hadn't thrown God away; He was her guide. Becca still prayed and read her bible daily, but it was not the *LV* bible she opened. And she did not interpret God's word in quite the same way her parents had. So, instead of homeschooling her siblings, she enrolled them in public school, where they played sports, went on dates, read books that interested them, and chose to wear what they liked.

When the last child left home, Becca was forced to sell the house. Even with two jobs, as an end-of-life care professional and a baker, she could no longer afford the mortgage. The house should have been paid off, but her father had borrowed against it so many times that even when it sold, there would be little money to carry her into the next stage of her life. The house was too large for her anyway, and bad memories hid everywhere, threatening to jump out and choke her.

On February 10th, her thirty-ninth birthday, with no more government help to pay the bills, Becca began preparing the house to sell. Three weeks later, there was only one room she had not readied, her parents' bedroom. When her parents were alive, no one had been allowed to enter. Even with them gone for over twenty years, the door had never been opened. It wasn't a shrine as much as a bed of quicksand. The horrific memories—of which Becca carried the most significant load— had the potential to suck her under and swallow her alive.

Off living their own lives, her siblings had virtually abandoned her. She had no regrets. That was her job, to prepare them to go forth and prosper—*not multiply* as her mother had. Success was what she wished for each. They were independent, strong-minded individuals who would do great things. She had saved them from a lifetime of misery and abuse.

The only one who ever returned was Daniel. But they never spoke of the past.

Holding her breath, Becca cautiously pushed the door open, half expecting to come face-to-face with her parents—not just crushing memories. Everything was the same as it was the day her parents died at the hands of a drunk driver. The green and brown patchwork quilt her mother had made covered the bed.

The last person to touch it had been her mom. Her father's reading glasses lay on the nightstand along with a leatherbound bible and a well-worn copy of *Life Vision—Basic Principles for Living by God's Word*. A thick layer of dust covered the book, making the top appear grayer than when her father was alive.

When Becca opened the closet, she shrank back. Her mother's drab dresses hung next to her father's work shirts and jeans. The contrast between the two was remarkable. The clothing looked like it had come from two entirely different decades. Men were allowed modern dress, to stand out, to garner attention from others. Women were not.

The room spun as Becca pulled a brown dress from the hanger and brought it to her nose. Instead of smelling like she remembered her mother—of soap and lilacs—it smelled of dust and cedar.

Her mother would have been sixty-five, her father sixty-nine. Compared to the other parents, they were old when she was born. But it had not stopped them from giving birth to nine children. When they died, they had been in their forties. It should have been the prime of their life—and yet, they seemed ancient. Her father, Robert, a mechanic at a garage in town, had hurt his back years before. He stooped like a man of eighty. The only time Becca saw him stand tall, shoulders back, was when he swung a belt at one of them. Katherine, her mother, was deathly thin and frail from giving birth to so many children. At the time of the accident, Baby Ten was close to joining the family. The baby would have been "buddied" with almost eight-year-old Leah.

Becca drew and released a deep breath before removing the clothes from the hangers. There was nothing she wanted, not a blessed thing. She grabbed boxes from the hallway and began sorting things. An hour later, all that remained was the bedding. She placed the handmade quilt in the dryer and put the sheets and her mother's nightgown in the washer.

As she walked into the room, a cardboard box caught her eye. It had been shoved so far under the bed that she might not have noticed it until she took the frame apart. The box was partially sealed with cracked, yellowed masking tape that had lost the fight to keep the box closed. Becca brushed her hand across the top, sending the dust flying. She sneezed as she sat at the end of the bed and ripped the top open.

Confusion coursed through her. The box held a gingham-checked quilt and a pink teddy bear. After removing them, Becca paged through the stack of old photos that lay beneath. They were in color but had turned orange over time. She had never seen them before and wasn't even sure who they were of. Her mother? A sibling? A child her parents had lost?

A large envelope lay in the bottom of the box. She tore the flap open and removed several sheets of paper. Becca's eyes grew wider as she read each page. She slid down the edge of the bed and landed on the floor. Her heart raced as she tried to make sense of the information.

What in the hell did this mean?

CHAPTER FIVE

BECCA HULLS

"Two days in a row, Dr. Olson? I don't recall Dr. Bonner coming that often." Joyce stared at Becca. Her nostrils flared, and her brows rose.

"I, ah…" She searched for words. "I had a cancellation this morning." Becca pursed her lips and swallowed hard. She looked down and pretended to dig through her jacket pockets.

"Did you misplace something?" Joyce stood to get a better look.

"I can't remember what I did with my keys." Seconds later, she held them up for Joyce to see. "Found them."

"Well, lucky for you." Joyce glanced over her shoulder before turning back and holding her index finger in the air. "Wait here." The woman hurried out of the room, calling, "I'll be right back."

The visitor's door opened just enough for Becca to see the guard's shoe on the other side. Since she was the only one in the waiting room, she stepped toward it, anxious to disappear before Joyce returned. Suddenly, the door flew open. Becca jumped back, trying to avoid a head-on collision with the woman.

Joyce's fingers were tightly wrapped around the camera lens. The guard pushed the toe of his heavy boot between the door and the frame. Becca's pulse raced. She knew he was listening. Were they both questioning her visit? If it was just the nosy woman, the guard would have let the door fall shut.

"Forgot to get a photo of you yesterday." Joyce raised the camera for Becca to see.

Becca's chin dropped. "What are you talking about? Why do you need a picture?"

The center of Joyce's lips pressed together, and the corners of her mouth turned down. "It's just something we have to do. You can never be too careful." Joyce gestured to the entry door, signaling for Becca to back against it.

"I, I don't like having my picture taken," Becca mumbled.

"How can that be?" She tsked. "The way you young people all use social media, I figured everyone under the age of fifty loved looking at photos of themselves."

"Not me."

Joyce shrugged. "To each his own, I suppose. But I still have to take it. Besides, it's not like we're going to use it in an ad for the prison." She released a weak laugh. "We just need to know who's coming and going. And like I said, you can never be too careful." She raised an eyebrow. "Not to mention, as Mr. Enderly's social worker, you'll become a regular around here. So, let's just get it over with." She tipped her wrist down and flapped her hand outward twice. "Go stand with your back against that door."

"Is this absolutely necessary? Could we do it next time? I don't really feel the best this morning."

Joyce lowered the camera. "I suppose you could plead your case to the warden, but I doubt…"

"Fine. Let's get it over with." Becca ran a hand through her hair.

"You look fine. Like I said, they aren't for public viewing." Joyce's eyes widened. "Unless, of course, you've broken the law." She lifted one shoulder in a half-shrug. "If that's the case, your picture will be on every TV station and post office from here to Texas. And your mug'll be everywhere on the internet. You'd be famous." Joyce sighed. "Have you? Broken the law,

I mean."

Becca felt the crushing weight of that question. Her heart pulsed in her throat, making it difficult to speak. She pressed her knuckle into the lid of her left eye, knowing the twitching would begin in a matter of seconds. "No. No, of course not. I, ah, just thought another day might be better since I didn't sleep very well last night."

Joyce smiled as she swung her fist through the air in front of her. "Well, nothing like the present. Now, let's get this picture taken before the lobby fills with visitors. Wednesdays are busy around here." She laughed out loud. "You'd think we were offering a two-for-one sale the way this place'll fill up in a bit."

Not wanting to be caught in the middle of a crowd, Becca backed against the door, contemplating how to quickly change her appearance. She hung her head before running her hand through the wig, sweeping the long red hair to the opposite side before tugging the fringe bangs down over one eye. Then, she narrowed her eyes and raised a brow slightly. She inflated her hollow cheeks and held them in that position as she dropped her mouth open a fraction.

Joyce tapped her foot. "It's not a glamour shoot, Dr. Olson. I just need a photo." She aimed the camera and clicked the button several times.

"Wait! I'm not ready. Why are you taking so many?"

Joyce paused and waited for Becca to repeat her routine before adding a head tilt and pursed lips.

"You're sure this is the photo you want me to take?"

Becca nodded.

Joyce rolled her eyes and snapped several pictures. When Becca swept the hair of the wig back to its natural side, Joyce took a few more.

"I thought you said *a* photo—one. You took way more than that."

"Don't you worry your pretty little red head about this. I'll pick the one that shows your true self the best, so the warden…"

Becca's neck stretched forward. "The warden?"

"Oh, didn't I tell you? The pictures get sent to everyone on the staff."

She nodded, more out of confusion than understanding.

As Becca moved toward the counter, she felt the heaviness of Joyce's statement—*her true self.* If anyone knew who she really was, they would despise her. The people who raised her had. And Mack Enderly had been the one to start that list forty-two years before.

Her anxiety swelled, and her left eye twitched rapidly. This time, rubbing it did not help. If she got caught trying to destroy the Enderlys, how would she explain it to her brothers and sisters? Suddenly, her shoulders fell, and she snorted. Why was she worried? They were her siblings in name only—which wasn't even her real name. Rebecca Hulls didn't exist. She never had. Wren Brigham Enderly did.

Joyce disappeared through the door before reappearing at the desk. "You may have a seat, Dr. Olson. I'm done with you." The phrase felt ominous, a foreshadowing of things to come. Joyce looked down at her keyboard and said in a voice that smiled, "I'm sure the guard will call you back shortly."

Becca chose a seat in the row facing the doors. It was preferable to seeing Joyce's judgmental glare. Until the door opened, she kept her face lowered. A woman barely out of her teens with part of her head shaved and tattoos running down each finger walked past her. She held the hand of a boy of about six. The pair looked like they were playing tug-o-war as he tried to remove her hand, and she dragged him to the desk. It was then that Becca noticed the height indicator taped on the door frame. The release of air she expelled was as close to a *give-up* as Becca had ever come. Not only did the prison have tons of photos of her, but they knew she was five foot four—in flats. For all Becca knew, there was a scale hidden in the floor that weighed her when she walked in.

"One-oh-seven," she whispered. "I'll save you the trouble."

"I'm sorry, Dr. Olson. Did you say something?" Joyce

poked her head out of her window, ignoring the woman with the little boy signing in.

Becca shook her head. Thanks to that bizarre woman, she had just given the police her life on a silver platter. The realization clawed at her. If Mack wouldn't talk to her today, she would have to find another way to destroy him.

CHAPTER SIX

BECCA HULLS

Joyce's eyes burned into the back of Becca's skull. The hair on the back of her neck stood at attention and her scalp tingled. The buzzing inside her grew louder as her brain short-circuited. She pressed the first two fingers of each hand against her forehead and slowly counted backward from ten, drawing a deep breath in, then releasing it before claiming the next number.

The longer she waited for the guard to call her name, the more Becca melted into the furniture. Her legs had turned to rubber. Anxiety caved her body inward, making her feel as if she were disappearing. In her mind, she had grown so tiny that she feared she might slip through the hole between the backrest and the seat of her chair.

Suddenly, Joyce touched her shoulder. Becca clapped a hand over her mouth.

"The guard's called your name three times now, Dr. Olson."

"Sorry," Becca muttered. Grabbing her jacket, she hurried toward the door. She had tucked her purse and gun into the sling beneath the front seat. Besides her coat, the only thing she carried was her fake ID.

"Use the bin," the hulking guard from the day before muttered. Becca knew he did not like her any more than Joyce did.

She tossed the lightweight jacket into the tub. "That's all I have."

"Don't really give a crap." He nodded toward the machine. "You know the drill."

Becca stepped into the X-ray machine, held her hands above her head, and grinned discreetly.

"Back up," the guard hissed. "Empty your pockets."

"But I don't have anything…" She reached into her pocket and removed the driver's license. "Oh, this is nothing." The guard held out his hand. "But…"

A deep V formed between his eyes. "Did you not hear me say I don't give a rat's ass?"

Becca sighed loudly and dropped the fake license into his palm.

The guard nodded toward the machine. "Again," he grunted.

This time, she was cleared. The door buzzed before it opened. The sentry on the other side led her to a different table than the day before. In a monotone, nasally voice, the woman repeated the rules Becca had heard the day before. Before she even nodded her understanding, the guard was gone.

She tilted her head down, wrinkled her nose, and quickly glanced around the table to see if anyone was watching. Then, she raised her right shoulder slightly and sniffed her armpit. The smell of perspiration attacked her. Fear, anxiety, and worry all smelled the same on Becca. Her father had once lambasted her, saying her B.O. smelled like she had been trapped in a Chinese restaurant for a week. At the time, she had no point of reference. She had never eaten or smelled Chinese food, but clearly, he had.

He broke the yardstick across her back before locking her outside to *air out*. It was only the first of many nights she spent curled up in the dilapidated doghouse.

Becca sniffed the other side and jerked her head back. If Mack got a whiff, he would know she was a fraud. She slid her chair back a good foot and pressed her arms tightly to her sides.

The prisoner door opened, and Mack stepped into the room. He took one look at her and spun around. The guard followed him. Becca stood and called his name.

"Sit down," the female guard snapped from the other side of the room.

Dropping onto the cheap plastic chair, Becca called Mack again. He turned around and spoke quietly to the guard. The man looked at her, nodded, and escorted him to the table.

"What in the hell are you doing here?" White foam emerged at the corners of his mouth. "I told you we were through talking."

"Mr. Enderly, I want to apologize for yesterday. I think we got off on the wrong foot. I'm new to this job." She tilted her head and blinked several times. "I-I can't lose it already. I'd never get another." She tipped her head to the right and softened her eyes. "You understand, right?"

Becca was met with silence. Finally, Mack swung a finger between the two of them. "If this is going to happen, there's going to be some ground rules. I never want to hear the name *Wren* again." He glared at her. "Otherwise, we're done. Understand?"

"Yes." Becca nodded at him. "All right, then, let's talk about your son."

"Already told you. It's a waste of time. He hates me more than I hate myself."

"I understand, but the more I know about you and your relationship with alcohol and your son, the more I can help you." She kept her arms pressed to her sides but turned her hands outward. "After yesterday, I pitched Chelsea's notes. That means we're starting from scratch." She watched him carefully. "Does that sound fair?"

Mack shot her a look of disdain. "Whatever," he muttered.

"Okay, so let's start with who you were before you started drinking."

"Who I was *before* I started drinking?" He huffed. "That was a hell of a long time ago. I barely remember *before*."

He stared over her head as he removed the cobwebs from that chapter of his life. Finally, he started talking. For the better part of thirty minutes, Mack recalled his life before and after alcohol held him hostage.

Becca listened intently, searching for places to insert questions about *her brother*. It was clear Mack carried an overload of guilt over how he treated Brian. Did he feel the same about her? Did he care that he had thrown her away? Maybe that was why he did not want to talk about her. Maybe the guilt destroyed him—made him drink to forget.

Suddenly, Becca huffed.

"What the hell was that?"

She shook her head. "Nothing. I was just thinking about *my* father." It was not a lie. She was thinking about Mack—her *real* father.

Becca poked at everything he told her. Perhaps, had she not been abandoned, she could have been the one to save them from living under a cloud of alcohol and rage. Her mother would not have been there, true, but Becca knew she was enough. *She* could have given them their happily ever after.

But there she sat with her father, carrying on about the son who no longer claimed him. How could he not realize his daughter was sitting right in front of him? Had he shown any remorse, she would have thrown her arms around him and never let go. But that would never happen. He could not even say her name.

As she listened, a realization dawned on her. Nothing she could do to Mack would have any impact on him. He had covered himself in armor to keep from getting hurt. The only way to punish him was to destroy his family—*Brian*. His son was his Achilles tendon.

Becca's brows furrowed as she nodded fake compassion. "Have you spoken to your son since you've been here?"

Mack cast his eyes downward. Becca watched the conversation of two years before play in his memory. The expression on his face hardened and softened as scenes flashed inside of him.

"Once." He glared at her. "But that was police business. It wasn't personal."

Becca clenched her jaw and stared at him. "How does it feel to be thrown away like that?"

Mack snorted. "How the hell would you feel, Miss…" He rolled his eyes. "*Dr.* Olson?"

Warmth rose from her neck to her cheeks. She leaned her chin into her left palm and covered her cheek with her hand to keep Mack from noticing the color change. "The same way you do, I'm sure."

"I doubt it. Did your father ever beat you? Take his revenge out on your mom or your brothers or sisters? Did he drink until he passed out, come to, and start the cycle all over again—every damn day?"

Her dead eyes and locked jaw concealed her emotions. It was something she had perfected as a child. She kept her breathing slow and shallow as she stared *through* her father rather than *at* him.

"Yeah, I didn't think so." Mack folded his arms across his chest and fell against the back of his chair.

While her face held no affectivity, her brain did not follow suit. The voice inside her screamed at her father, berating him for leaving her life to chance. *Fifty-fifty.* She could have ended up with a good family or not. *Not* had been where she landed. The man who raised her had been *sober* when he beat them. She shoved down the overflowing garbage that grew inside of her, biting her lip to keep the debris from exploding.

Mack huffed. "Obviously, you came from money and privilege. You even look the type. And being a doctor and all— I'm guessing your father doted on your mother. And I'll bet you never wanted for a damn thing."

Enough! The voice inside her screamed, begging her to wrap her hands around his throat and squeeze until he stopped breathing. She pictured it, watched him die in front of her, with others standing around, cheering her on. If she stayed one second longer, she feared her vision would become a reality.

Her father knew nothing about her life. *Nothing.* And yet he judged her through rose-colored glasses, believing everyone outside his house lived in a fairy tale of singing birds and Prince Charming. If he only knew the life he had condemned her to, what the man she called *father* and her disgusting brother, Daniel, had done to her, how she'd been kicked out of the family on her eighteenth birthday, and how she had raised all eight of her siblings with virtually no help. Yes, if he only knew.

Becca scraped the scab of those thoughts over and over again. She twisted her mouth, and swallowed past the cotton that had formed in her mouth. What? Did she expect him to care? He had thrown her out like garbage. That was what was written in the envelope she had found in the box under her parents' bed. Not those exact words, but she could interpret what happened.

Her head throbbed. With her thumb and finger, she squeezed the bridge of her nose. Rage had stolen her balance. She grabbed the edge of the table when she stood. "Well, Mr. Enderly, you'll hear from me soon." Her sneer turned into an evil smile. "I promise you that."

"Sit down," the guard hollered for a second time.

"I'm leaving. I don't feel well."

Typically, the prisoner was escorted out first, but Becca was already at the visitor's door. The guard pointed to Mack, indicating he was not to move until after she left.

On her way out, Becca picked up her license and coat without noticing someone else was stationed in the room. She passed through the exit and into the waiting room where she was met by two officers.

"Dr. Olson, we'd like you to come with us. We have a few questions for you." The whooshing in her head grew violent. She had been prepared to face the music. But she had not expected it to happen so soon—not before she got what she wanted.

CHAPTER SEVEN

BECCA HULLS

Becca's lips parted, and her shoulders rolled forward. A fractured sigh escaped. Suddenly, she lifted her chin and pursed her lips. If she had any hope of saving herself, she had to play the part of Dr. Jennifer Olson—calm, controlled, and confident.

She squared her shoulders. "How may I help you?" Her voice was pinched, less assured than she intended. "I was meeting with Mr. Enderly."

"Come with us, please." The female officer took her elbow and steered her past curious onlookers through the visiting room door and down a long hallway.

"I have another meeting. I don't…"

"It'll have to wait." The woman opened the door and directed Becca inside.

Becca fought the urge to jerk her arm from the officer's grip. She had to keep her wits about her, so she stared at the terrazzo flooring and counted her steps.

The room was no larger than a small walk-in closet. A half-circle table was shoved against one wall. Three lightweight chairs were tucked in tightly to make room to pass.

The male officer pulled out a chair on the far side and nodded for her to sit. Becca cautiously lowered herself into it. Parks, the female officer, chose the chair next to her, and the beer-bellied O'Connor sat near the door.

Becca's eyes anxiously darted around the tiny room. The white brick walls rapidly closed in. She tilted her face toward the tall ceiling to keep from panicking. But the grids on the small transom window near the ceiling made it worse. She felt trapped, like the tiny animals she had frightened away as a child. They had been weak and vulnerable—just as she had been. Retaliating against her father was not an option, so she took her anger out on everything else.

Between heavy, quick breaths, she mumbled, "I can explain."

The officers exchanged a curious look.

"Explain what, Dr. Olson?" O'Connor clicked his pen several times. "What can you explain?"

Becca shook her head. She looked from one officer to the other. "Why am I here?"

The female cop slid her chair back until it touched the wall. "What did you mean—explain?"

Becca clenched her jaw and stared at the table.

Finally, Officer Parks pointed to the man across from Becca. "We're officers O'Connor and Parks. We have some questions for you."

"I can read," Becca growled, staring at O'Connor's crooked name badge. "Tell me why I'm here."

Parks looked at her partner. "All in good time, Dr. Olson, but before that, it seems you may have some information for us. Let's go back to what you said. You can explain what exactly?"

Becca shook her head and folded her arms across her chest. "Nothing. I…" She refolded them. "I just thought you wanted to know why I was meeting with Mr. Enderly."

Lying was as natural as breathing. And why wouldn't it be? Her entire life had been one colossal lie made up of a million tiny ones that started with her birth parents, the Enderlys. That deception grew legs and led her to the despicable people who raised her. For forty-two years, she had not belonged to anyone, not really. It had all been a gruesome façade veiled beneath the

Christian cult known as *Life Visions*.

Officer O'Connor shrugged. "You're a social worker, correct?"

"Yes," she uttered softly. She tugged the sleeves of her sweater over her sweaty palms and rubbed them against her thighs before shoving her hands beneath her legs. "So, what exactly do you need to know? Is it something about my meeting with Mr. Enderly? Because…"

"We're not interested in Enderly." Without taking his eyes from her, O'Connor turned sideways and rested a booted foot across his thigh. "We'd rather talk about you."

Warmth mushroomed up Becca's neck and across her cheeks. For the second time that morning, she pressed her elbows onto the table and leaned her cheeks into her palms to hide the redness that would to bloom momentarily.

"Why me?"

Officer Parks pulled a small notebook from her pocket. "How about you tell us where you live?" The cop held her pen over the pad, rocking it between her fingers while she waited for an address.

Becca stretched her neck sideways, smacking her head against the unforgiving wall. One eye instantly closed as she kneaded the throbbing spot with her knuckles. The physical pain sent forth a burst of anger she could not control. "What business is that of yours?"

"There was…"

"Background check," O'Connor interrupted her. "Address, please."

Becca's eyebrows pressed together as she searched her brain for the fictitious address. "Dr. Jennifer Ann Olson. 415 Potter Road, Ashland, Wisconsin. I live there with three roommates—two females and one of their boyfriends. Happy?"

O'Connor's eyebrows rose, and he gave a long whistle. "That's like seventy-five miles from Duluth. Do you make that drive every day?" His eyes widened. "It won't be fun in the winter months. Are you new to the Midwest?"

Her eyes skittered across the scarred tabletop. "I don't usually work over here. But after Chelsea's death, I was hired to take over some of her cases. Typically, I stay in the Ashland area."

"Then you know about the lake-effect snow that gets dumped on us every winter." Officer Parks rocked her head back and forth. "And that car of yours doesn't look like it has that many more miles in it."

O'Connor dropped his foot to the floor and rested his arms along the edge of the table. "How about you tell us about that car?"

Becca's eyes widened. "My car? Why is what I drive a concern of the police?"

"Normally, it's not. But it's got expired Michigan plates, and you're telling us you live in Wisconsin. So, how about you stop asking questions and answer ours?"

Becca had settled on the vehicle because it was nondescript—an older, white, small SUV. It blended in with most of the cars on the road. Skating by unnoticed was an essential part of her plan.

She looked O'Connor directly in the eyes and lied. "It's my great aunt's car. I'm borrowing it for a while."

O'Connor nodded slowly. "Does she have a name, this great aunt of yours?"

Becca had memorized the name and the address. She'd even checked out the house online in case she was ever asked about it. "Millie Wagner. It's really Mildred, but everyone who knew her called her Millie."

"And she's related to you, how?"

"She's my grandmother's sister—on my mom's side."

"And where does she live?"

"Roseville. Michigan, not Minnesota."

Parks scribbled something on her notepad. "We assumed that since it's got Michigan plates. When did your great aunt pass away?"

Becca grew quiet. They already knew more than she had

anticipated. She slumped against the back of the chair. A tear rolled down her cheek and dropped onto her blouse. Making herself cry on cue was something she had practiced. Skeptics could question the sincerity of words and tone, but waterworks, if executed to perfection, were not as easy to deny.

"I'm sorry, Dr. Olson, but it's important to understand what you mean when you claim you *borrowed* a dead woman's car that's still registered to her. The title hasn't been transferred, and Wisconsin plates haven't been obtained." Parks looked at her notes. "So, how about we start with the word *borrowed*."

Becca's chin quivered; it was another trick she had picked up. She swiped her fingertips below one eye and then the other. "I didn't really mean borrow. Maybe *obtained* is a better word. I bought it from my Uncle Terry." O'Connor nodded. "Not renewing my tabs is on me, I'm afraid. I planned to do it shortly after she died, but…"

"And *when* did she pass?"

"A few months ago." Becca repeated the words of the man who had sold her the car. "His mom lived in Michigan and came to visit him, but she passed away in her sleep."

"I'm sorry to hear that. I'm sure that was difficult." Parks flipped through her notebook. "You say a few months, but it seems it's been almost a year."

Becca bit her lip. "Has it been that long? Goodness, I hadn't realized."

Parks nodded. "The title should have been transferred immediately."

"Oh, of course. I just got so caught up in…" She twisted the bottom of her sweater. "I'll do it today." Becca looked at O'Connor. "What made you even notice my plates?"

O'Connor tipped his head slightly to the left. "When we ran the plates, the car didn't belong to you."

Becca's brows pinched together. "Why'd you run my plates anyway? Is that something you always do?" She sighed loudly and fell against the back of her chair. "It was that woman at the front desk, wasn't it? She tipped you off, right? Oh, my God, she hates me. If I ever see her again, it'll be too soon. She's vicious. You should make *her* guard the prisoners instead of greeting the public."

"No, Doctor Olson. No one urged us to look you up. Your car was involved in an accident in the visitor's lot while you were meeting with Mr. Enderly."

Becca's eyes widened. "What? Is my car okay? Is it drivable?"

Parks shook her head. "We aren't really sure."

Becca jumped up and tried to open the door, but it was locked. "I need to get some things out of my car in case they have to haul it away."

"Such as?"

"Umm, my purse, suitcase, computer."

"You left those things in the car?" Officer O'Connor stood up and unlocked the door but stepped in front of it to keep Becca from leaving. "The owner of the other car is fully cooperating. I'm sure her insurance…"

"Move," she demanded. "I need to get to my car."

The officers shared a look before O'Connor opened the door and let Becca leave.

As always, Becca had backed into the parking spot. For a quick getaway, she aimed it down an aisle in case things went south. A tow truck circled the parking lot and pulled between the two vehicles. When it backed up, the beeping caused shivers to crawl down Becca's spine, and she pressed her hands over her ears.

Finally, she caught a glimpse of her car. The white noise in her head made her feel as if she had been standing in front of the speakers at a rock concert. Genuine tears dripped from her chin. To Becca, the car appeared worse than it was. Her baby was ruined. What she saw was a crumpled mess of aluminum. The bumper was pressed inward and barely clung to the car. The hood was pushed toward the cracked windshield. Was it a total loss? The driver had to have plowed into her at a high rate of speed. The other vehicle, a rusted Impala that had more holes than Swiss cheese, looked like it gave much worse than it got.

Becca unloaded her suitcase and backpack from the backseat. With significant effort, she opened the driver's side door. After checking the location of the officers, she reached under her seat and retrieved her purse. Leaning into the car, covering the front of the seat with her body, she reached into the sling for the gun but felt nothing. It could not have been thrown into the back seat upon impact; the holder had been designed specifically to keep that from happening. Becca felt again. *Nothing.* The gun was gone.

Her heart raced, and sweat beaded across her forehead. Someone at the station had taken it. Damn the broken locks. So much for believing the criminals lived *inside* the building. Becca could not report the weapon missing. She didn't have a license to carry it. The gun did not even belong to her. It was registered to her father, Robert Hulls—a man who had been dead for over two decades. It would be easy to trace it back to the Hulls of Carson Springs, Wisconsin. And the townsfolk hated her enough to give her up without a second thought.

Becca did not wait for the tow truck driver to tell her where her car was going, nor did she pause to speak to the Impala's owner. She gathered her things, hooked her backpack over the suitcase's handle, and pulled her purse strap across her body before heading across the parking lot.

With the double-timed beat of a timpani, Becca heard the slapping of feet closing in behind her. "Wait! We need to exchange information."

The woman moved around her and gave a venomous smile. She grabbed Becca's hand and pulled her so close, Becca could feel her hot breath on the side of her face. Whatever the woman whispered was lost in the whooshing inside Becca's ears. She leaned back and stared at her. Her heart jumped in her chest when the woman pulled her closer a second time and repeated, "I said, *Hello, Becca.*"

CHAPTER EIGHT

TERAH DIXON

Terah Dixon walked down the quiet street of Cedar Point, Minnesota. Trees canopied over the pavement, sheltering her from the warm September sunshine. Shadows danced, mimicking the brightly colored leaves overhead. Her long blonde hair fluttered in the breeze. A section of hair attached itself to the lip balm she had applied before leaving the house; she lifted it and tucked the stray piece behind her ear. A smile erupted on her face. Her heart puffed up and begged her feet to skip. She made a single hop before scolding herself. As a new resident of the small town, the goal was to fit in, not stand out. *Not ever.*

Never had Terah felt the arms of happiness wrapped around her as tightly as they had since her arrival in Cedar Point. Within *Life Visions*, back in Carson Springs, her dreams had been nothing more than childhood fantasies. The community had shut them down before she turned double digits. Only within the four walls of her tiny house did she feel safe to dream. Her mother listened, and her father indulged her aspirations for something bigger. But the elders dictated everything: what to believe, how to act, and when to speak. Under *Life Visions*, children were to be seen and not heard. Honestly, Terah was not even sure most adults wanted to *see* their children. Parents viewed them as a product of following the laws of the church, not as a want.

Before she *became a woman*, the elders had drawn a blueprint for her life. No suitable partner had been available in the community, so against her desires, she was shipped off to the homeschool conference in Illinois. There, matchmakers worked behind the scenes to ensure she would be married before turning nineteen. But Terah had sabotaged all plans made for her.

Friends since birth, the girls had attended the conference together. But while they had comparable tastes, they could never be described as two peas in a pod. They were more like a pea and an artichoke jammed into the same shell known as the small town of Carson Springs and the *Life Vision* community. Even though Terah fit in, she still longed to be free of the church's hold. Becca, on the other hand, was like the artichoke, bristly and sharp. No matter where she went, she did not fit in. A fish out of water, she was neither well-liked nor understood. Other than sharing a birthday, the only thing they had in common was their desire to leave the community.

At seventeen, the girls began planning their escape from Carson Springs. But leaving the church was not as simple as it sounded, at least not for Terah. If someone left, they were excommunicated from their family and the community for life. There was no Rumspringa like the Amish youth were granted. In or out—the decision was final. Once out, the person was never permitted to enter the Life Circle, an imaginary line surrounding the community, without being threatened or ignored. Some who left and returned met their *accidental* demise while there. But Terah's family accepted her wishes, promising they would always welcome her back and protect her from the church and the elders. Becca's did not; they *would* not. She would be dead to them.

While Terah spoke about the lights of the city, falling in love, and a fairy-tale wedding to the man of her dreams, Becca talked about power, being her own woman, and not needing or wanting a man. Every male she had ever known had been controlling. As far as she was concerned, no one would ever force their desires on her again.

The girls knew if they stayed, they would be married by twenty, mothers within the year, and live in cottages like the ones they grew up in. They would spend their lives serving their husband in the kitchen and the bedroom. It was not what either of them wanted. So, they made a pact to live outside the community. But for Terah, that agreement tugged at her heartstrings.

Unlike Becca, Terah adored her parents. She could not recall ever being disciplined, but then again, she rarely did anything wrong. In her household, the only abuse she witnessed was doled out by the church, aimed at her parents for not having more children. The way the elders treated them crushed Terah. Having few children was viewed as an embarrassment to the community. *Go forth and multiply* was something her parents could *not* do. No matter how hard they tried, no matter how many doctors they visited, it was not meant to be.

They had been called into multiple meetings with the elders and told they needed to get themselves right with God. Because, if they were right with the Lord, had not sinned against him, he would fill their home with children. Terah could not recall her parents ever sinning against God. She did not understand how the elders could accuse them of such a horrendous offense. No individuals loved God more than her mother and father.

Terah viewed *Life Vision* as a pyramid scheme. Those at the top controlled the power. The farther down the ladder someone was, the more the power diminished, and the responsibility burgeoned. They were the worker bees, the ones whose life mission was to grow the church. If the church expanded, the wealthier Andrew Godley became, and the more *bonuses* the elders were gifted. So, of course, the elders clung to every member with steel jaws.

Even within the hierarchy, there was a strong division. The men were virtually unidentifiable as *Live Vision* members on the street. They worked in the community, wore up-to-date clothing, occasionally ate in restaurants, had tasted junk food and alcohol. The women, in their long dresses and hair swept into a loose knot at the nape of their neck, sold baked goods, jams and jellies, fresh eggs, homemade toys, quilts, and furniture along the side of the road and in town. Terah would often help her mother bake but hated being on display for tourists. As a young girl, she would frequently hide behind her mother's skirt when a stranger approached.

Still, other than growing up under the strict guidelines of *Life Vision*, Terah had had an idyllic childhood. Her father adored her mother, and her mother reciprocated that adoration. At least once a month, her dad brought gifts for his girls, something that was against church teachings. *Gifts were reserved for the Lord.* If anyone had money to burn, it was expected to be given to the church.

Her parents loved the Lord with all their heart, and if they were faithful, they knew God would return that love tenfold. But what did faithfulness look like? Did it mean destroying the dreams of their only daughter? Yes, they had chosen this life, but shouldn't their daughter have the same choice? *Life Visions* or not? So, even after being accused of flagrant disobedience of God, they remained steadfast with the church and its teachings.

The love Terah felt for her parents was equal to what she felt for the Lord. They had given her everything she had ever wanted—and then some. She did not know her grandparents. Both sets had turned their backs on them when they joined *Life Vision*. As Protestants in good standing with the church, they could not understand the choices their son and daughter had made to raise their only child in a way of life that saw punishment as love. But Terah had never been punished a day in her life—not by the church and certainly not by her mother and father.

Then Terah became an adult in the secular world, and men began pursuing her—some as old as her father, many who had lost their wife or had never married, most well past their *best by date*.

By then, Becca had been forced to return to her home to raise her siblings, so if Terah left, Becca would be alone. Day and night, Terah weighed her decision. Finally, just after her nineteenth birthday, she left in search of something better. The expectations of *do this, wear that, speak this way*—or, better yet, *don't speak at all* had finally worn her down. And the men who had tried to force themselves on her even when she refused had been the icing on the cake. She had run in the middle of the night, under the brilliant stars and a sliver of moonlight.

When Terah turned her back on the church, she knew her parents would be ridiculed and punished for allowing *one to get away*, but she could not care, not if she were going to better her life.

Her parents had not disowned her. They told her she would always have a home with them and would be welcomed back whenever she needed or wanted to return. All they ever wanted was for her to be happy, and if leaving made her happy, then they supported that. They would always be her safe place to land.

So, she packed her things and headed to a place that was the exact opposite of Carson Springs, Wisconsin—*Minneapolis*. She was not adventurous in any sense of the word, but Becca had goaded her into taking a chance, living among the lights and music, live theater, and excitement. It had taken time to acclimate to the constant commotion. While she waited for Becca to finish raising her siblings, Terah quietly faded into the background of Becca's life.

When Terah first left, she and Becca communicated daily, but as the months passed, Becca found less time for Terah, and their relationship grew stagnant. Terah wondered if Becca would ever need her again.

Then, out of the blue, more than a dozen years since they last spoke, Becca contacted her, describing the perfection of a small town called Cedar Point, Minnesota. Trees, lakes, and nature were all Terah needed to hear. It sounded like the ideal location to spend the rest of her life. Nestled along the Long

Prairie River, which fed into beautiful Cedar Lake with miles of sandy beaches, and a half hour from Alexandria, it had everything she needed. Becca sold it as a beautiful location to buy a house and start their own restaurant. That was all it had taken. Terah had not realized how unhappy she had been until she was presented with the possibility of being together again. Prince Charming did not live in Minneapolis; perhaps she would find him in Cedar Point.

Within seconds of Becca's suggestion, Terah checked out the small town. After a couple of visits, she left the big city and moved into the lower level of a house owned by Rose Hill. Audrey Laine, a woman in her eighties, had occupied the upstairs for nearly three decades.

On her second day, she dropped her resume at Just Desserts and Pauline's Café. Then she walked into Knuckle Sandwiches. They were short waitstaff. Terah grabbed food from the heat lamp and asked the cook which table was number five. She worked the entire noon rush before meeting the manager. Terah did not need to make people love her; they just did.

The minute Terah moved to Cedar Point, she fell in love— not with one person, but with everyone and everything the town had to offer. It felt like coming home.

However, one thing gnawed at her stomach. At first, Terah had thought it was exciting, but after two decades apart, the closer it came to becoming a reality, the more it weighed on her. *Becca.* What would happen when she arrived?

Maybe agreeing to live together had been a mistake. Yet here she was—awaiting the person who had always needed her but only wanted her when it was to her advantage. During their time apart, just as Becca had faded into Terah's past, so had the bad. But the closer it came to settling in the same town, to sharing a house, the brighter the memories flashed—reminding her of the pain Becca had caused—*terrifying her.*

Terah expected them to share the apartment, work in the same place, and have the same friends, but Becca, as fickle and angry as ever, made only sporadic appearances in town. When she was gone, Terah felt like she could breathe. But if she knew Becca was within a hundred miles, she slowly disappeared into herself.

From the time they were children, Becca had to have everything Terah did. If she could not buy it, she stole it, often from Terah. It was one of those *What's mine is mine, and what's yours in mine* relationships. She had copied nearly everything, purchasing the same material for dresses, buying or stealing the same shoes, even loving and despising the same foods. Becca even faked having the same peanut allergy as her. It should have been endearing for Becca to imitate her, but instead, it was annoying. It was one of the things Terah had stuffed so deep inside that she had completely forgotten about it—until the day Becca purchased an identical car—a 2010 white CR-V. They owned matching vehicles, one housed in the garage next to Audrey's Escape and the other in the driveway. It irritated more than perplexed Terah; they were forty-two years old. Why would anyone in their right mind do such a thing? But then again, Becca was not in her right mind. Terah could either accept Becca's ridiculousness or make herself sick thinking about it Still, she had more angst than acceptance.

Their old baggage washed over Terah. Had she made a mistake? *Perhaps.* As long as Becca was absent from the small town, Terah's life was golden. And lately, she had been gone a lot. That gave Terah room to breathe and develop a plan to rid Becca from her life.

CHAPTER NINE

TERAH DIXON

One person Terah had grown close to was Brian Enderly, the chief of police. He frequented Knuckle Sandwich, typically ordering the beef commercial on the cook's *secret recipe* soft white bread. Enderly was usually part of the lunch crowd when the noon whistle blew at the Pallet Factory and Cedar Point Pipes. While waiting for his food, he often visited with other patrons, keeping his thumb on the pulse of the town.

Arriving just before the factory workers, the chief always sat in Terah's section of the restaurant—the last booth facing the door. He almost always came alone, but occasionally another officer or his wife, Jane, would join him.

Jane was a kind woman who rarely let her husband out of her sight. Anxiety was permanently etched on her face, ever-present in the lines around her eyes and those across her forehead. Loud noises made her jump. The week before, when a busboy dropped a bucket of dishes, she screamed and fell face down in the booth, as if attempting to hide. It seemed peculiar for the owner of Hallman and Carter, a huge Mid-West Human Resources firm, to be so unhinged.

From the small-town gossip mill, Terah learned the reason for Jane's social unease. Two years before, she had almost been killed by a man who turned out to be her half-brother. And her ex-husband, a high-powered attorney, had had his own plans to destroy her as well.

Sean Hart, Jane's ex, resided in a psychiatric hospital after losing all connection to reality. Kidnapped, or rather *sold* as a child, ignored by her parents, and sought by the high-powered players of Cedar Point for all the wrong reasons, Jane had become somewhat of a celebrity. Her story put Cedar Point on the map. It was broadcast on TV stations all over Minnesota and even hit *People magazine.*

That experience also made her fear almost everything and everyone in her life. The only people she trusted were her husband, Brian, and her adult sons, Cole and Luke. After Jane's mother was sent to prison for extortion and conspiring to murder her own daughter, word came out that the man she had called her father was not. That role was biologically assigned to Harrison Andrew Carter the Second. It was a shock to everyone. No, Doug Sterling was the man she had always known as her father. She had despised him nearly as much as she did her mother. However, when everything was sorted out, Jane realized Doug had been nothing more than a pawn in her mother's game of life, a game Viv, her mother, played with a vengeance. The more convoluted the lies, the more money they were worth.

If anyone understood complex lives, it was Terah. Becca had lived one as well. Many church members back in Carson Springs had suffered the same. Once Terah left, she realized that nothing was ever as it seemed. Secrets were kept behind closed doors. Even the self-proclaimed *holiest man of Life Visions,* Andrew Godley, the founder, had skeletons in his closet. In the past twenty years, many had been exposed, but Terah was willing to bet those that came to light were only the tip of the iceberg.

Terah poured Jane's coffee and refilled Brian's Diet Coke. Like her and Becca, the chief and his wife were as different as night and day. Enderly must have weighed over three hundred pounds. He was not fat; he was just a big man—someone you would not want to run into in a dark alley. Jane was his opposite.

A strong wind could have toppled her. She ate like a bird, picking at her salad with her fork while he shoveled in an overflowing plate of beef, potatoes, and gravy in minutes.

But they were in love. Terah could see it in the way they looked at one another. It was the passion she saw between her mother and her father, the love she hoped to find one day. But the clock was ticking. She was forty-two and had only been kissed by creeps. She was not a virgin, at least in *Life Vision's* eyes. In her second year in the city, she had been raped while on a date. If she still belonged to the church, they would have faulted her. It would have been something she had worn, something she had said that had caused it to happen. She had asked for it. Like any woman in their right mind would say, "Please molest me, rape me, and treat me like garbage."

The church taught that men could not be expected to stay away from women who "enticed" their inner demons to come out and play. Terah did not see it the same way. The guy was a monster who locked her in a public bathroom, pinned her down on the floor, and covered her mouth while he raped her. Then, he had the nerve to return to their table of mutual friends. When she stopped crying and pulled herself together enough to leave the bathroom, she saw him sitting there, laughing as if nothing had happened. She walked the four miles home, hiding in the shadows, hugging the buildings like a frightened animal. The monster had not only taken her sense of security, but he had also taken her purity, something she had saved for her husband. From that day forward, she feared men. Group outings were the only way she went out any longer, and even then, she never left the table unless she was with another female.

After that, Terah saw herself as weak. Had it happened to Becca—the man would have drawn his last breath before he had unzipped his pants.

CHAPTER TEN

TERAH DIXON

Terah glanced at the clock on the front of the microwave. It was four minutes to nine. She had expected Becca to arrive around dinnertime, but she had not made it. One small piece was missing from the pan of lasagna Terah had made. It was Becca's favorite meal. A piece of garlic toast wrapped in plastic sat atop a lidded bowl of Caesar salad. If things went according to plan, neither the salad nor their friendship would survive until the following day.

Terah clutched her phone, willing it to ring. All four texts she sent had gone unanswered, and her calls had been sent straight to voicemail. Terah was beyond concerned. Panic surged through her, squeezing her chest until she could barely breathe. It meant only one thing when Becca went off the radar: something bad had happened—or was about to. Over the years, she had seen Becca go off the rails more times than she could count. Everyone became a target, and anything a weapon. In one of her rages when they were children, she had thrown a cat off the rock wall when it brushed against her leg. When Terah closed her eyes, that movie played and replayed. No matter how hard she tried, she could not unsee it.

Terah shut off all the lights except for a nightlight in the living room. She paced through the kitchen and dining room, heading down the hallway and back up before beginning the trek again and again. At half past midnight, she lay on the couch, pulled a thick blue finger-knit throw over herself, and finally dozed off. She had propped herself up on pillows, facing the door. When Becca arrived—*if* she arrived—Terah would know immediately.

Just before dawn, when the house still hugged the darkness, Terah woke with a start. Had she heard something, or was it just her nerves playing tricks on her? Was Becca home? She wrapped the blanket around her shoulders and tiptoed down the hall. Praying she would find Becca asleep, she slowly turned the knob and peeked in. A strip of moonlight spread across the still-made bed. She sighed loudly. Her hand was wrapped around her phone. Her cramped fingers rebelled when she twisted the phone to check for a message. *Nothing.*

Terah stripped off her day-old clothes in the bathroom and crawled into the hot shower. It was her early shift. Baking bread was one of her favorite jobs, but today, it was overshadowed by concern about Becca.

She had no doubt that whatever had happened was Becca's doing, and it would be covered in a layer of ugly.

The restaurant was a five-minute walk from Terah's duplex. Dread clouded the joy she usually felt on her way to work. Her feet felt heavy as they moved along the sidewalk that had fallen into disrepair.

Only once, in the middle of a torrential downpour, had she driven. While Becca's car always remained outside, Terah's was protected in the garage. The van Audrey used for volunteering was parked on the street.

On rare occasions, Terah and her upstairs neighbor would make eye contact. For a woman in her eighties, Audrey Laine was a mover and shaker. If she was not volunteering, she was working in her gardens. A retired nurse, she now cared for flowers, plants, and those in need. During the cold winter months, when she was too frightened to drive on the icy roads, she found friends in her books. Terah was a fan of neither gardening nor books, so they seldom shared more than a few words.

When Terah removed the last loaves of bread from the oven, the restaurant was nearly ready to open its doors to the lunch crowd. A dozen times or more since arriving at work, she had checked her phone. She felt the noose of fear tighten with each passing hour.

One of the servers had called in sick, so Terah picked up her shift. It was not the money that convinced her to stay; it was the distraction. At home, she would stew about Becca—worry and wonder what she had gotten herself into.

Just after 7:00 p.m., after thirteen hours on her feet, Terah threw her apron into the laundry basket in the workroom and headed out the back door.

The headache battle that had started during the dinner rush had turned into a full-blown war. A misty haze circled the streetlights and swirled before her. Her stomach lurched, and she threw up in someone's yard, spraying vomit across their flowerbed. Wiping her mouth on her sleeve, she narrowed her vision until all she could see were the tiny hairs of her eyelashes and a slit of light. She placed one foot in front of the other, feeling her way along the cracked sidewalk.

Terah stumbled down the stairs and into their apartment before crumbling into a heap on the worn sofa. The last thing she saw before she passed out was Becca standing over her with a knife.

CHAPTER ELEVEN

CHIEF BRIAN ENDERLY

Brian pulled into the station just minutes after the noon whistle blew. He had driven up and down every street looking for the woman with the dark hair who had shown up at the station claiming to be his dead sister. But anyone who fit the description, he knew.

His brain buzzed. How could this not be a farce, someone playing an incredibly cruel trick on him? Wren Brigham Enderly had been nothing but a name, a secret his mother had shared with him on the day she was killed. The baby had never taken a breath and had never lived outside his mother's womb. That left him wondering—How should he refer to her if not dead? Unborn? Imaginary? Fictitious? A callous joke?

Suddenly, other thoughts bombarded him. How far along had his mother been when she died? Could she have been farther than he thought? Was it possible she had hidden the pregnancy from his father for months rather than just a day? That would not have been difficult. The man was drunk damn near all the time, and he rarely noticed anything except an empty bottle.

The noise in his ears intensified, and the vein near his temple pulsed. Memories flashed in time to his drumming heartbeat.

A few weeks before his mother told Brian he was going to

be a big brother, she had been hired to care for old Mrs. Paquette. She was bedridden and had no one to help her. Her children lived hours away, her husband had passed, and her sister was too old to care for her. If Brian had learned anything, it was that no matter how much money you had, it meant nothing in the end.

While his mother watched over the older woman, Brian would often go with her. It was better than dodging whatever his dad threw his way—physical or verbal.

A thought squeezed through the door and lodged in Brian's memories. The entire time he had been in the house, he had never actually seen or heard Mrs. Paquette. He had spent his days playing with his train or other toys his mother had packed in a paper bag, or he wandered the woods near the house while his mother dusted, cleaned, and cooked. Squeaky floors, broken windows, and dust gave the home the appearance it had been abandoned. But Brian knew better. While he did not see her, he heard crying and other noises from upstairs.

Then, one day, his mother told him he could no longer come. The end of the woman's life was nearing, and out of respect for the family who would be stopping in for their final goodbyes, she needed him not to be underfoot.

For over a week, Brian did not see his mother. He remained at the house, dodging his father. He spoke with his mom on the phone, but she did not come home. She said she *could not*.

Then, one day, she returned. She hugged him and went straight to her room, where she spent the next couple of weeks—too worn out from caring for the dying woman. When he asked her why she was sad, she said watching Mrs. Pauquette had taken a toll on her. Then she held his face between her hands and said something curious. *We don't always get what we want.* Brian's young brain took it to mean she did not want the elderly woman to die. Now, he wondered if they had been talking about two different things.

He kicked the garbage can. It slapped against the side of his desk, wobbling back and forth until it finally stopped. Was it possible the old woman had been a cover? Had his mother had the baby before she even told them she was pregnant? Had she given his sister away? Did Mrs. Paquette even exist? If she had used caring for her as a cover, why would she ever have told him she was expecting? Brian stared out the window. Had someone kept his sister until his mother could test the waters and see if her husband would turn his life around for another child?

Questions were a dime a dozen. What he needed was answers. Where would he get them? Could he track down the Paquettes? Would they know anything? If not, who would? If there was truth in any of this, his father had lied to him.

Brian shook his head. This *maybe* sister would have been born when? Forty-two years before—*1982*. Could he count on his eight-year-old memory? Could he really have a sister out in the world somewhere?

"Dammit!" This time, he sent the garbage can flying. It bounced off the wall and exploded debris everywhere.

"What's that bin ever done to you?"

Brian jumped at Mauri's sudden appearance. "You've got to stop doing that."

"What? My job?" She grinned before handing him a can of Diet Coke and a pink slip of paper.

"I swear you cut a year off my life every time you sneak up on me."

Mauri grinned. "Might wanna plan your funeral sooner than later, then." She patted him on the arm and disappeared.

Brian read the note she had handed him while he drank his soda. "What the hell is this?"

Mauri appeared at his door. "Point to the words you want me to sound out, Boss."

"You're hanging on my last nerve, woman."

She flashed him a look of disdain. "So, what exactly do you want to know, then?" She plucked the note from his thick fingers. "It says that Warden Harmon called and wants you to call him back."

He shot daggers at her. "I know that's what it says. I'm not stupid."

"Well, your previous question begs to differ." Mauri grinned.

Brian crumpled the paper and squeezed it until his knuckles turned white. "Any secretary worth their weight in gold would have asked more questions if a prison warden called."

Mauri's hands balled into tight fists. She climbed onto a chair and pressed her face close to Brian's. "Listen to me, Boss. First of all, I am not a secretary." She poked a finger into his chest. "I'm an administrative assistant. There's a big difference. I work for the entire squad, not just you. You just happen to be the asshole sitting in this office. And second, I only weigh a hundred and two pounds. So, if you want somebody better than me—someone worth 'their weight in gold', hire somebody fatter." She jumped off the chair and headed toward the door. "Oh…" She spun on her heels. "And if you ever call me *woman* again, I'll use a taser on you and pluck your nose hairs while you're struggling to breathe." She slammed Brian's door on her way out.

Seconds later, his door opened, and he walked out of the station, returning minutes later with a McDonald's bag and a tall takeout glass of ice.

Brian put them both on her desk before going into the workroom. He returned with a can of Diet Pepsi, popped the top, and emptied it into the glass. "One plain hamburger. Nothing on it. No french fries. A tall glass of ice with a cold Diet Pepsi." He stood before her with his hands folded.

Mauri scowled at him. "You think this is going to get me to forgive you for being a dick?"

Brian's head bobbed. "I was kind of hoping so."

The station door opened, and Deputy Porter sauntered in. He glanced at Mauri's desk. "What number is this, Chief?"

"Two," he and Mauri said in unison.

"It's only Tuesday, Brian." He looked at Mauri as she took a sip of her soda. "What'd he do this time?"

Mauri raised her eyebrows. "The usual. He stuck his size thirteen boots into that big mouth of his." She put her hand on Porter's arm. "Hey, would you let me borrow your taser some…"

"Do not let her touch that thing. Understand?"

Porter laughed. "I'm staying out of this." He followed Brian into his office. He sat across from the chief and grinned. "Hey, Mauri. I hear you can buy them on Amazon."

"Already found one."

"Shut the damn door," Brian told Porter.

Jeff got up and closed the door. "You two've been going at it a lot more than usual lately. What's going on? I haven't seen you like this since the whole incident with Drew and Sean."

Brian spun his chair around and stared out his window. His deputy respected the silence.

"Have you ever had a situation where you can't figure out what's real and what's not?"

Porter's brow creased. "You mean like in every case we've ever had to solve? Or are we talking about hallucinations?"

Brian turned his chair to face his deputy. "I'm not crazy—although I'm sure Mauri would tell you differently." He leaned toward Jeff. "Remember the name Wren Brigham from two years ago—the name my old man used when he set up Hart for trying to hire a hitman?"

"That's hard to forget. Cedar Point isn't exactly streaming with hitmen, fake or not. Why are you asking?"

"You know that was the name my mom planned to name the baby she said she was expecting just before she died, right?"

The deputy shrugged. "Yeah. Where are we going with this?"

"Something doesn't add up. Someone stopped in a few days ago claiming to be Wren Brigham Enderly—my sister."

"Are you kidding?" Jeff shook his head. "How is that possible?"

"Exactly. Now you know why I'm on edge."

"What'd she say when you asked her about it?"

Brian snorted. "That's the thing. I was off that day, and you were out on a call. By the time I got to the station, the woman was gone. The only person who saw her was..." He pointed toward the door.

Deputy Porter narrowed one eye. "You know damn well Mauri would never make up something like that just to get to you. She likes pranks, but she's not evil."

Brian nodded. "Yeah, but if she had, this would be over, and I could move on."

"There's something off with this," Jeff said. "It doesn't make sense."

Enderly nodded. "I know."

"Have you googled the name?"

The door opened, and Mauri strolled in. "I have."

Brian snorted. "Well, of course, you have." He gave Porter a knowing look.

"So far, I haven't found anyone with any combination of those names. I haven't gone through the police database yet, but I will if…"

"Do it." Brian nodded. "You're going to anyway. So, you have my permission."

Mauri's head bobbed as she turned to Porter. "Jeff, you want a *Diet Coke*?"

Porter laughed before placing a hand to his heart and role-playing utter shock. "Why no, Mauri. You know I would prefer a Diet Pepsi."

"Get out, both of you." Brian pointed to the door and waited for them to leave.

The deputy stuck his head back inside. "What about hospital records or birth certificates? It might be too long ago for the hospital to still have paperwork, but a birth certificate should have been filed."

Brian opened his mouth.

"On it," Mauri called from her desk.

"Damn, she's good." Porter laughed.

"You don't have to tell me." Mauri snickered. "By the way,

Jeff, would *you* say I'm worth my weight in gold?"

"Oh, my God!" Brian said. "Give it a rest, would you?"

CHAPTER TWELVE

CHIEF BRIAN ENDERLY

Brian shoved his door shut with his foot. He held the pink note in his hand. Why was Bob Harmon, the warden at Superior Correctional Institution, calling him? He had an urgent need to know, and yet he was afraid to make the call. They had worked together two years before, but he had not spoken to him since.

Truth be told, he liked Bob, but he was not thrilled with how he had manipulated him to talk with his father—locking them together in a conference room. Sure, it had helped get some things out in the open. And for the first time in twenty years, he saw his old man as he wished he had been when Brian was a child. *Sober*. But the way Harmon had gone about it had pissed him off. Plus, now that his supposed sister had appeared, he wondered if his dad had been honest with him.

Maybe Harmon wanted to talk about a case. Brian looked at a photo of him and his mom. Or perhaps it was something else.

Brian dropped into his chair. A long breath passed through his lips. More likely, it was bad news, something to do with his dad. Could he have passed away? His stomach flip-flopped. Two years ago, that news would have given him cause to jump for joy, but no longer. Today, he felt something he had not experienced in a very long time—at least where his dad was concerned—*worry*.

As a child, Brian lived in constant fear. He worried about everything. A day had not passed without him feeling the crushing pain of fear and uncertainty. But this fear was different. It was chilling and had wrapped itself tightly around his chest. Struggling for every breath, he leaned forward in his chair and breathed like his therapist had taught him nearly forty years before.

He picked up the phone and returned it to the cradle a half dozen times. Mauri opened his door. "Do you need me to dial that number for you?"

Brian's brows pressed together. "How in the hell did you know…"

Mauri tapped her leg with the fingers. "The phone light has gone on and off, on and off so many times it looked like a strobe. For a second, I thought I was going to have a seizure."

"Out! Get out! And shut the door."

Mauri grinned. "You've kicked me out more times today than usual, Boss. I'm thinking you might need some help."

Brian gritted his teeth and pointed to the door. He waited for the click before picking up the phone and dialing the ten-digit number. It was nearing the fourth ring when he heard Harmon pick up.

"Warden Harmon." The voice was commanding yet gentle.

Brian fought with himself not to hang up. "Bob." He cleared his throat. "Brian Enderly here."

"Just the man I've been waiting to hear from." Brian heard Bob shuffle some papers. "Hold on a second, okay? I'm digging for something."

Brian blurted, "Is my dad okay?"

"Of course, did… Ohhhh. You thought I was calling because something happened to him."

"It crossed my mind." Brian was not sure if he felt relief or disappointment. He hoisted his feet onto his desk and put the warden on speaker, knowing full well Mauri would hear every word, even with his door closed. This was far easier than trying to explain Bob's side of the conversation afterward.

"Sorry, I should have said that in my message. Your dad's fine. As a matter of fact, that's why I'm calling. Mack is actually going to be released within the year."

Brian's feet dropped heavily to the floor. "What? How can that be? He's got a hell of a lot of time left to sit behind those bars."

"According to the numbers, yes. He should be in a long time yet. But your dad's been a model prisoner. He's working the system. And, after his help with Sean Hart—or Hartung—or whatever he's going by these days, the parole board decided to look at an early release."

"I can't believe it. It doesn't seem right."

"You *can't*, or you *don't want to* believe it?" Brian could hear Harmon blow on his coffee. "The governor's new program to get nonviolent prisoners back into society is working. Our goal is to rehabilitate them. Your father is one of our greatest success stories."

"Success, my ass. That man's a murderer—not once, but twice."

"I know you think that, but he didn't actually murder anyone. Involuntary manslaughter—yes. But he's been sober for over twenty years. At this point, his rate of relapse is less than ten percent. And your dad knows if he does relapse, he'll find himself right back in here to finish off his sentence. Plus, we'll have support systems in place before he walks out that door." Brian heard Bob set his coffee cup down. "Besides, it's not like he'll just walk free. He'll do a year in a halfway house and three years of probation. He'll have to land a job, which means peeing in a cup weekly, and there'll be random alcohol checks."

Brian could not speak. He was not sure if he was angry or in shock. One thing was for certain; he never wanted to see his old man on the streets of Cedar Point.

"Your dad's been working with a social worker."

"I want their name and contact info." He wagged a pencil above a pad of paper.

"Hold on. Let me find it." More papers shuffled as Brian waited. "Here it is. Dr. Jennifer Olson. 607-555-1239."

"When will he be sprung?"

"Don't have a firm date yet. He has to finish up his program. Best guess—six months to a year. I wanted you to hear it from me, though."

Brian sighed loudly. "Thanks for that, I guess." He hung up the phone. "Mauri!"

The door flew open instantly. "Yes, Boss."

"Did you get all that?"

"What are you talking about?" She pressed a hand to her chest and scrunched her face. "Did you think I was listening to your private conversation—with the warden—about your dad?" She spun on her heels and headed out the door. "Yeah, I got it."

"I assumed as much."

Brian looked at the name he had written on the notepad. *Jennifer Olson.* "Well, Jennifer Olson, you and I are about to become really good friends. I'm going to be on you about everything. You aren't going to be able to fart sideways without me questioning it and how it's going to impact my father's release."

Mauri reappeared in the doorway with another Diet Coke. "How would you even know if she farted sideways? Is that even possible?"

"Get out!" Brian rethought his command. "Wait! Find out everything you can about Jennifer Olson. She's the social worker…"

"I'm already working on it."

CHAPTER THIRTEEN

CHIEF BRIAN ENDERLY

Brian paced the small waiting room outside his wife's office at Hallman and Carter Human Resources for nearly twenty minutes. Jane's meeting had gone much longer than she told him it would. While he waited, her assistant offered him coffee, soda, a magazine, a trip to the work lounge, and a handful of snacks, fidgets, and other things. He had turned down everything she presented. Brian knew he was making her nervous, but he could not help himself. Finally, she bid him goodnight and left. For that, he was grateful.

When Jane ushered the last employee from her office, Brian raced in and slammed the door. The loud bang made them both jump. Jane fell against the wall and released a long breath.

"I'm really sorry." He gave her a peck on the cheek and pushed past her, around the corner, and into the depths of her office, where he practically threw himself onto the couch like a toddler having a tantrum.

"What's going on?" Jane asked, settling next to him. "Something has you really upset."

Brian dropped his feet to the floor and sat upright. "Guess who I talked to today?" He did not wait for her to answer. "Bob Harmon at the Superior prison."

Jane gasped. "Does this have anything to do with Sean? Are they moving him from the psych hospital to the prison?"

Brian jerked his head back. "What? No. This isn't about your ex, Drew, or anybody related to what happened two years ago." He looked up. "Well, that's not entirely true."

"Well, what then? You're scaring me."

"Bob told me my dad's going to be released sometime in the next year."

"What? How is that even possible?"

He crossed his arms and nodded. "That's what I asked. After I talked to him, I did some research on early release. It's possible." He huffed. "Bob says Mack's been a model citizen who's—catch this—*working the program*." Jane laid a hand on his leg. Brian covered hers with his. "Before he went to prison, the only thing that man put to work was his elbow—hoisting a glass or bottle to his mouth probably a thousand times a day."

"Things change, honey. People change."

Brian grimaced. "And if I said that about *your* mother, the infamous Vivian Sterling, who's also sitting in prison for conspiracy to commit murder, would you agree with me?"

Jane laughed softly. "No."

"And why not?"

"Because she's *my* mother. She's evil. She always has been and always will be. I lived with her my entire life. I know how…" She smiled at her sudden understanding. "Got it."

"Bob says Mack's working with some social worker." He turned toward Jane. "Which is where you come in."

"What do you need me to do?"

"I need you to help me find out about a company called Thrive Mental Health out of Duluth. Have you ever worked with them before?"

"I've heard of them, but we don't usually do HR for companies that far away." She poked a finger into the air. "But Mark Jonas just joined an HR firm in Superior. I might be able to call in a favor or two. I just don't want to get him fired before he proves himself." She grabbed a notepad from her desk. "So, don't hold your breath." Brian nodded. "What specifically are you looking for?"

"Anything about the company: services they offer, ratings, why they work with the prison, the steps they go through to rehabilitate a prisoner, and anything else that might prove they can be trusted. I'm most interested in learning about a social worker they employ—a doctor named Jennifer Olson."

Jane scribbled notes on the same pad. "Jennifer Olson? Now, there's a name you don't hear every day in Minnesota." She rolled her eyes. "There's probably five hundred Jennifer Olsons in Minnesota alone." She typed the name into her computer search engine. "Seven hundred and one to be exact."

Brian's eyebrows shot up as he watched his wife over the top of her screen. "It's that last one I want to know about. The other seven hundred, I don't give a rat's ass about."

Jane sat on the edge of her desk. "Why are you worried about this woman? Are you afraid Mack will try to convince her to sign off on his release papers even if he's not ready?"

Brian nodded. "Convince her? No. Force her? Quite possibly. It's Mack. I don't trust him farther than I can throw him. I never have. I doubt I ever will." He stood up and wrapped his arms around Jane. "Now, let's get out of here and go have dinner at some romantic little restaurant in Alex."

"It's Alexandria, Brian. Romance and quiet aren't exactly what the town's known for. It's a tourist city."

He took her hand and pulled her toward the door. "Doesn't matter. As long as I'm with you, I'm happy."

Jane grabbed her purse and her jacket from the hook near her door. "Then table for two it is."

Nothing could dampen their mood, not even the woman with the dark hair in the parking garage watching them drive away.

CHAPTER FOURTEEN

BECCA HULLS

Anxiety swelled inside Becca. A zipline of fear raced the length of her body. *"Hello, Becca."* Her heart threatened to jump out of her chest.

How could that woman have known Dr. Jennifer Olson was a ruse? *How?* Becca had covered her bases so carefully, dotted every *I*, and crossed every *T*. She had left nothing to chance. That was why it had taken her two years to mold it into the perfect plan. Had it been destroyed in just a couple of words?

First, she had to know who the woman was and how she knew her as Becca.

Insurance and contact information were exchanged. It was an equal trade, a safe one—Becca's P.O. box in Ashland for the woman's P.O. box number in Duluth. There were no street addresses for either. Other than the city name, there was nothing to pinpoint an exact location. Not that it mattered; no one would find her in Ashland. Potter Street did not exist. She also questioned the validity of the woman's address.

Becca was a good judge of character. And this woman screamed trouble. Something definitely felt off.

The woman claimed full responsibility for the accident. But the account of what happened felt too rehearsed, over-performed, and the remorse too contrived. Becca listened as the lady clarified for the officers how her hairbrush rolled off her console and lodged beneath the brake. She explained she had attempted to slide it out with her foot, but her toe became trapped beneath the pedal also. Then, when she tried to dislodge it, she accidentally pressed the gas with her heel, sending her car forward. The tale was deceptively slippery, yet the cops bought every word. *Cut and dried*—entirely fabricated—at least in Becca's mind. She knew the woman was a liar. Terah often slammed her with "It takes one to know one." Every time she heard those words, she wanted to destroy her.

Becca didn't consider herself a liar. She was a *storyteller*—there was a big difference. Yes, she manipulated the facts, stretched the truth, and exaggerated even, but always for a good reason. Becca could see no motivation for *this* elaborate story—except to out her.

Becca's eyes narrowed as she stared at her. Suddenly, the woman returned to her car and fished a hairbrush from the floor in what was meant to be irrefutable proof. *An accident.* This time, Becca noticed something she had not seen before—a small cut on the lady's forehead, an angry red splotch, and a thread of blood that had not been there before. She winked at Becca before turning toward O'Connor, faking pain and discomfort. He expressed concern over her head, handed her a wadded-up tissue, and helped her to a car she could lean against.

With an act like that, the officers saw no need to check the cameras in the lot or to seek witnesses. And why would they? *Joyce* was on their payroll.

Becca's eye twitched. Joyce knew her identity—her true self, as she had said when she snapped her picture. Becca rubbed her eye and once again tried to leave the scene, but the police were not quite done.

Standing on the sidewalk, near the door, was the prison guard who had let her in to meet with Mack. When their eyes met, her breath caught inside her. The wag of his eyebrows and evil smirk sent chills down her spine. A band of tightness wrapped around her chest, and she could barely draw air in. Panicked, Becca spun on her heels and hastily wheeled her suitcase across the lot and through the prison gate. She moved so quickly that there were times when the two wheels of her suitcase never touched the pavement.

Listening for Joyce's henchman to approach from behind, Becca raced along the stone prison wall, keeping her face low, away from the cameras.

After several blocks, a dozen corners, and numerous back alleys, Becca stepped behind a tall hedge. She poked her head out, confirmed the intersection, and pressed several buttons on her phone. Satisfied, she returned it to her jacket pocket before removing her black slacks and tugging on a pair of jeans. She traded her red wig for a mousy brown one before turning her reversible jacket inside out and poking her arms through the sleeves. Finally, she pulled on a plain blue baseball cap and a pair of sunglasses with lenses so dark that no one could see her eyes.

As the driver approached, Becca stepped onto the sidewalk. She knew the area, the street names, and the escape route she had used. She had practiced it before. The accident had never been part of her plan, but the need for a quick getaway had always been a possibility. No good con left anything to chance.

Becca climbed into the Uber and contemplated the unfairness of her situation. She was not a con. She was the victim. Others were responsible for everything that was about to happen. The music they would face was dark—murkier than Guiseppe Verdi's version of the *Day of Wrath*. Fitting? Most definitely. It was her theme song. At 7:00 a.m. every day, she woke to the angry beat thundering inside her.

Now, everyone who made her suffer would hear it.

Canal Park was the destination she had entered into the Uber app. It was autumn, the time of year when tourists flocked to Duluth to delight in the brilliant colors of the changing season and the migration of eagles and hawks. Except for tugging her suitcase, she would easily blend in. The driver dropped her in front of the first of a long line of overnight accommodations. She got out and waited for him to drive away before walking a mile to an inn up the hill and away from Lake Superior.

Before entering what appeared to be a one-star hotel, she hid in a small jag in the building and pulled the gray-floral luggage cover from her suitcase and tucked it inside. She made a reservation under a new name and credit card. Today, she was Rachel Smith from Minneapolis, Minnesota. With one hundred forty-six Rachel Smiths in Minnesota, she was the proverbial needle in a haystack.

The clerk pursed her lips and informed her that check-in was not for another five hours. Becca waved a ten-dollar bill in front of her face and asked if she might change her mind. The woman checked her computer and offered to store her luggage until then. Another ten ensured it would be delivered to room 307 precisely at three. Becca had been willing to go five times that high, but the woman nearly drooled at the prospect of twenty bucks. *Pushover.*

While the woman watched, Becca slipped a small padlock through the zipper-pull holes on her suitcase and squeezed it shut. It was a silent message to the clerk that she did not trust her. Then, she walked out of the drab lobby and into the bright sunshine.

After purchasing a Duluth sweatshirt and cap from a tourist shop a block from the hotel, she waited for someone to leave the outdoor bathroom of a rundown gas station down the street. Becca grabbed the key from the hand of an unstable woman with a cane, offering to return it when she was done. She dug through her backpack, retrieving everything she needed. Becca tugged the sweatshirt over her black T-shirt and pulled a short blonde wig over her pinned up, capped, dark hair, before yanking on a brown baseball cap. After rounding the bill between her palms, she pulled it down to meet a different pair of sunglasses she had lifted from a convenience store a few days before.

Someone pounded on the bathroom door, but Becca ignored them. Staring at herself in the scarred mirror, she barely recognized Becca Hulls. But then again, that was no longer who she was. She was *Wren Brigham Enderly.*

The pounding started again, this time accompanied by yelling and a handful of unsavory words. She quickly shoved her jacket into a plastic bag and dropped it into her backpack. She lowered the bill of the cap once again before walking out.

"It's about time," the wild-eyed woman screamed at her.

Becca quickly closed the door behind her. She snapped her fingers and grinned. "Oh, shoot! I left the key inside."

The woman's mouth fell open, and her eyes narrowed. "You bitch."

Keeping her face down, Becca walked away as the woman continued to scream at her.

The hills were steep as she headed north-west away from the lake. Her breathing grew labored as she climbed two more blocks. Finally, she turned south-east and walked a handful of blocks along the level street, before turning north-west again. After a half mile or so, she tossed a plastic bag with some of her clothes into an open dumpster behind a small hardware store and continued a couple more blocks before making the trek back down to the canal via an alternate route.

Every step had been meticulously calculated. She had left nothing to chance. In the last two years, Becca had learned to think on her feet, weigh every movement, every choice she made. As a child, when she was in earshot of her family, she had been practically perfect. But she could turn on a dime, playing whatever role she needed. Mack Enderly had started the avalanche of hatred inside her, and her parents, *Life Visions*, the elders, and Daniel had widened it.

Becca would take no responsibility for anything she had done or was about to do. None of it was, or ever would be, her fault. It rested solely on the shoulders of Mack Enderly. He had forced her hand—left her entire life to chance on the steps of that church. If anyone should rot in prison, it ought to be the man who threw her away. What kind of a person did that? Not a *normal* human being. But then again, she had met him, and in her estimation, he was anything but normal.

CHAPTER FIFTEEN

BECCA HULLS

Canal Park was busier than usual, more active than any of the dozen or so times she had scouted the area. That worked in Becca's favor. She purchased a box of popcorn and a soda from a long-haired college kid in the vendor wagon before hiding herself on a bench in the crowd near the lake.

The first thing on her agenda was procuring a car. But not just any car would do. It had to be a white 2010 CR-V, the exact vehicle she had been driving. She checked the used car sites and the classified ads in the newspaper someone had tossed into a trashcan. *Nothing.* She called used car dealers but struck out again. One dealer told her it was a very popular car, as that exact make and model had driven off the lot not more than a half hour before.

In her mind's eye, Becca let loose. She screamed, yelled, and beat the man on the other end of the cement bench. Her hands trembled, and she curled them into tight balls. Closing her eyes, she drew deep breaths, reminding herself she had never failed and was not about to start now. Finally, she grabbed her bag, tossed the paper into the trash, and headed down the Lakewalk toward Fitger's.

Gobbling down a hot dog she bought from a street vendor, she headed toward her hotel, keeping her eyes cast downward. She took great care to ensure her steps were even, so her right heel always landed near the crack between boards. Only once did someone get in her way. After a thunderous sigh, she adjusted her steps and began again.

Finally, she veered off the boardwalk and headed along the street. The light at the intersection of Lake Avenue and East First Street was red. Becca's impatience swelled. Her entire life had been spent waiting—waiting for her dad to stop beating her mom, for him to come after her, to see where her brother went so she could disappear in the opposite direction, and to find out who she was. She had waited too long.

Becca pressed the button to cross the street. She cringed as she listened to the robotic command, "Wait! Wait! Wait!" Nearly a full minute passed before he announced, "Walk. Walk. Walk." Still keeping her face tipped down, she stepped into the intersection. Someone laid on their horn and swerved, narrowly missing her. She jumped backward and banged on the roof of the car.

"Asshole!" She flipped off the driver and screamed the insult again.

The car's brake lights popped on, and the driver veered across two lanes of traffic before making a sharp right. Becca froze. She was positive the car was circling back for her. Dashing across the street, she ran into the grocery store on the corner and raced toward the women's bathroom. Inside, she locked herself in a fully enclosed stall. Minutes passed. When no one entered, Becca's breathing slowed.

Suddenly, the bathroom door opened and closed. She held her breath as the person wiggled the door handle. The heavy footsteps entered and left once, then a second time. No toilet flushed; no stall doors banged shut.

For nearly an hour, Becca waited in the stall. The door had not opened, nor had she heard a peep. She silenced her phone and stared at a map. It was five blocks to the hotel, almost all uphill. Would someone be watching her? Waiting for her? Her gun was missing, but her switchblade was still in her backpack. Before opening the door, she pulled it out and shoved it in her front pocket. She would not go down without a fight.

Slowly, she cracked the door open and scanned the room. When she stepped out, she gasped. Her name was written in red lipstick on the bathroom mirror, printed as a kindergartener might. The word taunted her, sending her into a full-blown panic.

The walls were caving in. The air was being sucked from the room. She had to get out of the store.

People stared as she bounded down the aisle, knocking over a stack of cereal boxes arranged in a half-circle, stacked like Jenga blocks. The automatic door did not open fast enough; it caught Becca's shoulder. She cursed but did not stop running.

Her feet pounded the pavement with a steady beat as she raced toward the hotel, nearly tripping over the leash between a gray-haired woman with a walker and her bichon. She passed through the front door and ran up the three flights of stairs to her room. When it did not open the first time, she slid the card into the slot, kicked it, and swiped it again.

The slam of the heavy door echoed in her head as she twisted the deadbolt and pushed the swing bar in place. When she turned around, she nearly fell over her suitcase, which had been deposited just inside her room. Her shirt rode up her back as she leaned against the fake wood and dropped to the floor. Locking her arms around her legs, she pressed her forehead against her knees and sobbed.

An hour later, locked in the bathroom, she stood in a hot shower, letting the water wash away the frustrations of the day. Each time she shifted direction, the pitch of the water pelting the shower curtain changed. The sound was soothing. As a child, the bathroom was the only place she had felt safe.

When she turned off the faucet, her skin was a brilliant shade of red. She poked her hand around the end of the curtain, pulled a towel from the hook, and haphazardly dried off in the shower before throwing back the curtain. She screamed. Her name appeared on the mirror, in the same red lipstick and the same lettering as in the grocery store bathroom.

Someone had been in her room, picked the lock on the bathroom door, and stood five feet from her while she showered behind the gray curtain. Were they still there?

Becca pulled on the clothes she had discarded on the floor and slowly opened the bathroom door. She pulled the switchblade from her jeans pocket, popped it open, and palmed the handle as she searched the room.

The space beneath the bed was empty, as was the closet. And no one was hiding behind the floor-to-ceiling curtains that ran along one whole wall. Becca jerked out every dresser drawer, even knowing no one could hide in there. Logic and fear were enemies. There was no adjoining room, and the window and the door were locked. Even the swing bar was still in place.

She stood at the end of the bed and turned in a slow circle. Fear thundered inside of her. If everything was locked, how had someone gotten into the bathroom? Was it possible the writing had been there, and she had not noticed it? Had it been done when the suitcase was delivered? Goosebumps rose on her arms. Had the woman at the desk figured out who she really was?

She grabbed a box of tissues from the desk and headed to the bathroom to erase the evidence before someone else saw it. When she turned the corner, she gasped. Except for a wiped-clean spot in the middle of the mirror, the reflective glass was covered with steam, but her name was gone.

Becca dropped onto the cold, damp ceramic floor, curled into a fetal position, and bawled. What was happening to her? Was she losing it, or was someone playing tricks on her?

CHAPTER SIXTEEN

BECCA HULLS

All night long, Becca kept vigil, waiting and watching. Was she being conned? No. She was positive she had an enemy. Was it Joyce? Or maybe it was the prison guard. Or could it be Cedar Point's Chief of Police, her own brother, Brian Enderly?

The clock on the nightstand read *3:17 a.m.* Becca's body ached from lying on the cold floor. It was nearly midnight by the time she had moved to bed. But no matter how exhausted she was, sleep would not come, not one wink. She would not let it. Becca was afraid to even blink for fear she would miss the moment someone entered her room. Her racing heart had not slowed. She had to get out of the hotel and out of Duluth before anything else happened. If she left now, the cover of darkness would give her a head start. *How?* She did not have a car but knew how to hot-wire one.

Her hand ached from gripping the switchblade all night long. She set it next to her and rubbed her palm and the base of her fingers, stretching them outward until the stiffness eased and the pain dissipated. Still wearing the same clothing as the day before, she pulled on a pair of socks before tiptoeing to the bathroom to pee and brush her teeth. She shoved everything in her suitcase before unlocking the door and peeking into the empty hallway. Finally, she quietly lugged her suitcase down the stairs on the opposite end of the building and into the back parking lot.

When she opened the door, her eyes narrowed, and her heart raced. Heat flooded her stomach. She blinked rapidly, uncertain it was not a dream. A white 2010 CR-V, identical to her car, was parked three cars down from the door. Becca scanned the poorly lit lot but saw no one. Except for a lighted stairway on opposite ends of the building, the hotel was dark.

Cautiously, she approached the car and peeked inside. The car door popped open when she pulled the handle. A half-smile lifted one corner of her mouth. It was too good to be true. Confident it wouldn't work, Becca inserted the key for her now demolished car into the ignition and turned. The engine hummed to life. How could this be happening? Was she dreaming?

She jumped out and tossed her bag into the backseat. Before anyone noticed, she backed out of the parking space. Racing through the lot, she narrowly missed a burly man walking his dog. He looked directly at her and gave her that crooked smirk. Becca's heart banged against her ribcage. It was the prison guard.

Trying to distance herself from the man, she sped toward the freeway but thought better of it. Becca spoke into her phone, requesting directions to Cedar Point using all back roads. The phone told her that the four-hour trip would be double that. That did not matter. If it kept her off the main drag, she was all for it. She stopped only for gas, food, and bathroom breaks and never saw the guard again. By the time the police began searching for the stolen vehicle, she hoped to have enough distance between herself and Duluth that no one would connect the dots that pointed to a woman over two hundred miles away.

Around 10:30 a.m., as she walked out of the Holiday Station in Mora, a police cruiser rolled past the front door. She tilted her head down and raised a large glass of soda to her lips to cover her face. Instead of heading toward the gas pump where the stolen car was parked, she turned left, walked around the back of the store, and watched for him to leave. Becca drew a deep breath and released it when the squad car turned north on Highway 65.

Once he was out of sight, she rushed to the car and drove in the opposite direction. She had to be more careful, go deeper into the backwoods. Pulling down a side road, she rerouted to follow gravel roads through farm county. An hour outside Mora, she drove into what appeared to be an abandoned farm. The weeds were waist-high. A strong wind could have taken the buildings down, making it a safer place to hide. She eased the car through the yard and parked behind the barn. Tilting her seat back as far it would go, she checked the locks on her doors, closed her eyes, and drifted off to sleep.

Three hours later, she woke. She checked her route and made a few adjustments, hoping to enter Cedar Point just before sunset.

At 6:10 p.m., she drove into the small town. The sun was low in the sky as she approached a four-way stop. Becca scrunched down as Brian Enderly's squad car passed directly in front of her, heading north. She sat at the intersection, contemplating her move. The woman in the car behind her laid on the horn, sending her in the same direction her brother had gone.

Becca kept him in her sight the entire time, holding a consistent distance. Five minutes after she started following him, he drove into the ramp at Hallman and Carter. Becca parked on a side street and walked past the barrier arm into the parking garage. Hugging the side walls, she made her way to the back of the block structure. Brian had already disappeared into the building. A dozen cars were randomly parked in the ramp, including the SUV in the spot near the door, marked with the sign *Reserved for Jane Enderly*.

It was well past quitting time. But other than Jane, a small group of butt-kissing minions, all driving big-buck cars, and the cleaning crew, whose cars were similar to Becca's, everyone else had left the building. At this time of day, anyone entering would likely leave before long. She would wait.

Becca tested the door, but as she had expected, it was locked. She scanned the lot for a hiding place, eventually taking cover behind a column beyond the farthest car in the lot. Anyone leaving would go the other way. When all the newer cars had gone, she knew her brother and his wife would not be far behind. At quarter after seven, the door popped open. Laughter echoed through the open space. Holding hands, they walked toward their cars.

Enderly opened Jane's car door. "I'll pick you up at home in five minutes," he said. Then he leaned in and kissed her before she drove out of the lot.

Becca clutched the switchblade as she silently stepped from behind the pillar. She moved swiftly and silently. But her *brother*, the chief, was parked too far away. He was gone before Becca could leave her *message*.

Ten minutes later, angry as hell, Becca stumbled into the apartment she shared with her one-time best friend, Terah. Terah lay on the couch looking like death warmed over. As she opened her eyes, Becca leaned over her, popped the switchblade open, and almost drove it into her friend's chest.

Becca was done with her. Terah had held her back too many times. She was so tired of her sanctimonious drivel and goody two shoes attitude. But she could not do it. The woman with the unending positive outlook and an annoying smile might be helpful yet. Her shoulders folded forward, and she retracted the blade.

A new plan was already piecing together in the short trip to her bedroom.

CHAPTER SEVENTEEN

BECCA HULLS

By the time Becca rose, Terah was gone. Except on rare occasions, like the previous night, the two hardly ever connected. Becca was not sure Terah had seen her standing over her with the knife. If she had, she most likely would not have closed her eyes and gone back to sleep. She would have fought. But based on the bucket she had her hands wrapped around, the prescription bottle lying on the floor, and the beads of sweat that rolled across her forehead, Terah was undoubtedly suffering from one of her debilitating migraines. Nothing would have registered, and any memory of the night would have been sucked into the black hole of her empty head.

Terah's judgmental personality made Becca want to pull her hair out. She had forgotten how much Terah's righteousness angered her. If she had it to do again, she would never have invited her long-ago friend to Cedar Point. She would have left well enough alone.

Their hit-or-miss interactions made Terah tolerable. Lately, all they did was battle—via notes left on the kitchen table, text messages and glaring looks as they passed one another. Their lives orbited around the duplex in Cedar Point. Thankfully, they appeared to be on different courses, periodically colliding before setting themselves straight and heading in opposite directions.

Another thing that bothered her about Terah was that she always settled. Take her job, for instance. It was a menial position that brought in just enough money to pay her share of the rent and food. To Becca, it was a waste of time. A job like that was beneath her. Life was about getting what you deserved.

Money was pivotal to Becca. She did not waste it on things she could get in other ways, like stealing. Becca pilfered things she *needed:* food, personal supplies, and clothing. As for the rent, it was paid in gratis by an old woman she had cared for. With no family, she helped herself to the woman's bank accounts, jewelry, and anything worth selling. Becca had credit cards in a couple dozen people's names, including the old broad's, *Bernice Anttila.* As Bernice was dying, Becca withheld her pain meds until she signed everything over to her. That made Becca rich, filthy rich. But no one knew that, not even Terah.

Becca shoved the last bite of peanut butter toast into her mouth, licked her fingers, and typed *Jane Enderly* into the search engine on her laptop. Article after article populated the screen. Some she had read while researching Brian, but others were more interesting than she initially thought. To get to Mack, she had to get to Brian. To get to Brian, her easiest mark was his wife, Jane. Undeniably, the woman had a past deeper than she cared to admit—or knew about until the last couple of years. Through no fault of her own, Jane Enderly had lived a life of lies. And now that she had found true love, she may have let her guard down. Becca needed to strike while the iron was hot.

Hours passed as Becca outlined Jane's life. Her ex-husband, Sean Hartung/Hart, had been a huge part of her miserable existence since shortly after she was born. According to several articles, Sean's family had purchased her from Vivian Sterling for monthly installments. *Yes, purchased.* The papers from back then recounted a kidnapping by two men in a blue truck. But somehow, two years later, Jane, known as Emily Hartung—

sister to Sean—was found wandering the streets of Alexandria and returned to her birth parents in what was described as a miraculous reunion. No one was ever charged. Because no one knew she had ever been part of the Hartung family. Sean's family had kept her hidden indoors, away from the neighbors' prying eyes. After she was returned to her family, Sean's mother committed suicide, and he and his father moved to Duluth, where they began a life free of all Hartung women.

Somehow, Sean had reconnected with Jane/Emily, later marrying her. That made her his wife/sister. According to the news articles, Jane knew none of this. She recalled nothing about living with Sean's family. Several articles questioned why Sean married her. Was it to love or punish her for abandoning him with his alcoholic father? A quote from Jane stated the latter. Even as depraved as Becca was, she was sickened by the thought that someone would sell a child. Perhaps it was too similar to her own story.

But that was not the only tragedy in Jane's life, a tale resembling the madness of *King Lear*. Secrets were abuzz in the small town. It seems Jane had been born the love child of Harrison Andrew Carter II and Vivian Sterling. That secret was buried deep within the pair. Harrison, a founding partner of Hallman and Carter, never breathed a word of it. Neither did Viv. No one else would have known had it not been for Harrison's will.

Several articles told of the difficulty of Jane's life with Sean and her desire for an amicable divorce, but her husband would have no part of it. He stated he would kill her before he would let her leave him—again. It was clear he had never gotten over her disappearance as a child.

Warned by the FBI that someone was after her, she quietly disappeared before they could take her into protective custody. Jane was certain it was her husband who wanted her dead, but she had been wrong. The person who needed to destroy her was her half-brother, Harrison Andrew Carter III—Drew—a sibling Jane knew nothing about. After running his father's company into the ground, he needed every penny of his old man's inheritance to save it. However, the will stated the money was to be divided unless one sibling was deceased before their father.

Two, as Drew called his dad, was closing in on the finish line of his life. So, Drew conspired with Jane's mother for a price tag of five million dollars. Drew saw it as insurance money that would keep secrets from being revealed and would give Viv the nest egg she needed to live the remainder of her life in the lap of luxury. However, when the dust settled, Drew was dead, Viv was remanded to prison, and Sean snapped, remanded to a psych hospital where he remains today, and Jane became the sole owner of Hallman and Carter. She was a wealthy woman.

Jane's entire life had been puppet-mastered. To Viv, she was a *dammit* baby—a child who should never have been born. Sean saw her as someone he needed to punish. And Drew Carter had perceived her as a threat. After everything that happened, she admitted, she still lived in fear. That admission gave Becca the lead. It was her serve, and there was no way she could lose this time.

That was where Terah came in, not the real Terah, but a Becca-fied version of her. She would become Terah, Sean's long-lost cousin. Becca would not know until she spoke to him what he knew about his wife or if he could or would give her enough information to ruin her. All she knew was that she had to try.

CHAPTER EIGHTEEN

BECCA HULLS

After calling the hospital to inquire about visiting hours, Becca donned a navy floral two-piece dress. It was the homeliest piece of clothing Terah had in her closet. She selected a pair of low-heeled shoes—not so unlike the leather ones they had worn beneath their long dresses growing up under the rules of *Life Vision*. She stared at herself in the mirror as she applied pale pink lipstick and just a touch of mascara. Pinning her hair up and tucking it beneath a wig cap, Becca bent forward and tugged on the blonde wig. Standing, she straightened it, pinned it in place, and wove the long bangs into a small braid at her crown.

Becca sighed loudly. "Terah, you are most definitely a tiresome woman." She snapped off the bathroom light. "It's no wonder you have never had a boyfriend."

She slipped on a tan jacket and lifted the strap of a purse that held a duplicate of Terah's ID over her shoulder before moving toward the door. Stretching her neck upwards and pulling her shoulders back, Becca channeled Terah: the sugary smile, the positive outlook, and the childlike simplicity. For the next several hours, she would portray her one-time best friend better than Terah herself.

For thirty minutes, Becca practiced Terah's honey-sweet

voice and no-nonsense words. Upon her arrival at Serenity Park Health Hospital in Alexandria, she summoned Terah's movements. As she proceeded toward the front door, there was a spring in her step, almost a skip, but not quite. The receptionist directed her to follow the yellow line, explaining someone would help her when she reached the end.

"Thank you so very much. You were so helpful." Becca conjured a Terah smile and waited for the woman to respond.

"Oh, aren't you just the sweetest."

Becca smiled broadly and nodded before walking on the yellow line through the hospital.

"Good afternoon, ma'am," she said when she reached the end. "I'm Terah Dixon," Becca smiled. "Sean Hartung, I mean, Hart." She sadly shook her head. "I guess I'm not even sure what he goes by now."

The woman silently stared at her.

"Anyway, Sean's my cousin. I haven't seen him in years, but I was here visiting my mother, and she told me about his…" Becca looked around, then spun her index finger around her ear.

"Ma'am. We don't refer to patients as *crazy*."

Becca pressed a hand to her chest. "Oh, goodness. I'm so sorry." Becca's eyes softened as she looked at the woman and whispered, "That was something Sean taught me when we were kids." She cleared her throat. "Thank you for pointing that out to me. I'll be more aware."

"What's your name?" The woman's hands hovered above her computer keyboard.

Becca could feel her head sweat beneath the warm wig. The woman eyed her the way Joyce had.

"Terah. Terah Dixon," she said quietly.

Keys clacked as the woman typed her name and other information into the system.

"Three-nine-one Shady Road, Washburn, Wisconsin, five-four-eight-nine-one." It was a phony address Becca had used multiple times—one she could spew by heart. Then, she repeated a phone number that went to a burner phone that forwarded to her cell.

"All right, Miss Dixon. Have a seat. Someone will be out to speak with you shortly."

Becca smiled. "Thank you so much." She looked at her hands. "It's going to be so hard to see my cousin this way. But I feel I need to. We were so…"

The woman pointed to the small waiting room. "Have a seat," she said.

She backed into a gray two-seat sofa. Memories of waiting to speak to Mack flooded her. She tried to push them away before they sprouted roots and grew vines that choked her. But it was no use; the thoughts boomeranged back again and again. If Joyce had figured out who she was, could this woman? Her stomach fluttered. The toast she had eaten for breakfast suddenly felt unwelcome. If the hospital uncovered her lie, could they lock her away? Becca scanned the room, noting the exit doors.

"Miss Dixon?" A thin, brown-haired woman in a black pinstripe suit and white blouse held a door open as she looked around the room. "Terah Dixon?" the woman called again.

Becca squared her shoulders and walked toward the woman. "That's me," she said in a sing-song voice, mimicking Terah.

"I'm Doctor Hillary Evenson." Becca followed her through the hall. "I'm a little surprised. I didn't even know Sean had other family." She shrugged. "His wife, or rather *his ex-wife*, never mentioned anyone else. But then again, there were a lot of things he kept hidden." The doctor stopped at her office and pointed inside. "Let's talk in here, shall we? I'd like to get to know more about you before I decide if it's in Sean's best interest to meet with you."

Becca swallowed hard. "I completely understand. I only want to do what's best for my cousin."

"Good. Then we're on the same page. My concern is for Sean as well."

Dr. Evenson pointed to a chair on the opposite side of a

maple table. A box of tissues and a small bowl of chocolates sat on a tray in the center. Becca pulled out the chair and smoothed her dress before sitting.

"I don't know how much you know about Sean's state of mind."

Becca shook her head slightly. "My mother has said nothing to me. I'm not even sure *she* knows how he is."

Dr. Evenson nodded. "In Sean's mind, he is four years old. He's lost his entire life—everyone except his mother, father, and *Emily*, that is." The doctor stared at her. "I assume you know about Emily—or rather, Jane."

"I do." She folded her hands with the neatly trimmed fingernails. "Such a tragedy."

"Good. That will make seeing him this way a little less—*frightening*." She pressed a hand to the edge of the table and slid her chair back. "So, tell me about your relationship with Sean."

Becca cleared her throat, piecing together the story she had concocted the previous night. "Where would you like me to start?"

The doctor got up and grabbed a notepad and pen from her desk. "You say you are cousins." Becca nodded. "On your mom or dad's side?"

Two years. She had spent two years planning every conversation, every story—except this one. This was a spur-of-the-moment plan that popped up when she watched her pathetic friend the previous night. She had to remember everything she said, every lie she told, in case someone asked her to repeat it. But if Sean was as bad as the doctor claimed, there would be no way of checking on her tales.

"Our moms are sisters." *Give details.* "My mom was older by a year. So, they were very close."

Doctor Evenson scribbled down some notes. "Did they have other siblings?" Becca shook her head. "Well, then, do *you* have any brothers or sisters?"

Becca almost blurted out eight. But then she remembered

it was Terah's life she was describing. Sharing as many real facts as possible would make it easier to remember. "No, just me. It was the same with Sean, well, other than Emily. But I never knew her." She straightened her back. "That's why the two of us were so close." Quickly, she calculated that Sean would be about fifty-two. She aged herself. "We were just a couple years apart."

"Did you live near one another?"

She scanned her memory, attempting to recall all the details she had read about earlier in the day. "No. I never lived near him. But once he and his father moved to Duluth, we spent a lot of time together."

"Oh, so you lived in Duluth, then."

"Not quite. I grew up in Washburn, about an hour or so from there."

The doctor nodded. "It must have been terribly hard for your mother to spend time with Sean and his father after her sister committed suicide."

Becca twisted her hands. "It was. But she wanted to be there to support Sean and his dad."

"Your mom must have been a saint."

"Oh, she was." Becca wanted to scream, *Which mom? The one who gave birth to me? The one who raised me and was beaten daily? Or Terah's mom—the one who actually supported her daughter?* Instead, she nodded and added. "Definitely."

Doctor Evenson flipped over the notepad. "I think a visit from you might do Sean some good, Terah. Maybe your presence will spark some memories in him."

She stood, and Becca followed. "I won't listen to your conversation, but someone will always be watching through the one-way mirror. Since he has been here, Sean has never been violent, but you never know. Better safe than sorry."

They stood at the door and peeked in. Sean was lying on his bed watching a TV attached to the wall. A cat bounded across the screen, and he smiled.

"After I reintroduce you, I will step out." She studied Becca. "Do you have any questions?"

"I don't think so."

Becca closed her eyes and drew a deep breath. "Wait!" She laid a hand on the doctor's arm. "Do you think he will recognize me?"

The doctor shook her head. "I don't. When was the last time you were together?"

Becca's eye started to twitch. She rubbed it with her knuckle while she answered. "I was probably fifteen."

The psychiatrist shook her head. "Then it's not likely. Most people look a lot different than they did as a teenager." She smiled. "At any point you want out, just raise your hand like this." The doctor held her arm high in the air.

Becca nodded. She stood behind the doctor and watched her unlock the door.

"Sean, you have a surprise visitor. This is Terah, your cousin."

Becca studied his face for a flash of confusion.

Dr. Evenson stepped forward. "Do you remember Terah?"

Sean rolled over on the bed and dropped his feet to the floor. The corners of his mouth turned upward, and his eyes grew wide. "Terah. Terah. Terah." He smiled at her and grabbed her hand. "Cousin Terah." A huge grin crossed his face. "Want to play cars with me?"

"That would be fun," Becca said quietly. His quick acceptance unnerved her.

Sean pulled her to the corner where a black rug had been marked with roads. Small buildings had been painted on it. Becca recognized the town as Cedar Point. The hospital had recreated the town, perhaps hoping it would help Sean remember. Goosebumps rose on her arms as she watched him push the small cars down the road, calling out each place he passed.

Becca had been in Sean's room for under fifteen minutes when she raised her hand to be let out. It was extremely unsettling to watch a grown man play with cars and act in such a childish manner.

Before she followed the doctor to the door, he threw his arms around her and asked if she would visit again. Becca didn't have a choice. If she could learn even one thing from Sean, it would be worth however long it took. All she wanted to know was Jane's Achilles tendon—a way to get to her that would make Brian suffer. Whether he could give her that was debatable. For all she knew, Sean might not even remember Jane.

After debriefing with Becca, the doctor asked if she planned to return.

"I will. I'm hoping to catch a glimpse of the Sean I knew when we were kids." She looked toward the door. "I'm only here for a couple of weeks. So, is it too soon if I return tomorrow?"

"Not at all. Just make sure it doesn't get to be too much for you. It's hard to see loved ones struggling like this—and this is a rather unusual case." She patted Becca's shoulder. "Sometimes it takes a toll on us that we don't always see at first."

"I'm sure. But Sean and I were so close. I think maybe I can help him. And if I can, I want to."

The doctor crossed her arms. "That would be wonderful."

CHAPTER NINETEEN

BECCA HULLS

The following day, Becca arrived at 10:00 a.m. on the dot. Instead of a dress, she had on jeans and tennis shoes. The only way she would get Sean to talk to her was if she played with him.

"Sean, look. Your cousin Terah is here again."

A huge grin crossed his face. "Terah. Terah. Terah," he sang as he had the day before. He threw his arms around her shoulders and tucked his head into the crook of her neck. Sean made a noise as he squeezed her. Then, he dashed to the town and sat on his knees.

The rug was in a different location than it had been previously. It had been moved to the far corner of the room—opposite the observation window.

"Want to play cars again?" Sean held out a truck for her.

"I sure do." Becca smiled.

"Well, I'm going to leave you two alone," Dr. Evenson whispered. "Remember, someone will be on the other side of that mirror the entire time. If you need help…"

Becca nodded. "I know."

The doctor escaped through the heavy door. Becca heard the lock click. *Was this what prison was like—minus the toys? If she got caught, this could be her life—locked in a small room.*

Sean pushed the cars down the street. Again, he called out the names of the buildings he passed. When he approached the jail, he looked at Becca.

"That's where the bad guys go," he said. He tilted his chin toward his chest and looked up at her with his eyes. "Or the bad girls." His mouth flat-lined. "Are you a bad girl, Terah?"

Becca swallowed hard. "Oh, no, Sean. I'm a good girl," Becca assured him. "I'm a *very* good girl."

His shouldered rose. "Okay, then." He hummed as he drove the little yellow convertible down Main Street.

Becca picked up a truck and pushed it along a parallel road. Suddenly, Sean picked up his car and slammed it into her vehicle.

"Hey," he said. "I thought you were a good girl."

"I am, Sean."

"Well, good girls don't crash their cars." He grabbed his car and parked it in front of the police station. "The policeman needs to know you're not a good girl."

Instead of continuing Sean's story, Becca changed the subject. "Where does Jane live?"

Sean's eyes narrowed, and he glared at her. "I don't know no Jane." Then he maneuvered the little car down one street and up another. After a few minutes, the smile on his face grew evil. "Look, Terah. I found Jane's house."

Becca studied the street name. "How do you know that's Jane's house?"

Sean laughed. "Fooled you." He laughed louder. "I'm just teasing."

"You are a little stinker, aren't you?" She turned her back toward the one-way glass of the viewing room and pressed her shoulder against Sean's. "Jane was your sister Emily, but she ran away from your family." She set a hand on Sean's back. "Do you remember Emily, Sean?"

Sean's back muscles tightened. "I hate Emily. She left me. I hate Jane. Jane left me too."

"That's right, Sean. Jane left you. She's a bad person. But

Emily was just a little girl. She didn't know she wasn't supposed to leave."

Sean lay on his stomach on the rug. "I hate girls. I hate Jane, and I hate Emily." He scowled at her. "And I hate you."

"Oh, Sean, you don't really hate me, do you? I came to play with you. I'll come back tomorrow too, if you want me to."

Sean's eyes darted around the rug. "Yes. Come back tomorrow and the next day and the next day. I like Cousin Terah." He continued to sing those last four words over and over.

"It's time for your lunch, Sean. But I'll come back tomorrow."

"Okay, Emily and Jane and Terah. You can all come back tomorrow. I want to play with all of you."

As Becca raised her hand to signal her desire to leave, she knew exactly how to get into Sean's head.

Again, Becca arrived precisely at ten the following day. She wore a pair of dress slacks and a blazer—much like Jane might have worn when she and Sean were married. The two sat on the floor and drove around the replicated town of Cedar Point. Sean seemed to enjoy this more than anything else in the room.

Becca turned her back to the observation room again. "Sean, do you know who I am?"

He nodded. "You're Terah. Terah. Terah. Terah."

"No, Sean. Today, I'm Jane. My name is Jane."

Sean's jaw tightened, and he tilted his chin toward the floor. His eyes grew wide. "You are not Jane. Jane is icky. Jane is mean."

Becca rubbed his back. "Sean, let's just pretend I'm Jane. What would you say to her?"

He took several long, loud, and angry breaths. His nostrils flared. "Jane is bad. She left me."

Becca was afraid Sean would start yelling, so she changed direction. "Okay. I'll be Emily. What do you want to tell

Emily?"

Sean pressed an elbow into his thigh and rested his chin in the palm of his hand. "Why did you leave me? I thought you were sleeping. But you left me." Again, his eyes grew wide, and anger washed over him. "Bad Emily! Bad girl, Emily."

"I *was* a bad girl, Sean. I was a very naughty girl."

"I hate you, Emily."

"My name's Jane now."

Sean's eyebrows knit together, and his mouth curved down. He got up on his knees and stared at her. "I hate you, Jane. You're a bitch."

That was progress. The man-child was breaking out of his shell. He had just called Jane a name most four-year-olds would not know.

Becca continued to push. "I'm your mom, Sean."

Sean stared at her. His eyes were wet. "Mommy? Mommy, why did you leave me? Did you love Emily more?"

"I'm Jane again," Becca whispered.

Sean wiped the tears from his eyes. "I don't want to play no more." He got up and lay on his bed. "I wanna take a nap."

"Okay," Becca said, pulling the blanket over him. "I'll see you tomorrow, Sean."

But he did not respond.

CHAPTER TWENTY

BECCA HULLS

When Becca left the hospital on the second day, her phone had blown up with a dozen or more messages. Several were for her; others had been forwarded to her phone when her office telephoned her emergency contact, Terah Dixon. A few were for her fictitious references, trying to find out if anyone knew where she was. Everyone at the office of Thrive Mental Health was searching for her—or rather, *Jennifer Olson*—wanting to know where she was, if she was okay, and when they could expect her to return to work.

Concocting believable stories had quickly become Becca's specialty. Shortly after noon, she called the office from her cell phone, blocking the number with *67.

"Good afternoon. Thrive Mental Health Services. This is Bethany. How may I direct your call?"

"Hi, Bethany," Becca said. Her voice was airy and at a higher pitch than usual. She slowed and softened the tone. "This is Jennifer."

"Oh, my gosh, Jennifer. Everyone in the office has been so worried about you. Where are you?"

Becca wrapped her arms tightly around her stomach to keep from breathing deeply. The move caused her breaths to sound tight and shallow. "I've been in the hospital."

"The hospital. Are you okay?"

"I have a really bad case of mono."

"Mono? I didn't even know adults could get that."

"Me either. I just got home. I-I'm heading up to bed. Will you please let Karen know?"

"Absolutely. Can we do anything for you? Food? Flowers?"

Becca cut her off. "N-no. I won't enjoy them anyway. Maybe once I start feeling better…" The last thing she needed was for the office to attempt to send flowers to a street address that didn't exist.

"Of course, Jennifer. You take care of yourself. Let us know if you need anything at all."

"I will."

"Promise?"

"Yes. I have to go. I'm so tired."

"I understand. You go rest."

"I'm going to shut my phone off for a week or so."

"Thanks for letting me know. I'll let the others know."

"Thank you."

Becca hung up the phone and laughed out loud. Pulling the wool over Bethany's eyes was the easiest thing she had done since leaving the Carson Springs house. Either she was a damn good actress, or Bethany was dumber than a box of rocks. She wanted to believe the first but knew it had more to do with the receptionist.

Every day for two weeks, Becca arrived at the hospital mid-morning. Dr. Evenson told her that for the first time in almost two years, Sean was making progress that was not followed by a backward slide. There were no words Becca wanted to hear more. She was closing in on getting some tidbit from Sean— something she could use against Jane. The only person she really wanted to hurt was Mack Enderly. But playing with the others was a fun little bonus.

"Hi, Sean. It's me." Becca lowered herself to the floor and

sat with her back toward the mirror.

Sean glared at her. "Who are you today?"

Becca stiffened when she heard the hardness in his voice. His words did not sound playful like a child's but more like the fifty-two-year-old Sean's. Information was important, but she did not want to push him too far, too fast.

"I'm Terah, honey. Your cousin, Terah."

Sean nodded as he intently watched her. "Terah? My cousin?"

"Yes, Sean. Do you remember me?"

He nodded, picked up the truck she always drove, and set it in front of the police station. "This is where you need to stay today."

"In the police station? Did I do something wrong?"

Sean looked directly at the window before turning back toward the rug. He picked up his yellow convertible and drove it down Maple Avenue. He stopped in front of the park and pretended to get out and go to the playground. He alternated his index and middle finger to look like he was running across the park. Again, he turned toward the observation glass.

"Can I play with you?" Becca asked.

The manly voice that exited his mouth startled her. "I'm pretty damn sure that's what you've been doing for the past couple weeks."

Becca's eyes widened, and she gulped air. "What?"

"You heard me. Who the hell are you, and what do you want?"

She sat very still, aware someone was watching from the window. For the first time, she was grateful for the person on the other side of the mirror. Becca started to lift her hand, but Sean pressed his over the top of it and held it in place.

"I'll ask one more time. What are you after? Money? Information? Me? My ex? My sons? Who?"

Sean bounced his head like a child for the observer.

"I'm Terah."

"Like hell you are. I have no cousins—period. Now start

talking."

"I think I should go."

"No, you don't." He leaned on her hand harder. "You need to stay and tell me who the hell you are. Otherwise, I'll spill everything about you."

Becca grinned at him before driving her blue truck away from the jail with her free hand. "Wow! All this time, I thought you were some crazy-ass attorney who was just majorly effed up. Now I find out you've been hiding in here for two years, pretending to be four years old." She tipped her head closer to his and whispered, "You don't think that's not going to raise some flags?" She pulled her hand from beneath his. "What's your deal anyway?"

Sean stared at her before making a show of driving his car down the block. "It didn't start that way. For eighteen months, I was trapped inside that little boy." He took a deep breath. "Then, things slowly began to come back to me. It wasn't until you showed up and started pushing me to remember Jane and Emily that my full memory returned." Sean got up on his knees and drove his truck around the corner and down Main Street. He peeked at the window. "Keep up the act, would you? The last thing we want is for them to come in here."

Becca drove her truck down a road and pretended to go into the grocery store.

"So, who are you?"

She pressed her aching shoulder blades together. "Who do you want me to be?"

"Are you medical?" Becca shook her head slightly. "Law?" Again, a shake of her head answered his question. "Then what's your business?"

Slowly, she pretended to climb into the tiny truck. She drove her car next to his car. "I'm on a mission. I need to destroy someone."

"Who?"

Drawing a deep breath, she admitted her end game for the first time. "Mack Enderly."

Sean clapped his hands like a child. "Perfect. We're on the same page. I want that son of a bitch to pay also. So, how is this going to happen?"

Becca shrugged. "The only way I can get to him is through his son. And the only way I can get to his son is through your ex-wife."

Sean gave a deep growl. Becca jumped as he grabbed her hand and squeezed so hard that she was sure it would break.

"You touch one hair on my wife's head, and I'll kill you." He stared at her. "Understand?"

"Your *ex-wife*," Becca reminded him.

"That's only temporary."

Becca shook her head and reclaimed her hand. "I think you're delusional, Mr. Hart. Your wife's married to the Chief of Police now." Sean's eyes grew glossy as Becca grinned. "You've got your head up your ass if you think you're going to win her back."

Sean spoke very quietly, so softly that Becca had to lean closer. "It's been said that nothing is for certain except death and taxes." He gave a childlike howl of laughter. "And I doubt very much that a con like you pays taxes. So…" Sean scowled. "You best be looking behind you because death may be heading your way."

Becca's jaw tightened. His eyes said he was not kidding. She stood and waved her hand in the air.

CHAPTER TWENTY-ONE

JANE ENDERLY

Jane poked her head out of her office door and looked around before closing it. The click of the deadbolt rang in her ears as she made her way down the short hallway that led into the main part of her office. It was quiet, too quiet. The hairs on her arms rose, and she shuddered.

Glancing up at the black-faced clock, absent of hour and minute markings, she sighed loudly. It was *about* 6:25 p.m., but that was only a guess based on the position of the hands. She had spent weeks weighing whether the two-grand price tag was worth it. But the more she thought about it, the more she realized it symbolized her life. The years had passed without noting the minutes or hours. It was the days that stood out—both good and bad: giving birth to her sons, suffering Sean's daily abuse, being forced to give up her career on her forty-seventh birthday, facing her madman brother and mother on the day she nearly died, and the unveiling of secrets on that same day. Jane looked up at the clock again. It was definitely a conversation starter, but no matter who started the dialog, she shut them down if it turned to her.

Jane moved deeper into her office. Nearly everyone, except the cleaning crew, would have left the building. The solitude made her skin crawl. Place her in a room full of people in the middle of the day, and she was unruffled. But gradually empty the room, and her anxiety would surge.

The main part of her office was hidden from the narrow glass panels on the sides of her door. She had selected cloudy privacy curtains that let the light in but would not allow others to see through.

After passing through the third-floor security checkpoint and being interrogated by her assistant, visitors would enter through the door and travel down the sixteen-foot-long corridor before turning into the central part of her office. She was grateful for the unusual design that let her hide. But it was after hours, and the guards were gone for the day, which made Jane uneasy.

She instructed her digital assistant to play instrumental piano to drown out the quiet while she paged through the folder in front of her for the dozenth time in the past two hours. The meeting with the finance director had gone better than expected. Profit predictions were headed in the right direction. Resuscitating the company after Drew's poor management had not been easy. Her directors would be pleased. Raises, albeit small, would be forthcoming, leading to increased morale and the retention of employees who had been slipping closer to the door out of Hallman and Carter under her brother's mediocre leadership.

With Drew gone, Jane sat at the helm of the Human Resources company she had inherited from her *father*. Even two years after learning about her parentage, that word still made her breath hitch. The father she had grown up with had been detached and cruel. But that was before she learned her malevolent mother had forced him into that role.

After getting the company back on track, Jane made security a priority. It was not because the small town of Cedar Point was unsafe but because of the madness of what had happened to her two years before. She knew the odds of anything that horrific transpiring again were unfathomable, but she was not about to take a chance. Every employee underwent a yearly background check, and new hires were rigorously screened before being placed on the payroll.

Top-of-the-line security had been added before she returned to the office full-time. Before that, she worked from home, protected by cameras, alarms, and window grids. Those entering Hallman and Carter passed through a metal detector monitored by a security team before stepping foot inside. A biometric iris scan had been installed for employees. Her husband, Brian Enderly, and sons, Cole and Luke, had been added to the list of employees, allowing them to come and go at will. From a room near the entrance, two rows of cameras were watched during business hours. The entrance, hallways, conference rooms, and waiting rooms had cameras—with the sound turned *off* for privacy and security reasons. While there was a camera outside Jane's door, her office was devoid of surveillance. There were too many company secrets that needed to be safeguarded.

The next measure to be implemented was a twenty-four-hour security team. After all that had happened, Jane wanted her employees to feel safe. But even with all the processes and procedures in place, she would never let her guard down. A guard accompanied her to and from her car every day. And she was never to be alone in the building. If she needed to work on the weekend or after the cleaning crew left, she paid a security guard to be on staff.

It should have made her feel safe, but instead, it made her skin crawl to think she had to go to such great lengths to keep her sanity in check. She was confident her staff placated her even though they didn't know the whole story. However, her husband, the Chief of Police, felt the extra security was warranted, because he had been part of that nightmare.

Trees swayed, and clouds drifted across the darkening sky, casting ever-changing shadows on the surface of the lake and city below Jane's window. One after another, the streetlights made themselves known, illuminating the small town below. Sitting in the window seat she had installed when she redesigned the office, Jane felt safe. The glass was tinted to let her see out, but others could not see in. When it had been installed, she had not trusted it. She spent an entire week testing it from every angle. Brian had placed a large floral arrangement in the window and left a light on; then, for two weeks, they had driven around the town day and night, rain and shine, to curb Jane's fears. Finally, satisfied, she settled into the space that had once been her father's office.

A loneliness stirred inside Jane. Brian had left town to attend a small-town police training institute in Fargo. It was too far to drive back and forth. He would be home in a couple more days. In his absence, Brian had arranged for her boys to spend the night with her—in the fortress she had become accustomed to.

Jane had visited her sons' house numerous times since the *incident*, as it was whispered about around town, but she had not been there after dark, with the shadows and unknowns. The memories were still too fresh, too raw. They were so powerful, she could stand in the middle of their living room with her unhinged half-brother—recalling all that had transpired—the gunshot that nearly killed Hoss, Luke's Newfoundland, the fenced yard that hid Drew's entrance into the house, Drew's condescending words when he told her she had to die so he could inherit all the money from *their father*.

His words made no sense. They were incomprehensible, like listening to the TV and the radio simultaneously. Bits from each slammed together, creating a jumbled mess of sounds that had no meaning.

Jane was born a Sterling. How could they share the same father? Then, the realization struck her. Viv had lied. She had buried her indiscretions and secrets beneath stories and innuendos. Her unscrupulousness had started long before Jane breathed life. It was no wonder her mother hated her. Jane had been a reminder of the affair between Harrison and Viv.

As Drew held her at gunpoint, his mission had been clear— *she had to die*. But in her mind, that fact took a backseat to her

DNA. The floor gave out beneath her. She was *not* a Sterling by blood but a Carter of the extremely affluent Carters. Hallman and Carter was where she had spent twenty-five years, working side-by-side with the people she had not known were her family. That knowledge made her want to live. As a Sterling, the town despised her. Her mother had seen to that. As a Carter, she would have been loved and adored by the town, as they had with her brother—before he went off the rails.

Yet, there she had stood, face-to-face with her *brother*—a loaded pistol between them. She had bargained with him, offered her silence, even her part of the company, in exchange for her life. But the look in Drew's eyes had told her no deal would change his resolve to kill her. As she stared at him, watching the pistol bob up and down in his trembling hand, she wondered whether Drew Carter had been loved by anyone but his father. *Their* father.

Lies. Her entire life had been built on lies, and when the foundation cracked, it could not be shored up. Finally, the walls tumbled, crushing Jane beneath the heavy ruse edged with razor-sharp deceit.

The handle of her office door wiggled. Jane clutched the edge of the gray velvet window seat cushion and leaned forward to listen. Once again, she heard someone fiddling with the handle. Tiptoeing across the room, she grabbed a baseball bat from behind the lateral filing cabinet. She lifted the piece of aluminum onto her shoulder and waited. After a few seconds, there was a rhythmic knock to the musical couplet: *Shave and a haircut, two bits.*

"Mom! Yo, Mooooom! Security detail here to pick you up."

Jane released the breath she had been holding. The smell of fear hung in the air. She lowered the bat before tucking it behind the filing cabinet, drawing and releasing deep breaths to slow her racing heart. After slipping on her blazer to cover the stains beneath her arms and wiping her forehead with the back of her hand, she unlocked her door.

Luke planted a quick kiss on her cheek and brushed past her.

"Got anything to eat? I'm a growing boy, you know."

Jane's shoulders drooped forward. A shaky smile spread across her face. "You're already six foot four, Luke. If you grow any more, you'll have to duck to walk through doorways."

He plopped into her chair and rummaged through her drawers. "It's not my fault you make 'em big," he said.

Jane laughed out loud. "Just you. Your brother is not a giant. He never was."

Luke grabbed a handful of chocolate candies from her top drawer, unwrapped each, and popped them into his mouth. He chewed while he spoke. "True, but he also doesn't have the enormous brain I have, or my incredible good looks."

Jane rolled her eyes. "And *you* certainly don't have his humility," she teased.

Luke lifted one shoulder. "You don't need to be humble if it's true."

"You sure do. If I were the prettiest girl in the room…"

"Mom," Luke interrupted her. "You're the only girl in the room right now, so, by default, that makes you the prettiest."

Jane gave up. She knew she would never win. "Are you ready to go, son?"

Luke mumbled something unintelligible as he continued to search her desk. "Ah-ha. You've been holding out on me." He held up a small bag of chips.

She narrowed her eyes. "I don't remember…" She shrugged. "Seriously, are you ready? It's been a long day, and I'm ready to get out of here."

"Sure." Luke shoved the bag into his front sweatshirt pocket and offered his elbow to his mother.

"So chivalrous."

"Whatever. I just wanna get you home so we can eat. I'm starving."

"Did you cook?"

Luke laughed loudly. "What's the use in having a mom if she's not gonna make you dinner?"

Jane rolled her eyes. "I suppose that's true."

She grabbed her purse from her desk drawer and her jacket from the hook by the door. Tossing it over her arm, she turned off the lights and locked the door. She checked it twice, walked away, and then returned to check it again.

"Come on, already. It's locked. I watched you."

She nodded, took her son's arm, and headed across the open workspace. Luke asked about dinner, inquiring whether they should grab a pizza on the way home as an appetizer or dessert. Jane giggled, completely unaware they were not alone. When one of the cleaning crew stepped from behind a partition, she shrieked in surprise.

"Oh goodness. I'm as sorry as can be," the woman with the short brown hair said in a southern drawl. "I didn't mean to scare the daylights outta you. Shame on me."

"It's fine." Jane rehooked her arm in Luke's to steady herself. As they neared the woman, she pulled her head back in surprise. "Do I know you? You look so familiar."

"I reckon I do. I got the kinda face that makes ever'body think they know me."

Jane nodded. "Well, goodnight, then." She took a few steps and stopped. "Don't you work at Knuckle's?"

The woman shook her head. "Can't say as I even know that place."

'Hmm. You look very much like a woman who works there."

"Well, it weren't me you saw there. I just got into town not more'n a week ago. This is my first job in this sweet li'l town." She sprayed a bleach-smelling substance on a table and swiped at it with a white rag. "But if you're recommendin' I get a bite there, I maybe oughta check it out."

"Mom?" Luke pulled her along. "I've gotta eat soon, or I'm gonna collapse."

Jane sighed. "All right, Luke." She patted his arm and smiled at the young woman. "Well, we'll get out of your hair then."

The woman nodded and returned to her work. When the

elevator door closed, she threw the rag and bottle into the trash and raced for the stairs.
Becca was on a mission.

CHAPTER TWENTY-TWO

JANE ENDERLY

Luke scarfed down the bag of chips while he drove his mom home. Three handfuls and the bag was empty. He upended the foil pouch and shook the crumbs into his mouth.

Jane grabbed the steering wheel. "Watch where you're going."

Luke raised an eyebrow and turned onto her street.

After changing into jeans and a T-shirt, Jane washed her hands and put a leftover pan of lasagna into the oven. Cole and Luke sat at the counter and talked to their mom while she made a salad and set the table.

"You know you're the only one eating that crap, right?" Luke sat up, laid a hand on his stomach, and stretched uncomfortably.

"I assumed as much. There's corn for the two of you and garlic bread."

Suddenly, Luke laid his cheek against the cool quartz. "I don't feel so good."

"Well, I wouldn't think so the way you shoveled in that chocolate and bag of chips. You should consider chewing."

Cole clapped his brother on the back. "I doubt it's anything he ate. I've seen this boy polish off a large pizza and an entire gallon of ice cream and still search for something *to eat*."

Suddenly, Luke went limp beneath Cole's hand.

"Mom!" Cole yelled. "Luke! Luke!"

Jane looked at her son. His arms hung limp. She turned off the oven and moved toward him. "Luke! Cole, call 911."

Within minutes, the ambulance crew had Luke on a gurney and wheeled him out the door. Jane argued with the EMTs about riding in the ambulance; she refused to separate herself from her son. Without being given the okay, she climbed in, took Luke's hand, and spoke to him the entire trip. The paramedics worked around her. Cole followed, staying on the transport's bumper, passing through stop signs as the ambulance did.

In the waiting room, the ticking clock drove Jane crazy. Minutes turned into an hour and then two while they waited for the doctor. Jane raced toward Dr. Lofstrom when he appeared. He held his palm outward in front of him.

"Jane, Luke's going to be fine." She fell against the doctor in relief. Cole put his arm over her shoulder and pulled her back. I do want to talk to you, though." He pointed down the hallway. "But let's go to my office."

In the small room, Cole adjusted his mother's chair before sitting next to her.

"What's going on, Mark? What's wrong with Luke?"

The doctor cleared his throat. "It appears Luke was poisoned."

"Poisoned? As in—on purpose?"

"It could have been accidental," he said, crossing his legs. "The tests we ran showed it was some form of pesticide. That's what took so long. We had to know what we were dealing with before we could fully treat him."

Wrinkles deepened across Jane's forehead. "That makes no sense. Pesticides?" Jane looked at Cole. "Do you know anything about this?"

He shook his head. "No. How would he have ingested pesticides?"

"Has he done any yard work recently where…"

Cole snorted. "Are you kidding?"

"Did he eat anything that may have been stored close to pesticides?" The doctor folded his hands and rested them on the edge of the table.

Jane sighed. "Mark, you're talking about Luke. You know him. He eats everything."

"Has he eaten anything within the last few hours?"

"Well, he picked me up at my office. He found some chocolates and a bag of chips in my desk drawer and practically inhaled them."

"Fortunately, the amount he had in his system wouldn't have killed him…" The doctor looked from Cole to Jane. "But had either of *you* eaten it, it could have been a different story."

Jane slumped into her chair. "Oh, my God." She grabbed Cole's hand. "Mark, are you saying someone tried to kill me?" She started crying. "When is this ever going to end?"

He rested his hand over her free one. "We don't know that, Jane. It could have been an anomaly. I have someone on the research team looking to see if there have been reports of pesticides showing up in foods. Now that I know what he ate, they can narrow the search."

Cole slid his chair closer to his mom and rested his arm across her back.

"Do you have the wrappers from the things he ate? I'll have the lab run some more tests."

"I know the candy wrappers would have gone out in the trash by now, but the chip wrapper is in the bin at my house." She looked at Cole.

He nodded. "I'll go get it."

Jane swiped at the tears that heated her eyes. "I'll go with you."

"Wait, Jane. Where's Brian?"

"He's at training this week. The boys are staying with me."

The look he shared with Cole made Jane nearly jump out of her skin. "I think you're safer here than at your house." He shrugged. "Hopefully, this was nothing more than a freak accident. But we won't know until Luke wakes up."

Jane hugged her son. "Be safe, Cole. I mean it. Don't eat anything at home."

He nodded and disappeared.

"I'm going to call Jeff Porter and get someone down here to stand guard outside Luke's room." Mark sighed deeply. "I'd rather be safe than sorry." He moved toward the door. "For now, I want you to stay in Luke's room. Do not step foot outside of it. Understand?" Jane nodded slowly. "And call Brian. He needs to get back here."

CHAPTER TWENTY-THREE

CHIEF BRIAN ENDERLY

When Brian came through the door, it was nearly 2:00 a.m. According to the nursing staff, Jane fell asleep in the aqua-blue recliner after being covered with a warm blanket and drinking a cup of tea. Brian knew closing her eyes had been difficult. Even with the officer stationed at the door and him in the room, Jane would not feel safe.

Before entering the room, he had spoken to Officer Finley, one of Cedar Point's finest, at his post in the hallway. He had a lot of questions, some for Jane and Cole, but mainly for Luke when he woke. But for now, he only wanted to hold his wife.

Jane flinched when the door opened. In seconds, he was holding his sobbing, limp wife in his arms. He did not attempt to talk to her; he just held her, brushed her hair from her face, and let her cry.

Cole sat up and lifted his hand to acknowledge Brian's presence. "I sure am glad you're back. I've never been so happy to see anybody in my whole life."

Brian shifted his gaze to Luke. "Has he woken yet?"

"On and off. Not really awake, more aware, I'd say." Cole ran a hand through his hair.

The blood pressure machine hummed. Jane twisted out of Brian's arms. She watched and waited for the numbers to pop up on the screen. "Normal. Thank God."

"I spoke with Mark on the way over here. He said Luke is going to be fine." He wrapped his arms around Jane again. "I'm more concerned about you and how in the hell this could have happened."

She patted Brian's chest. "I'll be fine once I can talk to Luke."

"No, you won't, Mom. This is scary as hell." Cole moved next to Luke's bed. "Someone tried to kill you again."

Brian shot a warning look at his stepson. "We don't know that for sure. It could have been an accident."

"It wasn't an accident, Brian." Jane sniffed loudly and pressed her forehead against his broad chest. "Cole's right. Someone's trying to kill me."

Brian weighed his words carefully. "The most important thing is that the three of you are safe. And I intend to keep it that way." He dropped into the blue recliner and pulled Jane onto his lap. "I've got Jeff and a team over at H and C going through the place with a fine-tooth comb. The security team's been called in, and Canter's watching the videos with your surveillance guys." He laid a hand against Jane's cheek and gently turned her face toward him. "There's something you need to know. It *was* the chips. They found pesticides in the bag."

Jane swallowed hard. "I knew it."

"You don't even eat chips. How did they get in your desk drawer?"

Jane shook her head. "I don't know." She kept her eyes on Luke. "I honestly don't."

Brian stared out the window. "So, if *you* didn't put them there, someone else did. Cameras don't lie. Whoever did this doesn't have a prayer."

"Shuuuut uuup." Luke dragged out the words. His eyes were barely open. "Could you guys just shut up?"

Jane leaped from Brian's lap and dropped onto the side of the bed. She laid her head on Luke's chest. "Thank God you're okay," she said.

Luke raised an eyebrow slightly. "I don't feel okay," he whispered. "What happened?" He awkwardly patted his mom's back with his huge hand.

Brian stood behind Jane. "We can talk after you've had some rest. Just know you're safe."

"Safe?" Luke looked from Brian to Cole. He rubbed the front of his neck. "Safe from what exactly? What happened? My throat hurts like hell."

Jane took his hand. "They pumped your stomach, honey. I'm guessing your throat feels raw from the tube."

Luke looked at his brother. "Pumped my stomach?"

Brian shook his head at Cole. "How about we wait until we know more?"

"No. I want to know why I'm here and what was pumped out of my gut."

"Okay," Brian put his hands on Jane's shoulders, "but you have to promise you'll stay calm—no matter what I say."

"Way to put me at ease there, Brian."

Brian snorted. "Sorry." He frowned. "Those chips you ate last night…from your mom's office…" He waited for Luke to catch up. "They were laced with pesticides."

"What? How? The bag wasn't even open."

Brian tilted his head slightly. "I know. But when we looked at the bag, we found a small needle hole near the bottom seam that had been sealed with a rubbery substance. No one would have suspected anything."

Luke laid a hand on his forehead. "So, I ate pesticides? How did I not know? Shouldn't they have tasted weird?"

Cole smiled at his brother. "Because you'll eat anything. Because you swallow before you taste. Because you're a pig."

Luke gave him a crooked half grin. "Well, you're not wrong."

Brian nodded. "The thing is, Luke, those chips weren't intended for you." He glanced at Jane. "They were…"

"What? Someone tried to kill Mom?" He shook his head

violently. "Noooo. This can't be happening again. It can't." Luke repeatedly slammed his hands into the bed. He nearly pulled the IV from his hand.

"Cole, go get the nurse," Jane said, gesturing toward the door. "Honey, calm down. I'm fine, and you're fine."

"But someone's after you again, Mom. I can't lose you. I can't." His eyebrows pressed together, and he scowled at Brian. "What the hell are you doing about this? Maybe you should have been…"

"Luke, stop. This isn't Brian's fault."

Brian took a deep breath. "We're working on it, Luke." He laid a hand on his stepson's knee. "Listen to me; *you* may have saved your mom's life."

The nurse rushed in behind Cole. She checked Luke's vitals. His blood pressure had spiked.

"He's quite agitated," Jane said.

"I can see that." The nurse disappeared, promising to return in a few minutes.

"How? How did I save her?" Luke poked at a button on the remote lying near him. But as the head of the bed rose, the room started to spin, so he lowered it again.

"If your mom had eaten those chips, she wouldn't be here right now."

The nurse returned with a syringe. She shot it into the IV in Luke's hand. Almost instantly, he melted into the bed and drifted off.

Jane brushed his bangs away from his forehead. "Sleep, Luke. I'm not going anywhere."

Brian pulled Jane to her feet and backed her into the recliner. He covered her with the blanket and raised the footrest. "You need to sleep too, Jane. You won't be any good to anyone if you don't."

Within minutes, Jane's breaths were even and shallow. Cole had returned to the window seat, pulled a blanket over his head, and was softly snoring. Brian looked at the family he had grown to love. He vowed to protect them. He just didn't know who the enemy was.

The staff wheeled in a second recliner. Brian raised the footrest and searched his phone for information on pesticide poisoning.

It was just past sunrise when Jane stirred. The hospital was springing to life with the changeover of staff.

"I know you'll want to stay with Luke, so I'll bring you some decent coffee and a change of clothes before I head over to H and C. Cole, what's your plan?"

"I'm staying with Mom."

Brian kissed his wife. "That's probably a good idea." He moved to the door. "Do you want me to bring you anything?"

"Just a coffee," Cole said.

Jane shifted in the recliner and watched Luke. "Jane, sleep. Luke's fine. And you are all safe. I'm keeping an officer outside the door, and until you're all home, he's not going anywhere." Jane nodded and let her eyes fall shut.

Brian disappeared through the door. Officer Finley briefed Serrano, who was taking over the post. As the three men spoke, no one noticed Becca walk past them in her burgundy scrubs and short blonde hair.

CHAPTER TWENTY-FOUR

CHIEF BRIAN ENDERLY

Brian traveled the back way to Hallman and Carter, curious to see if anyone was watching from that side of the building.

Nearly a dozen cans of Diet Coke in the past twelve hours had quelled his need for sleep. At least half of those cans had been abandoned on the floor of the passenger's side of the squad. He could feel the caffeine, lack of sleep, and junk food gnawing in his stomach. What he needed was a steak dinner, a night with his wife, and a couple of bottles of beer, but that was out of the question. Not since Jane disappeared two years ago had he felt this bottomless pit of helplessness.

A steady stream of cars drove away from H and C. As people arrived, the security team sent them home, only saying the building was closed. The number of police vehicles parked out front had to have given some indication it was not a water main break or something equally as frustrating but fixable. While those in the know had been sworn to secrecy, it would not be long before word got out about the poisoning. It was a small town—with cracks. Whoever had their finger stuck in the dike, holding back the water, would soon pull it out, and word would flood the town. Half-truths and rumors would swirl in the rushing waters.

Several employees tried to get information, but the guards at the main doors shut them down, refusing to say anything other than, "Go home." No one was allowed to enter unless they needed to be there. The Alexandria police had been called in to assist, as had Moorhead.

On his way to H and C, Brian placed a call to John Wallick of the FBI. The two had worked together two years before when Jane went missing. This latest incident did not fall under the FBI's jurisdiction, but he thought John might have some insight. That was all he wanted. But within three hours, Wallick joined Brian and several other officers in Jane's office. He was committed to the Enderlys and the small town.

He waited while Brian spoke to his men, sending them off with new orders.

John bit his lip. "I have to wonder if there's any way those chips were intended for Carter—
planted long before Jane took over?"

Brian shook his head. "Not possible. It's a new desk. The entire office was redone. Jane wanted nothing that reminded her of Drew."

John nodded. "Okay, so someone on the inside put them there. But who? And why?"

Brian rolled his eyes. "And you're FBI? I asked that question *last* night."

"It was rhetorical. I was just thinking out loud."

Brian's phone rang. It was the station. "Enderly," he barked.

"Hey, Boss." Mauri coughed softly. "I wanted to let you know that a huge box arrived for you."

"Who the hell cares," Brian snapped. "I'm busy. Just put it in my office."

"Did I say *huge*? They used a forklift to unload it from the truck. It's actually sitting on the sidewalk outside the station, on a pallet."

Brian scratched his cheek. "How the hell big is it?"

"Almost as tall as me," Mauri told him.

"And it's a box?"

"Well, it's more like cardboard wrapped around it and then bound together with flat metal straps."

"Just leave it. I'll send somebody over to deal with it in a while."

"Okay. But it's blocking the sidewalk, so I just thought…"

Brian huffed. "Did you hear me? I said I'd send somebody over in a while. I'm kind of busy at the moment." He pressed the end button and grumbled about Mauri.

"As I recall, Mauri's a pretty decent assistant." John grinned.

"Just shut up, would you?"

Brian stormed out of the workspace with John on his heels.

Three hours later, Brian stepped into the hospital room and quietly closed the door. Cole held a finger to his lips and pointed at his mom. He glanced between his two stepsons, both wide awake.

"Luke, you look pretty decent, all things considered," he whispered. "How're you feeling?"

"Hungry."

Brian laughed. "Of course you are."

"And why should that surprise anyone?" Jane asked, stretching.

"Sorry, hon. I didn't mean to wake you."

"I've been dozing, not really sleeping." She snapped the footrest of the recliner down. "What's happening out there?"

"Well, you know how you've wanted to put in twenty-four-hour surveillance?" Jane nodded. "You need to. We came up with nothing. No one was in or out of your office during office hours unless you were there."

"So, whoever planted the chips did it after six, then?" Jane looked at him. "The only people there after 6:00 are the cleaning crew, and they've all been there forever."

Luke gently rubbed the front of his neck. His throat was still sore from the tube Dr. Lofstrom inserted to pump his stomach. "Mom, what about that woman who was there last night? The one you said looked familiar?"

Jane stared at her son. "Yeah, I've never seen her there before." She looked at Brian. "You know that waitress who works at Knuckle Sandwiches? The blonde with the long hair?"

Brian shrugged.

"The waitress? The one who takes your orders when you sit in the back section? Long hair? Ponytail?" Brian's face was blank. "Large breasts?"

He smiled. "Oh, her."

Cole and Luke laughed.

"Yes, her." Jane rolled her eyes. "Luke and I ran into a cleaner who looked a lot like her, but she had short brown hair and a strong Southern accent. She claimed she'd only been on staff for a week."

"Not true." Luke shook his head. "She said she'd only been in Cedar Point for a week or so. She didn't say how long she'd worked there."

"So, if H and C hired someone, there should be a file and a background check, right?" Brian pulled out a notepad and flipped it open.

"Yeah. I'll call Sara and have her email it to me."

Jane stepped into the bathroom to make the call.

"How's she really doing?" Brian asked.

Luke snorted. "How would you be if someone tried to kill you a second time?"

"I have no idea how this is going to affect her." Cole rubbed one eyebrow. "She was jumpy before, always looking over her shoulder, paranoid about every sound. I can't even imagine what it'll be like now."

Brian raised an eyebrow. "Here's the thing. We have to keep things as normal as possible. BUT…and this is non-negotiable." He glared at Luke and Cole. "You boys'll stay at the house until we get this mess sorted out. We've got the security system in place, but more than that, she needs to know you're both okay."

Luke nodded. "You're not gonna get a no from me. After this…" He swiped a hand through the air over him. "I need my mom."

Brian smiled.

"I took a couple weeks' vacation." Cole's voice cracked. "We weren't exactly there for her last time. We led that asshole *brother* of hers right to her." He glanced at Luke. "I want to be there for her now. I need to be."

"Good. I'm glad I don't have to fight you on this." He dropped onto the side of Luke's bed. "Rumor has it they're springing you tomorrow."

"That's what they tell me." Luke glanced toward the door. "But I sort of like the extra protection."

"Cole, I'm sending a uniform with you to get whatever you boys need for the next couple of weeks."

"I don't need an escort. I'll be fine. I'm not the target."

Brian cocked his head. "You'd like to think that, right? But you thought your mom would be safe there two years ago too. And that bastard Carter cornered you then, remember? We're not taking any chances."

Cole glanced at his brother.

"Just say yes, Cole. Why tempt fate?"

He nodded. "Will six tonight work? I can get what I need, deliver it to the house, and be back to pick up Mom around eight."

"I'll have someone drive her home tonight. You don't need to come back here." He turned toward Luke. "As for you, there'll be an officer stationed outside the door until you're released tomorrow. Then, you'll get a ride home too." He looked at his stepsons. "Are we good?"

"What are we talking about?" Jane stepped out and closed the bathroom door.

"The boys'll be staying at our house for a while."

Her shoulders drooped, and she cast her eyes upward. "Thank God. I..." She breathed a huge sigh. "Just, thank God."

CHAPTER TWENTY-FIVE

OFFICER JEFF PORTER & FBI AGENT JOHN WALLICK

Officer Jeff Porter and FBI Agent John Wallick entered the station just before 4:00 p.m. They had spent the last five minutes studying the package that hogged the sidewalk, forcing residents to step off the walkway to pass.

Mauri had positioned herself near the street to monitor the gawkers. "Keep moving," she told those whose curiosity got the better of them. "It's just a box." The message was different for her friends who appeared. She claimed it was an early birthday gift for her boss.

Rumors circulated. A handful of people gathered across the street to watch. No one knew what to believe. Everyone acquainted with Mauri knew she would give you the shirt off her back, but she was also full of a whole lot of crap. Eventually, they moved on and went about their business.

"Mauri, do you know if we have a pair of wire cutters?" Jeff asked.

"Seriously?" Mauri held up the cutters she had already placed in a box near the door.

"Damn," John said. "I sure could use a Mauri in my life."

She grinned and followed the men back outside.

Jeff cut the flat metal straps along one side and peeled back the cardboard.

"What the hell?" Wallick backed up. "It's diet soda."

Porter's head bobbed. "But not just any soda. It's Diet Coke." He looked at John. "Brian's favorite." He cut the straps on the backside. "Help me get the cardboard off."

The three removed the temporary sides and the straps of metal. When John hoisted the top piece from the pile, a sheet of white paper fluttered to the ground. He picked it up and read it silently. Mauri pulled his elbow down so she could read the message as well.

She tsked. "This makes no sense. What secret admirer would send…" She looked at the stack. "…like a bazillion cases of soda to anyone?"

A knowing look passed between the two men. "Someone who wants the chief dead." Wallick rubbed his chin.

"A secret admirer? Dead?" Mauri studied the stack. "That makes…Ohhhhhh." Her eyes grew wide. "You mean…"

Agent Wallick nodded.

Jeff folded his arms, turned his head sideways, and whispered to John, "So, if I'm reading you right, you're thinking one of these cans has poison in it." Wallick nodded. "I don't know, John. It doesn't seem to make sense. I mean, that's a hell of a lot of work to take one can out of a case, inject it with poison, somehow seal the hole, reseal the case, and hide it among a hundred cases or more." Porter looked at the stack. "Do you really think that?"

John methodically nodded. "FBI," he reminded Porter. "I've seen this before. And considering what went down with Jane's son, I don't think we can take any chances." He looked at Mauri. "They all need to be dumped—*every last can.*"

Mauri grinned. "I gotta tell you, I don't mind dumping Diet Coke one bit."

"Says the Diet Pepsi fan." Wallick laughed.

Jeff pulled the door open wide enough for the bottom edge to catch on the uneven sidewalk and remain open. He and John hauled cases inside while Mauri made sure none grew legs and walked away with the teenage boys watching from down the street.

John picked up two soda cases near the pile's center and drew a deep breath. "Oh, damn." Because his hands were full, he pointed with his chin. In the center of the stack was a single case of Diet Pepsi.

Mauri shrank back. "What the hell is that?"

Jeff wrapped her in a hug and gave John an unsettled look over the top of her head. "Mauri, stop overthinking this. Let's get the rest of these inside, and then we can talk."

Twenty minutes later, one hundred twenty-three cases of Diet Coke and the lone case of Diet Pepsi were stacked in the workroom. John had moved the wooden pallet to the back of the building and the cardboard into Brian's office in case it contained evidence. Porter hung an "In case of emergency…" sign on the station door, locked it, and lowered the shade.

"Well, we might as well start with the obvious." John picked up the case of Diet Pepsi, set it in the middle of a table, and walked around it. Suddenly, he stopped. "Look at this," he said, pointing to the end of the box. "See how the top flap is loose, not tight against the bottom flap?"

While Jeff and Mauri watched, John took several photos before opening the other end. He pulled on a pair of rubber gloves. As he removed each can, he ran his fingers along the sides, edges, and the top and bottom of each, explaining to Jeff and Mauri what he was feeling for.

"Found it." He raised the can and pointed to a tiny clump of sealant near the top of the can. "I'm guessing there's a hole beneath this."

John scraped the sticky clump from the can, exposing a pinpoint opening about a millimeter wide. "Bingo." After popping the top, he poured a small amount into a red plastic cup on the table. "Flat as can be." Wallick shook his head. "Obviously, the can's been opened."

"I think I'm going to be sick." Mauri moved to the door and curled her arms across her stomach. "Whoever sent this had to have known I like Diet Pepsi and that Brian wouldn't touch the stuff. They knew he'd pawn it off on me. Had I drunk it, I could be..."

"Don't jump to conclusions. We'll run some tests to be sure, but it might be nothing." He lifted her chin. "Besides, you never would have drunk flat soda."

She shook her head. "It's not *nothing*, Jeff. I know it, and you know it too."

Porter could hear the tears in her voice that had yet to fall. "I'm sorry, Mauri. This sucks. Everything about it sucks. But honestly, we don't know who they're after. From what I can tell, they're aiming at anyone connected to the station." He looked at John.

"Luke?" Mauri sniffed. "His only connection is being Brian's stepson."

Porter's eyebrows lifted. "Yeah, but Luke wasn't the target. It was Jane."

Agent Wallick tipped his head. "I'd say they're trying to hurt the chief by going after anyone important to him."

"I think we all need to be on alert," Porter said, looking at her. "All of us."

John placed the can inside the glass. Because of the narrow shape at the bottom, the can never touched the soda he had poured inside. "I'm taking this to the lab for testing." He looked at Jeff. "Check every can before you open them." He headed toward the door but turned around before he reached it. "Mauri, did you sign for the delivery?"

"No."

"Was there anything written on the side of the truck, or did you see the plate?"

She shook her head. "It was dark blue. There was nothing special about it."

"What about the driver?"

"I didn't recognize him. But he was a big guy. Six-four or five, brown hair, and had on a black T-shirt and jeans. I'd say he was in his forties." Lines grew across her forehead. "Wait.

He also wore a green jacket—maybe military or something."

Wallick nodded. "Good memory. What about the forklift?"

"It was one of those attached to the truck." Mauri sighed. "Honestly, he was probably here for three minutes, tops."

"Did you talk to him?"

"All he said was he was delivering a gift for the chief."

"Nothing else?"

"No. Had I not heard the commotion outside, I don't think I would have even known about the delivery."

John nodded. "That's not a lot to go on." He nodded to Porter. "After I drop this at the lab, I'll fill Brian in." Then he left, holding the plastic glass with the can inside as if someone's life depended on it.

Mauri locked the door behind him and leaned against it. Jeff watched her.

"It's going to be okay. We'll figure this out."

She sighed loudly. "I hope you do—before it's too late."

Porter wrapped his arms around her and held her tightly. His heart and mind raced. What in the hell was happening to quiet Cedar Point with its friendly people and carefree life?

Jeff hauled two cases to the bathroom while Mauri texted her husband she would be working late. Porter knew her well enough to know she would say nothing to him unless she had to. But almost dying...

While Jeff checked and dumped sodas in the bathroom sink, Mauri took over the workroom.

It was nearly 10:00 p.m. by the time every can had been checked and emptied. They had found nothing.

As Jeff slipped on his jacket, Mauri's eyes widened, and she swallowed hard.

"I have a target on my back." Her hand shook as she tried to poke it through her coat sleeve. "Will you walk me to my car?"

"Mauri, you don't think I'd let you go home tonight, do you? Brian and I talked earlier. Mike's already at my house."

"What are you talking about?"

"Until further notice, you'll both be under police protection. For tonight, that means you're sleeping with me." Jeff wagged his head and grinned. "Well, not literally, just at my house. Tomorrow, we'll make other arrangements."

Jeff nodded. "An officer from Alexandria will be stationed here tomorrow."

Mauri fell against the wall. Her shoulders sagged. "The Pepsi? Did you hear from John?"

Jeff's eyes were grim. "Let's not worry about that."

Mauri drew a deep breath and released it so violently that her lips vibrated. "That means you did."

"I don't want you to worry. For now, you're safe."

"For now?"

"That's just an expression. You're safe. *Period*. I'll make sure of it."

Porter locked the station door and walked Mauri to her car. He poked his head inside and checked the front and back seats. He took her keys and started it. "I'll follow you to my house. I'll be right behind you. Okay?"

Her chin quivered. She nodded because her words were buried in fear.

Mauri stopped and waited for a white CR-V to pass before she pulled out of the station parking lot.

CHAPTER TWENTY-SIX

TERAH DIXON

Terah rolled over and tugged the curtains together that hung over her bed. She fastened them in place with a spring-loaded clothespin. With each beat of her heart, her head pulsed like a drum. The tone had softened somewhat overnight, but remnants of her migraine remained, still begging for attention. Her headaches were coming harder and more often than they had in previous years. For a dozen years or so, she had not faced even a small one. It was only since she agreed to room with Becca that they had returned.

She fished two tan tablets from the prescription bottle and washed them down with a warm glass of water that had been sitting on her nightstand for an indeterminate amount of time. The dust from the combines that harvested the crops on the outskirts of town covered everything—including the water's surface.

With the blinding headaches hitting more often, Terah worried. The first one she ever experienced happened when she was four. Back then, they were nearly always brought on by the nitrates in the hotdogs, sausage, or bacon her mom cooked for almost every meal.

Rail thin but with breasts that could have their own zip code, Terah had watched everything she ate. Periodically, she would falter, thinking *maybe it would not be as bad this time.* But it always was.

After purging her stomach and what felt like internal organs, she would sleep for hours before it no longer felt like stakes were being driven into her brain. She never saw a doctor. Never took a pill until recently. Both were against *Life Vision* guidelines. Even though her parents were uncommitted to certain rules, that was one law where her father drew a line in the sand. "God will heal," he would say as he prayed over her tiny body, her head hanging over a huge green plastic bowl. Terah was certain more came out than ever went in.

Her mother, on the other hand, continuously fired back with a line she wrongly believed to be in the bible: *God helps those who help themselves.* They would loudly argue their side until Terah wanted to scream. Her father would not let up, asking her mother to show him the exact quote—but she could not. Still, she would not give in.

At the moment, their disagreement did not matter. All Terah wanted was for her father to pray over her and her mother to lay a cool compress across her forehead and hold her hand. But that was impossible. Her mother and father were gone. *Where?* No one knew for sure. Not long after Terah left Carson Springs, her parents disappeared. After a conflict with the elders, most likely over them allowing their daughter to leave the church, they vanished.

With cell phones being against *Life Vision* rules—because of their worldliness—Terah had no way to contact her parents. She had returned to Carson Springs twice searching for information, but no one would speak to a deserter. According to the church doctrine, by leaving, she had turned her back on God, so the members were forced to turn their backs on her as well. And they did. They were fearful of being associated with a sinner such as herself.

The second time she returned, lights burned brightly in her family's home. Had her parents come back? She pounded on the door and asked for her mother and father. She could see strangers moving around in the house, but they would not allow her entrance. Evidently, they had been warned about the blonde-haired traitor who chose the world over God.

Her parents' disappearance haunted her. They were the least worldly people Terah knew. Their knowledge of life outside their small town was limited to their minimal interactions with the townspeople of Carson Springs. She wondered how they would survive. Who would teach them? Who would help them navigate life at their age?

In the first few years after she left, she searched for them online but found only one matching name for her father. But the man had grown up in Alaska—far from the tiny town of Big Falls, Wisconsin, where her father had been raised. Maybe they had joined another religious group or went into hiding from the leaders of *Life Vision*. Or perhaps they were buried in the church's cemetery in a nameless grave marked with only a large boulder. Had that been their fate, she was to blame. No one left the church without consequences. Terah figured her parents had paid for her escape.

As the headaches worsened during her teenage years, the possibility of something being seriously wrong with her haunted her sleep. Too scary to contemplate, with each headache, she would bury the thought until the next one slammed her. She had convinced herself the headaches were God's way of punishing her for not wholeheartedly accepting the—*cult*. There. She said it. *Cult*. There was no other word to describe their lives, the rules, the control. Until she moved away, she had never heard that word. The meaning was as distant as Andrew Godley himself.

Cult: a small religious group whose life choices and practices appear unusual or sinister to others; a group who places their admiration and worship on a person or thing.

Call a spade a spade. That definition described the small community, a few miles southwest of Carson Springs, to a T. They followed Dr. Andrew Godley, a man known worldwide for his teachings. They worshiped him and his principles, falling to their knees to thank him for turning them toward God. While the members lived in modest homes, Godley grew richer. He justified his house by claiming it was the golden palace meant to glorify God, the place he spoke with Him. Everyone was in awe. God's pleasure and trust in this one man was to be revered and celebrated. How dare anyone speak out against a man the Lord had chosen to lead the world. So, the people stayed, followed, and prayed not only to God but to Andrew Godley as well.

It made Terah sick. Everything that was done under the guidance of Godley and in the name of the Lord was a farce. It could not have been further from the truth of the loving God she had come to know since her departure from *Life Visions*.

Still, it was hard to separate herself from her past.

As the room spun and her head throbbed, Terah was confident the church, the elders, and even Andrew Godley himself were praying evil on her. At times, she was sure she could feel their macabre prayers.

Terah checked her phone. *Two hours.* If she fell asleep instantly, those two hours would be the difference between working her shift with a smile and throwing up between customers in the claustrophobic bathroom at Knuckle's. She bargained with God, begged him for ninety minutes, then an hour, then fifteen minutes—she would take whatever He would allow. But sleep would not come.

As she climbed out of bed, fighting a wave of nausea, she wondered if God even recognized her anymore. She was not the same young girl with the angelic voice who praised Him in word and song. Church could only be seen in her rear-view mirror. Oh, she still believed—more than ever before—but she no longer allowed Godley and his followers to water down the love God had for the world.

Terah rested her forehead against the cheap acrylic shower wall, letting the scalding water wash over her until her skin was red and raw. Soap had not touched an inch of her skin. The energy it took to bend over, shave her legs, or wash her hair was beyond her capability.

She dressed in her uniform: black jeans and a pale blue T-shirt with the restaurant's name emblazoned on the back. Her stomach ached, but all she dared give it was a cup of hot peppermint tea before heading to her eight-hour shift that began at dawn.

By 10:00, her morning jobs were completed. The bread was baked. Meats and cheeses were sliced. And the desserts were thawed, cut, and ready to serve. It all happened between trips to the bathroom.

At 11:00, the lunch rush began. They had received a large order from the police station, courtesy of Chief Enderly. Terah wondered what was going on that would account for nearly two dozen sandwiches. Training, perhaps? A meeting?

As she slapped the ingredients together, she popped a couple more pills and encouraged them to work with a heavy dose of caffeine in the form of a large cup filled with Coke and ice.

Enderly entered the sandwich shop precisely at noon. Terah carefully set three bags of sandwiches on the counter before retreating to the back for a case of soda and a bag of plastic glasses. Her third trip was for a large bag of ice for the cups and another with paper products and condiments.

She touched each, explaining their contents. "Sandwiches, soda, ice, and all the paper products." She smiled at the chief. "Including the mustard and mayo and additional plastic knives."

"Thanks." Brian stared at her as he pulled out his wallet and handed her a credit card.

"You must be feeding a small army today, Chief. Visitors?"

He ignored her questions and instead looked at her name tag. "Terah?"

Terah looked confused. "Terah Dixon, yes."

"How long have you been in town?"

She shrugged. "Several weeks."

Brian nodded. "Do you like our small town?"

"I do. It's so different from Minneapolis."

"I take it that's where you lived before coming to Cedar Point." Brian hooked a hand through two bags.

Terah nodded. "I lived there for over twenty years."

"And before that?"

"A tiny, tiny town in Wisconsin." She shook her head slightly. "It's just a speck on the map really. It's one of those places that has a bar, a grocery store, and a gas station. Very unremarkable. I doubt you've ever heard of it."

"Try me."

"Carson Springs." Terah cleared her throat. "I didn't live *in* town, though. And I never really associated with the townsfolk. Our—ah, *neighbors* kept to themselves."

"Have you always lived in the Midwest?"

"Uh-huh. Born and raised."

"Any siblings?" Brian tucked the case of soda under his arm and hooked another bag with his index finger.

She shook her head. "No. I would have loved a brother or a sister, but I'm an only."

"I know the feeling," Brian told her.

"Here. Let me help you, Chief."

Terah picked up the bag of ice and the remaining bag. Brian pushed the door open with his back and held it for her.

Once his hands were empty, she handed him her bags.

"Gosh. I've never seen the inside of a police vehicle. They really do have a partition between the front and the back." She smiled at him. "Well, have a good day."

The chief held up a finger. "Hold on a minute. I need to respond to a quick text, and then I want to give you a tip."

"You don't have to do that. It was my pleasure."

"I know I don't have to, but I want to."

Brian pretended to respond to a text, but instead snapped a photo of her face. He shoved his phone into his pocket and fished a twenty out of his wallet.

"That's too much. I can't take that."

He held up his hand, palm out. "Keep it. We'll call it a

housewarming gift." He cocked his head slightly. "Did you find a place to rent? There aren't many around here. People come, but they rarely leave."

Terah nodded. "Oh, yes. Over on Hanley."

"That's good." He opened the driver's door of the Explorer. "Well, welcome to Cedar Point, Terah from Carson Springs, Wisconsin via Minneapolis, who lives on Hanley."

She pulled her head back in surprise. "You don't forget anything, do you?"

"Rarely."

Terah smiled as she watched the Chief of Police back out and drive away. What a nice man. And what a wonderful town to have settled in.

For the first time in nearly two days, her head was not throbbing. Maybe Becca had been right. Perhaps Cedar Point was where she would find her Prince Charming after all.

Or maybe not.

CHAPTER TWENTY-SEVEN

TERAH DIXON

Terah walked out of Knuckle's at 2:17 p.m. She had worked longer than expected, but she needed the money. And as her headache slowly abated, she felt like a different person. The colors returned, as did her smile.

The azure sky, lined with puffs of white, hovered above her as she walked home. Terah was in no hurry to lock herself away in that basement apartment. It was a perfect fall day to be outside. The temperature did not call for a jacket, and the breeze felt warm against her cheeks.

Suddenly, she felt the urge to lie on her back and watch the clouds float across the sky, put names to the shapes, and laugh as she had with her mother and father back in Carson Springs. Oh, how she longed to be young again. To feel their arms encircle her. To smile and laugh at the silliest things. To stand on her father's feet and dance to songs forbidden by the church. To belt out songs while her mother played melodies of long ago on their ancient, out-of-tune piano. To collect the colorful leaves of the fall and press them between pieces of wax paper. Terah's heart ached for her childhood when her biggest concern was battling Becca for the mother role when they played house.

But it was impossible to go back—not just because she was an adult woman in her forties but because there was no one to return to. Her parents were lost among the seven-point-eight billion people on Earth. It was like trying to find a diamond in a boulder pile. She had thrown a few Hail Mary passes, going around the elders by contacting the police and hiring a private investigator, but nothing came of it. As much as she did not want to accept her parents' abandonment, she had no other choice.

Her memories slid from light and joyful to dark and grim. Miserable yet grateful for the release of the migraine's grip, Terah stopped on the sidewalk, closed her eyes, and drew a long breath, trying to summon back the joy of her childhood.

The earthy aroma of the small town filled her soul. It was something she had never experienced living in the city. She was grateful for the final hurrah of the autumn leaves, a burst of color as they faced their final days. A decaying scent hung in the air around the trees. The sweet smell of hay swirled in a dust cloud as the farmers prepared the land for the long winter's rest. Terah pictured the changeover of the season. Soon, woolen sweaters, mittens, scarves, snowballs, sledding, holiday music, and decorations would lay claim to the days.

While the memories were meant to take her back to the safety of her mother's arms: strawberry shampoo and warm bread coming out of the oven, and to the joy of her father: whisker rubs, tickle tortures, and roasting marshmallows over orange flames in the fireplace—they did not. They layered sadness on her, crushing her beneath the reality that she would never see them again. And in her forties, without a partner, the likelihood of recreating those moments with her own children was passing quickly.

Terah opened her eyes as a woman pushing a stroller passed her. The little girl wiggled her fingers in greeting and called out, "Hi, lady." It was a stark reminder of all she would likely never have.

She stepped off the sidewalk and plucked a perfect red leaf from a maple tree. She spun the stem between her thumb and finger as she walked toward home. The short section of uneven sidewalk, raised under the roots of a wayward willow tree, garnered her complete attention. Terah was not about to let it trip her as it had the week before. Eyes cast downward, stepping carefully over the broken concrete, she missed the car across the street, the man with the camera and long lens, and the woman in the passenger's seat.

Her stomach lurched as the house at 539 Hanley Street, which she shared with Becca, came into view. Becca's anger and violence had been out of control since her arrival in Cedar Point. There was little she did not destroy in her fits of rage. A broken TV screen, a flooded kitchen, a cracked window, four chair leg holes in the wall, and a busted bathroom mirror were the biggest of Terah's concerns. Not a confronter, Terah patched, replaced, and cleaned up what her irrational roommate destroyed. As for the TV, she left the broken one in the living room and purchased a smaller one for her bedroom. Every time she left the apartment, she padlocked her door. Terah knew the lock stood no chance against Becca if she truly wanted in, but it might make her think twice about entering.

Fortunately, the last two nights, Becca left and never reappeared. Terah was grateful for the quiet during her migraine. At times, she wondered if Becca was the cause of her hellish headaches, the auras, the pain, the nightmarish nausea. Stress had always been a contributing factor, sometimes bringing them on at the drop of a hat. As odd as it sounded, the only place Terah felt stress-free was at work.

The people of Cedar Point had hearts of gold. They were so kind to her and welcomed her with open arms. She could not ask for a better town, but she could, however, ask for a better roommate.

Becca's appearances were so rare that Terah had yet to confront her behavior, but she was getting closer to letting the words spill. When she did, it would not go well. That was decidedly so. Becca had gone completely off the rails since moving to Cedar Point. Terah had never feared her until recently.

Dreams and reality often blended during her migraines; she was not sure what was real and what was pain-induced. But there was a moment she swore Becca held an open knife over her. But, even as frightening as Becca's behavior had become, Terah could not imagine she would ever hurt her.

Growing up in Carson Springs, they had found their stride. Terah kept Becca in check, and Becca pushed her out of her comfort zone. The children of the community were homeschooled three days a week and sent to the small cooperative school the other two. The school days were separated by gender.

The girls were brainwashed with images of Satan entering their bodies and minds for harboring impure thoughts, dressing inappropriately, or doing anything that was unbecoming of a young lady. When not being beaten with the club of fear, they attended art and music classes centering around God and respect for the hierarchy of *Life Visions*. On the flip side, the boys were trained to use tools, administer discipline, and shoot to kill—*animals and people*. At the age of twelve, a boy became a man. On that birthday, they ranked above everyone but their father.

Terah had not chosen Becca as her friend, nor had it happened the other way around. They had not naturally gravitated toward one another. They were pushed together because of their matching birthdays, similar looks, and parents who viewed them more as sisters rather than friends.

In the small school, desks were limited, so the two shared a small table in the back of the room. Side by side, they could have been twins. Terah's blonde hair and Becca's dark hair were the only physical characteristics that set them apart. But based on their dissimilar personalities, they should have run from one another. And at times, Terah did. Even back then, it had not gone over well. Because of her high-strung personality, people feared Becca; they avoided her, ducking out of sight or choosing not to engage. To no avail, Terah had attempted all those things. Becca clung to her, reeling her back in when she tried to run. Fear was how Becca controlled her. Terah had always been too weak to stop her.

Years apart had faded the memories of their complex relationship—so much so that when Becca called, Terah's stomach surged with excitement instead of dread. Surely, Becca was not the same person. After all, she had cared for her siblings for a dozen years or more. A lifetime of responsibility had to have matured her.

But she had never been more wrong.

CHAPTER TWENTY-EIGHT

TERAH DIXON

As Terah walked down the steps into the lower duplex, she counted the stairs. It was a habit that took over when anxiety exploded inside of her. Her heartbeat pounded in her ears, and she cautiously opened the door.

"Becca?" She listened before calling again. "Becca?" There was no response.

Her shoulders drooped, and she released a long breath. *Relief.* She wandered through the house, checking each room because she did not trust her roommate. But nothing was out of place. It remained as Terah had left it.

After turning the key in the silver padlock on her bedroom door, she removed it and set them both on her dresser. As she turned toward the window, she had the oddest sensation someone was watching her. Goosebumps rose on her arms, and she crossed them and ran her hands vigorously up and down her pale skin as she quietly stepped toward the window.

A sudden rap on the door caused her to shriek. She slapped a hand over her mouth. What would the neighbors think, hearing her scream like that? What would the visitor think?

A second knock was louder, more urgent. Terah hurried to the door and opened it to a woman with a badge. Her hand was on the handle of her pistol.

"Are you okay, ma'am?" Her voice was almost a whisper as she scanned the apartment. "Is someone here with you?"

Terah locked her hands together and twisted them nervously. "No." She let go of a long sigh. "The knock scared me. That's all. Honestly, you're the first person to knock on my door since I moved to Cedar Point." She pulled her shoulders back. "Is there something I can help you with?"

"May I come in?"

Pulling the door inward, Terah stepped back. "Yes. Of course." She pointed to the living room. "Please, have a seat."

The officer nodded and sat on the couch, facing the door. "Thank you. I'm Officer Diane Collins. I work for the Cedar Point PD."

"Welcome. I'm Terah Dixon. But you probably already know that since you're here." She tipped her head slightly. "Or is this a *welcome to the neighborhood* visit?"

The officer smiled. "The latter. It's a small town. We just like to know who lives here. It keeps us all a little safer."

"Oh. That's so nice." She glanced toward the kitchen. "Can I get you something? A soda, water, or maybe some iced tea?"

"No, thank you." Officer Collins pulled a small notepad and a pen from her shirt pocket. "So, you said your name is Terah Dixon. Is that correct?"

"Yes. Terah. T. E. R. A. H."

"Interesting spelling. I don't know if I've come across that before."

"It's biblical." She tipped her head and turned her hand over. "And in the bible, Terah was a male. But my mom liked the spelling."

"I don't think it matters. My grandfather's name was Tracy. And I have a female friend named Mitch."

"Now that you say that, I suppose there are a lot of names like that."

"There are." Collins nodded slowly. "Cedar Point's a rather small town." The officer poised her pen over her pad. "What brought you to our neck of Minnesota?"

Terah's eyes darted across the brown carpet, which should have been cleaned before they rented the place but was clearly not. If she told her about Becca, it would ruin any chance of acceptance she had, and she was not interested in opening that can of worms.

Finally, she raised her chin and made eye contact with Officer Collins. "Well, I grew up in a small town in Wisconsin. When I left home, I moved to Minneapolis." One shoulder nearly touched her ear. "Now, it seems stupid, but back then, I was young and looking for something different, I suppose. I was there for a long time before I realized it wasn't for me. So…" She squared her shoulders and lobbed a lie at the officer. "I laid out a map and picked a town near water."

"Weren't you worried about finding a job?"

"Not really. I figure everybody needs waitresses and cooks."

"Well, that's certainly true." The officer stretched her neck to one side. "I heard Hallman and Carter are looking for cleaners. Have you ever considered working there? I'm sure they pay considerably better than Knuckles."

Terah held her hands out to her sides. "Look around. I'm neat, not necessarily clean." She pointed to the coffee table. "Check out the dust on the glass tabletop." She laughed aloud. "I can't believe I just pointed that out to you."

Collins laughed too. "My house looks the same. Well, if you're ever interested in making a change, H and C is always hiring for something or another."

"Where are they located? I've heard people talk about them, but I haven't driven by the building." Terah twisted her mouth slightly to the left. "I have to be honest with you. I haven't ventured out to see much other than what's right downtown."

"It's just to the west of Cedar Point."

"Hmm. I'll have to check it out sometime."

"It's unusual to see something so big in such a small town." Terah nodded. "I'm sure."

"So, why did you come here instead of returning to…

Where did you say you were from?"

"I'm sorry. I don't think I did. *Carson Springs—The Town That's Always in Season.*" She swung her fist in front of her when she repeated the tagline. "It sure is—if you like mud, cold, and ice—and about a week of summer."

"That bad, huh?"

"It's pretty and all, for about ten minutes, but there are a lot of in-between days that are not really so nice. Winter's too long, and fall's too short. Many years, winter refuses to let go so spring can bloom. It's not worth a visit—or that tagline." Terah giggled.

"It sounds like I should cross it off my bucket list."

"I doubt it's on anyone's bucket list. I told the chief it's just a blip on the map." She shook her head and sighed loudly.

"I get the feeling you didn't like Carson Springs."

Terah's shoulders fell. "Honestly…" She drew a deep breath and vigorously released it. "Honestly, I grew up in a cult."

Officer Collins twisted her neck slightly. "A cult?"

"Well, *they* wouldn't call it that, but that's what it is. My family and neighbors all belonged to *Life Visions*. Maybe you've heard of it."

"Andrew Godley." The officer nodded knowingly. "He's got his hands in a lot of…things. He likes to stir the pot. I can see why you call it a cult."

One corner of Terah's mouth lifted slightly. "He's a *do as I say, not as I do* kind of leader."

"I've read some about *Life Visions*." She tapped the tip of her pen on the paper. "What about the rest of your family? Did they stay?"

Terah twisted her lip and bit down. "I don't know. When I left, my parents told me I could always come home. But I could never get a hold of them again. My calls to their house were answered with *No longer in service*, and my letters were all returned unopened, stamped with *No one here by that name*. The first year after I left, I returned to Carson Springs a couple of times, but someone else was living in our house. People just turned their backs on me." Her chin fell, nearly touching her chest. "I don't know where they are. Maybe they joined another cult or went into hiding from the church. Or maybe they were…"

"What?" Officer Collins looked at Terah. "Were what?" Terah ran a finger across her neck. "Killed? Are you saying someone might have murdered them?" Officer Collins scribbled something on her tablet.

"Maybe. Outsiders wouldn't think things like that could happen in a *religious* group. But they do. Or at least I think they do. I guess I can't be sure, but I've always had my suspicions." She tilted her eyes upward. "I know other people who disappeared from the community. They questioned things and were called in to see the elders." Terah crossed her legs and locked her hands over her knees. "We were always told they *left.*" She wagged her eyebrows. "Like *the middle of the night* left." She eyed the officer. "And here's something else I know. There are an awful lot of what appear to be unmarked graves just outside the *Life Visions* cemetery."

"So, you think someone may have killed your parents?"

Her head bobbed, unsure. "I don't know. I just know I can't go back there. I won't go back there. I guess I have to wait for my parents to find me."

"What about your siblings?"

Terah pulled her hands back and twisted them. "I'm an only child." She cast a tight-lipped smile at the officer.

"That must be hard—to feel so all alone."

"I used to think of myself as an orphan. Now, I see myself as a free spirit—a nomad. I can live anywhere I want. That's why I came to Cedar Point."

A commotion outside made the hairs on the back of Terah's neck stand at attention. *Please don't let it be Becca,* she begged God. The worst thing that could happen was to have Becca walk through that door.

"Officer Collins, I, ah, need to run some errands this

afternoon." She uncrossed her legs. "Is there anything else you need to know?"

The first threads of a migraine wove through her head. Her temple throbbed, and she leaned into her fingertips and rubbed hard.

Officer Collins stood and returned the pad and pen to her pocket. "Welcome to Cedar Point, Terah." She reached out and shook her hand. "I'm sure you'll love it here. I appreciate having the opportunity to speak with you this afternoon."

Terah followed her to the door and pulled it open, half expecting to see her roommate on the other side. The door creaked, sending shock waves through Terah's pulsing head.

"Oh," Officer Collins turned before heading up the stairs, "one more question. Do you live here alone, or do you have a roommate?"

The throbbing intensified. "No. It's just me." The lie squeezed across her chest. Flashing lights from her headache impeded her vision, and she clung to the door for support.

"Well, it was good to meet you." The officer turned and started up the stairs.

"Same here." Terah closed her mouth tightly to keep her stomach from lurching.

Because she could make out only the shadow of the officer amid the aura of her newest migraine, Terah waited for the outside door to close before shutting her apartment door.

She raced to the bathroom and deposited her lunch in the toilet bowl. After a few minutes, she crawled to her bedroom and climbed under the covers, forgetting to lock her bedroom door.

CHAPTER TWENTY-NINE

TERAH DIXON

Before Terah drifted off, she popped two of the tan tablets into her mouth and washed them down with a mouthful of flat soda from an open bottle.

Within minutes, her dreams exploded. They were vibrant and horrifying. Terah often dreamt in black and white, but her migraine and the meds almost always amped up her nightmares, sending them into technicolor.

An adult game of hide-and-seek kept her running. She tried counting the steps, but it was impossible. Her feet were cartoon swirls like the Roadrunner's, and she could not get a count. Her breathing quickened, and her chest felt like it would explode— a bomb. *Tick. Tick. Tick. Tick.*

Unlike the childhood game, *It* was armed with a machete. Except for the dark hair, *It* could have been her.

Terah ran and hid in every nook and cranny in the town of Cedar Point: boathouses, bathrooms, behind trees, and in cellars. She was a lightning rod, attracting the attention of whoever wanted to destroy her. No matter where she hid, she was discovered because someone always gave up her location, and the chase would begin again. The friendly town did not seem as welcoming as it once had. Each time she was spotted, laughter echoed in her ears.

Suddenly, a giant hand lifted her from the ground, lifting her nearly into the clouds before letting her go. Terah screamed. She swam through the air and kicked her arms and legs to keep herself from falling so quickly. Then, just as she prepared to hit the ground, the hand grabbed her again and set her in front of an enormous building. Giant silver letters spelling out *Hallman and Carter* were attached to the side of the modern-looking building. Hearing footsteps behind her, Terah raced inside as someone exited.

Running and hiding. Running and hiding. Running and hiding. Terah was exhausted. All she wanted was to rest, to feel safe. Her side ached, and her stomach roiled. Footsteps sounded in the hallway behind her. She raced through an open room. Spotting an office marked *Jane Enderly*, Terah pounded on the door, keeping watch over her shoulder, hoping *It* had turned in a different direction. Finally, the door opened, allowing her entrance. Terah slammed the door behind her and pressed her head against it, drawing several deep breaths. But when she turned around, it was Becca she saw—Becca and her machete.

Screaming, Terah sat upright. Gratefully aware the events had been only a dream, she wrapped her arms around herself and attempted to slow her breathing. But, because of her anxiety, it was nearly impossible to gulp enough air. Finally, she had to choose between air and her stomach's losing battle with nausea. The green bowl won out as she retched into it multiple times before collapsing onto the sweat-soaked sheets and closing her eyes.

Exhaustion overtook her, and she fell into a deep sleep devoid of images and events.

Suddenly, Terah felt something sharp poke into her side. *Intense pain.* She kneaded the spot with her fingertips, but her hand came away wet. She brought it close to her eyes and screamed. *Blood.* Sticky red liquid ran down her arm and dripped from her hand. Everything moved in slow motion. Terah turned and stared at the shadowy figure in burgundy scrubs hovering over her bed. Becca held the butcher knife

above her head and plunged it into Terah's side again.
Terah gasped, and her world went dark.

CHAPTER THIRTY

CHIEF BRIAN ENDERLY

Officer Collins settled into a chair in Brian's office. She leaned back and crossed and uncrossed her legs.

"Cup of coffee? Water? Soda?" Brian stood and headed toward his door.

Diane ran a hand down her throat. "After the whole Diet Coke and Diet Pepsi delivery, I'm not sure I'm drinking anything that comes out of this office again."

Enderly shrugged. "Suit yourself." He left and returned with a can of Diet Coke. His chair groaned under his weight. He popped the top and guzzled nearly half the can before setting it on his desk. "So, did you learn anything new about our newest resident?"

Collins crossed her legs again and leaned forward. Loosely laying her arms across her knee, she sighed softly. "Not much more than you already told me."

Brian fell against the back of his chair and pressed his fingertips together. "Either she's clean, or she's really good at covering her past," he said.

"There might be a reason for that."

"Oh? Please share."

The officer flipped her notepad open and glanced at her notes. "Terah Dixon—T.E.R.A.H."

"Interesting spelling. I saw that on her name tag at Knuckle's. I figured her parents were hippies."

"Yeah…" Collins rocked back and forth. "Something like that." She eyed Brian with frustration. "Can I finish?"

Brian locked his fingers together over his stomach. "By all means."

"Dixon came to Cedar Point via Minneapolis. Arrived about a month ago—give or take a few days. I didn't get an exact date." The officer scanned her notes again. "She lived in the metro for over twenty years." Diane tapped her finger on the notepad. "She told me she was born and raised in Carson Springs, Wisconsin."

"Same info I got."

"Yes, but she shared something I thought was interesting." Collins perused her notes yet again. "Did you know there's a cult in Carson Springs?"

"A cult?"

"*Life Visions.*"

"Seriously? I thought Godley was only interested in big cities with money." Brian shook his head. "Doesn't seem like a speck on the map would be worth his time."

"Now that he's been indicted, do you suppose he's got flunkies running branches in these small towns?"

Brian grabbed his Coke and finished the can. "I suppose anything's possible. Someone else could be helping him hide money in these places. I mean, the guy's been named in a dozen lawsuits. There's probably a line a mile long waiting to file more lawsuits." He tossed the can into the recycling bin. "Nobody would be looking for him in the backwoods."

"I suppose that's true."

"What did she tell you about living there?"

"Her family was all in."

"Part of the cult, you mean?" Collins raised her eyebrows in confirmation. "Terah Dixon looks like a carpool mom—not a cult member. She doesn't seem the type."

"I would guess she grew up in it and knew nothing different.

That's how they trap these kids for so long. No computers, no televisions or radios, no cell phones, and no social media. Other than the occasional trip into their small town, they have no idea what's happening outside their little corner of the world."

"Well, somehow, *she* knew there was more outside of Carson Springs, or she'd still be there." Brian spun his chair around and stared at the grassy field outside his window. "I can't imagine being that naïve—to believe there is nothing beyond the trees, beyond the fields outside their back door." He turned around again. "Maybe she's more worldly than we know."

"I'm assuming that's why she left. Otherwise, wouldn't you stay? Marry, have kids, and raise them in the only way you knew? From what I can tell, it's a lot like being Amish. The difference is that once you leave *Life Visions*, you're banned for life. At least the Amish allow their young adults to sow their oats outside their community before committing to the church."

"It's control. Andrew Godley wants power and money. You get that by controlling people." He pressed his lips together and tipped his head to the side. "And you lie to them."

Collins nodded and leaned forward. "But get this, Chief. About a year after she left, she went back to find her family, and they'd vanished. They'd moved out of the family home and evidently out of the area. Terah said an elderly couple was living in the house she grew up in and wouldn't give her the time of day. They wouldn't even answer the door."

"Do you suppose they left the cult too?"

Diane hiked one shoulder. "Well, she couldn't locate them in Carson Springs, *and* she hasn't been able to find them anywhere else in the past twenty years." She tightened her mouth and glanced at him over the rim of her glasses.

"What's *that* look for?"

"Terah thinks they may have been killed by the elders and buried just outside the *Life Visions* cemetery."

"You're kidding, right? This is the stuff of movies, based on a true story where only one small piece is the truth, and everything else's been altered to protect the *innocent*." He scoffed. "If they're innocent, don't be making movies about 'em. Leave 'em the hell alone."

"I didn't get the feeling Terah's life was a story. But if it were, I'd say romance meets psychological thriller."

The chief nodded. "So, she really has no idea where they are?"

Diane shook her head. "No. I've read a lot about this group, and I've seen documentaries on TV. It wouldn't surprise me if what she said was true. Just the fact she even suspects they were murdered tells you what the organization is capable of."

Brian pulled his chair close to his desk and touched his trackpad. Painstakingly slow, he entered the town of Carson Springs into the search engine. He smiled when the town's website popped onto the screen. *"The town that's always in season."* Enderly looked at Collins over his screen. "I've passed through there once or twice on the way to a buddy's cabin. It's been a while, but I always thought it was a dump."

"That's what Terah claimed too."

"So, I get not returning to Carson Springs, but why Cedar Point? Does she have family here? Friends? Had she even driven through the place before she came?"

Collins shook her head. "Just needed a change, I guess. Said she laid out a map and picked a small town on the water."

Brian smirked. "It's Minnesota. She could have moved anywhere." He stared at the Minnesota map on the wall of his office. "What I want to know is why here?"

"All I can tell you is that she was ready for something else."

"Does she have a roommate we could talk to?" Collins shook her head. "So, she moves to a small town where she knows absolutely no one and takes a job as a waitress?" Enderly twisted his mouth in question. "Did you get the feeling she's running from something—or someone?"

"Honestly? No." Diane shook her head. "I believe what she said. She came here for a fresh start."

"Did you ask about Hallman and Carter?"

"I did. She didn't even know where the building was located."

"And you trust that?"

"I had no reason not to. Listen, she was very forthcoming about her life. She answered every question, made eye contact, and the pitch and tone of her voice were level. I never once sensed she was hiding anything or lying to me."

Brian typed *Terah Dixon, Minnesota,* into Google. His search came up empty. "Nothing. Not even a matching name."

Collins moved behind him. "It's an unusual spelling. She may be the only one in the Midwest."

He changed Minnesota to Wisconsin but again came up empty.

"Try just Dixon, Carson Springs."

Still nothing.

"I doubt a specific Amish person would appear in a search either. It's like they don't exist to the rest of the world."

Brian held his hand out to her. "Want a bet? Ten dollars says I can find Joe Yoder of Harmony, Minnesota."

"Who's Joe Yoder? And how do you know him?"

"He built some of the cabinets in our house." Brian grinned. "Anybody who has a business needs to be on the Internet."

Collin met his hand with hers. They shook. "You're on. I say there's no way you'll find the Joe Yoder you're talking about."

Brian typed *Joseph Yoder, Harmony Minnesota, builder* into the search. The screen populated, but he saw nothing about the man who had done the beautiful cabinetry Jane had purchased.

Diane held out her hand, palm up. "I'll take that ten now."

Brian rolled his eyes and plucked a ten-dollar bill from his now-empty wallet. "That was supposed to buy me lunch," he said, slapping it into her palm.

Collins laughed. "I've seen you eat. You'd need about three of these."

Brian made a face at her before looking back at his screen.

"Terah lived in the city for twenty years, you said. Shouldn't there be something about her from then?"

"Not necessarily. Maybe she still flew under the radar. Maybe she doesn't use social media."

"Right. Like that's possible. A young adult never using Facebook or Instagram? Highly unlikely."

"True, but possible. Or, hear me out; maybe her real name isn't Terah. Maybe it's Theresa or Teriah or some other variation."

Brian folded his arms across the edge of his desk. "I suppose that's possible, but if my name was Teriah, I doubt I'd go by a nickname one letter shorter than my original name."

"I suppose. But I still think it could be Theresa or a similar name from the bible." She held up a finger. "Wait a minute. Look up *Life Visions*, Carson Springs, Wisconsin."

Brian typed in Collins's suggestion. Pages of links populated the screen connecting the cult and the town. He looked at his officer. "It would take me forever to dig through all of this just to see if I could find anything on Terah Dixon— or any other Dixon, for that matter." He closed his laptop. "I think we just need to take her at her word. Maybe the woman Jane saw at H and C just happened to be her doppelganger."

"Doesn't it seem strange to have two people who look so much alike in the same small town, Chief?"

"That's why we have to find the woman who was at Hallman and Carter. If it wasn't Terah Dixon, then who the hell was it?"

"I take it you haven't heard from H and C about someone being recently added to the cleaning crew."

"Oh, I heard. I just didn't like the answer."

"Why?" Officer Collins tucked the pad back into her pocket.

"Because nobody hired her."

"So, this person just got into the place for, like what, a couple of days, and pretended to be on the cleaning crew?"

"More or less. They were going to be short-handed. One of

the crew was telling a friend at the grocery store, and this woman happened to overhear and volunteered to come and help for a few days—for cash."

Collins's eyes bulged. "So, she just showed up to clean?"

"Looks like it."

"No background check?" Brian shook his head. "A name?"

"Oh, there was a name, but it's no one anyone's ever heard of." He looked at the yellow notepad on the corner of his desk. "Tia Donnely."

Collins shrugged. "Not a name I've come across."

"Me either." He stood. "But until further notice, Jane will not step foot in that building."

CHAPTER THIRTY-ONE

CHIEF BRIAN ENDERLY

Brian felt like he was following a ball of yarn made of hundreds of tiny pieces—short strands rolled together to give the illusion of wholeness. Just when he felt he was closing in on an answer, the string ended, and another started, sending him in an entirely different direction. Some threads were solid and could be woven into a piece of fine fabric that told part of the story. Others were frayed and fell apart when they were stretched.

Frustration swelled inside him.

There were tangible clues wound in with a surplus of red herrings and dead ends. Each had to be followed from start to finish. But some findings twisted into a noose, choking away the hope he had just seconds earlier.

4:47 a.m. The dawn was still asleep, hidden well below the horizon. Thick clouds blocked the moonlight. Except for the light cast downward from a half-dozen streetlights, one on each block of Main Street, the town was disturbingly dark when Brian entered the station, locking the door behind him. The last thing he needed was somebody with a loose screw and a gun to surprise him while he worked.

Refusing to turn on the front office light, letting others know he was already at work, he relied on memory to get to his office:

"

thirteen steps and then a right. After he closed the door behind him and flipped on his light, he nearly jumped out of his skin. Someone was in the corner of his office, lying in a ball on the floor behind his recliner. The bulky quilt moved again.

Brian aimed his gun toward the pile. "Who's in there? Show me your hands," the chief ordered.

"Don't shoot, Boss." His administrative assistant poked her head from beneath the blanket. Her hair was a mangled mess, and she had huge bags beneath her eyes.

"Son of a bitch, Mauri. What the hell are you doing? You almost gave me a heart attack." He shoved his gun back into his holster. "And you almost got yourself killed."

Mauri sat up and leaned against the wall. She eyed the bare windows for a few seconds. Finally, she crawled to the door, pulled it open, and crawled out of Brian's office. He trailed close behind.

"What are you doing?"

She plopped into her chair, plucked a chunk of hair from the corner of her mouth, and tucked it behind her ear.

"I asked what you're doing here. You're supposed to be at Jeff's, under police protection, in case you forgot."

Suddenly, Brian's cell phone rang. For the second time in less than five minutes, he jumped.

"Hello," he barked into the phone, listened, and gave Mauri a dirty look. "Yeah, she's here—

at the office." With his mouth poised to speak, he was silent for a good ten seconds before he shoved his question between Jeff's words. "What kind of cop lets their charge escape?" He made faces as he listened.

"Doesn't... No one... Jeff... Jeff..." Finally, he hollered, "Stop talking!" He waited for the silence. "Let Mike know she's fine. Once I figure out what's going on, I'll call you."

Brian ended the call and shoved his phone into his shirt pocket. "Now that you're awake, how about you tell me how in the hell you ended up here instead of under my crappy deputy's watchful eye."

"It wasn't Jeff's fault. It was mine." Mauri's head barely moved. "You won't understand."

"Try me." Brian dropped into one of the visitors' chairs. He folded his arms across his chest and waited.

"Seriously? It's not even light outside, and I slept on the…" Her head wobbled. "That's not true. I didn't sleep. I was on the floor, curled up behind your recliner for the past several hours." She swept her hair back with her hand before combing through the snarls with her fingers. "And you want to have a conversation now?"

"Uh-huh. Start talking. Because you were supposed to be at Jeff's where he could keep an eye on you." He scowled. "You make a better criminal than he makes a deputy. Did Mike know you left?"

Mauri snorted. "He didn't. But, based on what you told Jeff, I'm thinking he does now." As if on cue, her desk phone rang. "Can I text Mike from your phone? I left mine…" She waved a hand in the air. "I can't talk to him yet. I'll tell him I'll call him in a while."

Brian handed over his phone and waited for her to finish texting. "So?"

Mauri released a forceful breath. Her neck popped as she stretched it one way and then the other. Pressing her hands into the chair seat behind her, she arched her back. She rolled her neck but stopped when she saw his face.

"Fine," she grumbled.

Brian's phone buzzed again. Mauri picked it up and read the message from her husband. A tender smile crossed her face as she laid the phone face down on her desk.

"I went to Jeff's like a good girl," she said sarcastically.

Brian planted his feet wide and punched a fist into the palm of his other hand. "Well, look at that. You *can* follow directions."

"You don't have to be such an ass."

"And you don't have to be such a pain in mine. Just tell me what happened before I die listening to you."

Mauri pressed her lips tightly together, and she sneered at him. "Sometime around midnight, I got up to get a drink."

"Water? Or something stronger?"

She huffed. "Could you blame me if I needed a little something to take the edge off?"

Brian shook his head. "No."

"Just water. While I was standing at the kitchen sink, a vehicle drove slowly past, turned around, and drove back the other way." She raised two fingers slightly. "Twice, that happened."

"Did you see what it was? Make and model? Car? SUV? Truck?"

Mauri shook her head. "Smaller SUV, maybe. I was too freaked out to notice much more." She drew a deep breath and released it slowly. "When it drove by the second time, I ducked below the cupboard and sat on the floor for a long time. I was too afraid to move." She closed her eyes for several seconds. "Finally, I got up and hid in the shadows of the cupboard, just watching. I didn't see the car again, but a package appeared in the middle of the sidewalk while I was hiding on the floor." She scowled at Brian. "And before you ask, no, it was not there before."

Brian huffed. "You went out to take a look." Mauri nodded. "Do you have any idea how stupid that was?" He stared at her. "You've worked here long enough to know better. Anyone could have been out there waiting for you. Anyone."

"I know. But this *what if* kept running through my head. I'm sure you would have had the same thought. What if it was a bomb or some other explosive? I didn't want everyone in the house to die because someone was after me."

Brian's face softened. "Okay, so you went outside to check it out." Brian's eyes narrowed. "Doesn't Jeff have a security system? Cameras? Anything?"

"No." Mauri shook her head.

"I probably shouldn't have sent you home with him then."

"As a cop, you'd think he'd have 'em everywhere, wouldn't

you?" She folded her hands and laid them along the edge of her desk, bent forward, and pressed her chin into them, almost as if she were praying. "He does, however, have automatic locking doors." She eyed her boss. "So, once I walked out…"

Brian nodded. "The door locked, and you couldn't get back in. So, why didn't you ring the damn doorbell or pound on the door?"

"And run the risk of Jeff shooting me? That wasn't something I wanted to chance."

"So, you got in your car and came here." Brian looked slightly upward. "But I didn't see your car in the lot."

"I drove Mike's. I parked it in the grocery store lot. I didn't want anyone to know I was here."

"Wait. You got locked out without a way to get back in, but you just happened to have your husband's car keys? How'd that happen?"

She looked down. "I didn't have his keys either. But Mike locks himself out of his car at least once a week, so he's got an extra hidden inside the fuel door."

"Right. Because that's safe." Brian rolled his eyes. "So, you drove here instead of calling me?"

Mauri pointed to his phone. "No phone." She bit the side of her cheek. "And it's not exactly like Cedar Point's teeming with payphones. Nor did I have two quarters to throw inside of one." Brian nodded knowingly. "In case you haven't noticed, I'm still wearing my pajamas." Mauri stood, folded her arms across her braless chest, and pointed to her gray T-shirt and black knit shorts.

Brian disappeared into his office and returned with an extra sweatshirt he kept at the station. He handed it to her. Mauri pulled it over her head. The bottom band came to the middle of her shins, and the sleeves nearly touched the floor. Before folding them up, she crossed her legs and tugged the bottom of the sweatshirt over her bare feet.

"I had a really hard time seeing the code on the back door. I figured if I hit the wrong buttons enough times, you'd get a notification." She looked at him. "Is that why you're here?"

"No. I came in to figure out how to get you out of town."

Mauri nodded. "Once I got here, I figured I'd be safe. I tried to sleep in your recliner." She snorted. "I know no one can see in your windows, but I could see out, and that made me feel like a sitting duck. So, I finally gave up and curled up with your quilt behind the chair." Mauri grimaced. "By the way, that blanket needs to be tossed out…or given a good bath. It smells like sweat and dirty feet and…."

"My mom made that quilt."

"Oh. Sorry. Maybe I'll wash it for you."

Suddenly, he slid to the edge of his chair. "So, what *was* in the package?"

Mauri dropped her chin slightly. "It wasn't a bomb…at least not one that ticked. I didn't touch it. I didn't want to mess with evidence."

Brian grabbed his phone and called Jeff. Mauri folded and unfolded her hands as she listened to Brian's side of the conversation and speculated what Porter was saying.

He pressed the end button and stared at her. "Soda. That's what was in the package." He swallowed hard. "Diet Pepsi."

Mauri dropped her head against the back of her chair. "Why is this happening?" Grabbing the arm of the chair, she pulled herself upright. "Did Jeff check the cans? Like we did before?"

"He did."

"And?"

Brian did not answer. Mauri's face fell.

"Listen. We're going to get you and Mike out of Cedar Point until this all blows over. The last thing I need is to worry about you too. I have enough on my plate with Jane and the boys."

"Thanks, but…"

"I mean it, Mauri. You're leaving town. Go to your sister's or take some trip you and Mike have always wanted to go on. But you're getting the hell out of Cedar Point."

"And what if this person follows me?" She tilted her head. "Because I don't want to put my family or anybody else in danger."

"I honestly don't believe it's you they're after. I think this is a warning to me." He sighed. "Think about it. Every person they have gone after has been close to me. I just don't know what the warning's about." He rested his ankle on his other thigh.

"Agent Wallick said the same thing. He said it was anyone connected to you."

Brian nodded. "Yeah." The word sounded more like a breath. "But while I figure it out, I want everyone I love to be safe."

Mauri gave him a sideways grin. "Ah, you love me."

"Shut up." The corners of his mouth lifted slightly. "To make sure you're safe, though, we'll set up a decoy—just in case. Like I said before, that's why I came in so early."

Mauri pulled her arms inside the sweatshirt and hugged herself. "I'm scared, Boss. Really scared."

Tears rolled down her cheeks. She tipped her head down and wiped her face on Brian's sweatshirt. It unnerved Brian to see Mauri like this. She was always so tough. He pulled her to her feet and held her while she sobbed.

"Are you done yet?" He smiled down at her. "My shirt's covered in snot and tears." He chuckled.

Mauri rolled her eyes and rubbed her nose across his shirt.

"That's disgusting."

"Yeah, well, if you ship me off, I won't be around to bug you. I have to get my licks in while I can—just in case…"

"Don't even say that shit." He pulled her close to him again. "I know I give you a lot of crap, but you really are important to me. I don't want anything to happen to you."

Mauri pressed her face against his shirt again and hugged him. They stood in silence for almost thirty seconds. Finally, Mauri whispered, "I knew you'd miss me."

"Damn right." He grinned down at her. "Who'd bring me my Diet Coke every day?"

Mauri slapped his arm and returned to her desk.

Jeff unlocked the door and stormed into the station. "What the hell, Mauri? You don't just sneak out…"

"We're good, Jeff." Brian held a restraining hand in front of his deputy. "Right now, you and I have to create a diversion to get Mauri and Mike out of town."

Porter let go of a long breath and threw his arms around Mauri. "Thank God you're okay." Then, he followed Brian toward his office for a planning session. "But do that to me again, and I'll kill you myself."

"I love you too, Jeff," Mauri said.

It was still over an hour before the station was to open. Mauri checked the front door to make sure it was locked. Then she tiptoed back to her chair and fell into it. She glanced toward Brian's office.

She picked up the phone but slammed it down when Brian bellowed from the other room. "No personal calls on that phone. We can't take the chance of having someone listen in."

"But it's the office phone."

"Doesn't matter. We're not going to chance it."

Mauri folded her hands and silently sat at her desk. Her head spun, and her heart ached. While Brian and Jeff planned her escape, she pondered the secret she was keeping.

CHAPTER THIRTY-TWO

ADMINISTRATIVE ASSISTANT MAURI LOCKE

Six hours later, Officer Diane Collins, dressed in Mauri's clothes and donning a brown wig cut to match Mauri's hair, was in the passenger seat of Mauri's Ford Focus. Officer Lance Finley, a near-body double for Mike Locke, wore Mike's favorite baseball cap pulled down over the pair of Oakley sunglasses Mike always wore. Jeans, a Columbia sweatshirt, and a black and gray North Face jacket completed his ensemble. The officers were headed for the airport in Fargo, driving Mauri's blue Ford Focus with the personalized license plate, *M & M*. The fake couple had loaded a pair of matching suitcases into the car as they gushed about their long overdue trip to Hawaii for their tenth anniversary.

The suitcases were empty, and the trip was not real—at least not the one to Hawaii.

After loading everything, they drove through Cedar Point and headed west. No. They were not the Lockes, but with careful planning, they looked an awful lot like them. They were decoys.

Suddenly, Officers Serrano and Higgins pushed two handcuffed men and a woman into the station. A loud argument ensued, drawing the attention of those on the street. One of the men was a deeply disguised Mike Locke.

Once inside, Mike was uncuffed, and the second part of the plan went into motion. He held his wife tightly while the blonde-haired woman changed clothes and deposited those she had worn on Mauri's desk. Mauri quickly changed into those of the woman before pulling on the blonde wig. Her husband slipped on a paramedic's uniform and traded places with a fake EMT who entered the station five minutes after the three were brought in. A third EMT was hiding in the back of the ambulance.

None of the players were real. They were officers from surrounding stations brought in to assist.

Minutes later, the blonde, AKA Mauri, was loaded into the ambulance by two attendants and whisked away. The sounds of the siren could be heard crossing town. Brian and Jeff stood on the sidewalk, watching the ambulance disappear, loudly discussing how out-of-towners created so many problems.

Lights flashed as the ambulance headed toward St. Cloud. At the hospital, they drove into an underground parking garage and appeared to unload a blonde female, when in all actuality, their patient was nothing more than a pile of blankets and a blonde wig. Mauri and Mike hid in the back while the paramedics pretended to do their job.

Ten minutes later, the EMTs returned. The ambulance drove away from the hospital, stopping at a McDonald's at the edge of St. Cloud. The driver parked in a ramp near the restaurant in a space that had just been vacated by a large black van. To the left of the ambulance was an SUV with dark windows. Shortly after they got out and walked toward the restaurant, a pair of small cars exited the ramp.

Mauri and Mike carried one burner phone. Their real phones were headed west. A text popped onto the screen. *Go time*. Mauri and Mike passed into the front of the ambulance, exited the driver's side, and climbed into the back of the waiting SUV.

Jeff Porter was in the driver's seat. He drove out of the ramp and headed toward Minneapolis. Words were scarce on the hour-long trip. Jeff dropped them in front of a car rental on the west side of the metro. For the first time since leaving Cedar Point, Mauri almost felt safe.

As Mike sped along Interstate 94, she fell into a restless sleep. Her dreams tormented her—visions of Brian in danger, images of his wife staring down the barrel of a gun, Cole and Luke fighting for their lives, and a casket being lowered into the ground.

The headstone read *Enderly*.

CHAPTER THIRTY-THREE

CHIEF BRIAN ENDERLY, JANE ENDERLY, &
HER SONS,
COLE & LUKE HART

Mauri was safe, at least temporarily. Now, Brian could focus on Jane and anyone close to him who might be in the line of fire. He was in the dark as to who was toying with him. What went down two years before had ended with Jane's ex-husband hospitalized for the long haul, her mother in prison for the remainder of her life, and her half-brother six feet under. Brian wondered if Viv, Jane's lowlife mother, could be pulling strings from inside the prison.

He stood in front of the whiteboard in his office. The day before, Deputy Porter had listed cases that might have strings attached: someone angry about the outcome, threats received during the last few years, or crimes the department was still digging into. Brian uncapped the pen and added the woman claiming to be his sister. He scratched his head. The odds of that being the case were a million to one. He erased it, stared at the emptied spot, and rewrote it.

Jane and Sean were not the only ones who were haunted by their pasts. The tangle of overgrown weeds from his was overwhelming. There was no time to get sucked into that mess.

Honestly, he barely had time to take a leak lately. His phone had not stopped ringing since Luke landed in the hospital.

Two years before, no one had made a move without checking in or awaiting directions. It was the same today. Cedar Point was a small town. His team typically handled parking and speeding tickets, a few domestics, and noise violations. Periodically, something bigger unfolded, but that was rare and did not involve attempted murder. The town was a haven of good people, so his deputies had minimal knowledge of dealing with something so savage. With the last attempt at poisoning Mauri, the FBI had gotten involved. Agent John Wallick and two others from Minneapolis had joined Brian's team. Finally, he had someone who thought outside the morals of Cedar Point.

He texted Jane to check in. An instant response pinged. Her thumbs up and a red heart let him know she was good. Her messages were always short and pointed. Brian knew she felt his frustration and fear, understood his lack of sleep, and knew he did not have time for anything that was not vital. As long as she was safe, that was all he needed to know.

Cole and Luke were with her at the house, secured inside the fortress protected by cameras and locks. The lower-level windows and doors had internal wrought-iron grids that opened and closed like shutters. They folded into the walls when Jane felt safe and pulled out and locked over the windows when she did not. Since Luke had been poisoned, Brian was unsure they would ever open again.

Two hours later, Brian stopped at the house for a quick check-in. It was nearly dinnertime. If he had planned his arrival right, he could shovel down a plate of food and make it back to the station before Jeff returned from Minneapolis to fill him in on Mike and Mauri.

Instead of building out in the country, as Jane and Sean had done when they married, Jane opted for a house in town, surrounded by people. To Brian, that translated to—*someone to hear me scream if needed.* She insisted they build in the center of a block of existing homes, not on a corner or in a new development.

Long before they married, she had purchased a ramshackle early nineteen hundreds house that appeared to give up the fight a little more each day. The coned roof on the turret had caved in years before, and the roof that remained sagged deeply.

Jonas and Anna Maja Johannson, the first family of Cedar Point, had built the house. Jonas had served as mayor for nearly twenty years. When he died, his daughter, Emma, moved in to care for her mother. After Anna Maja passed, Emma remained there, but she never married. She was over one hundred when she drew her last breath. When she was gone, the house sat empty for over twenty years before Jane bought it and built what her sons called *Fort Mom*.

Some might have considered the measures she took to protect herself excessive, but they gave Brian much-needed comfort. The last thing he wanted was to lose her again.

When he walked into the kitchen, his wife's eyes were wide. Her sons flanked her—Cole to her left and Luke to her right.

"What? What's going on?" Brian stepped toward Jane.

She opened her mouth, but no words came out.

"It's Dad," Cole said, tightening his grip on his mom's elbow. "Dr. Evenson just called."

Brian shrank back. "Did something happen to your dad? Is he dea…"

Luke answered with a quick shake of his head. "He's remembering stuff—like Mom."

"Are you serious? A few weeks ago, he had no clue who she was." He rested a hand on his wife's cheek. Still, Jane did not speak. He looked at Cole. "Did he ask for your mom or…Emily?"

Cole's eyebrows pressed inward. "Mom. *Jane.*"

Brian's mouth dropped open, and he grabbed the edge of the counter. "I suppose this is good news, but…"

Luke scowled at his stepdad. "But what, Brian?" He glared at him. "Dad's remembering." His head bobbed. "Sure, he was a major asshole to her and almost everyone else, but he's still our dad."

Color raced up Brian's cheeks. "No, Luke. I didn't mean it the way you think. I'm happy for you and Cole and your mom. It's just bad timing. We're trying to keep your mother safe from some nutjob, and now her psycho husband wants to see her."

"He's not a psycho." Jane's voice was shaky as her first words surfaced. The volume was soft. "He had a breakdown. That's very different. He was a victim of his childhood just like I was."

"Honey, I couldn't agree more, but *you* got help. Instead, he continued to perseverate on it and take his frustration out on you. Remember?"

"Maybe so, but…" She sent him a warning, pointing at her sons with her eyes. "He's getting better. That's what matters. He's getting the help he needs now."

Brian raised one shoulder. "You're right. Boys, I'm sorry. Your dad needed help, and he's getting that." He laid a hand on Luke's shoulder. "I'm happy for you both."

Cole rubbed his chin. "No. He *was* a psycho. Let's not pretend he wasn't." Squeezing his mom's hand, he turned and faced her. "He beat you for years. And he wanted you dead." His cheeks expanded with the release of a long breath. "Just because he shot your crazy half-brother instead doesn't mean he wouldn't have done you in had the cops not stopped him."

Jane's eyes softened. "I know, honey. But your father's been through a lot. I'll always have a soft spot for him because of the things he suffered." She smiled at Luke before meeting Cole's eyes. "And he gave me the two of you. For that, I'll always love him."

"It's a damn good thing we take after you and not Dad." Luke grabbed his beer from the counter and finished the last swig.

Jane snorted. "My side of the family doesn't exactly resemble the Cleavers." She smiled at Luke. "Ward and June were perfect. My family was perfectly awful. I was the product of an affair, had a money-grubbing evil mother, and a half-brother who tried to kill me."

"Well, Grandpa Doug's okay."

"He is. But Grandpa isn't a blood relative, Luke."

Luke smirked. "Still, he's not an ass."

Brian gently kissed his wife. "I'd say you boys are lucky to have an amazing mother who rose above her crappy life." He winked at Jane. "And you have to admit, you have one hell of an incredible stepfather."

Cole smiled. "That's *your* opinion."

Brian laughed. "I'm starving." He sniffed the air. "What's for dinner?"

"Pizza. Luke was going to order when Dr. Evenson called."

He looked at his stepson. "Are you sure you're okay—for pizza, I mean? You've been out of the hospital for like a minute."

Luke frowned at him. "It's pizza, Brian. Besides, I asked the doctor, and he said I could have all the pizza I wanted—and beer." He lifted his empty bottle in the air, set it on the counter, and grabbed another.

Brian nodded. "Okay, then. I'll grab something to eat on my way back to the station."

"Seriously? You're going back to work? Tonight?" Jane's voice cracked, and her chin trembled.

"I don't have a choice." He grabbed a Diet Coke from the fridge and upended it. "So, when do you want to see Sean?" He leaned against the counter. "Or maybe you don't?"

"I do. I feel like I need to."

"Okay." He looked at his watch. "You're not thinking of going tonight, are you?" Jane shook her head. "Can you wait a couple of days? There's so much going on right now that I don't know if I can spare an officer to go with you. And I don't want you going anywhere alone."

Jane nodded. "Saturday? Does that work?"

"That should be fine. I'll find somebody who can take you."

"I'll let Dr. Evenson know I'll be there at 10:00 on Saturday."

Brian kissed the top of Jane's head. "Don't wait up. I have no idea what time I'll get home—or if I'll make it home tonight."

"Check in occasionally, okay?"

"I will. But I don't want to wake you either."

"Then, let me know by midnight if you'll make it home."

Brian nodded. He pointed toward the front door. "This goes without saying, but do not open that door for anyone."

"Except for the pizza delivery." Luke smiled.

"I supposed that's okay." Brian rolled his eyes. "The delivery guys don't usually carry guns, so I think you're safe." He pitched his soda can into the recycling bin. "Lock the door and set the alarm behind me." Then he was gone.

An hour later, the doorbell rang.

"Pizza's here," Luke announced.

Cole looked at the clock on the stove. "That was a lot faster than they said but still a lot longer than it should have been."

"Just shut up and be grateful." Luke pumped his arms into the air and danced to the door.

He disarmed the alarm and turned all three locks before opening the door.

A woman in a red T-shirt, jeans, and baseball cap held three white pizza boxes. "Two large sausage and pepperoni and one small veggie." She looked at the top tag and announced, "$54.87." She waited for Luke to give her money before handing the boxes to him.

Luke handed her three twenty-dollar bills. "Keep the change."

"Thanks." The woman smiled at him. "You look like you could eat all three pizzas by yourself." She tipped her head to the left and tried to peek into the entry, but Luke and the stack of pizzas blocked her view.

Luke pressed his lips together and nodded. "Normally, but tonight, I'm being forced to share."

"I'm guessing the veggie's not for you." She laughed.

"Do I look like I eat veggies?" He grinned. "That one's all

Mom's."

"Good to know." She winked. "Enjoy your pizza. I hope your mom enjoys hers too."

Luke watched her climb into her white SUV and drive away. Something felt off, but he could not put his finger on it.

He set the boxes on the counter, opened the lid, and grabbed the biggest slice. The doorbell rang again.

Jane pressed her back against the fridge. Her voice trembled. "Who would that be?"

Luke dropped the slice of pizza and headed toward the entry. "Don't eat without me," he said. Again, he disarmed the alarm and unlocked the door.

"Hey, Luke." Jack Draper balanced a green pizza bag near his shoulder. "Got your order."

Luke's eyes grew. He bolted into the kitchen and swiped the pizza off the counter and onto the floor. "Don't eat that!" Cole was chewing. "Spit it out, now!" He slapped Cole on the back of the head. "Get it out of your mouth." He looked at his mom. "It could have been…"

Cole launched himself across the wide island on his stomach and spit everything into the sink. He stuck his head under the faucet and swished the water in his mouth before expelling it with such force, it splashed onto the quartz top. He wiped the inside of his mouth with the dish towel, gagging as a corner touched a tonsil. Luke dropped to his knees to scoop the pizza from the floor.

Jack appeared around the corner. "Do you guys want the pizza you ordered?" His eyes were wide when he saw Luke gathering the other boxes.

Jane slid down the front of the fridge and dropped onto the floor. She wrapped her arms around her legs and pressed her head to her knees. She held her breath and counted to ten before releasing it.

"Mom?" Cole put a hand on her arm. "Do you want me to call Brian?"

Her head still pressed to her knees, she whispered, "Yes."

CHAPTER THIRTY-FOUR

CHIEF BRIAN ENDERLY

Brian was positive his chest was going to explode. He could hear the rush of blood in his ears as he drove toward the house, rolling through stop signs and taking corners much too fast. The siren screamed, and the lights flashed. Still, Marilyn Gershan, a ninety-seven-year-old lady who should have given up her license years before, did not move out of his way. Instead, he raced around her, squeezing the steering wheel tightly to keep from flipping her off as he passed her green 1971 Chrysler Newport in the middle of Merkler Street.

The unexpected call from Cole made him realize Jane and her sons were not safe anywhere. They could not even trust food prepared outside their home. That meant Knuckle's and the other hometown hotspots were off the table—at least until they caught the son of a bitch who was screwing with them. Clearly, the mastermind of this plan had hacked Luke's computer or his phone.

He rolled into the driveway and reached the door in half as many steps as usual. With the side of his fist, he pounded on the door. Cole jumped. His eyes widened as the banging continued.

"Jane!" Brian hollered. "Boys, it's me. Brian. Open the damn door."

Cole ran through the entry, disarmed the alarm, and stepped

back as Brian burst through the door.

"Jane!" He moved through the kitchen and into the living room.

Jeff pushed through the door just as Cole was shutting it.

Jane was on the couch, clutching a small brown paper bag. It inflated and deflated as she drew and released long breaths. Brian sat next to her and grasped her other hand. "Just keep breathing, hon," he said.

Jeff dropped into an overstuffed chair and jerked his head sideways, indicating for Cole and Luke to join them in the living room.

After plucking a small pad from his back pocket and a pen from his shirt, he looked at all three victims. "Tell me exactly what happened."

Luke glanced at Cole. "Well, after all that crappy hospital food, all I wanted was pizza."

Porter snorted. "Of course you did." The corners of his mouth lifted.

Luke turned his palms up in question. "Why does everyone say that?" He shrugged. "Well, I ordered pizza. Two large sausage and pepperoni, and a small veggie for Mom."

"From where?" Officer Porter scribbled the order on his notepad.

"Caruso's."

"Online or by phone?"

"Online."

Jeff looked at Brian. "That means someone intercepted the order. How'd you order? Phone or computer?"

"Computer. It's easier."

"I need to see the computer you used to place the order."

"I'll get it." Cole headed toward the basement, where they were camped out for as long as it took to get rid of the creep who was after their mom.

"Okay, keep going."

"Well, the pizza showed up—early. Which was odd because the place said they said they were short-staffed, and it would take about an hour and a half."

Cole raced up the steps two at a time and set the computer on the floor near Deputy Porter. "And it wasn't what we ordered," Cole said.

Luke pulled his head back. "Well, no shit. We didn't ask for poison."

"That's not what I meant. The order was wrong. It wasn't sausage and pepperoni. It was just pepperoni and looked like a frozen pizza stuck in a greasy box." He looked at Brian. "I remember thinking the box looked like it had been used before, but…" Cole glanced at his mom. "I was hungry, so I ate it anyway. I didn't open the other boxes. They're on the kitchen counter."

Porter finished writing. "So, you ordered sausage and pepperoni and a veggie."

"Two." Cole held up his index and middle finger. "Two sausage-pepperoni and one veggie. And the one I opened was only pepperoni." Cole sat on the loveseat next to Luke.

"Wait. There's something else that was weird too." Luke closed his eyes and rubbed his temple.

"Are you okay, Luke?" Cole asked.

"I'm thinking."

"Well, that's something new."

Luke snarled at him.

"What is it?" Jeff slid forward in his chair.

"The woman who delivered the pizza wore a red cap and shirt. Caruso's is green and white. She also didn't have an oven bag. Caruso's always uses them." He shook his head. "I think I was so hungry, I didn't notice." Luke stared at the wall above his mom. "And this may be nothing, but I don't remember seeing the pizza sign on her car either."

Porter looked at the chief and then back at Luke. "We'll check the house cameras when we get back to the office." He made a note on the pad. "So, the person who delivered it was a female?" Luke nodded. "What'd she look like?"

Luke's eyes darted around the room. The edges of his mouth

turned down, and one shoulder lifted. "I don't know. She was like old, and I was hungry."

"How old?"

"I don't know. Like in her forties, maybe."

Jane's head was pressed against Brian's shoulder. "Thanks, Luke."

"I didn't mean *old*. I just meant too old for me to care what she looked like."

Porter nodded. "Do you remember anything about her? Hair color?"

"She was blonde. Definitely blonde."

"You're sure?" Brian wrapped an arm over his wife's shoulder.

"I'm positive. The wind blew a chunk of hair across her face, and she pulled it back and tucked it behind her ear."

"Okay." More pen scritches sounded on the notepad. "How tall would you say she was?" Again, Luke shrugged. "Stand up." Porter waited for him to follow his directive. "Now, imagine you're standing at the door talking to her. Where was the top of her head?" He held a hand near the middle of his chest. "All right. Was she heavy?" Luke shook his head. "Average?"

"No, she was super skinny, incredibly sickeningly so. Bony. She almost looked anorexic."

"So, a skinny blonde that was about five foot five." Porter raised an eyebrow. "That's nearly half of the women in Minnesota."

"Anything else you can remember?"

"Yeah."

"What?"

"She had really big…" He held his hands in front of his chest. "You know."

"Breasts?"

"Sure. Go with that."

Brian let go of Jane and leaned forward. He rested his elbows on his knees and locked his hands.

"Have you seen her before?" Brian asked.

"No." A strange look crossed Luke's face. "Wait. Maybe? If I did, I don't know where."

"So, she wasn't someone you knew by name or saw around town often?"

"I don't think so. I'm pretty sure I'd remember those…"

Porter interrupted him. "So, what made you suspect the pizza had been tampered with?"

Luke drew a long breath, held it briefly, and brought the memory to life. "Just minutes after she pulled out of the driveway, Jack knocked on the door with our pizzas." Lines ran across his forehead. "I remember seeing the sign on the top of his car. And that's when I knew something was wrong."

"Jack?"

"Jack Draper. He's been delivering for Caruso's for the last few months."

Porter's head wagged. "He's delivered to my place a couple of times."

"What can you tell me about the woman's car?"

Luke nodded. "A white CR-V with the plate hanging sideways."

Porter grinned. "Oh sure, that's what you remember."

Brian's eyes widened. "A CR-V? Do you know the year?"

"I'm a mechanic." He huffed. "I know every car. It was a 2010."

"Shit." He gave Porter an uneasy look.

"I saw that car the afternoon Mauri said some woman claiming to be my sister was waiting for me."

"I thought she was gone when you got back." Porter looked confused.

"She was. But when I went out to look for her, that car—or an identical one—drove past the station. The woman was blonde." His nose crinkled. "She looked right at me—or rather, through me. It was incredibly eerie." Suddenly, he slammed the heel of his hand across his thigh. "Oh my God. That woman looked like Terah Dixon." He turned toward his stepson. "Luke, if I showed you a picture, could you tell me if this was the woman who delivered the pizzas today?"

"Maybe," Luke said, non-committal.

Brian poked a button and flipped through a few pictures on his phone. He stared at the photo of the woman he had taken in front of Knuckle's. How could anyone so sweet be so evil? Finally, he stood next to Luke and handed him his phone.

"Is this the person who delivered the pizza tonight?"

"I…" He turned his head. "Well… It…" He deflated. "I don't know. I don't think I looked at her that closely."

Brian looked at Porter. "I want Dixon brought in for questioning—tonight."

Porter nodded. He returned the notepad and pen to their respective pockets and scooped Luke's computer off the floor. "I need to take this with me. I'll get it back to you as soon as possible."

Everyone followed Porter into the kitchen. He flipped a box open with a knife lying on the counter. "Cole's right. It does look like frozen pizza. He lifted the corner of another box. It was the veggie. "Brian, I think we need to get the detectives from Alex back here tonight. I don't want to touch these. We can maybe get some prints from the boxes."

Brian nodded. Exhaustion was suffocating him. All he wanted to do was protect Jane, but he was too tired even to do that.

Porter stood up. "Leave the pizzas where they are." He texted something. "Someone'll be here in a few minutes." He turned toward Luke. "Did the woman say *anything* else that you can recall?"

Luke bit his lip and stared at the jumble of boxes. "Yeah, but I thought she was just being nice." He shook his head. "She asked if the veggie pizza was for Mom."

Brian looked at Jeff and growled in a low voice, "I want that pizza tested tonight."

"Which do you want first?"

"Dixon. I want Dixon."

CHAPTER THIRTY-FIVE

BECCA HULLS

In the dark, illuminated only by the spotlight of oncoming cars, Becca's mind raced with the events of the last few hours.

After untethering her life from Terah's, Becca breathed a sigh of relief. Yes, they had been friends. And she had needed her in the past, but that was no longer the case. Terah was a chain around her neck, weighing her down, always judging, always wanting to know more than Becca was willing to share. She could hear her whiny voice. *Why? Why? Why?* Terah was the quiet and sweet one; at least, that was how everyone viewed her. But Becca was the one who got things done. She never feared stepping over the line.

The two of them looked like twins. She had seen people whispering behind their hands, *wondering.* Always secretly questioning how the two of them could look so much alike. Becca wondered about it herself. Two girls from the same small town, the same cult, who shared the same birthday and looked nearly identical but were seemingly unrelated—was it an anomaly, or had the evil of the elders and the church been at play? All Becca knew was that she fluctuated from hating stick-in-the-mud Terah to needing her. Terah may have been the only reason others tolerated Becca.

Terah had served her purpose. Becca had gotten everything

she needed from her. Now, her birthday was hers alone. She was the only one with that face, that turned-up nose, the hollow cheeks, and the thin body. And the one thing Becca loved about her body was her breasts. They would draw men's attention to her, not to her friend with the baby blonde hair and favorable personality. She would be the center of attention from now on.

While Becca stared at her computer, flipping back and forth between screens, she had packed everything she owned in her car. The rental had come fully furnished, so little belonged to her—a plastic bin of personal items and wigs, a suitcase of clothes, a backpack, and her purse. There was one item—the cardboard box with the baby clothes, quilt, and information about her birth that, since the accident, lived on the floor of her new-to-her car. Everything she left belonged to Terah. But then again, dead people did not need *stuff*. So, she had helped herself to a red glass heart she had always envied—a gift from Terah's parents on her thirteenth birthday.

Suddenly, the precise details she had been waiting for popped onto her screen. It could not have happened any better. She raced downtown, returning minutes later to prepare for her final performance in Cedar Point.

While she waited, she had taken one quick walk around the house, making sure *Becca Hulls* had been fully erased. Finding her would have been very unlikely, however. It had not been Becca, but Terah who had joined the community of Cedar Point, fully expecting to spend the rest of her life there. *And she had*. Poor Terah had no way of knowing how short that time would be.

Becca was not like Terah. She was a free spirit, a woman who came, took, and left. Her intent had never been to stay in one place—least of all Cedar Point. Her only reason for being there was to find a way to destroy Mack Enderly. She had invited Terah to move to Cedar Point as a cover. No one ever suspected they were two unique people.

Becca had tugged on a clean red polo shirt that belonged to Terah and checked her phone before grabbing the boxes from the pile near the garbage can and heading out. She had driven the ten blocks in record time, slipping in and out of the car, keeping her face tilted down and the cap low over her eyes when she made the delivery.

It had been easy to disguise the cyanide crystals. They looked like salt. Little by little, Becca was leaving a trail of destruction aimed directly at Mack Enderly.

Perhaps she should give him one more opportunity to make things right—to admit he had wronged her. But then again—did he deserve that?

Becca settled in for the long ride to Duluth, grateful for the cover of darkness. Her shoulders fell forward, and she felt a joy she had not experienced in a very long time. The waiting during that first half hour after she had dropped off the pizzas had almost put her over the edge. The sirens told her that her mission had been a success. Before, she had nearly killed Mack's step-grandson. Jane had been her target, but her big-ass baby had ruined that. This time, she had not failed. Neither of those boys would eat that veggie pizza. It was all Jane's.

An evil smile crossed her face. She looked at her reflection in the rear-view mirror. Even in the dark, she saw success.

She flapped a hand through the air. That woman at the police station had been an accidental bonus. By messing with her, it appeared someone was after Brian. After all, he was the Chief of Police. She was sure he had a target on his back. Someone he had arrested, a person he had sent to jail—maybe even his own father—all had reason to want to destroy him. Why would anyone suspect a new resident of Cedar Point, least of all the sweet blonde waitress at Knuckles? Yes, Terah had come in handy. But enough was enough.

If she stayed in one place too long, she was bound to be caught.

In St. Cloud, before driving up to the fuel pump, Becca parked on the dark side of the building, behind the car wash. She pulled off the blonde wig, tossed it into the plastic bin, and ran a hand through her dark hair. Then, she removed her shirt, exposing a tight-fitting black T-shirt. Becca tugged on a matching sweatshirt and zipped it halfway up. Finally, she balled up the red shirt, shoved it into an old fast-food bag, and rolled the top over. She switched baseball caps and looked at her face in her side mirror. Satisfied, she drove around to the fuel pumps. The first card she slipped into the slot at the pump, *Michelle Larson*, was rejected. The second card, *Lisa Hanson*, nearly filled her gas tank. She dumped both cards into the garbage and hit the can with her hip so they would fall through the garbage and land near the bottom of the bag. Then she pushed the fast-food bag with her shirt inside into a different can.

Inside, she skirted around shoppers, making sure not to draw attention to herself. She poured a thirty-two-ounce soda and grabbed a bag of chocolate chip cookies. Stress had kept her from eating for nearly two days. Truthfully, she rarely ate at all anymore. Her clothes almost fell from her bony frame. She was a walking skeleton with boobs. After losing weight, they looked like two huge headlights on a Fiat.

Becca and Terah were alike in that way too. It was another of the reasons the pair had bonded. *Life Visions* required modest dress. Hiding a pair of basketballs was virtually impossible. Loose-fitting tops did not help. It just looked like a tablecloth—*out and down*. Eventually, the pair had taken to wrapping their chests with elastic bandages—layer over layer, pulling them so tightly, they could barely breathe. But once they left the church, Becca wore tight-fitting T-shirts and clothes that showed off her figure. Terah, on the other hand, preferred the loose fit of men's shirts and baggy clothes. She was such a prude.

Fortunately, she was no longer Becca's concern.

As she headed northeast, Becca snapped a cookie in half and shoved the oversized piece into her mouth. It was soft and crumbly, sending small bits down the front of her shirt. With the side of her hand, she sent the crumbs flying to the floor of her car. Another two bites and the first of three cookies was gone. The other two met their demise in the same frantic way.

The soda was nearly empty when she pulled into a small gas station in Mora to relieve herself.

After parking on the side of the building, near the back corner, where the cameras were pointed toward the dumpster, not toward her, Becca pulled her hair into a ponytail and wound it into a knot. She snagged a different cap from the passenger's side floor and pulled it on before tucking her hair inside. Checking herself in the mirror, she tugged the bill down over her blue eyes. She intended to get in and out as quickly as possible.

The bathroom was opposite the entrance of the store. As Becca made her way in that direction, she kept her eyes low, pretending to look at items on shelves. Conflicting plans swam through her head as she peed. Would leaving the store without buying something be more memorable for the only clerk? Or would making a purchase stand out more? While washing her hands, she opted to buy something.

Becca bagged three more cookies and carried them to the counter. The clerk, half her age, had his back toward her when she approached. He was watching something on a small TV screen behind the counter. He snapped a photo with his phone before scribbling something on a sheet of paper before turning around.

"Be careful out there," the man in jeans and a red fleece said. "The police are looking for a woman with long blonde hair." He swallowed hard. "For attempted murder." The boy's eyebrows shot up. "It didn't happen close to here, but still, you never know. She could be headed this way."

Becca tipped her head down and said, "Scary." Anger swirled inside of her. *Attempted* murder? How could that be? The plan had been perfect.

"I used to think small-town Minnesota was safe. I don't think that anymore." He looked at her. "Do you live around here?"

Her face grew warm, and she tipped her head toward the back of the store. "Over a couple streets."

"I go to college in St. Cloud," the clerk offered. "I chose to stay in Mora because I didn't want to deal with the lowlifes in the city." He turned his palms up and raised his shoulders. "I mean, I know ninety-nine percent of the population are wonderful people. It's that one percent that scares the crap out of me. I guess I really am a small town per…"

Becca dropped three dollars on the counter, picked up the bag of cookies, and headed toward the door.

"Wait," the clerk said. "I'll give you a deal. They'll be day olds in a few hours anyway." He rang up the order. "Three cookies—a dollar and a half. I'm sorry I talk so much. I get so bored when I'm here by myself."

Becca handed him two bills and waited for her change. She rocked back and forth between her toes and heels while he fished two quarters from the register drawer.

He dropped them in Becca's hand. "Have a good night. And, like I said, be careful out there. You never know when you might cross paths with this woman. Do you want her license plate number?"

Becca turned toward the door. "Nah, I'm good."

When she exited, she turned left instead of right and walked around the store, pressing herself against the building as if she were prey, keeping out of view of the cameras. Her heart thudded in her chest, threatening to catapult its way out. He saw her. He could identify her if anyone came looking.

When she reached her car, she glanced at the license plate hanging by one screw. The day she stole the car from the hotel parking lot, she had switched the plates. The best thing her father ever did was collect old license plates. They had lined the walls of his shed. Becca had removed some before she burned the place down but kept a few with similar number sequences just in case. That shed had needed to go. As the first place her brother molested her, it was a constant reminder of his repeated attacks.

Becca took out a screwdriver and removed the plates from the only other car parked behind the store. She assumed it belonged to the kid, but after having to listen to him, he owed her.

She walked around her car and switched the back plates as well. Then she tossed her old plates into the dumpster. Unless she was stopped for some vehicle violation, she would be safe, and she was not worried about being stopped. Yes, she was a criminal and now a murderer, but she was also an incredibly safe driver. It was one way she could fly under the radar.

She climbed into the car, drove out the back exit, and headed toward Duluth for one final chat with Mack Enderly—this time as Becca Hulls.

The phrase *attempted murder* ran through her head. Son of a bitch! How had she failed again?

CHAPTER THIRTY-SIX

DEPUTY JEFF PORTER

Deputy Porter walked into Knuckle Sandwiches, looking for Terah Dixon. Often, she worked a double shift. If he were lucky, she would be there tonight. He tried picturing her in other places, but he could not. How was it in a town where you could throw a rock from end to end, the restaurant was the only location he could recall seeing her?

If he walked in with guns blazing, asking a million questions, it would only cause undue concern. Maybe the townspeople should be concerned. Someone was attempting to poison innocent people. They *should be* watching their backs. Regardless, that was not his call to make. Brian wanted Dixon, and he was trying to avoid panic. So, even if he found her, there would be no handcuffs or Miranda rights until they arrived at the station. If she were as sweet and honest as Officer Collins suggested, she would go with him willingly.

Jeff slid into the booth in Terah's usual section. He plucked a menu from the stand and laid it on the table, knowing he did not plan to eat. It would create less suspicion if he appeared as just a hungry cop.

Ellyn set a glass of water on the table in front of him. "Hey, Jeff. Are you eating alone, or are you meeting someone tonight?"

"Just me." He glanced down at the menu and pretended to peruse it. "Where's Terah? Isn't this her section?"

Ellyn raised one shoulder. "She worked the morning shift."

Jeff bit the corner of his lip and returned the menu to the holder. "Maybe I'll just have a coffee to go. I'm not really as hungry as I thought."

The waitress patted his hand. "How about I bring you a pastry too." She smiled. "On the house, of course."

"You don't have to do that." He grinned. "But I wouldn't turn it down."

Five minutes later, he was in his squad, trying to save his uniform from the strawberry jelly that threatened to fall from the second of the two donuts she had bagged for him. He had not fooled anyone with his *not-hungry* statement. He was starving, but waiting for a burger was out of the question. That was why he had not turned down the pastry.

Porter parked two doors down from 539 Hanley. Licking the stickiness from his fingers, he kept his eyes on the lower-level apartment. After a few minutes, he climbed out of the squad and walked toward the duplex. When Jeff opened the door to the porch, he weighed going immediately downstairs or gathering information. The decision was quick. He climbed the eight steps and knocked softly.

"Jeff?" Audrey pulled her head back in surprise. "Are you here to arrest me?"

Porter grinned at the sweet old woman and asked softly, "Should I be? Have you been misbehaving, Audrey?"

"Well, I tested a grape or two at the grocery store yesterday before I paid for them." She winked.

"I think we can let that slide," he said, pointing into her house. "Mind if I come in?"

Audrey stepped back. "Yes, of course. I'm so sorry. Where are my manners?"

He chuckled. "Perhaps you should have asked yourself that before you ate those grapes."

"I guess I'll have to watch myself from now on."

"You won't have to do that, Audrey. I'll be watching you." A wide smile spread across his face.

"What can I help you with, Jeff?"

"Do you know the woman who lives downstairs? Terah Dixon?"

"Yes, of course." She raised her shoulders and smiled. "What a wonderful woman. So kind and sweet."

"How well do you know her?"

"Oh, we wave from occasionally, and she's brought up my newspaper and left it at my door several times."

"Have you spoken to her?"

Audrey shook her head. "No. Not really—not other than a few words here or there. But I'm sure your mother told you actions speak louder than words. Didn't she?"

Jeff nodded. "So, she keeps to herself and is rather quiet? The kind of neighbor anyone would like to have?"

"Well," Audrey tilted her head down and looked at Jeff over the top of her rimless glasses, "If I'm being honest, sometimes there are some weird noises coming from down there."

Jeff cocked an eyebrow. "Weird? How? What kind of noises are you talking about?"

"Just…well, like things breaking. Once, I heard someone screaming."

"Screaming?"

Audrey nodded. "Angry screaming. Like someone was having a tantrum."

"Do you think it was Terah?"

She shook her head. "No. One time after it happened, I saw a dark-haired woman leave the house. Another time, it was a redhead."

"So, Terah has visitors often?"

"Mmm." She weighed the question. "No. I wouldn't say often. But it seems like every time there's been a commotion coming from down there, there's been an extra person who has come and gone."

"Do you know who these people are?"

"No. I never see their faces. Because of how the house sits compared to the driveway, I only see their backs—leaving and turning the corner. And by that time, they're too far away."

"What about a car?"

She shook her head. "The driveway is on the side street. Because of the stairs, I don't have a window on that side."

Porter glanced at his watch. "Do you know if Terah's home now?"

Audrey shrugged. "I'm not sure. I was over at the church most of the day today. We're getting ready for the Fall Festival." Jeff nodded. "Then I went to dinner with the girls. I haven't seen or heard her since she left for work early this morning." Suddenly, she looked at the far wall. "Wait. That's not true. I think someone left her place about an hour ago."

"Terah?"

She turned her palms upward. "I don't know. I heard a commotion."

"What kind of commotion?"

"Like someone was moving furniture. It also sounded like something broke. But it wasn't as noisy as usual, and it didn't last nearly as long."

"Then what happened?"

"Well, then it got quiet, and a little while later, I heard the door close."

"What time was that?"

"Oh, I'd say around six-thirty or so."

"So, you think she's gone?"

"Based on the noise, I would say one of her visitors left. I can't imagine that nice woman would act like that if she were alone." She eyed Jeff. "Now, I'd like to ask a question." Deputy Porter nodded. "I have a feeling I should be worried. Is my neighbor in some sort of trouble?"

"No," Porter lied. "We just like to keep track of who's living in Cedar Point. After what happened a couple years ago…"

"But, Jeff, those idiots were all locals. Everyone knew them. It wasn't like someone new came to town and tried to kill Jane."

Jeff laughed out loud. "Tell me how you really feel, Audrey."

"I'm just saying. You seem to be worried about this sweet woman when maybe it's the locals you need to know more about. I'm sure these people who keep showing up at her house aren't coming from far away. They're here way too often."

Deputy Porter nodded. "You may have a point." He turned and walked to the door. "Thanks, Audrey. I appreciate the help. Let me know if there's anything else you remember."

He opened the door and stepped out.

"You mean like the smells?"

Jeff stepped back inside and closed the door. "What smells?"

Audrey chuckled. "It was nothing, really. But tomorrow, I'll be making myself a frozen pizza because the smell from downstairs was so strong, it made me want one."

Jeff went white. "Pizza, you say?"

"I haven't had one in years. I imagine you eat them often."

"More often than I should." He rubbed his stomach, not to indicate his overeating but because a buzzing sensation sounded an alarm. "I appreciate your help, Audrey."

He ran down the stairs and knocked on Terah's door. Ten seconds later, he rapped harder and longer. Still nothing. He pressed an ear to the door but heard only silence.

"Police! Open up!"

The elderly woman's door opened, and she peeked over the railing.

"Go back inside, Audrey."

She raised one eyebrow. "I don't think you told me everything, Jeff."

"You'll be safe as long as you stay in your apartment."

Audrey went inside and shut the door. The sound of the deadbolt echoed in the stairwell.

Again, he pressed his ear against the door. He put his hand on the doorknob and attempted to turn it, but it would not budge.

He exited the building and walked around the house, trying

to peek into the windows, but the blinds were closed, and all the lights were off. Either no one was home, or they were hiding.

Getting a search warrant tonight would be impossible. Judge Halverson was impossible to track down once she left for the night. First thing tomorrow morning, he would be in her office. Then, they would know what Cedar Point's newest resident, Miss Terah Dixon, was up to. But tonight, they needed an unmarked patrol car to sit watch.

CHAPTER THIRTY-SEVEN

BECCA HULLS

Before Becca reached Duluth, she drove north and turned right on Skyline Drive. The streetlights were surrounded by a ghostly mist that engulfed the light. A chill ran down her spine, and she shivered. Was she making a mistake?

She pulled off the narrow road into a makeshift parking lot edged with sizable boulders to keep the drunks and halfwits from driving off the cliff. Stupid people did not deserve to have a warning. She snorted. Of course, that was what she planned to give her father—one last warning, one final attempt to take responsibility for his actions, to let her know giving her up had crushed him, but he had no other choice. Maybe meeting with him was a mistake, or perhaps she feared he had a heart of stone. Either way, in less than twelve hours, she would have her answer.

From the top of the hill, the familiarity of watching ordinary people going about their lives washed over Becca. Between the city lights below and the stars above, they pulled her back home—not *home* as in warmth, but rather a location, a place where one laid their head. As far back as she could recall, home had never been warm or filled with love. And when she did lie down to sleep, it felt neither peaceful nor safe.

The town of Carson Springs was nestled in a valley

surrounded by steep rolling hills on three of the four sides. To the west was what looked like a lake but was a sewage pond surrounded by a massive treatment plant. It was another deception that outsiders saw as beautiful—*from afar*. But when they entered the town, they learned the truth. It was the same for the hills. From the road, they were breathtaking, but hidden in the winding gravel roads were decaying houses and people who lived in constant fear of the outside world.

Life Vision members inhabited the tallest hills to the southwest of the town. *Closest to God.* It was one of the laws of the organization, or rather, of Andrew Godley. It did not matter that he resided in Los Angeles, near the *base* of Mount Lukens, in a multimillion-dollar mansion. Becca's entire house was most likely smaller than his guest closet. The roof leaked, and many of the windows were boarded over. But that did not matter to the church. Money mattered. Control mattered. Following the rules mattered. Andrew Godley mattered—at least according to him.

After leaving the church, she did a great deal of research into the head of *Life Visions*. The man had misled and deceived people for nearly sixty years. Now in his late eighties, Godley spent most of his time defending his organization and hiding bad press from his followers. Or rather, he paid attorneys and top-level employees to protect the organization in return for a fat paycheck. His questionable policies and unfavorable publicity were the main reasons he isolated his communities, did not allow technology, and forbade newspapers or other *garbage* that might bias members—*with the truth*. It was the only way he could keep people from discovering he was a crook.

For an hour, Becca sat above the city and watched. Her life replayed amidst the lights of the cars and the boats below. Suddenly, a rusted heap of junk in dire need of a muffler repair drove into the lot. Becca's breath quickened as she kept her eyes on the car. All she saw were shadows moving on the inside of the fogged-up windows. If they were doing what she suspected, she doubted they were watching her as intently as she was watching them. It was possible they did not even know she was there. Still, she was afraid to stay but more afraid they might follow her if she left. Becca slid down in her seat and debated her choices. Finally, she sat up, raced out of the lot, and drove toward the northeast end of Duluth, constantly checking to ensure she was not being trailed. It was silly. Could that car even travel that far?

Finally, Becca slowed, searching for the road that headed north through Lester Park. With no one around, she turned onto a street in serious need of repaving. Fury grew as she repeatedly slowed for potholes and cracks in the pavement, afraid of losing an axle. After following the winding road for just under two miles, she drove into a deep pull-off along Seven Bridges Road. She cut the lights and sat in the dark, *waiting* to be discovered or killed. Her entire life had been built on worst-case scenarios. It was how she survived.

Finally, she laid her seat back and closed her eyes. Thoughts stomped through her head, reminding her of all the evils she had done. In her wildest dreams, she would never have thought she was capable of murder. But obviously, that was a lie. What would happen when her brothers and sisters discovered who she really was? What if someone turned her in or the police got wise to her? Or what if she died before she made Mack Enderly pay for his sins? That last thought was the one that agitated her the most.

If she stopped now, there was a strong possibility she could walk away and not look back—live her life as a free woman. No one would connect her to the murder of Terah Dixon, the attempted murders of her sister-in-law and her brother's assistant, or the nearly accidental death of her nephew. If she continued, the chance of getting caught and spending the rest of her life behind bars increased significantly. But if she stopped, where would she go? Her family had disappeared, scattered like dandelion seeds in the wind. She could not return to Carson Springs. The elders had made that abundantly clear. And if she stopped, she was no better off than when she started this mission. Mack Enderly would never be forced to acknowledge his choices, and Becca would still be alone.

As she lay in the dark, she bounced from one ending of her life to the other. Becca never seriously believed she would or *could* stop, for that matter. Mack's family needed to know he had done her wrong. *She* was family—more so than his step-grandsons or his daughter-in-law. The only person who was on equal ground was her brother, Brian. Yes, she was family, and family did not treat one another that way. Becca laughed out loud. *Her family excluded.* They had treated her horribly. But then again, she was not a blood relative.

She did not deserve the life she had been delivered to by chance—the despicable father, the abusive brother, the mousy mother, and the condemnation of the *Life Vision* elders and the church members. It had all been heaped on her by the man who delivered her into evil but saved her older brother.

Becca and her brother were as different as night and day. Brian was the Chief of Police. He upheld the law. She was a lowlife criminal who *bent* it. They were opposite sides of the same coin. But it felt as if Brian's side had minted perfectly, and the press died partway through when it was her turn. Then again, maybe she was looking at it all wrong. Brian had turned out like their dead mother, and she had been cut from the same cloth as her father. That was obvious, since he was sitting in prison. Mack looked out for no one but himself. In actions and thoughts, they were carbon copies. Except he had chosen the life he was condemned to. She had not.

For two years, Becca shaped her plan and put the pieces into play. She anticipated every scenario and laid out a pair of divergent paths with *just-in-case* trails leading off. One path was easy, the other not. They were on the latter. She had not wasted time asking herself how things would have been different had she been raised by her biological father and brother. The answer was always the same—she *would never know*. No one had given her the choice.

There was only one way to know even a small piece of what her life would have been like—ask her brother. But every time she got close, she backed away. The day she showed up at the station, she had taken a half tablet of Valium and paired it with a glass of wine. The combination had calmed her but had slowed her reflexes. Almost everything moved in slow motion. When she turned her head, her surroundings moved in a white fog, a second or two behind reality.

Becca wanted to meet her brother, get to know him, and let him introduce her to their father. But while she waited, she got cold feet, and the drugs and alcohol made her second guess herself. The longer Becca sat in that office, sipping her Diet Coke, staring at his administrative assistant nervously carrying on about the arguments she and Brian had had over which diet soda was better, the angrier she became. How dare this woman discuss their petty disagreements when Becca's entire life had been a lie? No longer able to listen to the drivel, she gave in to her fears. Her shoulders tensed, and she tossed out the excuse of retrieving a photo album from her car. She was gone long before her brother arrived.

Her heart raced as she replayed that moment, her anger fired in a barrage of unforgiving waves. If she were going to get any sleep, she had to put it to rest. She closed her eyes and imagined herself sitting in a black room. Counting to three, she drew air in through her nose. On four, she sucked in a long quick breath and held it. Then, she pursed her lips and slowly released the breath to the count of eight, drawing two long breaths before beginning again. Soon, she was focused on only her breathing, not her brother. She repeated the cycle over and over until her brain pixelated and her body grew numb. As she dozed off, the only thing she saw was a picture of her mother—as she imagined her to look.

CHAPTER THIRTY-EIGHT

BECCA HULLS

The morning sun soaked through the windshield, warming Becca's left cheek. The minute her eyes popped open, her bladder begged for relief. Except for a watered-down sip, last night's soda was gone. Becca scooped up the cheap brown napkins from the gas station, shook the cookie crumbs off, and shoved her car door open. Feeling the sloshing of her bladder, she gingerly moved to the nearest bush and relieved herself behind it. She swiped at her privates with the sandpaper napkins, tossed them near the base of the bush, and breathed a heavy sigh of relief as she pulled up her jeans. If only everything in life could bring that much comfort.

Once inside the car, she drank the last of the soda and scarfed down the remaining cookie. She knelt on her seat and snagged a clean T-shirt and a hairbrush from the outside pocket of her suitcase. Using the rear-view mirror, she applied just enough makeup to accentuate her blue eyes, high cheekbones, and full lips. More than anything, she wanted Mack Enderly to see the *trash* he had thrown away.

A phone call to the prison the day before had told her Joyce, the visitor's receptionist, was on extended leave. What *extended leave* meant was anyone's guess. Becca knew it worked in her favor. It was why she had chosen to return to Duluth that day.

Without stirring suspicion, there was no way to know when the woman would return.

That left the security guard with the draconian personality and the beady eyes. Since she could not remember his name, Becca could not ask if he was at work. If he were, she would have to initiate Plan B. Becca could count on one hand the number of times she was forced to follow a Plan B. She did not like them. It meant something had gone wrong. And she despised *wrong* more than she hated Plan Bs.

Without thinking, Becca looked up and called out to God but stopped just shy of begging for His help. For as long as she could remember, praying had been her go-to. It had been as natural as breathing. She had been taught to turn to the Lord in times of darkness. And if this did not qualify, she didn't know what did.

Her gut roiled. The cookie and soda partied inside, threatening to return. Becca had no need for prayer because it was a waste of time. After discovering she had been adopted by a wicked man and his spineless wife who cared only about their biological children, she no longer believed in God. He had let her down too many times. Besides, even if this so-called God was real, why would He help her carry out her evil plan?

At 7:05 a.m., Becca guided her car along the narrow road. Ten minutes later, she drove into the parking lot of Elite Car Rental in the middle of a strip mall. After parking in front of another store, she entered the small brick building, filled out the paperwork under the name Rebecca Hulls, and left ten minutes later in a gray Mazda 3. If she drove into the prison in her white CR-V, after the crash with Joyce, the guard might remember her. Even though she had been a redhead at the time, and had gone by the name Jennifer Olson, there was always the chance he was one of those people who never forgot a face.

By 7:30, Becca was parked on a side street a block from the prison gate. She kept her eyes on the traffic, watching for the guard of her nightmares to drive through the tall columns and barred entrance. 8:00 a.m. was literally the changing of the guards and everyone else who worked there. She never saw the man enter or leave. Becca closed her eyes and relaxed, grateful Plan B was off the table.

At half past eight, she passed through the gates. She handed the license, claiming her to be Rebecca Hulls from Carson Springs, Wisconsin. The guard typed the information into the computer and sent her into the lot.

Ten minutes later, she was checked into the prison by an older man wearing a plastic name tag labeled Oscar. Sitting in the visitor's waiting room, she hoped she was not making the biggest mistake of her life. No. That ship had already sailed. A grin inched up the corners of her mouth as she thought about Terah.

Becca was not on Mack Enderly's visiting list, but Oscar was not the hard-ass Joyce had been. He saw no problem in letting a *pretty young thing* in to see a man who encountered only one woman a day—*typically heavyset and butch*. He had winked at her when he said it. Had Becca not needed to see Mack, she would have slapped him into yesterday. She had neither time nor patience for men who were pigs.

The door creaked open, and a female guard called her inside. Her shoulders drooped forward in relief. Becca picked up her bag and headed through the door. She did not wait to be told how the process worked. She emptied her pockets and dropped her purse, phone, and everything else into the bin before stepping into the X-ray machine.

Her heart raced. She could feel it pulse in her throat, creating a tightness that made it hard to draw a full breath or even swallow. Her eye twitched as she stood near the door, waiting for another guard to take her inside. She rubbed it and reminded herself she was there to tell the truth, to speak *her* truth, for the first time in her life.

The door opened, and the guard led her to a table. In his monotone, *this is the millionth time I have said this* voice, he told her the *cans and cannots* of visiting the prisoner. He walked away before Becca could even acknowledge her understanding.

Folding her hands in her lap, she waited for Mack. The urge to pray pressed on her heart, but she pushed it down.

A door opened, and she heard footsteps moving toward her. She kept her eyes focused on the gray tabletop. Mack sat opposite her but said nothing. Finally, she looked up at him. His mouth tightened, and he narrowed his eyes.

"Who the hell are you?" Mack leaned back in the plastic chair and folded his hands in front of his stomach.

It was apparent he had not recognized her, although, Becca figured that it might be a different story once she spoke.

"My name is Becca Hulls." Still, his eyes remained unchanged. "I'm from Carson Springs, Wisconsin."

Enderly shook his head. "So?"

"I'm here because…"

"Wait." Mack leaned forward. "There's something familiar about you. Have we met?"

She wanted to scream. *Yes, we've met, you bastard. I have your DNA. I'm your daughter—the one you didn't have the time for. The one you left outside a church while there was still snow on the ground.* Instead, she weighed whether to admit the truth or to lie. Honesty could backfire. A lie might get her further in finding the truth about why he tossed her away.

"It's unlikely. I've never been to this prison before." Her eye twitch returned. She pulled her lower lid down, hoping to halt the involuntary movement.

"Well, what do you want?" Mack slouched in his plastic chair. The back nearly folded over against his size.

Becca opened her mouth, but no sound came out. She had pictured this moment so many times, yet she had never imagined the exact words she would say. It had always been like a silent movie—one where he took her in his arms and told her it had all been a huge mistake.

"Well?" Mack's knee bounced, jostling the table.

"I, ah, I, um…"

"What the hell's wrong with you? You act like you've never spoken to a person before." He switched the bouncing to his other leg.

Becca shook her head, gulped a mouthful of air, and puffed out her cheeks as she slowly released it.

"I'm Becca…"

"You already told me that." Mack glared at her and snapped his fingers. "Let's move on."

"Your wife…"

"My wife's dead." He scowled at her, warning her with his clenched jaw.

"I know. She, she was my…" Becca swallowed hard. "My m-mother."

Mack never blinked. "I don't know who the hell you think you are. But this is bullshit." He stood. "Guard!"

"Wait!" She grabbed the edge of the table. "I'm Wren." Becca nervously stared at Mack. "And you're my father."

Mack's mouth dropped open, and he fell into his chair. He waved a hand at the guard, sending him away.

"How is that possible?"

"How?" The anger in Becca returned with a vengeance. "How? What are you asking? How did you get your wife pregnant? How did I figure it out? Or how could I possibly be the daughter you disposed of in Carson Springs?"

Mack repeated the word. "H-how?"

Becca's neck tightened. "I'll throw it right back at you, *Father*. What the hell's wrong with *you*?"

"I, I don't believe this."

"Well, you better believe it because I'm a walking, talking, breathing Enderly with *your* DNA." Mack shook his head. "And you threw me out like garbage because you didn't want to raise a reminder of your dead wife." She tightened her jaw and glared at him. "Isn't that right, *Dad*?"

"No. That's not what happened." His eyes narrowed, and his brows pressed inward.

"Bullshit. Let me remind you. You left me on the steps of a church in Carson Springs on February 10, 1982. I was hours old, wrapped in a pastel gingham-checked quilt. I assume my mother made it." Mack slowly shook his head. "What? Are you denying you left me? Are you denying I'm the daughter you threw away? Seems odd that you tossed me to the curb but kept my brother, the Chief of Police in Cedar Point, Minnesota." Mack's mouth fell open again, and his eyes grew wide. "Why? That's all I want to know." She ran her hands down her arms.

Mack let go of a long breath and stared at Becca. "Believe me. If you really are my daughter," he swallowed hard, "who you are claiming to be, then you were a hell of a lot better off than you would have been had you been raised by a drunk like me."

Becca laughed out loud. The guard at the desk looked up. She leaned in and whispered, "Let me tell you about my life, *Dad*." She held up a fist and raised a finger with each item she listed. "Hateful father. A mother who would not stand up for me no matter what. A brother who sexually abused me every chance he got. Grew up in a cult. Never accepted by anyone in the town or in the church." She lowered her fingers and started again. "Kicked out of my home when I was eighteen because I didn't have a marriage prospect. Six months later, I had to raise my siblings when my so-called parents were killed in a car accident. And I put my entire life on hold for a dozen years to raise my eight siblings. The corners of her mouth turned down. "I could go on and on, but I think you get the picture." She leaned so close to him, her head nearly touched his. "So, when you say I would have been better off without you, you don't know what the hell you're talking about."

Mack stretched his neck and pressed a fist into one hand. "You may have had a shitty life, but ask your... Ask Brian about *his* life. I'm pretty damn sure he has you beat in the *crappy father department*."

"Screw you, old man."

Mack tipped his head slightly to the right and stared at her. "You look just like... Shit. You were here counseling me about getting out of prison. You said your name was..." He looked up. "Dr. Jennifer Olson." He shook his head. "You impersonated a social worker. That makes you a...”

"And you're a poor excuse for a human being.” Becca leaned back and crossed her arms. "I must have inherited my criminal streak from you.”

Mack stood up. He booted his chair across the room. "Guard. Get me the hell away from this lying bitch.”

"Truth hurts, doesn't it, *Dad*? It's hard to unknow the truth once you know it.”

The guard clutched Mack's arm and escorted him back to the prisoner's exit.

After the door closed, Becca remained in her chair. The cockiness she had felt moments earlier fell from her face. A lone tear tumbled down her cheek, leaving a thin, faded line in her blush.

All she wanted was for him to acknowledge her and to apologize. Had he done that, none of what Becca was about to do next would have to happen. Her old man was pushing her toward it. Mack was making her destroy her brother and his family. It was all on him.

She smiled as she stood and looked around the gray prison walls with the barred and locked doors. They were not so different after all.

CHAPTER THIRTY-NINE

CHIEF BRIAN ENDERLY

The sky had opened overnight, dousing Cedar Point with over two inches of rain. Thunder shook the house several times as the storms blew through repeatedly. The western side of Minnesota had taken the brunt of the storms, while the east saw peeks of sunshine. And even though the turbulent weather had played a part in preventing Brian from getting a few winks, it was not entirely to blame. He could also not fault Jane's restlessness. It was his alone. His mind had raced all night, fitting the pieces together like the second-hand Lincoln Logs he had played with as a child.

Brian was running on empty. The last two nights, he had torn the sheets from the mattress. His brain was a spin cycle of thoughts, the biggest of which was how to keep his wife safe and sane while he attempted to figure out the *whodunit* in the case that mimicked a TV movie. The only problem was this was real life. Jane had run before. He had no way of knowing if she would again.

He watched his wife pretend to sleep. Every time she rolled toward him, Brian closed his eyes, slowed his breathing, and drew shallow breaths to mimic sleep. His wife worried about everything. If she thought he had not slept, it would be another rabbit hole she would fall into, checking on him every chance she got. In the beginning, she tried to hold off, but during the last day, her anxiety had knotted itself into a zillion tiny battles she felt the need to fight. Brian did not have time to reassure every fear. Jane was the love of his life. She always had been. But if he was going to keep her safe, he had to work the case and lean on the boys to protect their mother.

By 4:23 a.m., his body argued the need to rise. His back and shoulders ached. He rolled his neck, but not without it complaining when he turned to the left. Jane had finally dozed off. Her soft snoring told him she had let go enough to finally sleep, at least for a few minutes. If she kept this up, she would collapse before nightfall. He was the police chief. The community expected him to keep going no matter how exhausted he was—even if they had no clue what was happening in their own small town. He had taken an oath.

In his three-minute scalding shower that turned his skin an angry shade of red, Brian created a mental list of what needed to be done before the station door opened at eight. He missed Mauri. On typical mornings, by the time he reached the office, she would have been sitting at her desk in the dark, searching for the information she anticipated he would need. His administrative assistant would have handed him a stack of notes organized by importance. Mauri would have already perused the Department of Motor Vehicles records for Dixon's car, left a message for the judge to get a search warrant, and found Terah's elusive phone number. She would have done a deep, *deep* dive into the Dixons of Carson Springs and *Life Visions*. And more likely than not, she would have called Andrew Godley—and God Himself—if that was what it took.

She was the finest assistant he had ever had. *Humble?* Not even close. *Excellent at her job?* The very best! She anticipated his every need before it crossed his mind. But what he missed most was the cold Diet Coke or excellent cup of coffee sitting on his desk when he walked into the station, day or night, and those during the day, when she knew he was in desperate need.

Yes, she was annoying, *more* than annoying—*infuriating,*

obnoxious, and frustrating. But more than any of those, she was dependable, his right hand. He would never concede that information right now because she would figure out a way to get back to town before he got to the station. She wanted to be needed; she *needed* to be needed. But it was more important that she and Mike were safe in Wisconsin at her sister's, while the rest of Cedar Point believed they were off on a wonderful anniversary celebration in Hawaii. Word of their safe arrival had come from the police chief of Elizabethton. He had only met him once, but that once was enough to know he could trust him. At least, he hoped.

Brian stepped into his closet and put on a clean uniform. Before heading to the kitchen, he peeked at Jane. She was still asleep. He silently shut the door behind him, facing his morning with a chasmal breath.

He flipped on the cabinet light above the coffee counter and stared at the day-old brown liquid. A warmed-up cup would do, but the aroma would wake Jane, so he opted to grab one or more on his way to work. There was no way he could drink the mud the fill-ins at the station made numerous times a day. Anyone who referred to that crap as coffee needed their head examined.

Grabbing a pack of sticky notes from the counter, he left a message for Jane and her boys. *Do not leave. Lock doors. Set alarm. No one enters except an officer.* Then he left a separate note for his wife: *Jane, I love you. Do not worry.* That last line was a waste of ink. Telling his wife not to worry was like telling the moon not to shine.

When Brian backed onto the street, the sun was still asleep, but the sky no longer hugged the darkness so tightly. Periodically, he drove through clouds of ground fog as he wove toward the Daily Grind, making a slight detour past 539 Hanley.

The previous day, he and three of his men had pounded on Terah Dixon's door to no avail. Not a sound came from within. The house was old, and the doors were hollow. It had not taken much for the door to give up when Brian ran his shoulder into it.

With a search warrant in hand, they warned her they were coming in, but she still had not answered. Four officers searched the house but found no sign of Terah. One door was padlocked, creating suspicion and a modicum of fear. After cutting the lock, with one hand on the handle of his gun, Brian slowly pushed the door open.

He shrugged when he looked at Porter. Who locked a bedroom with a padlock? The other bedroom door had been left open. A bed, dresser, and small rocking chair were the only furniture in the large room. Except for the unmade bed, the room was tidy. Enderly ran a finger along the top of the dark dresser. Dust clung to it. So, she was not clean, but she was orderly.

Officer Duncan stood at the front door, watching in case Terah or someone else suddenly appeared. Deputy Porter moved next to the bed. Beneath the worn pink, seafoam-green, and white quilt was a lump, the size and shape of a body. Confident they were facing a homicide, Brian took a breath and slowly peeled back the covers.

Pillows—nothing more than pillows. A joint sigh of relief exploded in the small room. While standing guard, Officer Duncan noticed the dark spots trailing across the carpet and into the bedroom. Brian squatted and touched one of the spots. Red clung to his fingers. He lifted it to get a better look. *Blood.*

Brian looked at his officers. "Shit." Porter repeated it, as did Duncan. It was the only word that came close to describing the magnitude of the scene.

Porter lifted a pillow from the bed to expose more of the same. On the cotton sheets, the blood had dried and was a deeper brown color. Bloody fingerprints and one handprint had been pressed beneath the pillows. A quick search uncovered the bloody knife beneath the bed.

The one thing they never found was the victim. Was Terah the target of some depraved murderer? Had someone gotten to her, or had *she* killed someone else? Based on their interactions, he believed the first. There was no way a woman who could not have weighed more than a hundred pounds soaking wet could have removed a body from the lower level without someone noticing—unless the person walked out on their own accord. But with that amount of blood, that was highly unlikely.

Brian texted John Wallick, the FBI agent who had helped with the last big case, before calling the Bureau of Criminal Apprehension. John had gone back to Minneapolis, but he promised to return by noon. The best part was the FBI could pull strings to get information that the small-town cops could not.

They had no body, no way to know if anyone had been murdered, but there had been enough questions to summon the higher-ups.

By noon, the BCA and the FBI were on the case. Brian stepped back and stayed out of their way, offering his assistance only when asked. The Alexandria police department sent an officer three times a day to sit in the station, monitor phones, and document information. They did little else—except make atrocious coffee. It was a body with a gun at the station.

Brian spent his time trying to find out where Terah Dixon might have gone. *Dead? Running? Or hiding?* No matter which it was, he had to find her.

CHAPTER FORTY

CHIEF BRIAN ENDERLY

If the blood was Terah's, someone had gotten to her before Brian had. However, the chief was more concerned about what had transpired if it belonged to someone else. Audrey had been gone all day. Something must have gone down during that time. Was Terah Dixon a cold-blooded killer? Had he been wrong about her all along? Repeatedly, Brian second-guessed himself. What was he saying? Of course, she was. She had attempted to murder Jane, not once, but twice. What would make him think otherwise? Clearly, she had had help.

Brian pulled up to the curb on the street opposite 539 Hanley and stared at the house. Yellow police tape was wrapped around trees and temporary stakes, encircling the 1970s two-story duplex. Was it a crime scene, or had what happened here been nothing more than an accident?

He had met Terah a dozen times or so. She had always been kind. If she had been the victim, what could she have done to make someone want to kill her? If she was the murderer... Brian could not even force the thought. There was no way she would have killed anyone. He flip-flopped again and again.

Regardless of who the victim was, the amount of blood was concerning. Brian had dumped the job of calling every clinic, urgent care, and emergency room within an hour's drive of

Cedar Point on the officer stationed at Mauri's desk. What that officer did not finish became the job of whoever was next at the post. Thus far, the results have been disappointing. No one with long blonde hair and a significant stab wound or cut had walked, been carried, or rolled through their doors. Today, he wanted the circle widened.

The house was dark. The night before, Deputy Porter had moved Audrey to the Moonlight Inn to secure the house and to keep her out of harm's way. Completely out of character, she had not argued.

As Brian rounded the corner, he noticed a new red SUV with a temporary license plate parked near Terah's driveway. It could have belonged to anyone on the block. But something did not sit right. Why would anyone park a new car so close to a house under investigation? The pieces did not fit.

The car did not belong to Audrey. Because of her volunteer work, which included delivering meals to shut-ins, transporting people to appointments, and hauling furniture for the free store at her church, she drove a minivan. She also had an older Ford Escape that she used on longer treks. Brian could only hope to be as civic-minded and active as her when he reached his eighties.

Was it possible Terah had returned? Or did the vehicle belong to one of the many friends who visited Terah, the ones Audrey had told Porter about?

Smart enough to wait for backup, Brian called Porter. After the arrival of a second police cruiser, a dozen people gathered across the street, many still in robes and slippers, continuously moving to warm themselves in the cool morning air. The busybodies were at it early this morning. Many had likely made several calls or sent a handful of messages. But, then again, he could not blame them. Cedar Point was a humdrum town where the biggest secrets were revealed at little league games, in the salon, or on the street corner where neighbors met while walking their dogs. Police tape was a flashing beacon, begging for attention.

Brian shook his head at Porter. The pair walked to the center of the street. "I know this seems really interesting, folks, but I need you to return to your houses. This is police business." He glanced at his watch. "It's early. Go inside, love your kids, and get 'em to school."

"What's going on, Brian?" Jake Marsh stepped to the edge of the curb. "The police were here all day yesterday, but not one of them would spill." He tipped his head. "Is it even safe for our kids to go to school?"

Brian nodded. "I can assure you it is."

"When are you going to let us know what's going on?" Grace Berkoff bounced her chubby toddler on her hip. "I didn't sleep one wink last night." She looked at her son. "And it wasn't Rowan's fault."

"Soon. We'll let you know soon. But right now, we have work to do, and you can help us by clearing out." He stepped on a still-burning cigarette butt that had been tossed into the street.

"That's easy for you to say," a woman grumbled. "You've got a gun."

Brian looked directly at her, committing her face to memory. He shifted his eyes toward Jeff. Pointing toward the woman with a slight jerk of his head, Brian gave him a look only they understood—the one that asked *Who the hell is she?*

Porter answered with a nearly invisible shake of his head and a slight rise of one shoulder.

The chief stepped forward. "I'm sorry, ma'am. I don't recognize you. May I ask your name?"

The woman stepped closer to an extremely tall, burly man. She wagged a finger between them. "Just passing through."

Porter stepped forward. "I believe the chief asked for your name?"

Afraid they might be linked to the woman and the mastodon on her right, the crowd separated.

The man gently pressed his elbow into her side. She scowled at him before answering, "Joyce." She cleared her throat and spoke louder. "I'm Joyce, and this is my son, Tony."

"What brings you to Cedar Point?" Brian crossed his arms and absently twisted the toe of his boot on a small rock.

"Like I said, just passing through."

"Kind of early for a visit. Don't you think?"

The man slung his arm behind the woman's neck and rested his hand on her shoulder. Brian saw him squeeze it tightly before she squirmed away.

"We spent the night in town."

"At the Moonlight?"

The woman twisted her mouth to one side. "I don't see where we stayed is any business of yours."

The hair on the back of Brian's neck slowly climbed. "As the chief of police, I make it my business to know everything that happens in this town."

"Ma'am, the chief's just trying to keep the town safe." Porter eyed her son. "You can answer the question he asked, or you can come down to the station and let me get to know you both a lot better."

Joyce shrugged. "Yes."

Porter tipped his head. "Yes, what?"

The woman released a sigh of exasperation. "Yes, we stayed at the Moonlight."

"Now, that wasn't so hard, was it?"

The crowd sidestepped in both directions, leaving a more prominent spotlight on the pair.

"The Moonlight's on the other side of town. If you don't mind me asking, what are you doing on this side of town this early?"

"We're out for an early morning walk before we take off."

"Do you have family or friends in town?"

Joyce gave Enderly a hard stare. "I told you. We're just passing through."

Brian shook his head. "Well, then, since you'll be on your way shortly, you needn't worry about what happened here." He turned his attention back to the crowd. "Like I said, folks, head on home and go about your day. We'll release a statement soon."

As the whispering crowd dispersed, Brian and Jeff headed across the street.

Brian leaned his head toward Jeff's and whispered, "Go around the right side of the house and across the back. Get a picture of the license plate on that new car sitting near the driveway. Be discreet. I don't want anyone to see you take it." He tipped his head backward slightly. "Especially our visitors across the street. I want to know who it belongs to. I have a feeling they aren't just passing through." He sighed. "When we're done here, I want you to head over to the Moonlight and see what Nancy knows about his pair."

Jeff took off around the right side of the house. Brian turned his back toward the house and pretended to check his phone. He had an eye on Joyce and Tony. If he was right, and that was their car, they would not go near it while he stood out front.

A minute later, Jeff returned from the direction he had disappeared. "Back door's locked, and the tape's secure all the way around the house." Brian could not have cared less, but he knew it was Jeff's coded way of telling him he had gotten the photo.

Brian nodded toward the front door. The pair ducked under the tape and headed inside.

Cautiously, Brian opened what remained of the splintered door of the lower apartment. He had done quick work of destroying the hollow wood panel. He had barely felt it when he grabbed his wrist, lowered his head, and plowed through it. But today was a different story. He felt it from his neck down to his elbow.

The blinds were still closed, preventing even the early morning streetlight from entering the apartment. Jeff flipped on a light. "What in the hell happened in here?"

Paint drips ran from four words spray-painted on the once-white wall separating the living room from the kitchen: *You're a dead woman.*

Jeff's mouth hung open. "I don't think Dixon's our perp." He huffed.

Brian nodded slowly. "That's what I was afraid of." He slipped on rubber gloves and gingerly picked up the spray paint can from the floor. "If she's not dead already, whoever wrote this will make damn sure she is soon."

CHAPTER FORTY-ONE

CHIEF BRIAN ENDERLY

Brian inserted a key into the lock of the station door and tried to turn it. To his dismay, the door was already unlocked. The cop was just a fill-in from Alexandria until they solved this case, but no one would leave the station open all night, especially with the possibility of a killer on the loose.

A soft noise shattered the quiet and drew Brian's attention when he opened the door. Pulling his gun from his holster, he guardedly stepped into the hallway of the station and held it in front of him. He held still until it sounded again. Finally, he reached a hand around the wall and flipped the light switch on. The night officer was lying on the floor. Blood oozed from the back of his head.

"They're gone." The officer's voice was barely audible.

Brian dropped onto his knees beside the cop as Porter entered the station.

"Why's the door unlocked?" He stopped when he saw Brian and the officer on the floor. "What happened?"

"Grab me some paper towels," Brian said.

Jeff raced into the workroom and returned with a roll. He whispered to Brian, "Did you do this?"

Brian unrolled a couple of feet, folded them, and pressed them to the back of the man's head. "No, I didn't do this," Brian snapped. He turned his attention to the bleeding man. "Can you sit up? Do you need an ambulance?"

"No," he whispered. "I'll be okay." The officer slowly rolled onto his side, pushed himself upright, and sat against Mauri's desk.

"Keep pressure on that cut. You're going to need a few stitches."

The man held the towels against his head.

"Lock the damn door," Brian hollered at Porter. "Otherwise, we're inviting trouble, and we sure as hell don't need more than we already got."

While Jeff headed toward the door, Brian settled on the floor close to the man. "Let me know when you're ready to get up." The officer nodded. "What's your name?"

"Ben. Officer Ben Dillard. One-zero-one-three."

"This is a hell of a way to meet the guy handling the office." Ben tried to smile but grimaced instead. "So, can you tell us what happened, or do you want to go to the hospital first?"

"I'd rather get it over with."

"When did this happen?"

"Not long ago. A half hour, maybe." Ben moaned slightly. "I answered the call from you…" His mouth fell when he looked at Brian. "But it wasn't from you, was it?"

Brian pushed a fist into the palm of his hand. "Those bastards hacked my phone." He held the power button down and turned it off. "Jeff, call Jane and tell her not to answer any calls from my number."

"On it." Porter disappeared into his office.

Brian hoisted himself from the floor and went into the workroom, returning with a few painkillers and a glass of water. "I think you're gonna want these," he said, checking the back of the officer's head. "At least the bleeding's slowed some." After tearing off a few more sheets of towel, he traded the officer.

Jeff joined them. He looked at Brian and tipped his head forward. "Done. Jane knows."

Brian lifted his chin in thanks and returned his attention to the officer on the floor. "Tell us exactly what happened."

"Like I said, I got the call from what I thought was you saying you were in a hurry." He started to shake his head but thought otherwise. "Well, not *you*, but the person I thought was you. Anyway, the man on the phone barked the order to have the door unlocked when they got here."

"And you believed it was me?"

Officer Dillard lowered his neck into his shoulder blades. "I've never talked to you until now, so I wouldn't have recognized your voice." He looked at the floor. "But I've heard you can be kind of a hard-ass."

Brian nodded. "Yeah, I've heard that before, too."

"The guy sounded big, and he was."

Brian looked at Porter. "Put an APB out on…"

Porter shook his head. "That red car didn't belong to anyone named Joyce, Tony, or Anthony. I checked before I left the duplex. It's registered to a Robert Harmon of Duluth."

Brian's shoulders fell forward. "Are you kidding me? That's the warden at the prison."

"I knew that name sounded familiar." Porter scratched his cheek. "Why would someone be in Cedar Point with the warden's car? His wife, maybe?"

"I doubt that. Find out if that car was reported stolen."

"Do you have his number?"

"It's on the bulletin board behind my desk."

"Got it." Porter disappeared into Brian's office.

"Okay. So, what happened?"

"I came back to the desk and started working on digging into Terah Dixon's background." Ben touched the back of his head and released a long breath. "I heard the door open and assumed it was you. I turned around to pick something off the printer…"

"…and that's when someone hit you. Did you get a look at the person?"

"Two. Two people." Officer Dillard looked toward the

hallway. "After I got hit, I let them think they knocked me out. I know I shouldn't have done that, but that guy was huge."

"How big?"

"Six-four and probably three-hundred and fifty pounds. *Big*."

"Let me guess, the other person was a woman about five foot six."

"Yeah, that sounds about right."

"I know exactly who hit you." He twisted his mouth slightly. "I wouldn't have taken them on had I been you either."

"You know who they are?"

"Only first names: Tony and Joyce, but that should make them easier to find." He slid out in front of Dillard. "Did they ever say names? Maybe a last name?"

Ben stared at the wall behind Brian. "No, but I'm pretty sure he called her Ma."

Enderly sighed. "Yeah, same two. Do you know what they were after? Did they take anything?"

Porter came out of Brian's office. "Where's your laptop?"

"Dammit! Dammit all to hell. Those bastards took it." He raced into his office, cussing as he looked at the space where his computer had been. "Jeff, was that car reported stolen?"

"Called Harmon at home. Get this; he loaned it to a woman who works at the prison. She had an accident in the parking lot there a couple days ago. Harmon saw the commotion out his window and realized it involved this woman. Because he was heading into a meeting, he offered her his car so she could pick up a rental. He said she told him a friend would meet her at the rental office, and she would drop his car off before he headed home." "I take it she never took it back."

"Correct. That was a few days ago."

"So, it's listed as stolen?"

Porter shook his head. "Nope. He's been trying to get a hold of her. Wanted to give her the benefit of the doubt since she's been a faithful employee."

Brian ran the name through his head. "I remember her.

Harmon told me how good she was. I remember thinking she was a lot like Mauri. Anything else I should know?"

"I told him you'd call him in a while." Porter looked at Dillard. His eyelids dropped, and his head rolled forward. "I think I need to get him to the ER."

Brian helped his deputy move Ben to the squad car. He returned, locked the door, and headed to his office. Enderly dropped into his chair and looked at his empty desk. "Son of a bitch." His chair slammed against the wall when he stood. He was across his office in five steps and out the door, staring at Mauri's empty desk. "Those sons of bitches took hers too."

Brian radioed Officer Serrano. He pushed the button and barked, "Serrano. Station. Now!"

Almost instantly, he heard, "Ten-four."

By the time Officer Serrano arrived, Brian was fit to be tied. He had checked his watch a dozen times in the eight minutes and twenty-three seconds it took Carlos to get there. Brian opened the door and locked it behind him.

"Office."

Serrano followed him. "You're a man of few words this morning, Chief. What's going on?"

Brian waved his hand across his empty desk. "Do you see my computer anywhere?" The officer shook his head. "Did you see anyone sitting at that desk out there when you came in?" Again, Serrano responded with a shake of his head. "Exactly. Some bastards robbed us. The night officer was attacked, and the assholes hacked my cell phone."

"Shit," Carlos muttered under his breath.

"No kidding." Enderly held his hand out, palm up. "I need your phone. And then, I need you sitting at that desk out there. Got it?"

"Yes, sir." He handed over his phone and looked at Brian. "What the hell's going on?"

Enderly tipped his head. "When I figure it out, I'll let you know."

CHAPTER FORTY-TWO

CHIEF BRIAN ENDERLY

Within the hour, Chief Enderly had a new cell phone, number, and laptop. A police tech out of Alexandria sat in Porter's office setting up both. The tech's first job was to block access to everything the thieves got their hands on. Small towns had their advantage.

He had learned from Porter that the pair had never entered the workroom or Porter's office. They would not have gotten Jeff's computer anyway. It was an appendage. He was never without it. While the police tech worked, Brian went through the station with a fine-tooth comb and a bug scanner in search of cameras or listening devices but found none.

By the time he was done, the tech had reinstalled all the information, locked everything down tighter than before, and made a list of files the crooks had accessed. The tech had left a back door open enough to see what the two were searching for but not enough for them to sneak through the firewall to see anything else from their side. He was still trying to get a read on their location.

From the searches, it appeared the pair was looking for information on someone named Rebecca Hulls. That was a new name for Brian. Did she have something to do with Terah Dixon? Perhaps she was one of the people Audrey had seen leaving Dixon's duplex. Or was it all an unrelated coincidence? Either way, he wrote the name on the top of his notepad and circled it several times.

Before Brian phoned Warden Harmon, he called Jane. He gave her his new number and again warned her about keeping the door locked, alarm set, and not allowing anyone access. Because of the phone hack, he told her to block his old number and be wary of unknown callers.

Nearly three hours had passed by the time Brian got Harmon on the line.

"Bob, Brian Enderly here."

"That took a while. I've been waiting to hear from you." Harmon cleared his throat. "Hold on a second. I want to close my door." Brian clicked the end of a pen while he waited. "Okay. I'm back." He let go of a deep breath. "I hear you saw my car this morning."

"I did. I also saw your right-hand, Joyce, and her overgrown son, Tony."

"Son? Tony? What are you talking about? As far as I know, Joyce never had kids."

"This guy was like six-four, three fifty, and he called her *ma*."

"Tony Manderley?" Brian added the name to his yellow tablet. "He's a guard at the prison. He took a sudden leave of…"

Brian set his pen down. "And?"

"You've got to be mistaken. It can't be the same Tony who works…" Several seconds of silence passed. "Crap."

"So, it is?"

"Oh, Lord. How in the hell did that slip through? A mother and son working together—same shifts, same area of the prison." Brian heard him groan. "I would never in a million years have let that happen."

Brian leaned back in his chair. "Yes, I saw your car and the thieves—Mommy and Clyde."

"That might be funny if it wasn't so true," Harmon admitted. "Damn! This makes me so mad. I trusted her—trusted both of them."

"Did you report your car as stolen?"

"I did after your deputy called me. I also put an APB out on Joyce, but I'll add her son."

"What's her last name?"

"Man." His frustration floated across the phone line in a long sigh. "How in the hell did I not see that?"

"You mean Manderley and Man—two names with literally the same first three letters? I don't know. How *didn't* you see that?" Brian shook his head and scribbled Joyce's surname on the tablet.

Enderly explained to Harmon about the attack of Officer Dillard, the stolen computers, the hacking of his phone, and the search for information on someone named Rebecca Hulls.

"Do you know Rebecca Hulls?" Brian picked up his pen again. "I mean, if two people from Duluth are searching for her, might she be connected to the prison?"

"I suppose it's possible. Let me check."

Brian could hear the computer keys clicking. He wondered how the prison had hired relatives—a mother and son, no less. Obviously, they had hidden their relationship from the start.

"No Rebecca Hulls." More typing. "There's a list of Hulls who have visited the prison in the past few years, though." He raced through the list, reading it aloud. "Aaron, Ardis, Barb, Becca, Bernice…"

"Wait." Brian leaned forward. "Becca Hulls."

"Becca. That makes sense, I suppose." Harmon snorted. "How does she spell her full name?"

Brian looked at his notepad. "R. E. B. E. C. C. A."

"Spelling matches." Harmon cleared his throat.

"Do you take pictures of visitors?"

"Not unless we suspect something unusual."

"Okay, email me everything you have on Becca Hulls. Also, send me a picture of Joyce and her son." Brian sighed. "Oh, thanks to your friend, Joyce, I have a new email address too." He said it slowly and then repeated it.

While the men were on the phone, Brian's email dinged with a message from Harmon. Sure enough, the pair on the screen were one and the same—Harmon's employees and Brian's criminals.

"That's them," Brian said. "Let's get back to Rebecca Hulls. What was she doing at the prison?"

Harmon clicked several keys. "Oh, wow," he whispered.

"What?"

"She visited your dad."

Brian's mouth dropped open. "You've got to be kidding me? How in the hell did she get in? She can't be on his visitors list."

"I don't know, but I sure as hell am going to have a conversation with Joyce's fill-in."

"Now what's that son of a bitch gotten himself into?"

Harmon coughed softly. "I wouldn't be so quick to blame him. It's possible he had no idea."

"I'm not buying that for a second. I told you he couldn't be trusted."

"Brian, we don't know…"

"*I* know." He held the I long enough to make Harmon understand. "I know enough." Brian looked up at his whiteboard. "Do you have anything on a woman named Terah Dixon? Spelled T. E. R. A. H."

More clicks before Harmon spoke. "Nothing. There aren't any Dixons in the system."

"I figured that was a long shot."

"Brian, do you want me to ask your dad about his visitor?"

"No. I'm coming up. I'll be there tonight."

"I'll be here. Give me a heads up when you plan to arrive."

"I will."

Brian pressed the end button. Nothing having to do with his father was easy. *Nothing.*

With Porter in charge and a clean shirt on the seat beside him, Enderly started toward Duluth.

CHAPTER FORTY-THREE

BECCA HULLS

The sun dipped below the horizon just minutes before Becca reached the small town of Mora on what would be her final trip to Cedar Point. She had already pushed the limits, meeting with Mack Enderly under her real name. No. That was not true. Wren Brigham Enderly was who she was, not Rebecca Ann Hulls. That had been a placeholder, a giant patch on a playground ball. As Wren, she would be whole again. But once the final pieces of her plan were set in motion, would she ever be able to claim it? Or would her life be spent hiding?

She said her name out loud. The sound was sweet, like a bouquet of honeysuckle, lavender, and jasmine. Rebecca Ann Hulls was sawdust-in-her-mouth boring. *Wren Brigham Enderly*. Unique *and* beautiful.

But why Wren? It was such an unusual name. Had she been named after someone? Was Brigham her mother's maiden name or her grandfather's first name? Questions she would never have answers to rose like bile in her stomach, causing her significant discomfort.

Becca knew she was out of control. The world spun around her, and she hung on like it was a carnival ride—laughing and screaming, enjoying every second—never wanting it to stop. No matter how often she tried to convince herself to leave well enough alone, to walk away before someone popped the last few pieces of the puzzle into place, it would not happen. It was a powerful tsunami, a freak of nature. She could not stop it, nor did she want to.

Her entire life had been spent walking away from her adoptive father's rage and control, her brother's abuse, her mother's inability to protect her, and the church's judgment. Everything that happened sent her fleeing in the opposite direction, eyes closed and head down. She was a second-class citizen in her own home. Then again, it wasn't her home—not really. The people she believed were her blood had been nothing more than strangers. In no sense of the word had they treated her like family. She had been a babysitter, cook, maid, and night nurse. Never was she considered a daughter or sister. She had been a square peg in a round hole. *A misfit.* She was done, beyond done. No one, biological or not, would treat her that way again.

Her heart pulsed in every part of her body: her fingertips, chest, ears. *Nothing.* The word swelled with each beat. Rage pounded on the bass drum. *Noth-ing. Noth-ing! NOTH-ING!* As she pumped gas into her car, she fought the urge to light a match and send the whole town up in flames, but she only allowed it in her imagination.

If she died, her *father* could not have cared less. That word shoved the other thoughts aside as it thrust itself in, pleading for her attention. The only thing Mack Enderly had ever done for her was fertilize the seed she came from. It was one more reason to hate the man.

Father. It was a word she had grown to hate. The only other man she knew by that word was the dirtbag who had raised her—or rather, ignored her unless she was at the end of a willow switch or a belt. She was the whipping girl, the one who took the punishment for all his perfect children. He withheld meals, locked her in her room, and chose her siblings over her.

His headstone in the *Life Visions* Cemetery in Carson Springs read *A man of great honor, integrity, and love.* It had been scripted by the elders. She had had no input. Those words would have never come out of her mouth.

And that was why she hated Mack Enderly. He had abandoned her and imprisoned her in that life. He deserved to pay. Her *real father* deserved everything he had coming.

The pump shut off with a bang. Becca jumped and looked around her. This gas station in Mora was much larger than the other she had stopped at. It was easier to hide in the crowd. Best of all, the young man who had felt the ridiculous need to engage her in conversation at the other station did not work here.

With her chin nearly pressed to her chest and her eyes aimed downward, she zigzagged across the store and into the multi-stall bathroom. She waited for the conversations to end and the room to fall silent before she left. Finally, she headed toward the door with a large Diet Coke and a bag of cookies. Tossing them on the counter, she held out a ten-dollar bill but did not make eye contact. Her heel bounced as she impatiently waited for her change. Shoving it into her pocket, she pushed through the exit door and wove between three rows of cars.

Warmth ran up her cheeks, and her eye twitched as a police cruiser pulled up to the pump directly behind her. The bold, navy lettering on the side of the car read *Cedar Point Police.* Becca turned her head in the opposite direction, but not before catching a glimpse of the lower half of a large man climbing out of the squad. There was no doubt that she had stumbled into her worst nightmare.

Her chest constricted, and she fought for a breath. As she slammed her car door, she tipped the glass of soda, soaking the front of her jeans. While daubing the wet spot with a dirty shirt she scooped from the passenger's side floor, she checked the rear-view mirror. *Chief Brian Enderly,* the brother she did not know but despised deeply, glanced in her direction. Heart racing, she drove out of her spot, careful to use her blinkers and check for traffic, just in case. Giving any cop a reason to stop her was akin to committing mission suicide. Again, she checked her mirror. If he was after her, he was in no hurry.

Becca's heart pounded against her ribcage and screamed in her ears as she turned south and headed toward the intersection that would take her toward Cedar Point. Just before the crossroads of Highways 65 and 23, Becca hung a left on Dala Lane, narrowly escaping the front end of a jacked-up pickup truck with a bull bar. The warning horn faded as the driver continued north. Immediately, she veered into a parking lot, drove behind a cluster of storage buildings, and parked to the side, hidden in the shadows of the trees. If the chief was heading home, even if he helped himself to a sit-down dinner, Becca calculated he would turn onto Highway 23 within the hour, so she watched.

Hypervigilant, Becca kept her eyes on the intersection. She barely blinked as she shoveled in the cookies and guzzled her soda. An hour passed and then a second, yet there was no sign of her brother. She started her car and headed across the highway toward Cedar Point.

If Brian was not heading home, where was he going? He was a long way from Cedar Point—too far to be working on a local case unless… Suddenly, a sinking sensation beset her. The one thing she had not considered was a trip to Duluth. Had he connected the dots? Was he on his way to talk to his father about the crazy woman who had first appeared as Jennifer Olson, later emerged as Becca Hull, and finally claimed to be Wren Brigham Enderly?

Becca pressed the accelerator, setting the cruise at four miles an hour over the speed limit. If he was on his way to Duluth, she had a minute window of time to put her plan into action before he sicced the rest of his force on her like stink on a pig.

She had to get to Sean Hart before Brian got to her.

CHAPTER FORTY-FOUR

BECCA HULLS

At 9:13 p.m., Becca drove past the *Welcome to Cedar Point* sign. The heavy rain that had begun to fall near St. Cloud slowed the farther west she got. The aura of the streetlights made her stomach tighten. An ominous feeling washed over her. It was impossible to put her finger on it, but something bad was about to happen. She was sure of it.

She drove down Hanley toward her house but stopped a block away. Even with the thick, sticky air, she could make out the yellow police tape surrounding the duplex. Both levels were dark. Did she dare go inside? Had the police found Terah? How was that possible? It had not been that long since she had shut the whiny bitch up for good. Who would have missed her in that short time?

Becca surveyed her surroundings through each window as she pondered her dilemma: should she sneak into the house or spend the night in the car? Neither option was ideal. The air was crisp. As September transitioned into October, it was too cold to sleep outside without a sleeping bag. Still, it was better than getting caught before her mission was accomplished.

Turning down Main Street, Becca drove west and out of town. Three miles from the edge of town, she pulled to the side of the highway and backed down what appeared to have once been an old logging road. She cut the lights and locked her car doors.

She could have spent the night in Alexandria, but she had seen the Alex police car in front of the station. Maybe her brother had kept the news of the murder out of the gossips' mouths, but it was apparent he had shared it with the neighboring towns.

Becca retrieved the new gun she had stolen from a homeless man from beneath her seat and laid it on the dashboard. It had been an easy snag. The empty bottle of booze told her he was not in any shape to defend himself. Goosebumps rose on her arms, and she rubbed them vigorously to warm herself. Finally, she knelt on her seat and pulled two sweatshirts from her suitcase lying on the backseat. The larger of the two, she tugged over her head. The other she laid across her lap. She grabbed the small pistol and slid it inside the kangaroo pocket of her oversized sweatshirt with the *Up North* logo. Tipping the seat back as far as it would go, she stuck her hand inside the pocket and curled her fingers around the handle. If she had learned anything, it was that it was better to be safe than sorry.

Becca dimmed the light of her screen before scrolling through her phone, searching for news of Cedar Point. She entered the keywords: Terah Dixon, murder, Cedar Point, Rebecca Hulls, and, of course, the names of her brother and father. For nearly an hour, she opened and closed sites but found nothing. Her brother was good. She would give him that. He had successfully made the people of the town believe they were safe. A crooked grin eased up one corner of her mouth. The silence worked in her favor. It made her plans much easier to pull off. Relieved, Becca closed her eyes and hoped for sleep to come, but it did not. Her mind wandered, thrashing angrily.

Chief. Enderly. Brian. Brother. Traitor. Asshole. Becca was not sure how to refer to him. Right now, the last two seemed most appropriate. He had to have known about the birth of his sister. How could he not? Surely, his—*their*—father would not have kept it a secret all these years. Yet, when she arrived at the police station, claiming to be his sister, Wren, the woman at the desk seemed confused, shocked even. She kept digging for information that Becca was unwilling to divulge. She wanted to meet her brother on her terms, not under pressure from anyone, least of all one of her brother's minions.

Before the woman phoned Brian, she stood before her with two cans of cold soda. It felt like a peace offering for being such a nosey bitch. Becca had accepted the Diet Coke. She drank most of it while the woman—*Mary, Marcy, Maria*—something like that—drank her Diet Pepsi and continued to dig for information hidden amidst talk of the weather, Cedar Point's Oktoberfest, and the ongoing argument between her and the chief over diet sodas. Small talk made Becca nervous as hell. And this woman was hanging on her last nerve.

Finally, Becca asked for her brother's cell phone number. The woman said she would have to ask Brian before divulging it. Then she disappeared inside the chief's office, closed the door partway, and made a call. Becca stood outside the door, listening to the woman's side of the conversation. From her words, it was evident her brother's assistant did not trust her. But then again, that was a two-way street.

When Becca heard the phone hit the cradle, she practically ran back to her chair. She picked up the soda and finished the last of it. When she heard her brother would be there in fifteen minutes, she panicked and made up the story about retrieving a photo album from the car. She had not parked in the lot but on the other side of the grocery store, where her car could not be easily seen. A maze of dumpsters and flattened boxes hid her disappearance.

Becca pushed that day from her mind. Rolling onto her left side, she continued to clutch the gun as sleep finally won out, and dreams of her past flooded her.

Suddenly, she woke with a start. What was that? The noise reverberated inside her. Was someone outside, or had the loud noise been part of one of her all-too-real dreams? She waited, listened, and ran through multiple scenarios.

Afraid to let anyone know the car was occupied, she pulled her head inside her sweatshirt and checked the time—*3:48 a.m.* The sky was still dark. She felt an intense urge to leave immediately.

Maybe it had been nothing more than her internal alarm that woke her. All those years, getting fully dressed in multiple layers of clothing before Daniel forced his way into her room and, on top of her, had trained her to wake early, to hope for the best and prepare for the worst. Becca almost always experienced the latter.

Becca slowly raised the back of her seat and frantically looked through every window but saw nothing. Unable to stay there a minute longer, she started the car and drove down the rutted field much faster than was safe. She bottomed out once before pulling off the grassy road onto the trafficless highway. Had she left a few hours later, exiting the logging road in the middle of morning work traffic, she would surely have attracted attention.

Headed in the opposite direction of Cedar Point, Becca felt only relief. A trip through an all-night coffee drive-thru for a large mocha latte with a double shot of espresso gave her the boost of confidence she needed. While it should have sent her into a hand-shaking, heart-racing state, instead, it calmed her nerves.

But it was not confidence she needed. It was luck.

CHAPTER FORTY-FIVE

BECCA HULLS

With the large coffee tap-dancing in her stomach, Becca meandered down dirt roads, stopping twice to relieve herself. Just before 8:00 a.m., she changed clothes, pinned her hair under the wig cap, and pulled on the long blonde wig. A thin coat of mascara, a swipe of blush, and a bit of lip gloss transformed her into Terah Dixon. It appeared the public had no clue that Terah was dead. If she stayed away from the police, she would be safe. Besides, this would be her last visit to Sean Hart.

Becca headed toward Alexandria. She turned into the Serenity Park Health Hospital parking lot and backed into a spot on the left side, hidden between two large SUVs. Like before, she checked in at the desk before claiming a seat and waiting to see Jane's ex-husband. She scrolled the local headlines but, again, found nothing.

The last time she was at the hospital, Sean had called her out, admitted his memory was returning, and told her he would reclaim his ex-wife. He demanded to know who she was and what business she had visiting him. In the last few days, Becca knew what she needed from him. Today, she planned to offer a solution that would benefit both of them.

"Terah." Dr. Evenson looked directly at her. She held the

door open and waited.

Becca pulled her purse over the shoulder of Terah's disgusting pink, ruffly blouse and made her way to the door.

"It's so good to see you. Sean has been asking about you."

Becca gently pressed a hand to her chest. "About me? Really?" Tiny beads of sweat grew beneath the wig. Scratching would have felt so good, but she could not. She laid a hand on her head as if surprised and poked a finger through the hair, digging it into the spot that itched the most.

"He missed you. You haven't been here for a few days. I thought you may have left."

Becca nodded. "I've been a little busy."

"I'm sure you have." Dr. Evenson's heels clicked as they walked down the wide hallway.

Becca stopped. "What does *that* mean?"

The doctor turned around. She shook her head and blinked rapidly several times. "I just meant that we all have days like that."

Becca smoothed the front of the hideous blouse. "Yes, of course. I'm sorry. I've just been so busy with…" She tried to recall the lie she had told when she first started coming to see Sean.

"With your mother, I'm guessing."

She nodded with relief. "Yes, my mother has not been doing well. It's so hard to deal with an elderly parent." Becca continued to walk so the doctor would not see her face. "I'm just so tired."

"I'm sorry to hear that." Dr. Evenson joined her for the short walk. She rested her fingertips on the handle of Sean's door. "Well, are you ready? I know he will be happy to see you." Becca nodded.

With the turn of the key, she was inside the room. She heard the echo of the lock clicking behind her.

Sean looked at her and lifted his eyes toward the mirror. "Terah. Terah."

His voice was not as childish as she had recalled, but it did not have the deep tone of an adult male either—at least not the one she had heard him use when he interrogated her the last time she visited. Becca knew *this* Sean was all an act.

"Come, play with me." He took her hand, squeezed exceptionally hard, and pulled her toward the rug.

"That hurts," Becca whined.

"Tough shit." He positioned himself with his back toward the observation mirror. "So does being locked in this room for two years."

Once Becca sat down, he handed her a car and growled, "Why are you here? What is it you want?" Even though she knew the other Sean had been an act, his deep voice startled her.

"As I recall, you said you wanted to reclaim your wife—your *life*. Right?"

"Yes, but what the hell does that have to do with you?"

"Well, I have a way to make that happen."

Sean drove his truck along the road. "Drive," he hissed. "They're watching. They're always watching." Becca pushed her car until she came to the police station. "And what is this brilliant idea?"

"You let me worry about the details. Just know that it involves getting rid of my brother."

"Your brother?" Sean pulled his head back in confusion.

"Chief Brian Enderly—your wife's husband."

Sean's mouth dropped open. "Are you serious? Enderly's your brother?"

Becca nodded. "He is." She drove her car off the road and plowed it into what was labeled as the Police Station. "At least for now." She smiled.

"What are you planning to do, kill him?"

Becca lifted one shoulder in a half-shrug. "It's a win-win, don't you think? We both get what we want."

"And what exactly are *you* getting?"

Her shoulders fell as she sighed. She put a hand on Sean's arm. "I get to stick it to my asshole father."

"Mack Enderly. But why?"

"That's not really your concern now, is it?"

Sean shook his head. "I don't like it. I ended up here because of a deranged bastard. I sure as hell don't want to deal with another one—named Terah." He bobbed his head like a child. It was a show for the man behind the window. "I want to do this on my own terms this time."

Becca laughed. "Rather odd you'd call Drew Carter deranged when you're the one who snapped."

"Shut up. Just shut your effing mouth. You don't know anything about me or what happened."

"Mmm. I know enough." She drove her car down the carpeted street. "Besides, this time, I'll be doing the shooting."

He shook his head. "And I'm supposed to trust you?"

"I don't think you have a choice."

Sean stared at her. "And how do I know you won't hurt Jane or my boys?"

Becca turned her palms up. "You don't. You're just going to have to have faith that I know what I'm doing."

Sean snorted. "Right. I don't even believe your real name's Terah. So, who the hell are you anyway?"

"Let's just say I'm your guardian angel."

Sean pushed his truck closer to Becca's. "I have a feeling you're the spawn of Satan."

Becca tipped her head. "Believe what you want." She pinched his cheek and smiled. "But when this is done, Brian will be gone, and you'll be free to pursue your wife again."

Sean bit his bottom lip. "And what exactly do you need from me?"

"I just need you to keep your mouth shut."

He glared at her and shook his head.

Becca laughed and clapped her hands once. "Well, there's not a lot you can do about it, is there? You're in here." She pointed to the barred window in the door. "And everything that's about to happen is out there." Again, she laughed. "There's no way to stop me."

Sean shook his head. "I don't know if that's true. What

happens if I spill everything I know?"

"I've thought about that—you squealing on me, trying to get someone to believe some cockamamie story about Terah who told you she was going to kill the Chief of Police." She laughed again. "You're locked up in a psych hospital. Do you really think anyone's going to believe you?" Becca pointed to her chest. "I played my part so well that they love me here. They think I'm helping you." She poked a finger into his chest. "You're the nutcase who lost touch with reality."

Sean grabbed her hand and started yelling at her. Becca wildly waved her hand to be let out. Within seconds, Dr. Evenson and a man in blue scrubs raced into the room. The man pulled Sean away from Becca while she ran out of the room. This time, she was not acting. She *was* terrified, panic-stricken, that Sean was not only going to hurt her, but he was going to grab her wig and expose her as a phony.

Becca watched through the small window in the door as the pair wrestled with Sean. Finally, the man, nearly twice the size of Sean, held his arms behind him while Dr. Evenson injected a needle into his arm. It had taken only seconds for his body to melt into the man's arms.

The door opened, and the doctor stepped into the hallway. "Are you okay?" Becca nodded. "I'm so sorry. I've never seen him go off like that. It doesn't make any sense. He talks about you all the time." She laid a hand on Becca's shoulder. "What happened?"

Becca shook her head. "We were just talking. I told him I loved to keep visiting him. Then I touched his chest and asked him if he liked it when I came to see him." She blinked several times to stop the tightness of her eyelid that would soon become a full-blown twitch. "Sean growled and then attacked me."

"I don't understand." She looked at Becca. "You're sure he didn't hurt you?"

"I'm fine. Just a little shaken. I thought Sean was making such great progress." She tipped her head and cocked an eyebrow. "I guess that's not the case."

Dr. Evenson peeked into the room. "He was supposed to see his ex-wife this morning. That's not going to happen now."

Joy danced inside Becca, but she lowered her shoulders and raised her chin to keep the delight out of her voice. "Jane?"

"So, you know her?"

Becca nodded. "I do. We're meeting for brunch in…" She glanced at her watch. "Goodness, I'm going to be late." She looked at the doctor. "I can let her know what happened. We talk after every one of my visits. She likes to know how they went."

Dr. Evenson pulled her head back in surprise. "Really? It's wonderful Sean has so much support." She opened the door and let the man in the scrubs out before locking it again. "Thank you for relaying the message. I'm late for a meeting too." She looked at Sean, asleep in his bed. "I hope this little episode doesn't deter you from visiting again."

Becca shrugged. "I don't know. He was making some pretty wild accusations."

"Like what?"

"It was like he didn't recognize me. He kept calling me *Emily*." Dr. Evenson shrank back. "What is it?"

"You don't know?" The doctor sighed softly.

"No," Becca lied. "Who's Emily?"

Dr. Evenson shook her head. "For now, let's just leave that question unanswered." She released a deeper breath. "I'm afraid your cousin has just taken a few steps backward again."

"Oh, no." Becca stepped to the window. She kept her back toward the doctor as a vile smile spread. "That's terrible news."

"I agree. I thought we were finally getting somewhere."

"Thank you, Dr. Evenson. I'll understand if you think it's better for me not to come for a while."

"I'm afraid I do."

Becca shook her hand, turned, and practically floated down the hallway and out of the hospital.

CHAPTER FORTY-SIX

BECCA HULLS

It was seven minutes to ten when Becca pulled on the pants and zipped them. She poked her arms through the freshly laundered sleeves of a blue shirt and buttoned it to the top. Studying herself in the gas station bathroom mirror, she looked *passable*. The uniform was a little on the large side, but it would get her through the door. That was all she needed—a foot inside.

She squeezed her size seven feet into the too-small, black tennis shoes she picked up for eight dollars from a discount rack at a chain store. They were as ugly as sin, but they completed the uniform. On her front pocket, she pinned the realistic-looking badge she had pocketed at the toy store in Alexandria. After adjusting the nondescript reddish-brown wig she had pulled into a ponytail, Becca straightened the collar of her shirt, brushed a hair from her arm, and nodded her approval.

The cleaners would have given the uniform to anyone with a twenty-dollar bill. Becca was sure of it. She had not even offered them a name—just claimed she was there to pick up her police uniform. They happily handed one over. It was kismet. Hopefully, Lady Luck would continue to shine down on her. The plastic bag she had been handed with the uniform held a service cap. Becca was prepared to go without one, but this made it so much better. The bill would cover her face until she was through the door. It was going to be a serendipitous kind of day.

After abandoning her street clothes and the plastic cleaner's bag in the bottom of the garbage can, Becca covered them with layers of wadded paper towels before passing through the store and out the front door.

Once inside the car, she pulled on the sweatshirt she had used to cover herself the previous night. The peaked cap and her gun remained beneath her seat as she drove the half hour back to Cedar Point. If she were stopped, all they would see were the blue pants and the ugly shoes. Many people dressed that way. She would not arouse suspicion.

In Cedar Point, Becca parked on the street, out of view of the Enderly front door. She picked up her loaded gun, held it in her hand, and debated where to carry it. Sticking it into the waistband of her pants would have been a dead giveaway. So, she opted for the front pocket. The gun was small, and her pockets were deep. It would be unnoticeable.

She adjusted the cap, climbed out of the car, and headed toward the house she had delivered the pizzas to just days before.

Her heart thudded in her chest at the thought of carrying out something so heinous. Still, she kept walking. Suddenly, she was outside the heavy wooden door. Her finger wagged as she held it an inch from the doorbell. Was what she was about to do worth it? Was it worth possibly dying? Going to prison for the rest of her life? Living the next forty or more years on the run, always looking over her shoulder?

She stretched her neck one way and then the other before pulling her shoulders back until they popped. Making Mack Enderly suffer was worth whatever happened to her in the next seven bullets. That was all she needed to make her asshole father understand he should not have left his child to a family of monsters. In the house she grew up in, the boogeymen were not just under her bed; they were in her face every minute of every day. This was payback.

The dual-pitch doorbell reverberated in the large, covered porch. The noises inside let her know someone was home. It did not matter who. Anyone would make her point.

A male voice came through a speaker. "State your business."

Becca knew they could see her. She tipped her head down slightly and lowered her voice. "Officer Bryn Everly." She had purposely chosen a name similar to her brother's. She hoped the familiarity would work in her favor. "The chief sent me to update you."

Silence. Uncomfortable with the lack of response, Becca counted in her head. Suddenly, the door opened to reveal a man in his twenties.

"You can give me the information, and I'll share it with the others."

"Others?" Becca was so busy trying to look inside that she missed what he had said.

"My mother and brother."

She nodded. "Yes, of course." She squared her shoulders and looked over her shoulder. "Cole? You are the oldest son, correct?" He nodded. "Cole, it would be much better if we talked inside, away from the gossiping neighbors." Becca tipped her head slightly. "You know as well as I do that your stepdad is trying to keep this away from the public for the time being."

Cole stepped back and opened the door wide enough for her to enter. Becca stepped into the foyer and waited to be directed into the house. If this was going to work, she had to play the part until the right moment. After he reset the alarm—*five, five, nine, eight*—she followed Cole down the hallway and into the living room. Jane and her younger son, Luke, were seated on the couch.

Becca nodded to them. "I'm Officer Bryn Everly out of Fergus Falls." She wanted to say more, but rattling on would create suspicion.

Jane's eyebrows knit together. "Have we met? You look familiar."

Becca tipped her head lower. "I don't believe so. This is my first trip to Cedar Point." She flashed a crooked smile. "But people always say I look just like someone else they know. I must have one of those faces."

Jane glanced at Cole and then back at Becca. "I didn't realize Cedar Point was working with the Fergus police."

Becca folded her hands and pressed them low across her stomach to cover the bulge in her front pocket. "Yesterday was our first day onsite. It took us a day to get up to speed." Jane nodded. "Your husband asked me to update you on some new developments."

Jane looked confused. "Bri...I mean, Chief Enderly's in Duluth." Becca nearly smiled. "I didn't know he was..."

"Oh, he checks in multiple times a day."

Jane's eyes narrowed. "I thought you said you just started yesterday. How would you know that?"

Becca cleared her throat softly. "It's just part of the process, ma'am. The chief must be available at all times."

Jane bobbed her head slightly. "I suppose that's true." She pointed to a chair. "Please, sit down, Officer Everly."

"Thank you." Becca backed into the leather recliner and shifted her weight to one side, hiding her hip with the gun behind the arm of the chair.

"So, what are these new developments?" Cole sat on the opposite end of the couch from Luke—bookends protecting their mother.

Becca watched them, lined up like bowling pins waiting to be knocked down. They could not have positioned themselves any better. She reached into her pocket, pulled out her gun, and clutched it with both hands. The small weapon bobbed as she moved to the middle of the room and aimed it directly at Jane.

"This." She nodded toward her gun. "This is the new development, Mrs. Enderly."

CHAPTER FORTY-SEVEN

BECCA HULLS

Becca swung her gun from Cole to Luke and back again. "One word of advice." She sneered at each of Jane's sons. "Do *not* try to be a hero." She looked at their mother. "I doubt either of you want to be an only child or…*worse*." She laughed. "Do what I tell you, and nobody gets hurt."

Cole slid closer to his mom.

"Look at that." Becca rolled her eyes. "Such a good son." Becca's words dripped with sarcasm. She lowered her arms a shade and pressed her elbows to her sides.

Becca looked at Jane. "Well, here's something you might be interested in. I don't have any news from the chief. Never did. But I do have a message from that sick ex-husband of yours."

"Sean? How do you know him?" The wrinkles on Jane's forehead deepened, and her lip quivered.

"Oh, didn't he ever mention his *cousin Terah*?" She snickered.

"Terah?" Jane's eyes grew wide. "You're the waitress from Knuckles. The one they're looking for."

"Hardly."

"But you just said…"

"No. I'm not Terah. She's a simple little bitch who isn't

worth the air she breathes—or *used to* breathe." A vile smirk crossed her face, and she wagged an eyebrow.

Jane glanced at Luke. "But you look just like her."

"Huh. They say everyone has a doppelganger." She swung the gun toward Luke, who had been slowly sliding his hand into his pocket. "Don't even think about it, fat boy. Cell phones—in the middle of the floor, now. Toss them." All three phones landed near Becca's feet. "Good. From now on, keep your hands where I can see them." She looked directly at Luke. "Especially you, big boy. Got it?"

"So, who are you, and what do you want?" Cole squeezed his mom's hand.

The corners of Becca's mouth turned up slightly, and her eyes held a look of disdain. "You'll find out soon enough," she snorted loudly. "Your family needs to learn they can't toss people away and think they're gonna get away with it."

"Cryptic, aren't you?" Luke spat the words. "This is ridiculous. What exactly are you after?"

"Shut up!" Becca took a step toward Luke and aimed the pistol between his eyes, keeping enough distance so he could not grab her gun. "Unless you have a death wish."

"Just tell us what you want," Cole said. "I'm sure whatever it is can be fixed."

A dry, bitter laugh filled the room. "Fix it? You can't retrieve something forty-two years after you gave it away and think all will be forgiven." She swung the gun toward Cole. "But then again, how would you boys know anything about suffering? No one tossed you out on your ass, took away your family, or made you believe you were nothing every day of your life." She wagged her head at Jane. "And I'm pretty damn sure Mother Dearest here never abused you."

Jane looked from one son to the other. "No, I didn't. But *I* was abused."

Becca huffed. "Yeah, I know your story." She pressed her lower lip out in a phony pout. "Poor little rich girl gets richer when her real father dies and leaves his entire empire to her.

How does that even equate to anything I've been through?"

Jane sat up. "So, tell us your story."

"Ha!" She pointed the gun at Luke and then at Cole. "You boys can call me Aunt Wren." Her jaw tightened. "That's all you need to know."

Jane's jaw dropped. "You're Wren, Brian's sister?"

"Sister? Please. That would mean we grew up together." She blinked slowly. "We might share the same DNA, but I'm not family in any sense of the word."

The wrinkles at the corner of Jane's eyes deepened. "How is that even possible? His mother died before…"

"And there it is—the ten-million-dollar question." Her cheeks puffed out as she exhaled. "That would be a good question for your father-in-law, Mrs. Enderly."

Jane's lips parted. "Are you saying Mack has known about you all this time?"

"What do you think? Do you really believe I'd be standing here if he didn't?"

Luke slid closer to his mom. "So, what do you want from us?"

"A trade," Becca said.

"For what?" Jane grabbed Luke's hand with her free one.

"Brian or Mack," she wagged her head from side to side, "for your lives." She let the offer sink in before she looked at Jane. "And if I were a bettin' woman, I'd venture you'd offer up Mack before your husband." Becca watched them squirm. "I hope you're ready to play the game."

She picked up Jane's cell with the lacy-patterned cover. "Give me the code to unlock your phone."

"One. Three. Five. Seven," Jane blurted.

Becca entered the code, but nothing happened. She pointed the gun at Jane. "Stupid woman. Pull that shit again, and you won't be needing a phone."

Jane's neck swelled as she swallowed hard. "Nine. Three. Six. Two."

Becca entered the new code. This time, the screen opened.

She pressed the text icon and searched for a conversation with Brian. There were two. One had a long string of posts; the other contained two cryptic messages.

"What the hell is this? They both say *Brian*."

Jane's brows hiked upward. "You should know. You hacked his phone this morning."

Becca wagged the phone at her. "Like hell I did." She raised her shoulder and flashed a crooked grin. "But it sounds like your husband has more enemies than friends." Her eyes narrowed. "And that bodes well for me. Maybe someone else will kill him before I do." She leered at Jane. "Now tell me which to use?"

"The short one."

Becca held the gun on her prisoners while she typed with her left thumb. When she looked up, Luke had moved to the front edge of the couch.

"Didn't I tell you not to be a hero?" Becca shook her head. "I don't get it. It's like being poisoned wasn't enough for you, *nephew*."

"You did that?" Jane dropped her son's hands. "Why? What did you hope to gain by trying to kill me or my boys?"

Becca smirked. "For a smart woman, you sure are dumb." She rolled her eyes. "Let me draw you a picture—one your teeny tiny brain can understand." She karate-chopped the air in front of her with each word. "*Boys. Jane. Brian.* All of you are important to Mack. Hurt one of you, hurt him." She pulled her neck down into her shoulders. "I just have to decide *how much* pain I want to inflict on my father."

The hairs on the back of Becca's neck stood on end when she looked at Jane's phone and saw no response from Brian. "Looks like your husband just answered that question for me. He's not replying to your sweet message." She looked at Jane. "So, we turn up the heat." She swung the phone back and forth. "And if I don't hear something soon, the stakes increase." Becca eyed each of her hostages in turn. "And it sure would be a pity to leave him without *any* family, wouldn't it?" After pressing buttons on the phone again, she looked at her captives. "Settle in, *family*." Becca scowled. "I have a feeling we're gonna be here a while."

CHAPTER FORTY-EIGHT

ADMINISTRATIVE ASSISTANT MAURI LOCKE

Mauri paced the hardwood floor of her childhood bedroom. It creaked in the same spots it had when she and her sister used to sneak out of her second-floor window and climb down the rose trellis to hang out with their friends in the nearly non-existent town of Elizabethton, Wisconsin. Back then, they had committed to memory every squeaky board. This morning, the moans barely penetrated her anxiety.

She and her husband had been holed up in the small town for almost a week now, and it was driving her crazy. Mauri prided herself on knowing everything that happened around her. As Cedar Point's go-to person for information, she was more accurate than the local news. People told her things they would not confide in anyone else and asked her to verify gossip. And if it was to be kept a secret, no one could jimmy that lock open. But here she was, in a desert of information, hiding from an unknown assailant who had tried to kill her—not once, but twice. Even though it set her on edge, it was the least of her concerns.

After her mother's death, her sister, Meggie, and her husband, Cory, moved into the 1930s Cape Cod-style house with gray shake siding. Meggie, the more nostalgic of the two, refused to change anything in the main bedrooms. For six months, Meggie and Cory slept in her room, with the canopied full-size bed and the ruffly curtains that covered the yellowed and brittle roller shade. During that time, Cory, a contractor, remodeled the attic, turning it into the owner's suite. Mauri knew Meggie would eventually make changes once she had kids. If her sister's grin was any indication, Mauri could be an aunt in a year or so.

For now, posters of Boys II Men, the Backstreet Boys, and New Kids on the Block lined Mauri's lime green and pink wallpapered walls. The mattress of her pencil-post bed, covered with the homemade quilt that matched the wallpaper, looked the same as it had the day she went away to college. The only thing that had changed was the sheets—at least, she hoped they had.

Mauri ran a hand over the wallpaper. It had been put up in her neon life stage—about a handful of years later than it was popular. Color was how she referred to her life. After college, but before Mike, it was her blue stage—and afterward—yellow. She wore those colors and changed her couch pillows to match. Mauri had never admitted her need to match things to anyone; she had not confessed it to Mike when he asked why she had a closet full of pillows. She just closed the door and told him to mind his own business—which he did. If she were asked her color today, it would be a double: black and red. *Depression and anxiety*. And being alone this morning increased their intensity.

Cory and Mike left before dawn, traveling from one job site to another. Since Mike was not from Elizabethton or Wisconsin, and since they had not married in Elizabethton, no one would recognize him as her husband. But if Mauri showed her face, everyone would know her.

Meggie had left to run errands in a nearby town. She promised to be quick, but after days of not setting foot outside the house, Mauri convinced her to take the day to herself.

"Be my eyes and ears. Let me know what's happening..." Mauri pointed toward the curtained window. "Out there." She sighed. "I'll live vicariously through you."

After hemming and hawing, her sister finally agreed to get a haircut, go to lunch with a friend, and pick up some groceries. Even with her anxiety, Mauri could not have been more relieved.

While Meggie was out in the real world—with people and stores and fresh air—Mauri dug through her mother's bedroom closet until she located the ten-year-old laptop.

It had been a gift for her mother, something to keep the Wetherby women connected. They emailed like others texted, multiple times a day. Her mother's bad eyes and arthritic, misshapen hands kept her from texting, so they settled on email—with a program that allowed her mother to speak her messages.

Before wrapping it, Mauri had set it up in the simplest way possible. Even though her mother had been gone for four years, Mauri continued to email her every Sunday. It was therapeutic, a way of journaling about her life.

Once the computer sprang to life, the first thing she did was update it. Over two hundred unopened emails populated her mother's inbox; almost all of them were from her. Reading her letters, she laughed and even shed a few tears as she imagined her mother's snarky or comforting replies—depending on the situation.

Meggie, who knew little about computers, would have been horrified that Mauri had touched it. She would have thought just turning it on would send flares above the house, signaling the person who was trying to kill her. But Mauri was a techie. Her sister was not. She knew she was reasonably safe.

After logging in to the fake email account she had created, Mauri began to pace. She kept her eyes glued to the screen no matter where she was in the room. Her head swiveled with each turn. She waited for the email to pop in. A couple of junk mail false alarms sounded, so when the third one pinged, she had convinced herself it was more of the same. But when she saw the sender, her heart raced.

She stared at the screen. Once she opened the email, there

was no going back. It felt wrong, as if she were entering Brian's house for the sole purpose of snooping. Only this was not that, not even close. She reminded herself of the importance of knowing the truth. Jesus said the truth shall set you free. Brian needed to know.

She drew a long breath, expelled it harshly, and clicked on the message. Mauri scanned rather than read it. There was only one sentence she needed to find. And there it was, the information she had been waiting for.

Unrelated.

Mauri released a full morning of stress in one long breath. Several pieces of paper fluttered from her childhood desk to the floor. The woman was *not* Wren Brigham Enderly. Praise the Lord. She had not liked that woman from the minute she set foot in the station. Something about her was off. But…

She picked up her phone and scrolled until she found the picture she had accidentally taken. It was a gift. Out of sheer boredom, Mauri had spent a morning cleaning up her phone, organizing and tossing apps and photos. Most of the pictures she tossed were out of focus, no longer meant anything, or were unbecoming of the subject. It was rare for her to take photos. With just her and Mike, no kids—yet, her mother gone, and rarely spending time with her sister, there was little need. But then she came to one of her blunders. For Brian, it was a gift.

On the day the woman claiming to be Brian's sister walked into the station, Mauri had been on her phone. She jumped before dropping it on her desk—but not before capturing an off-kilter, somewhat fuzzy shot of the woman. The quality was not good, but at least Brian would know what the liar looked like in case he wanted to pursue her.

Mauri studied the computer screen. A wave of nerves stomped through her. She would have to answer to the chief about using the police lab to run *personal* tests. But more importantly, she would have to deal with the—*You're always poking your nose where it doesn't belong*—conversation Brian would throw at her.

Yet she was as stubborn as the chief. No matter how much yelling her boss did, she would defend her decision to send the pair of soda cans belonging to Brian and the woman claiming to be his sister to the lab to see if there was any truth in her claim. And clearly, she had made the right decision. The woman was a fraud, a bottom feeder who got her jollies from toying with other people's emotions. Mauri bit the inside of her cheeks. Yes, she and the chief had their moments, but she cared for him and would never let anyone hurt him.

The bigger issue was how to tell Brian about her discovery—not just about the woman lying, but how to get word to him when she was supposed to be in hiding.

Once again, she paced the room. Two creaks each time she traveled the fourteen feet from one side to the other. *Step. Step. Step. Creak. Step. Creak. Step. Step. Turn.* Ten times, she counted those creaks as she crossed back and forth. Then, an idea came to her.

She sat down at the computer and searched for a phone number.

Before noon, a small cardboard box sat on her sister's front step. Inside was Mauri's favorite sweater, the DNA results, and a printed, grainy photo of the woman claiming to be Wren Enderly. A sticky note with the handwritten letter M was the only other identifier of the sender. The box was devoid of a return address; it showed only the destination.

For the next hour, Mauri watched through the curtains, praying Sam would pick it up before Meggie got home and put an end to her plan.

Sam had been Meggie's high school boyfriend. He drove a delivery truck that traveled into Minneapolis and back daily. Fake coughing and sneezing through the phone call from the house phone, Mauri convinced Sam she was Meggie and was too sick to mail the package, a surprise for her sister's birthday. She asked him to send it upon entering Minnesota, where rates would be cheaper. She explained it was going to the Chief of Police where Mauri worked and that her boss would wrap it for her and leave it on her sister's desk on her birthday. Sam happily agreed to help and offered to drop it at the police station on his way to Fargo—a trip he made weekly. He even accepted that she would leave it on her front step for him to pick up. Being *sick*, she did not want him to catch anything she might have.

"Come on, Sam," Mauri whispered under her breath. "Hurry up."

Finally, the big white truck with black lettering pulled up in front of the house. Sam scaled the six stairs in three steps, scooped up the package, waved at the shadow behind the curtain, climbed into his truck, and drove off in thirty seconds.

Mauri breathed a massive sigh of relief, but she knew it was only temporary. She would have to face the music and deal with her boss's wrath at some point. Everything inside her hoped the end justified the means.

CHAPTER FORTY-NINE

CHIEF BRIAN ENDERLY

By the time Brian was dressed in his street clothes, morning had not yet announced its arrival. He pulled the blackout curtain away from the hotel window and stared into the rain that had started while he and Bob had met with his dad the night before. They were set to pick up where they left off at 8:00 a.m.

There were two messages from Jane. Fear of his phone being hacked again and putting her in danger kept him from responding. He knew she was worried, but she knew where he was and who to contact if anything was seriously wrong.

The only light in the room bled through the sheer curtains beneath the thick ones he had left open. No natural light seeped in, only that from the streetlights. He wandered around the room, grateful to be on the main floor where his heavy footsteps would not wake anyone below. For nearly an hour, he traveled the same path, glancing at the barely audible early morning news each time he passed the television.

Questions badgered him. Who was Rebecca Hulls? Did she really believe Mack was her father? Was that even possible? But more importantly, was she connected to Terah Dixon?

The previous night's encounter had lasted until nearly midnight. His father had been less than forthcoming. Brian could tell he was harboring secrets. His old man had promised to be honest two years before, but he was lying. Even Harmon doubted him.

Today, he wanted answers—real answers, not some made-up crap or a stack of excuses.

"Son of a bitch," Brian grumbled, grabbing the miniature coffee pot from the counter. Did this hotel think they were renting rooms to gnomes who drank caffeine by the thimble? He was a grown-ass man, and he wanted a pot of coffee that would fill his stomach and could peel paint from a car. But he gave in. His jaw tightened as he made a pot of what looked like someone had sloshed their dirty feet in it. When it was done, he poured it into a ceramic mug and started a second pot.

Ten minutes later, Brian headed out of the hotel with his backpack. He dropped his keycard into the basket on the counter and stepped into the steady rain in search of real coffee.

After starting his squad car, he turned on the seat and steering wheel heaters and waited for the window to defrost. His phone signaled a text. Only Porter, the desk at the station, and Jane and the boys had his new number. Unless it was an emergency, he was not going to answer anything. Jane would have to wait. Brian leaned back and pulled it from the front pocket of his jeans. It was his wife.

Why haven't you called?

There was no doubt Jane needed him right now, but the boys were with her, and they were safe inside, while the evils of the world loomed beyond those walls. For now, the BCA and FBI were in charge of the possible murder of Terah Dixon and the attempted murders of Jane and Mauri. Luke rode the edge of attempted murder after being poisoned, but he had not been the target. Having others on the case gave him time to figure out who the woman was, who alleged she was his sister, the one who had visited his dad, claiming him as family. Were they the same person, or were there more sociopaths hiding in the shadows of Cedar Point?

Of course, there were. Joyce and the goon qualified. Why the hell were they hanging around the small town anyway?

Stealing police computers and knocking an officer senseless had at least pointed him in the right direction—toward Rebecca Hulls. They were the reason he was meeting with his dad. Besides, he had left Porter in charge. His deputy would be all over them like flies on shit. Unless they had some connection to Terah Dixon, they were the least of his worries.

Brian returned his phone to his pocket. Through the nearly clear windshield, he could see the pinkish light of day breaking the horizon. But even so, according to meteorologist Dave Anderson, the day would be a washout. He slipped into his brown canvas jacket, buckled his seat belt, and drove out of the lot.

London Road was nearly empty, as were many streets heading up the hill. Fortunately, the early morning commuters would not hit the road for almost an hour.

Driving calmed his nerves. It meant he was in control. It also put him closer to the possibility of an open coffee shop. By 6:30 a.m., he had found one, ordered two large black coffees, and sat in their parking lot, drinking one of them before killing time driving the side streets of Duluth.

CHAPTER FIFTY

CHIEF BRIAN ENDERLY

Brian drove toward the prison at 7:45 a.m. under a short burst of rain. By the time he reached the gate, the rain had returned to a steady drizzle.

After parking, Brian ran for the door. He hoped no one saw his version of running. Honestly, he was not sure what to call what he just did. *A fast walk? A trot? A gallop?* It definitely was not a skip; he knew that for a fact. Skipping was something he had never mastered.

When he arrived at the front door, as promised, Warden Harmon was waiting. His lips were sucked inward, and his brows pressed together.

Harmon flung the locked door open. "Nice...skip?" He could no longer hold it inside. His laughter echoed in the entryway.

"Shut up." Brian's scowl turned into a grin.

"Little wet out there?" The dark circles under the warden's eyes meant he had not gotten much sleep either.

Enderly frowned. "Are you asking or telling?"

"Just making small talk." Bob walked toward the same conference room they had met in the previous night. "So, what's your goal today? What are you hoping to walk away knowing?"

Brian's eyebrows shot up. "*The truth.* I want to know how my mother could have died the night she told me she was pregnant, and yet, somehow, there was a baby born that my father seems to know something about."

Harmon unlocked the door and headed through. Brian followed. He crossed the room, settling into the same chair as before.

"So, let's play this out. Let's say your mom didn't die. She was alive and had the baby. How does that change anything?"

Brian pulled out a chair and fell into it. "What do you mean? It changes everything." He ran a hand through his hair. "It means my mother abandoned me. She left me with that bastard rather than protecting me from him." He pressed his elbows onto the table, locked his fingers, and rested his chin on them. "And if that's the case, she can rot in hell right along with my dad. And I'd have a lot more hatred for her than I do for my so-called father." He slammed the side of his fist into the table.

"Okay, hold on. That was only hypothetical. I'm just trying to understand where you're coming from." He handed Brian a Diet Coke. "I'm guessing you've had more than enough coffee this morning." Brian nodded. "I figured you're ready to move on to something else."

"Thanks," Brian grumbled. He popped the top and took a long draw.

"Are you ready for Mack?"

"No. I doubt I ever will. The bastard didn't come clean last night. What makes you think he'll tell me the truth this morning?"

"I don't know. But I do know he's trying to be a better person." Brian snorted his disagreement. "Maybe you should try appealing to *that* side of him. Don't blame him, and don't bring up last night. Tell him you appreciated the conversation. Be direct. Ask what you want to know." The two men locked eyes. "He may have had enough time to think about things. I don't think going off on him will accomplish anything."

Brian's eyes flitted across the room but focused on nothing.

"You may be right."

"What?" Harmon smiled. Patting his chest, he winked at Brian. "I'm good at some things." He cocked his head. "Want me to teach you how to skip?"

Enderly scowled his answer.

The warden's smile faded as he tipped his head down and stared at Brian over the top of his reading glasses. "Are you ready?"

"I suppose." He drew a long breath and released it as he spoke. "I know what I need to do."

Harmon picked up his cell phone, texted a message with one finger, and returned it to the corner of the table between them. Minutes later, a handcuffed Mack Enderly entered the room. Behind him was a man dressed in a gray shirt and black pants.

"Cuffs on or off?" The guard looked at Harmon.

"Off's fine. I'm sure we can trust Mack."

The guard nodded and unlocked the cuffs. "I'll be outside watching." He poked two fingers toward his eyes and then at Mack. "I've got my eyes on you. If anything happens, I'll know."

Mack shook his head. "Nothing's gonna happen."

The guard nodded at the warden and left. Brian heard him lock the door.

"That's just Buzz being Buzz," he said to Mack. "He's afraid if he lets go of that tough guy act, he'll lose all respect."

"Respect? He's kind of an asshole," Mack said as he turned and looked at the one-way glass.

Harmon's head bobbed. "I won't disagree. It's what makes him a good guard."

"Listen." Brian nodded to his father when they made eye contact. He opened his mouth to say more, but Harmon laid a hand on his arm and squeezed.

Bob tucked his head down between him and Brian. "Gentle," he whispered.

Brian looked toward his dad, who was sitting on the opposite side of the table. "Thanks for meeting with us again. I appreciate it." He glanced at Bob, who nodded approval. "But I still have some questions.

"I figured you would." Mack leaned back, pressed his elbows into the arms of the chair, and folded his hands across his stomach.

"And I need honest answers." His jaw tightened. "Not the bullshit you were flinging last night."

Bob leaned forward. "Okay. Let's try that again." He frowned at Brian before turning toward Mack. "Brian has some questions about this woman, Becca Hulls, and how she could possibly be your daughter." Harmon paused. "You've been a model prisoner, Mack. Within the next year, you could be back on the street. But lying or refusing to answer questions won't look good to the parole board." Harmon held Mack's eyes. "Besides, we will learn the truth—from you or from someone else. It'll go a long way if we hear it from you."

Mack looked from Brian to Harmon and back. "Fine." Defeat sagged his shoulders.

A lump swelled in Brian's throat. After forty-two years, he was finally going to know the truth.

His old man drew a long breath and released it between the narrow opening of his lips. "It's possible that this woman is my daughter." He peered at Brian. "Your sister."

Brian felt his body go limp. "How? Mom died the day she found out she was pregnant."

"No." Mack looked up at the ceiling. "It's a lot more complicated than that."

Brian's eyes widened and his pupils became black specks. "Two years ago, you said you would never lie to me, and now you're…"

Mack nodded. "I lied because I didn't want to hurt you."

A sharp laugh came from Brian. "Really? You beat the shit out of me for years, and now you don't want to hurt me with a bunch of words. I call bullshit."

"Believe what you want, son." Brian grabbed the edge of the table. Mack shrugged. "I think what's going to hurt you more is knowing she didn't die the night of the accident."

Brian shoved his chair back. "What? So, she walked away from me? She left me to rot under your… I can't even say it—*care*." He shook his head. "You didn't *care* about anything or anybody other than your bottle of booze."

"You aren't wrong. But it wasn't like that." He stared at the table. "She would never have left you—at least not with me. Brian, your mom didn't die that night." His voice cracked. "But she wasn't really alive either." He sighed loudly. "She was taken to a hospital in Minneapolis and eventually moved to a nursing home, where she remained in a coma for almost two years. She never regained consciousness."

"What? You let me think she was dead, you bastard."

Mack kneaded his hands. "I had to. I didn't have a choice. I couldn't let you see her like that. She wasn't your mom anymore—not the mom you knew. According to the doctors, she'd never hug you or tell you she loved you ever again." He stared out the window behind his son. "They said the likelihood of her ever returning to us was virtually nil."

Brian's phone buzzed with a text, but he did not look at it. "You're lying. This can't be true."

"Well, that's how it was. After the accident, you were in the hospital for three weeks. During that time, I sat with your mom and begged her to give me a sign that she was in there, but she didn't."

Harmon looked at Brian before turning to Mack. "They kept the baby alive and growing that whole time?"

Mack nodded. "Yeah. The kid was born six months later. She was so tiny when they placed her in my arms. She looked like a miniaturized version of you." He sucked in a ragged breath. "I cried, knowing this little girl would never have her mom to save her from me." He looked toward the ceiling. "So, I prayed. I asked God what I should do." His head wobbled back and forth. "Can you imagine? What would a drunken bastard like me do with a baby? At least *you* could take care of yourself."

"So, what *did* you do?" Brian stood and leaned in toward his dad.

A deep sigh cut through the room. "I filled out the birth certificate. I gave her the name your mom picked out, *Wren Brigham Enderly*, and instead of heading back to Cedar Point, I drove toward Madison. A few hours later, I entered a small town in a deep valley. I drove into the hills. When I got tired of listening to her cry, I fed her with the formula and bottle they gave me at the hospital." His chin quivered. "Then, when it got dark, I left her on the steps of a tiny little church." Mack stared out the window. Brian turned to see what he was looking at, but there was nothing but a memory. "One of the nurses told me about the church—said it was a drop-off site for unwanted babies."

"So, you just left her there?" Brian wrapped his arms over his head and growled his frustration. "By the way, asshole, she wasn't *unwanted*." He poked a finger into his chest. "*I* wanted her."

Mack ignored his son's comment. "I wrapped her in one of the quilts your mom made and scribbled a note on the outside of a McDonald's bag. I said her mother died, and I, as the father, was relinquishing my rights as her legal guardian. I asked them to find her a good home." He snorted softly. "Then I kissed her, left her on the step, and walked away."

"My sister. You left my sister to whatever pervert might happen by and pick her up." Brian spun around. "And you wrote this on a fast-food bag covered in grease." He kicked the table leg. "That's sick." Brian pointed at his dad. "You're sick."

His dad shrugged and nodded. "That's true. But, Brian, how was I going to take care of her? I sucked as a father."

Brian poked a finger into his chest again. "I could have taken care of her. Me."

"You weren't even nine years old yet. You could barely take care of yourself when I was drinking."

"Which was all the damn time," Brian muttered.

"I'm not going to deny that. I was a shitty husband and an

even worse father."

Brian rolled his eyes. "Don't I know. I was there, remember?" His temples pulsed. His phone rang, but he ignored it. Something buzzed his cell a minute later. Brian was unsure if it was a text or a voicemail, nor did he care.

The warden looked at Brian, but he was lost inside. "So, Mack, your visitor, Becca Hulls, pretended to be a social worker named Jennifer Olson. Is that correct?"

"Yeah. She came twice."

"And when she came back the third time, that's when she said her name was Becca Hulls?"

"Didn't we cover that last night?"

Harmon uncrossed his legs. "We're just trying to make sure we have the whole story."

Brian joined the men at the table. "Did this woman say where she was from?"

Mack nodded. "Carson Springs, Wisconsin. It…"

The color drained from Brian's face. He grabbed the Coke and upended it.

"What?" Harmon looked at him. "What's going on?"

Brian held up a warning hand. "Is that the town where you left…*my sister*?" Mack nodded. "So, it's possible this Becca Hulls really is…Wren."

Mack tipped his head. "Yeah, it's definitely possible. The pieces fit." He looked at Harmon. "But there's something else you need to know."

"What?" Brian leaned forward.

"If any of this is true, I'm…" Mack's voice trailed off.

"What?" Brian ground his teeth together. "What?"

Frown lines grew on Mack's forehead. "The woman claimed she grew up in a cult. She also said her father beat her."

"Doesn't sound a lot different than how I grew up, does it, *Dad*?" Suddenly, Brian turned toward the warden. "Carson Springs. That's a few hours from here, right?"

"Give or take. Why?"

"There's a group up in the hills known as *Life Visions*."

Harmon nodded. "Yeah, I know them well. Andrew Godley's been spreading his wings, grabbing every penny he can. A small subsection of that group started not far from here."

"The woman in Cedar Point…" Brian looked at his father before leaning closer to Harmon. "The case the BCA's working on," Harmon nodded, "she was from Carson Springs too."

"Are you thinking they may be connected?"

"It's possible." Brian looked up at the ceiling. "I want any information on this cult in Carson Springs. And I also need the contact info for the company that employed Rebecca Hulls when she was Jennifer Olson."

"I can have Amanda get that."

Suddenly, the door opened, and the guard who brought Mack Enderly into the room entered. A young woman in a uniform followed him.

"Warden Harmon, sir. There's a call from a woman named Becca Hulls." She nodded toward Brian. His eyes widened. "She said she's been trying to contact Chief Enderly. Her exact words were, 'If I don't talk to Enderly soon, he can kiss his wife and stepsons goodbye.'"

Brian's chair flew into the wall when he stood.

Amanda grabbed the phone from the counter behind the warden, adjusted the cord, and set it on the table. "Line two."

Harmon looked at the guard and nodded toward Mack. "Take him back to his cell."

"I want to stay. She'll listen to me."

"Nobody's gonna listen to you. This is your doing, old man. If this woman touches a hair on my family's head, I'll kill you myself."

CHAPTER FIFTY-ONE

CHIEF BRIAN ENDERLY

Warden Harmon moved the phone to the corner between himself and Brian. He glanced at the chief before pushing the red blinking button and putting the phone on speaker.

"Harmon here."

"It's about damn time someone picked up." A tangle of rage and frustration buzzed across the line.

"Is this Becca? Rebecca Hulls?" Bob laid a hand on Brian's arm as a warning.

"Actually, it's not. My name's Wren. Recognize it?"

Harmon glanced at Brian and squeezed his arm harder. "Okay, Wren. What is it you want?"

"What do I want?" She huffed. "What I *wanted* was taken away from me forty-two years ago. What I *wanted* was a father who didn't beat the shit out of me just for the hell of it. A brother who didn't molest me. And to grow up in a family where I was loved."

"I'm sorry for…"

"Put my brother on the line," Becca bellowed.

"I'm here," Brian said, pulling his arm from beneath Harmon's grip and leaning toward the phone.

"Well, well, well, brother. I've been messaging you for the past twelve hours, and I've not heard a damn thing from you."

"I didn't know the messages were from you. I thought they were from…"

"Check your damn phone."

Brian scrolled through his messages. They had all come from Jane's phone. The wording of the last three made it clear they were from Becca.

"I'm sorry. I was in a meeting."

"There are things in this life that are a hell of a lot more important than meetings. Like maybe the life of your wife and stepsons."

Harmon pulled out his phone and texted. The woman who had informed him of the call entered with a notepad and pen. The warden pressed one finger to his lips and moved his thumb and finger through the air to mimic writing. She pulled out a chair with her foot, sat down, and scripted everything the woman said while Harmon recorded the call.

"Where are you?"

"I'm sitting in your living room having tea and biscuits with your wife." She grunted. "Where the hell do you think I am? Did you think I was just calling to chat?"

Harmon shot a look at Enderly. "Brian knows you mean business."

"You know what, brother dearest? You forgot one thing when you reinforced this place. Sometimes, the biggest threats walk in through the front door." Her evil laugh sent chills through Brian. "I know you would love to see what's going on, but that's impossible. Your techie stepson shut the cameras down, so you're out of luck."

Brian scrolled through his phone and pulled up the video from inside the house. From multiple views of the room, he could tell Cole had shut the pinpoint light off but kept the cameras rolling. He could see Jane and the boys huddled together on the couch. "I want to talk to my wife. I need to know they're all right." He had to keep her in the dark about the camera.

"There's a lot of things I want too, but I'm not going to get them—so neither are you. You'll see them when you walk through this door—*alone*. Got it?"

"But I'm in Duluth. Cedar Point is almost four hours from here."

"I'm not going anywhere, and neither are these three." She laughed loudly. "But if you aren't here within, let's say, four and *a half* hours, your family won't be either." There was a short silence. Becca sighed. "Well, they'll be here, just not how you want them to be."

Brian gritted his teeth. "DO. NOT. HURT. MY. FAMILY."

"Oh, Brian. *I* am your family. Don't you get it?"

"Jane?" Brian yelled.

"Brian, I'm…"

"Shut up, bitch." Brian watched Becca bean Jane with one of the heavy decorative balls she plucked from the glass bowl. "That was a bad move, brother. Now, turn that siren on and get your ass back here before you make me do something I don't want to."

"I'm coming. Just don't hurt them."

"Listen to me. If you put one cop anywhere near this house, they're all dead. So, whether I hurt them or not is up to you. At this point, I've got nothing to lose."

The line went dead.

Harmon grabbed the pad and pen. "I'm going with you. I'll make calls and watch the camera while you drive."

Brian's heart raced. His words could not escape his sister's stranglehold.

CHAPTER FIFTY-TWO

DEPUTY JEFF PORTER

Officer Keith Harlow was so new to the brotherhood that his umbilical cord had not yet been cut. Someone checked on him multiple times a day, giving the Cedar Point Police Department a little freedom. Borrowing officers from Alexandria meant you got whomever they sent. Jeff and Brian were just grateful to have someone sitting at that desk twenty-four hours a day—even when the station was closed.

It was unlikely Harlow would make it through his first year. When Jeff entered the station at 9:00 a.m., the officer stood on a chair, playing with a lime-green yo-yo.

Porter crossed his arms and leaned against the doorframe of Brian's office. He watched the man complete several tricks while he waited to be noticed. Minutes passed. With each one, Jeff grew more and more angry. Finally, he stepped forward and tapped the officer's shoulder. He ducked when the hard plastic double disc swung in his direction.

"Shit!" Harlow nearly dumped the chair as he fell from it. He pulled the earbuds from both ears. "Sorry. I didn't know anyone was here."

"That's apparent." Jeff tipped his chin down. "But for future reference, this is a police station, not a venue for a yo-yo competition. Besides, with everything going on right now, you always need to be on your toes."

The inexperienced cop nodded once. "Got it. But give me a break, man. Officer Delaney called in sick for her shift, so I've been here for almost sixteen hours."

Jeff held his palms out in front of him. "Not my problem. Respect the uniform, *man*. You're damn lucky it was me who walked in here and not the chief." He cocked his head. "Or worse. I could have been the murderer."

Harlow picked up the chair and put it back against the wall. "Right." His sarcasm was thick. "You don't even know if someone was actually murdered. You're just guessing."

Warmth rose on Porter's cheeks. He had no time for this smart-ass kid. You could bet he would be placing a call to the Alex station to file a complaint. No one wanted a wanker like Harlow defending anything. And Barney Fife sure as hell should not be carrying a gun.

Porter stepped toward the chief's office but turned back toward the uniformed jerk. "Not my call. The BCA's on it now. All I need is for you to be a warm body sitting here in case something happens."

"And that's what I was doing."

"With headphones in? How in the hell could you even hear the…" An exasperated breath inflated Porter's cheeks.

He picked up one of the cups of coffee he had placed on the lateral filing cabinet and set it in front of the man before heading into Brian's office with a matching one. On the desk was a box addressed to Brian. It had no return address, postmark, or tracking information. Porter backed toward the door, unsure of the contents.

"What's with this box in here?"

Officer Harlow appeared in the doorway, nearly crashing into Porter. He shrugged. "Ah, some guy delivered it last night around seven."

Porter eyed him. "And you didn't think to let someone know?"

"What for? The guy said it was a package the chief already

knew about."

"Shit." Porter moved gingerly toward the desk and leaned in. "At least it's not ticking. But that doesn't mean diddlysquat."

"What are you worried about? The guy seemed trustworthy."

"Yeah, and a skunk's cute, but I wouldn't trust it." Porter scowled at the man. "I need to give the chief a call." He nodded toward the door, indicating for the officer to leave, but he did not take the hint. "No problem," Jeff mumbled sarcastically. "I'll just go to my office and make the call." He disappeared out the door.

"Okay," the officer said. "But I don't know why you don't call from here."

Porter rolled his eyes and slammed his door.

"No answer," he said as he rounded the corner back into Brian's office several minutes later. "What the hell?"

Harlow stood next to Enderly's desk. While Jeff was making his call, the dipshit had opened the package and dumped the contents on the desk. "See? Like I said, nothing to worry about." He turned the empty box toward Porter.

"Is your head up your ass? Had there been a bomb in there, you would have blown us both up." Porter rubbed his temple. "And not only that, but you've tampered with evidence and made it difficult to get fingerprints."

Harlow waved his hand over the desk. "For this?"

Porter snapped his fingers and pointed toward the door. "Get out," he growled.

"But…"

"Now," he hissed. "Get out before I throw you out."

Harlow pointed a finger toward the floor and then at the door. "Do you mean out of this office or…out-out?"

Porter huffed loudly. "Station. Cedar Point. Minnesota. GO! And don't cross paths with me again."

When the station door closed, he sighed deeply. "What a friggin' moron."

He dropped into Brian's chair and picked up a yellow

sweater. He recognized it as the one Mauri always had draped over the back of her chair. The deputy rolled his chair sideways and looked out the door. The sweater was gone. It made sense that she would have taken it with her when she went into hiding, but it also concerned him greatly. Had someone gotten to her? Was this their way of letting them know? A bright pink sticky note with the letter *M* written in black marker was stuck to the sleeve. It looked like Mauri's writing, but one letter was not enough to be sure. And even if it was, it could have been proof she was being held captive.

Porter lifted the sweater. Beneath it was a white sheet of paper folded in half. He dropped the sweater into the cardboard box and opened the paper. It was DNA results from the Minnesota Forensic Lab. Not knowing who it was for, Jeff gleaned that *Male A and Female A were unrelated.* Holding the paper, he flipped through cases in his mind that would have had Brian searching for relative information between a male and a female. But try as he might, he could not come up with a single case.

He set the information on Brian's desk and tried to piece the mysterious contents together. Porter picked up the paper again. The requesting officer was listed as *M. Locke.* Jeff rubbed his forehead in disbelief. Mauri had made the request. This was not going to go well with Brian. The chief's assistant had not only impersonated an officer, but she had requested testing for personal…

"Oh my God," he mumbled as he shrank into Brian's chair. His arms hung at his sides in disbelief.

This was *about* Brian—Brian and the woman claiming to be his sister. Jeff stared at the results again. *Unrelated.* So, the woman had either been mistaken, or she was after something. But what?

Jeff plucked Mauri's sweater from the box and shook it. A small sheet of paper fluttered to the floor. It was a black and white photo printed on a LaserJet printer. Porter's jaw dropped when he looked at the grainy photo. *Terah Dixon.* There was no mistaking it. The woman who had either been murdered *or had committed a murder* had been the woman who claimed to be Brian's sister.

The deputy moved to the window and tilted the paper toward the light. Only in this photo, she had dark hair, not blonde.

CHAPTER FIFTY-THREE

BECCA HULLS

It was sixteen steps from one side of the living room to the other. Becca had walked and counted it at least a hundred times, trying to stay awake. As she passed the couch, she turned and moved sideways, always keeping her eyes on her three captives. She had hoped to find Jane home alone. That lightweight would have been an easy hostage. Even Jane and Cole together would not have been difficult. But that big guy made her nervous as hell. The only advantage she had was the gun.

With the open kitchen and living room, she could keep an eye on her hostages while fetching a drink from the fridge. The caffeine from her brother's Diet Coke supply helped her stay awake while she waited for him to return and face the music. And music, which would sound a lot like gunfire when Brian walked through the door, was inevitable. From the far side of the living room, she had a direct line of sight to the front door. All she had to do was wait.

Becca checked the clock. It was still at least two hours before he would hit the *Welcome to Cedar Point* sign. *Welcome?* That was laughable. Becca was about as welcome in the small town as a root canal.

She stood behind the island and adjusted her pants. *Soda in—pee out.* The adult diapers solved that issue, but they were uncomfortable as hell. She knew how long they would last before they gave up. It was one of the advantages of working as a personal care assistant. She laughed. No one ever claimed she was good at her job.

When the boys claimed the need to take a leak, she threw the large kettle that hung over the stove at them. The big one used it, but the little one did not.

Jane had said nothing. She had been reticent for hours. Since Becca beaned her with the heavy ball, she had not made a sound. *Concussion? Fear?* Neither mattered to Becca. One less whiny asshole to listen to.

Cole and his mother had fallen asleep. From what she could tell, the boys were taking turns keeping watch. Fear was good. It was to her advantage they believed she would kill them. At this point, it was her brother she wanted. They were just bait. But if things went south…

Becca's plan was playing out perfectly. She was so close to the finale that she could see the curtain open for the final act. A smile spread across her face as she imagined it.

"Let Mom go," Luke whispered. "You can hold me and Cole hostage until Brian gets here."

"Shut up," Becca hissed. "Just shut the hell up." She pointed the gun toward his face. "Do you think I'm stupid?"

She rubbed her forehead with her thumb and index finger. The early threads of a headache knotted in the back of her head and pulled across her forehead.

Becca smacked her lips. "Get me another Coke," she told him. "And don't wake anybody up, or you'll be the first one I kill."

Luke tipped his mom's head onto Cole's shoulder, rose from the couch, and did as he was instructed. Becca waved the gun between him and the sofa.

"Put it on the table next to that chair and get your ass back on the couch."

When he returned to the couch, his mother stirred. "Shh. Go back to sleep," he whispered.

His mom gently touched the angry lump on her forehead and winced before laying her head on Luke's shoulder, but she did not open her eyes. Luke watched her until her breath was even and shallow.

"If we really are your family and you want to have any kind of relationship with us, maybe you should let us go."

Becca dropped into the chair opposite the couch. "You don't get it, do you? That's not how this is gonna go." She laughed softly. "For the moment, you and your brother are my step-nephews." Becca swung the gun toward Jane. "And she's my sister-in-law." Glancing at her watch, she smiled. "But soon, I won't be related to any of you anymore."

"So, you're planning to kill Brian." Luke's jaw tightened.

"Look at that. You're not nearly as dumb as you look. You figured that out all by yourself." Becca clapped one hand against her wrist. She had no intention of killing them, but threats made for compliance.

Luke winced as the gun bobbed. "Be careful with that thing."

Becca smirked. "Why? Are you afraid to die?"

Cole opened his eyes and stretched. He noted his mom was still asleep. "So, you kill Brian—and maybe us," he whispered. "How does that get you what you want?"

Turning her gun toward Cole, Becca raised her eyebrows. "Look who's been awake and listening."

"Do you really think Brian's dad's going to accept you if you kill his son?"

The thudding in Becca's ears turned to rage. She pressed the heel of her left hand against her temple. "Shut up! Just shut the hell up!" Her head throbbed.

Becca could barely keep her eyes open. There was a freight train running through her head, and every time those two imbeciles spoke, the engineer laid on that damn whistle.

A large crystal bowl filled with more heavy silver balls of varying sizes sat in the middle of the Brazilian rosewood table Jane had taken from her birth father's house. Besides his money and his company, it was the only thing she had kept. The house and all the furnishings had been donated to a church that turned the mansion into transitional housing for the homeless and those in need.

With the gun still aimed at her hostages, Becca began emptying the bowl and tossing the silver balls onto the floor. Before it was empty, she vomited into it. Luke, an empathetic vomiter, closed his eyes and plugged his ears while Becca emptied her stomach into the thousand-dollar bowl. She wiped her mouth with her sleeve and dropped back into the chair. Exhaustion, lack of food, and the blinding headache were a gut punch she had not anticipated.

"That's disgusting." Cole bent forward and plugged his nose just before a bullet flew over his head. "What the hell is wrong with you?"

Becca pressed an elbow into the arm of the chair and leaned her cheek into her hand. "I told you to shut up," she hissed.

"Do not hurt my boys," Jane seethed. "If you do, you'll have to deal with me."

Another shot hit the wall over their heads. This time, it shattered a large mosaic mirror trimmed in black crystal. Shards of glass rained down onto the floor behind the couch.

"Finally found your voice, did ya? Well, keep talking, and I'll kill all three of you and still have two bullets left for my effing brother."

Luke glanced at Cole.

"What was that?"

"What?" Luke asked.

"That look." Becca pressed a hand to the back of her head. "What was it?"

"Just a look." He looked at Cole again. "I wanted him to shut up."

"Smartest thing you've done all day." Becca's voice pinched. The pain ran from the top of her head to her toes.

Cole pressed his shoulders together. "Can I stand? My back hurts from sitting here all night."

Becca stared at him and contemplated the small one's request. If he tried anything, a single bullet would be all it took. "Fine. But do not move from the front of that couch."

Cole stood. Luke followed. Another bullet hit the wall near the ceiling. Jane screamed, and Luke dropped onto the couch.

"What the hell are you doing? I thought you didn't want to hurt us."

"Did I say *you* could get up? The next time you do something stupid, you'll be lying on the floor permanently."

Jane slid to the front of the couch and folded her hands in front of her. "Let the boys go, Wren. Hurting them isn't going to have any effect on Mack. He doesn't even know them."

Becca mimicked Jane, repeating the same sentence in a snotty voice. "Do you think I give a damn what you think? Mack Enderly would do anything for his son right now. As long as I have his family, I have leverage."

"How do you know that?" Jane tilted her head slightly.

"I know because I spent time listening to a crapload of hogwash about how bad he feels about hurting him. It made me want to puke."

Jane's eyes narrowed. "When did you see him?"

Becca tried to chuckle, but the pain was too intense. "Didn't you know? I was his social worker."

"You're a social worker?"

"No, but I'm a damn good actress."

"And a liar," Luke muttered. He ducked as two bullets whizzed over his head. He raised both hands. "Sorry," he grunted.

Becca pressed a hand to her forehead and growled. The pain was intense. All she wanted to do was close her eyes, but she could not. She leaned against the back of the chair and blinked slowly several times. Luke raised two fingers and whispered to his brother.

Becca stood quickly, too quickly. She leaned against the chair and steadied herself. "What the hell was that?" She mimicked Luke's gesture. "What did you say to him?"

Cole pulled the collar of his T-shirt away from his neck and wiped away the sweat that beaded on his upper lip. "It was a peace sign." Cole glanced at his brother. "He wanted me to stop talking."

She wagged the gun toward Luke. "He's the asshole who should shut the hell up."

Jane slid forward again. "Wren…"

"Move your skinny little ass back onto that couch before I shoot you."

Jane did not move. "Wren, listen. I know you're hurting. I understand rejection more than anyone."

"Waa-waa-waa. I don't give a shit how much you suffered, lady. All I care about is that your family hurt me—and now I get to retaliate."

"*We* didn't hurt you, Wren. That was Mack."

"Exactly." She rubbed the back of her neck. Her stomach churned again as another wave of nausea threatened to appear. Becca swallowed it down.

"So why are you doing this to my family?"

"Did you just hear yourself? *My* family? You just alienated me, made me feel like I don't belong."

"That's not what I…"

"Shut up. Just shut up." Becca vomited into the bowl again. Dry heaves clutched her gut.

Luke jumped up and dove at her. Becca lifted the gun and shot, and Luke dropped to the floor.

CHAPTER FIFTY-FOUR

CHIEF BRIAN ENDERLY & PRISON WARDEN ROBERT HARMON

The siren blared as Brian raced south on Interstate 35. The sound echoed inside him, piercing his soul with the sharp, ominous high-low repetition. By the time he turned off the exit ramp for Highway 23, heading toward Mora, he was numb. The sounds had faded to white noise. All he could see was his wife and stepsons being held captive by his sister, a woman he had never met.

Warden Bob Harmon rode shotgun. Keeping an eye on Brian's phone, he gave the play-by-play of events as they unfolded. His periodic reports were not enough for the chief. He wanted to see everything.

"What's going on?" Brian asked.

"It's fine. Everybody's okay," Harmon lied. The last shot had Luke on the floor, holding his leg and writhing in pain. It was the last thing he wanted Brian to know. He looked at the time on the screen. "We've got about two hours. Just keep driving. I'll let you know when to worry."

"I think I need to call her."

"Who? Jane or the woman?"

Brian snorted. "You mean my *sister*? Yes, her."

"Think carefully about that. It could set her off. Jane and the boys are holding their own—for now." Harmon continued to watch the events unfold on the tiny screen, praying the bullet Luke had taken had not hit an artery. The phone vibrated. "You've got a phone call coming in from your deputy again."

"Don't answer it. She was very clear. No cops. She wants me—and only me." He shook his head. "Porter'll want to go over there and play hero. It's my family she's holding. I can't let her harm one hair on their head."

Harmon raised an eyebrow and gave him an ominous look. *It was already too late.*

"What?" Brian asked.

Harmon shook his head. "Nothing. Just keep driving."

The siren echoed through the two-lane, tree-lined roads and the small towns between Mora and St. Cloud as they headed toward Interstate 94. It was not the most direct route, but it was the fastest.

"One more," Harmon muttered under his breath. "Come on, boys."

"What the hell does that mean?" Brian laid on his horn and skirted around a car that had not pulled over.

Once the Explorer was under control and Bob no longer feared for his life, the warden released a long breath. "Bullets."

"She's shooting?" Brian banged the steering wheel with his palm. "What the hell. Why didn't you…"

"She's not shooting *at* them," Harmon lied again. "They're just warning shots."

"Can you tell what kind of a gun it is?"

"I can't, but I'd say from the size, it's a Beretta. It's small. I can barely see it."

"If so, it's seven rounds. How many shots has she fired?"

"Six," Harmon said as he prayed for Luke to get up.

"One more."

They both knew that was all she needed to destroy his family.

One.

CHAPTER FIFTY-FIVE

DEPUTY JEFF PORTER

Deputy Porter had tried to contact the chief for the past three hours, but it was as fruitless as trying to get in touch with his teenage son. There was no response. For some reason, he had gone off the grid. Most likely, he and Harmon were still meeting with his dad to discuss the woman who had visited Mack. He refused to leave a text about Mauri digging her hands into Brian's past.

By eleven, someone new was stationed at Mauri's desk. From the looks of it, the officer was close to retirement. He was bald and had a paunch that weighed down on his belt so heavily, it had the potential to snap it in two. But in the fifteen minutes Jeff spent with him before heading out on rounds, the guy seemed to be the most dedicated employee he had seen yet. Evidently, the message he had left with the chief at the Alexandria station had had an impact.

Porter drove to the city limits on each side of town. As Brian had instructed while standing outside 539 Hanley, the people of Cedar Point were going about their daily lives. Even with the added police presence and the cordoned-off house, life went on.

He turned down a side street past Enderly's house. An older white CR-V was parked near the driveway. It most likely belonged to a friend of the boys who was there to game. If anything had been wrong, he would have heard about it.

The deputy slid into a booth at Knuckles and ordered a BLT on sourdough and an order of tots. The waitress had just walked away when a man in a dark sports jacket, white shirt, and blue checked tie scooted into the booth across from him. He set his half-eaten roast beef sandwich and glass of soda in front of him and grabbed a couple of napkins from the basket.

"David Hunt, BCA."

"Badge?"

The man pulled his jacket open to expose the shield clipped to his inside jacket pocket.

"Deputy Jeff Porter. What can I do for you?"

"I know who you are." Hunt looked behind him, leaned toward Porter, and spoke softly. "I was recently brought in to look at the Terah Dixon case." Porter nodded. "I need to get a look at the crime scene."

"Have at it. The door's already open." The right corner of Jeff's mouth lifted upward. "Well, whatever's left after the chief took it out."

"I was hoping you could talk me through the case."

Porter looked at his watch. "I can head over there with you after lunch."

Hunt nodded. "That'll work." He picked up his sandwich and took a bite. "Nice little town you have here." He retrieved his napkin and wiped the ketchup from his upper lip. "I spent most of my life in Minneapolis. I worked there and in Rochester for a decade and a half before moving out to God's Country." Hunt smiled. "Turns out God's been keeping Cedar Point a secret."

"How long have you been in Alex?"

"Hmm. About six months, I'd say."

The waitress set Porter's food in front of him and laid his check at the end of the table. "Anything else you need, Jeff?" He shook his head. "Enjoy."

Ten minutes of small talk was all it took for Deputy Porter to devour every crumb on his plate.

Hunt snatched Porter's check before he could grab it. "I got this." He untangled his thin six-foot-four frame, stood, and drank the last of his soda.

"I appreciate that," Porter nodded. "That's more than I get from the chief."

Hunt grinned. "You might need to tell him to step it up."

Porter rubbed two fingers and his thumb together. "Just tight."

"Seriously? I heard his wife's loaded."

Jeff nodded. "He's a man's man. It's her money. Not his."

"Good to know," Hunt said as he headed toward the register.

The sun was warm, but the breeze was cool when they stepped outside. Colorful leaves rustled in the trees. It was the first day Porter conceded autumn was winning. Shotguns blasted in the distance as hunters hoped to fill their freezers with wild game.

"Five-thirty-nine Hanley," the deputy said as he stood outside Knuckle's. "You can follow me." He looked around. "Where're you parked?"

Hunt pointed with his forehead. "Across the street. Silver Charger."

Jeff nodded once. "Nice. I'll circle back."

Porter headed to his cruiser, pulled left out of the lot, and slowly drove past Hunt's vehicle. In four stop signs, they were on Hanley. Porter turned on Clark, the street the driveway was on, and drove onto the asphalt pad at the end of the house. Hunt parked next to him.

The men ducked under the police tape. Jeff led the way down the stairs, through the shattered door hanging by a single hinge, and stepped into the apartment.

"So, Dixon lived down here?" He pointed toward the ceiling. "Who lives…"

Suddenly, there was a crash in the back of the house. Jeff

felt the hair on his arms stand at attention as he and Hunt reached for their guns.

"Who's there?" Porter hollered. "Come out and keep your hands where we can see them." He waited, but no one appeared.

Cautiously, the men headed in the direction of the noise. Porter pushed the bedroom door open, but the room appeared empty.

Hunt pointed toward the bed. The deputy checked beneath while the BCA agent covered him. Jeff shook his head. This time, Hunt jerked his head sideways toward the double-fold closet doors. He pointed at the doors while Porter stepped aside and yanked one open.

"On the floor. Both of you," the agent directed. "Now."

"Hands out," Porter said. He and Hunt each swiped a foot across the giant man's leg and took him down. The *oof* from the giant could have been heard at the station. "Fancy meeting you two here. Just passing through, my ass. Seems you found a reason to stay. I can't wait to hear what it is."

Joyce leaned on the bookcase and got down on her knees before lying face down on the floor. After handcuffing them, they confiscated two guns and a knife.

The woman kicked at Porter. "You're making a big mistake…"

The deputy shook his head. "I don't think I am. Let's see— just for starters, you're in possession of a stolen vehicle belonging to Warden Harmon."

"I take it you've met." Hunt jerked the giant man to his knees. "Get up."

"Yeah, we've met. Joyce and Tony—car thieves, assaulting a police officer, theft of police property, trespassing, and now, resisting arrest." He looked down at her. "Wanna add anything else?" Porter pulled her to her feet. "If I were you, I'd keep my mouth shut and your feet to yourself until you find a lawyer dumb enough to represent you."

"This is all a misunderstanding. I know…"

"Shut up, Ma," the big man hissed.

"Ma?" Hunt jerked the man's hands higher up his back. "Which one of you led the other into this life of crime?" Hunt snorted. "You're both pathetic." He pushed the man up the stairs and shoved him into the back of the squad car. "Move over, sonny. Make room for Mommy."

Porter slammed the door once they were inside. "They were here a few days ago—just passing through, they said." He grunted softly. "Those two have to be tied to the disappearance of Terah Dixon."

Hunt glanced into the back of the squad. The pair had their heads pressed together, whispering. "I'll follow you to the station. Once they're locked up, I'd like to come back and check out the place."

"Suit yourself, but your guys went over it with a fine-tooth comb."

"I'm sure they did, but sometimes fresh eyes see things others miss." Porter nodded.

Five minutes later, the two were locked in side-by-side holding cells at the back of the station. A block wall separated the pair.

Porter and Hunt stood in the hallway so they could see into both cells.

"Don't you two worry," Porter said. "You'll get used to living apart in about ten to twenty years."

CHAPTER FIFTY-SIX

CHIEF BRIAN ENDERLY, JANE ENDERLY & SONS, COLE & LUKE HART

Jane screamed when Luke dropped to the floor. She leaped from the couch and tried to comfort her son, who was writhing in pain. Luke was curled in a ball with his hand pressed against his leg.

Cole was on the other side of his brother. "Come on, buddy. Hang in there."

Like a wounded animal, a howl rose from the other side of the room. "Do you see what you made me do?" The pitch of Becca's voice was incredibly high. She pressed the heel of her left hand against her forehead. The gun bobbed up and down as she waved it between them. "This is on you," Becca yelled. She pointed the gun directly at Luke. "You. I would never have hurt any of you. I just wanted Brian." Her hand trembled as she swung it wildly. "*You* made me do this." She glared at Luke.

Luke's eyes widened as he looked at his brother. It was clear he wanted to tell him something. Cole bent closer to Luke. "Are you okay, buddy?"

Luke curled his head into his shoulder and whispered, "One bullet left." Then he moaned loudly. He had not taken his eyes off the woman who claimed to be his aunt. Cole watched as his brother slowly cupped one of the smaller silver balls on the floor and slid it to his side.

The woman closed her eyes, pressed a fist into one eyeball, and let out a bloodcurdling scream. Luke pitched the ball toward the hallway. Startled, Becca turned and shot in the direction of the noise.

"Now," Luke whispered.

Cole jumped up and moved toward her. Becca swung the gun toward him and pulled the trigger, but he did not flinch. Realizing it was empty, she threw it at him, but he ducked as it whizzed past. It slammed into the wall and slid down behind the couch.

She turned to run, but before she even took one step, Cole raised the vomit-filled crystal bowl and smashed it over Becca's head. Her eyes rolled back, and she fell, slamming her forehead into the solid coffee table. Cole grinned. "Strike three."

Luke sat up and leaned against the couch. He let go of a deep breath. "Nice hit, Cole." The brothers laughed.

Jane looked from one to the other. "What just happened?"

"Same page." Luke wagged a finger between him and Cole.

She looked confused. "We need to get you to the hospital before you lose any more blood."

Luke pulled up his pant leg. "Look, Mom. Not a scratch."

Jane's brows folded together. "You were faking it? You practically gave me a heart attack. I thought she actually shot you."

He nodded toward the lump on the floor. "She did too. I had to make you all believe it was real."

Cole knelt next to his mom. "Luke was counting rounds. Getting her to empty the gun was the only chance we had."

"She had to keep one shot for Brian, and she had two left. I had to get her to shoot one of them…"

His mother slapped his arm. "And what if she had killed you?"

Luke grinned. "She wasn't that good of a shot. Believe me. Dad taught me to shoot. She always shot to the right."

"I don't know whether to punch you or hug you."

"I'll take the hug." Jane threw her arms around Luke's neck and squeezed tightly. "Enough already," he grumbled as he pushed her away.

"I'd take one of those," Cole told her.

Jane pulled him into a hug. When she let go, she looked at Luke. "If you ever pull something like that again, I'll shoot you myself."

Luke pointed to the scattered glass balls. "I didn't have a choice. I had to get to the floor so I could grab one of these." He picked up a heavy ball, tossed it into the air, and caught it again. "I knew if I made a noise in the entry, she'd turn and shoot, thinking it was Brian. Once she shot that last bullet," he grinned, "it was all over."

Jane shook her head. "So, all this time, you were trying to get her to shoot at us?"

Luke's head bobbled. "Well, yes and no. I had to get her to waste bullets, but I knew she'd miss. I don't think she really wanted to kill us. You saw how she reacted when she thought she shot me."

Cole grabbed his phone from the floor and called 911 before tossing it onto the couch.

"Ambulance will be here shortly."

Jane looked from Luke to Cole. "You two are something, you know that?" She leaned against the couch and pressed her head to Luke's shoulder. "But just so you know, you're paying for the repairs to my wall, the mirror, and the silver balls." She took Cole's chin in her hand. "And you owe me one glass bowl and a new coffee table."

The three were still laughing when the front door opened. Brian scanned the room. Harmon stepped around him to get to Becca. "Wow! I can't leave you guys alone for a minute."

Jane jumped up and threw her arms around her husband. He lifted her off the ground and twirled her in a circle before setting her back down.

"Who was the genius who figured out how to disable the light without shutting the cameras off?"

Cole waved his hand. "Did you really think Luke could have done that?"

Brian smiled. "That was brilliant." He looked at the woman on the ground. "Is my sister…" The word stuck in his throat. Brian shook his head. "Is she alive?"

Cole looked at her. "Unfortunately, she's still breathing."

Harmon nodded. "She's going to have one hell of a headache when she wakes up."

The front door opened, and two EMTs wheeled a gurney into the house. Jane looked at Brian, confused.

"I watched every second," he waved a palm over the room, "of this, from the time we left Duluth. Brian's right. You guys were brilliant," The man said. "By the way, I'm Bob Harmon."

Jane hugged him. "Thank you." She looked at her husband. "Thank you for staying with him."

"Any time. I've actually come to like this guy in the last couple years."

Jane laughed. "Me too."

Brian stood next to the gurney and stared down at his sister. A lump the size of a lemon swelled in his throat. It was not love but disgust for everything she had put them through. Still, they had shared the same mother, the one person who had been there for him for the first eight years of his life.

The men wheeled Becca toward the door. "She needs to be handcuffed to her bed. I'll send an officer to take care of that and stand guard outside her room."

One of the paramedics smiled. "I don't think you need to put a rush on it. Based on the size of that lump, I'm pretty sure she's gonna be napping for a while."

Deputy Porter stepped out of the way as the men and the gurney exited the house. "I got word an ambulance was headed this way. Looks like you found Terah Dixon."

Brian shook his head. "That's not Terah. It's Becca Hulls. Terah's still missing."

"Are you kidding me? They look like they could be twins."

The chief nodded. "I know. It's shocking. Want to know

what's even more disturbing? That woman's my sister."

Porter shook his head. "Ahhh. No, she's not."

Brian nodded emphatically. "Yes, she is. My dad admitted it."

"Brian, you're not going to like this, but Mauri…"

Enderly sighed. "You're right. I already don't like this. If it involves Mauri, there's always trouble."

"I know," Porter agreed, "but you need to hear this. Mauri sent one of your soda cans and the one the woman drank from to the police forensic lab for a DNA test." He shook his head. "Doesn't match. She's not your sister."

"Are you kidding me? We're not related?"

"No."

"That woman practically destroyed my family because she thought we were siblings, and we're not?"

Porter folded his arms across his chest. "There's something else you should know. Mauri claimed to be Officer M. Locke to get them to run the test."

Warden Harmon clapped Brian on the back. "Sounds like you've got one hell of a good assistant there, Chief—much better than Joyce."

The corners of Porter's mouth lifted slightly. "Oh, speaking of Joyce, I have her and her ogre-looking son in lockup." He grimaced slightly. "But I haven't located your car yet. I know it's around here somewhere. The town's not that big."

Harmon smiled at Porter. "Good work, Deputy. I can't leave until you find it."

Jeff scanned the room. "You stay here with your family. I'll assign an officer to stand guard at the hospital." He turned toward the door. "Oh, I almost forgot. There's a BCA officer over at Terah's apartment right now looking through the crime scene."

"I thought the BCA moved on. What's this guy's name?"

"David Hunt."

Brian gave Porter a hard look. "I know every single person in the Alexandria office. I've never heard of David Hunt."

"He said he's new.

"How new are we talking?"

Jeff shrugged. "Six months."

Brian shook his head. "He's not one of theirs. They laid two guys off three months ago. I'm going over there to find out what the hell's going on." He turned toward the warden. "Bob, you can wait here."

Harmon shook his head. "Not on your life. I haven't seen this much action since my days in the department. I'm going with you."

Brian looked at Porter. "No sirens."

CHAPTER FIFTY-SEVEN

CHIEF BRIAN ENDERLY

Enderly and Harmon met Porter down the street from the duplex. They quietly passed by two houses before ducking under the police tape and taking the stairs two at a time into the basement apartment.

"Hunt? You here?" Porter called, peeking into the apartment with his gun drawn.

"Back here," the man called.

"It's a set-up," Brian whispered. "Let me go in alone."

The men waited. When Enderly reached the bedroom, he lowered his gun slightly and signaled the others to join him. The man was sitting on the edge of the bed with an open photo album.

"Are you carrying?"

Hunt pointed toward the dresser. "There's my gun."

When Porter and Harmon entered the room, Enderly waved his gun from his deputy to the man. "Frisk him."

Porter did as he was told. "He's clean."

"You're not Agent David Hunt, so who the hell are you?" Brian lowered his gun to his side but did not return it to his holster.

The corners of the man's mouth turned downward, and his shoulders fell forward. "My name's Daniel Hulls." Brian looked at Porter. "Becca Hulls is my sister." He tapped his finger on a photo. "This was me and Becca when we were young." He shook his head. "That was taken weeks before everything fell apart."

Bob Harmon stepped forward. "Pretending to impersonate an officer is a crime, Mr. Hulls."

"I am with the BCA." He looked at Deputy Porter. "Just not out of Alex. I work in Minneapolis."

Warden Harmon nodded. "I think you better keep talking."

Daniel closed the album and eyed Porter. "I think we should go to the station. Those people you're holding are involved with this too."

"Joyce and her son?"

Daniel's eyes were glassy. "Yes. They'll be able to explain the pieces I can't."

Porter scratched his neck. "But I didn't think you knew them."

"They weren't supposed to be here when we arrived before."

Enderly nodded. "All right, this is how it's going to go. You'll ride in the back of the squad car."

Daniel nodded. "I figured."

Chief Enderly opened the cell door of the goliath-sized man, cuffing him before he led him into the conference room. He attached the handcuffs to the thick metal ring on the top of the heavy table and sat down. Porter entered with a handcuffed Joyce. They put her on the opposite side of her son but left her untethered.

"Why are we in here?" Joyce asked. "Are you arresting us?"

Bob Harmon walked in with Daniel Hulls.

Joyce's face fell. "Oh, shit. I can explain."

Harmon nodded. "That's what we've been told. So, go ahead." He looked at Joyce's son. "First, I want your real name."

"Jake."

"Same last name as your mother, I presume?"

He shook his head. "It was, but I had to legally change it to Manderley to get hired at the prison." His booming voice matched his size.

Harmon frowned. "Which should never have happened."

"I know. But…"

"Right now, that's neither here nor there. We'll deal with that later."

Brian folded his arms and leaned them on the edge of the table. "Somebody better start talking."

Joyce looked at Daniel. "Let me start." She locked her fingers and twirled her thumbs. "Rebecca Ann Hulls is my niece, but she doesn't know that. Her mom was my older sister, Jeanne. Shannon Jeanne Mason was Becca's given name." Joyce's shoulders lifted as a sob tore through her. "I loved my sister more than anyone in the world, but Jeanne had a mental illness." Her voice broke. "From the time she could walk, she practically lived in one hospital or another. Every doctor swore they had the right combination of medications to help her. They'd send her home and hope for the best." She looked at Harmon. "But nothing ever worked for longer than a few weeks, and my parents would go see another doctor." Joyce shook her head. "My father referred to it as ping-pong doctoring." Another sob grabbed her voice. "Back and forth it went for her entire life."

"I'm sorry. It sounds like your family went through a lot," Brian said.

"Jeanne…"

"What was her last name?" Harmon poised his pen above a legal pad.

"Parker. We were known as the Parker sisters: Jeanne and Joyce." She twisted the handcuffs. "After a while, the community started referring to us as *the crazy and the normal one.*" Joyce bit her lip and stared at the far wall. "It was cruel.

Jeanne went through a lot. Her day-to-day struggles were something no one should have to endure. At times, I wondered how she could keep going." Joyce let go of a long breath. "Then, when she was sixteen, during one of her months out of the hospital, she got pregnant." She looked at Harmon. "It was the worst thing that could have happened. My father wanted her to have an abortion, but my mother fought against it. She thought maybe it was God's way of letting something good come from all their suffering." Joyce shook her head. "But it wasn't. Because Jeanne had to go off many of her meds, she was hospitalized for almost eight months." Tears rolled down her cheeks. "I saw her once, but she was so out of control that my parents refused to let me return. Much of the time, Jeanne was sedated."

Harmon rested his hand on Joyce's. "Do you want some water or something?" She shook her head.

"I just need to get this out." She sighed loudly. "On February 10, 1982, Jeanne's baby was born. My sister named her Shannon. She swore she would be the best mom in the world." Joyce slid her chair away from the table, crossed her legs, and rested the link of the handcuffs against her knee. "The doctors said that little girl couldn't grow up and have a normal life if Jeanne was around her at all. So, after a lot of conversations with my parents' pastor, my mother forged my sister's name on a stack of papers, and my father put the baby in the car and drove her to a town a good two hours away, hoping no one would notice the resemblance between the child and my sister."

"Where did he take her?" Brian already knew the answer but needed to hear Joyce say the words.

"It was a small town called Carson Springs, Wisconsin. Babies were often left on the steps of the church with the gold cross on the door. Because of the masses of people living in the hills around the small town, the church had luck finding homes for the babies." She pressed her thumb against one of the handcuffs.

Joyce nodded toward Daniel. "And that's where Daniel's family came in."

CHAPTER FIFTY-EIGHT

CHIEF BRIAN ENDERLY, WARDEN ROBERT HARMON, DEPUTY JEFF PORTER, JOYCE MAN, TONY MANDERLY, & DANIEL HULLS

Daniel folded his hands and stared at them through several deep breaths. "Much of this happened before I was born." His eyes narrowed. "My folks had been married for several years but could not conceive. The church…" He huffed. "It's hard to believe they called themselves that." He swallowed hard before meeting Brian's eyes. "Their mission was clear—*go forth and multiply*. If a couple couldn't have children, the church believed they had sinned against God." Daniel snorted. "And there were consequences for that."

"Consequences?" Brian leaned forward.

"Bullying by the elders. Shunning by friends and neighbors. Being forced to leave the community. Losing the house assigned to them by the church. Working as a servant for the elders. Or…"

"Or what?" Porter asked.

"Disappearing." His glance went from Harmon to Brian. "We're *not* talking by choice either."

"Death?"

Daniel nodded. "Disgusting, right?"

"Andrew Godley's a sick bastard. I hope he rots in hell."

As Daniel clenched his teeth, his jaw pulsed. "The community was filled with pregnant women and babies. But many didn't survive because seeing a doctor was forbidden. Families were told the sick or injured were in God's hands. Whatever happened was His will." He raised an eyebrow. "But I think it had more to do with the money. If people paid for care, it meant less for the church, less in Godley's pockets." Daniel looked down and sighed loudly. "And those children who were not perfect often died in...*accidents*." He drew air quotes around that word.

Joyce's eyes narrowed. "But how did Shannon, er, *Becca* survive, then."

"My folks hid her illness. Whenever she went off the rails, they hospitalized her immediately." He raised one shoulder. "She was gone a lot. They hid her absences from the community by claiming she was spending time with her grandparents—which was also against the church's laws—but somehow no one ever challenged it."

"Didn't she attend school?"

"It only met two days a week. Becca went when she was healthy, but girls only attended through 5th grade, so people didn't really notice how often she was gone. And she didn't become violent until after that."

"I can't believe how much you suffered because of my sister." Tears rolled off Joyce's face and landed on the table.

Daniel shook his head. "No. Your sister may have had a mental illness, but what Becca was dealing with isn't inherited. It's a coping mechanism victims use to deal with trauma. With Becca, it was sexual abuse."

Harmon's eyes narrowed. "Your father?"

"No. It was one of the elders who my mother was forced to clean for before Becca came to live with them. To the church, adoption was unnatural. Those who created their family that way were considered failures. Extra bodies helped them grow membership, but in their eyes, those children did not belong to the church."

"But that's not true." Joyce slapped the table. "Children, whether through adoption or naturally, are God's children." She laid her hand on her son's. "Tony was adopted."

"I agree, but the church did not. Therefore, until the child grew up and had children of their own, they were kept at arm's length. And because of that, my mother was forced to continue working for Mr. Crasser. Mom would take Becca with her every day. While she worked around the house, he would invite Becca into his study and..." His body collapsed forward. "It's sick. That whole group is sick."

"And he didn't touch you?"

"Oh, he did, but it didn't last as long because I was bigger than him by the time I was ten. My sister was tiny. She could be controlled."

"Terah...*Becca*, I mean..." Brian exhaled loudly. "She referred to it as a cult. Would you agree?"

"Oh, hell yes." Again, Daniel grew silent. The others watched him and waited. "Our lives were controlled in the name of God. Members didn't realize the mission of *Life Visions* had little to do with the Lord. It was meant to line the pockets of Godley and his minions."

"I'm sorry." It was a blanket statement. Brian was sorry for every part of Daniel and Becca's life, everything they had gone through, and what it had done to their family.

Daniel frowned. "So, since my parents couldn't bear a child, they opted to adopt." He unfolded and refolded his hands. "I know this sounds unbelievable, but there were three babies left at the church that week." He shook his head. "The pastor and his cronies were getting rich selling these children to the highest bidder. But my parents didn't have that kind of money, so my father helped around the church in exchange for a child."

Deputy Porter's jaw tightened. "Was Terah Dixon one of those babies?"

Daniel opened his mouth but closed it again. He was silent

for several seconds. "That's complicated." Leaning an elbow on the table, Daniel rubbed his forehead. "Because my dad was at the church when Becca…" he looked at Joyce, "*Shannon* was dropped off, he chose her because she had the same dark hair as my mother." He blinked slowly. "I honestly think she would have been fine had she not been molested."

Deputy Porter handed him a bottle of water from the small fridge.

"Thank you," Daniel said. He took a drink and recapped the bottle. He stretched his neck and shoulders. "Becca was three when things went south. Her imagination was off the charts. She made up wild stories." He folded his hands. "I was too young, but from what my mom said, the stories started around the same time as the abuse. She started hearing voices too, voices that told her to do awful things." He stared at the tabletop. "My parents began sleeping with their bedroom door locked." Daniel pressed his elbows to the table and leaned his forehead into them as if he were praying. "I slept in a small bed in their room until she moved away." He exhaled loudly. "When she started school, everything fell apart. Kids started to steer clear of her." He eyed Porter. "And *that's* when Terah arrived."

CHAPTER FIFTY-NINE

CHIEF BRIAN ENDERLY, WARDEN ROBERT HARMON, DEPUTY JEFF PORTER, JOYCE MAN, TONY MANDERLY, & DANIEL HULLS

"So, it was Terah who accepted your sister? Was she Becca's only friend?"

Daniel guffawed. "No. Terah didn't like Becca at all. But…"

"Then how did they become friends?" Harmon asked.

"Because they had to be." He slid his jaw back and forth. "Terah wasn't real."

"What do you mean she wasn't real?" Brian's booming voice made Joyce jump.

"Initially, my folks thought Terah was just Becca's imaginary friend. But as things got out of control, the doctors diagnosed her with Dissociative Identity Disorder, commonly called DID."

"What is that?" Brian stared at Daniel.

"It's where a person has multiple identities," Harmon said. "We had a prisoner with it."

Daniel nodded. "A person with DID can have from two to any number of personalities. They're referred to as alters or parts. Except on rare occasions, Becca was either herself or

Terah Dixon." He traced a wood grain line on the table. "When Becca was Terah, she was wonderful—sweet and kind—everything Becca was not, including blonde. Somehow, Becca got her hands on a wig. That was how Terah came to have blonde hair."

Brian looked at Porter. "Wow," he whispered. "When I spoke to her at Knuckles, she was so sweet."

"Yeah." Daniel shook his head. "Sometimes *Terah* would stay for weeks, other times, just a day or so. When she was there, the days were wonderful. We felt like a normal family. But when her headache started, we knew Becca was returning." He ran his tongue over his lips. "It wasn't easy for any of us. Terah and I got along so well, but when Becca…" He sighed. "Becca was evil. There's no other way to say it. As she got older, she accused me of all kinds of things that weren't true." He shifted his gaze to Porter. "Instead of blaming the church elder, she claimed *I* abused her. But I didn't. I swear. The thing is, she wasn't lying. It's what her mind saw as the truth."

"Did your parents know about Becca's abuser?" Porter asked.

"They did, but, like I said, Crasser was an elder. He would have destroyed them if they came forward." Daniel drew a deep breath and let it explode in a thunderous sigh. "And he did once Becca moved away. My sister hated growing up under the laws of *Life Vision*." A half-grin crossed his face. "As you've probably figured out, she's not exactly a rule follower. When she turned eighteen, she left home and moved to Minneapolis. After she left, my parents approached another elder about the abuse. That was a huge mistake. Becca wasn't the only child being abused, and Crasser wasn't the only scumbag in the church." A ragged breath cut through him, and his voice cracked when he spoke again. "Two days later, my parents were killed in a car accident driving into the valley." His face went white. "On a sharp corner, their car went over a cliff. Turns out, their brake line had been cut."

Joyce pressed her hands into the tabletop and turned toward

Daniel. "Oh my God. That's horrible. Did the police find out who did it?"

Daniel huffed. "Not in Carson Springs. Money buys silence there. And Godley and his underlings have money to grease the right hands." He looked at Brian. "And the right hands were… Well, you know."

"That shit pisses me off." Brian shook his head. "A few bad cops make us all look bad."

"I know," Daniel nodded. "I'm one of the good ones."

He folded his hands behind his neck, leaned into them, and stared at the ceiling. The silence in the room was deafening while they waited for Daniel to continue.

"Because of my parents, I was marked as a troublemaker. They placed me in the home of an old couple who never had kids. When I was old enough, I left and earned my GED. I was determined to become a cop and go after Godley and his cult. I moved to Minneapolis to attend school and to keep an eye on Becca. I became a police officer and then moved on to the BCA." He snorted. "But keeping an eye on my sister barely left me enough time to go after the church."

"It sounds like you gave up a lot to take care of her," Jeff said, touching his shoulder.

Daniel huffed. "I gave up *everything*. My wife divorced me and took my son and daughter to Idaho because she said I wasn't dependable. She said I chose Becca over them." He closed his eyes for several moments. "And she was right. I haven't seen my kids in almost three years." Daniel turned toward Harmon. "They didn't need me. Becca did."

"I'm so sorry." Joyce's voice cracked. "If Jeanne had never gotten pregnant, you…"

Daniel shook his head. "No. I made those choices. I could have let her go." His lips pressed tightly together. "But I chose her over my wife and kids. I live in constant fear she's going to hurt someone else."

Porter folded his arms and laid them against the edge of the table. "You said you worked out of Minneapolis and Rochester.

Is that because…"

"I followed her. I had to."

Joyce cleared her throat. "I guess that brings the story back to me."

CHAPTER SIXTY

CHIEF BRIAN ENDERLY, WARDEN ROBERT HARMON, DEPUTY JEFF PORTER, JOYCE MAN, TONY MANDERLY, & DANIEL HULLS

"Shannon," Joyce hung her head before mouthing an apology to Daniel, "I mean, *Becca* somehow got the idea that Mack Enderly was her father. To get to him, she forged a college degree, resume, and impeccable references good enough to get her hired by Thrive Mental Health out of Duluth. After Mack's first social worker died, Becca somehow got herself assigned to his case."

"Wait," Daniel said. "Mack's social worker died?"

Joyce nodded once. "I almost guarantee Chelsea's fall down the stairs wasn't an accident."

Daniel tightened his fists until his knuckles turned white. "I was so busy with a case that I lost track of Becca for a week. What could happen in a week? I thought." He clenched his teeth.

"This is not your fault," Harmon said. "None of this is because of anything you did or didn't do."

Joyce bit her lower lip. "The first time Becca showed up,

the hairs on the back of my neck stood at attention. On her second visit to the prison, I took her picture and laid it next to a photo of my sister at about the same age. They were nearly identical." Joyce's eyes were glassy as she looked at Harmon. "Her erratic behavior, mannerisms, and anxiety took me back to my childhood with my sister—which made my heart race."

"Is your sister still…"

Joyce shook her head. "No. She drowned a few years ago. She was sure she could walk on water during one of her hallucinations."

"I'm sorry," Harmon said. "I didn't realize."

"I didn't want you to know. It was easier to say goodbye quietly than try explaining about Jeanne." She kept her eyes on him. "I had been following Becca's life from afar. I didn't know what she looked like, but I knew my father had left her in Carson Springs. I spent years searching for information." She patted Daniel's hand. "As a matter of fact, I met your father years ago."

"What? How?"

"He was sitting at the counter in a bar, talking to the bartender."

"*Life Visions* allows drinking?" Deputy Porter asked.

Daniel nodded. "Men can do whatever they please. Women were barely allowed out of the hills."

"That's quite the double standard."

"That's Godley's ways—not God's," Daniel said.

Joyce crossed her legs and turned toward Daniel. "I heard your father mention his daughter *Becca*. I'm not proud of this, but I flirted and bought him drinks until he opened up. Then, I pried information from him." She twisted her hands. "I knew the Becca he described as his daughter was my niece. I asked to see a picture, but because *Life Visions* doesn't allow cameras, he didn't have one." Her hands shook uncontrollably. She clasped them together. "But I knew. I knew I had found her."

Harmon scribbled something on his notepad before looking up. "It must have been unnerving to realize the person claiming to be Mack's social worker was your niece."

Joyce nodded. "There's no way to explain it." She pressed a hand to her lips. "But there's more. That accident in the parking lot at the prison?" Harmon nodded. "I ran into her on purpose. I had to stop her long enough to talk to her. I mean, it was nothing more than a fender bender really, but it sure messed up my heap of junk. Her car was fine, though." She twisted her hands in front of her chest.

Daniel swiveled his chair toward Joyce. "I guarantee she thought her car was totaled."

Joyce shrugged. "Maybe, but I think I spooked her when I spoke to her. I called her *Becca*, thinking maybe she'd talk to me if she realized I knew who she was, but she ran." She turned toward Brian. "We lost her for a while, but eventually, she returned for her car. "And we followed her to Cedar Point. I had to save her from herself. It hadn't been that long since Jeanne died, and seeing her daughter made me realize I had to do what I couldn't do for my sister." She raised her eyes toward Harmon. "That's why we didn't return your car."

Daniel rolled his shoulders backward. "She's good at that— running, I mean. Becca always had these hallucinations and stories. None of them were real. She would tell elaborate stories about going places or doing things when she'd never left her bedroom. But like I said before, to her, it was all real. She was also extremely paranoid. She thought people were watching her, following her…" Daniel shook his head. "But almost none of it happened. When I followed her in Minneapolis, I would see her talking to herself on a bench, turning pages of an invisible book, or sitting in the middle of a baseball field picking a bouquet of imaginary flowers."

Harmon pressed his hands against his chest. "I can't even imagine how hard this was on you both."

Daniel nodded. "It almost killed me. I'm sure Joyce felt the same way with her sister." His voice was throaty. "But I had to protect her."

Brian cleared his throat. "Daniel, when we were searching

Becca's bedroom, we found a lot of blood on her sheets." He tipped his head slightly. "Would Becca have tried to kill herself?"

Words were elusive. Daniel shook his head until he could organize them into an explanation. "That was Terah."

"Wait. Terah?" Brian raised his palms in question.

Daniel's head bobbed. "When Becca gets extremely angry, she kills Terah."

"But…" Lines deepened across Porter's forehead. "Aren't they the same person?"

"They are. Now you see why this is so hard." His throat swelled as he swallowed the lump that was growing. "From the time she was young, Becca carried a knife. Every time we took it away, she'd get her hands on another one just as fast. When she was angry with Terah, she would…" his head bobbed, "*kill* her. One doctor explained it as if Becca were standing above Terah, looking down at her in a sort of out-of-body experience." His head dipped to one side. "The blood most likely came from Becca stabbing herself—imagining she was killing Terah."

"Are you kidding?" Brian shifted in his chair. "That's frightening."

Daniel glanced across the table at Porter. "Call the hospital and ask them if Becca has any fresh stab wounds."

Enderly nodded at Jeff. The deputy disappeared from the room, closing the door behind him.

Harmon slid his chair forward. "For my sake, can we review what I have so far?" He met everyone's eyes as he scanned the table. After flipping back several pages, he began paraphrasing. "Jeanne Parker was sixteen years old when she gave birth to a baby girl she named Shannon on February 10, 1982. Because of her lifelong struggles with mental illness, the baby was forcibly taken from her. Jeanne's mother forged her daughter's signature, which was needed to relinquish her rights to the child. Her father left the child on the steps of a church in Carson Springs, Wisconsin, claiming her name as Rebecca or Becca." He looked at the group to make sure his information was correct. No one disagreed.

"Jeanne's struggle with mental illness continued until the day she drowned a few years ago. Her daughter was adopted by the Hulls family of Carson Springs, where Rebecca Ann Hulls, her new name, was raised with a younger brother, Daniel, under a group of so-called Christians who followed the laws of Andrew Godley and *Life Vision*." He drew a deep breath. "Are we good?"

Daniel looked at Joyce. "So far."

Harmon scanned his notes. "After being sexually abused by a church elder, at a young age, Becca began experiencing multiple personalities—namely one—Terah Dixon." One eyebrow arched. "Daniel, were there other personalities?"

"Periodically, a new alter would pop up, but they never stayed for long."

"Could Becca summon Terah, pretend to be her?"

Daniel nodded emphatically. "Oh, yeah. She was extremely manipulative. If it would get her what she wanted, she became Terah."

Harmon wrote a couple words on his pad. "So, she also had several short-term personalities. She was diagnosed with Dissociative Identity Disorder or DID and was hospitalized much of her life." He scanned his notes. "Here's what I don't understand. What made her think she was Wren Brigham Enderly?"

"I can answer that." Tony's voice was deep. "I did a lot of digging into that church when Ma told me about Shan..., er, Becca. Daniel said they received multiple babies the week she was dropped off. I looked into several other cases from that church where parents claimed the child they adopted was not the one described on the birth certificate or as described based on birthmarks, eye color, size, and other things. So, I'm guessing the papers were accidentally switched."

Harmon narrowed one eye and tilted his head slightly. "Or *purposely* switched." His jaw tightened. "If you want someone to pay big money for a baby, you don't tell them the mother has a mental illness, nor do you hand over a child without background information. It's possible there were duplicate papers made from one of the other girls, and the originals for Becca were destroyed."

"How would the church have even gotten that information if a baby was dropped off?" Daniel stared at Harmon.

Joyce tilted her eyes upward. "The doctor filled out the paperwork with everything but the baby's *real* name. I'm sure my dad left the paperwork on the church steps with Shannon." She turned toward Daniel. "Sorry. *Becca*. I'm guessing they found out about Jeanne's background."

Harmon nodded. "And that's not something you want prospective parents to know."

Brian's eyes narrowed. "But my dad had no paperwork. He said he wrote his release on a McDonald's bag. I am guessing he just left her name and his signature."

"In that case, I would guess the church created paperwork or duplicated another child's—using the name your dad wrote. My guess is the people adopting these children were paying a pretty penny to that church. As I said, they needed to make that child look as good as possible—beautifully dressed and wrapped in a handmade baby quilt. And the paperwork had to make them appear perfect."

"That's disgusting." Brian gritted his teeth. "How did the law not get wind of this church in such a small town?"

Harmon looked at Brian. "Are you really asking that? *Money*. Money passed under the table. You'll be happy to know that church no longer exists. It was shut down over twenty years ago, and the people overseeing it disappeared." He scowled. "It's amazing what money'll buy you."

Porter walked into the room. All eyes turned in his direction. He held a sticky note between his fingers. "Recent stab wound just above the hip." He looked at Daniel. "The doctor also said there were multiple old scars that looked about the same size."

Porter waited for an explanation. "Every time she got angry

with Terah, Becca stabbed herself." He shook his head. "I know this is hard to believe, but unless you've lived with someone with DID, there's no way you can truly understand."

"So, since Becca and Terah are the same person, and Becca's in the hospital, the BCA's out hunting for no one. Correct?"

Porter poked a finger into his chest and then toward the door. "I'll go."

Brian tipped his head toward him. "Let Audrey know she can move home and that she has nothing to worry about. I'll replace the basement door tonight. Write up a press release, but I want to see it before it goes public." He glanced at the group. "We're going to have reporters all over this town in a matter of hours."

Porter nodded. "I'll run by your place too."

"Thanks. Tell Jane I'll call as soon as I can." Brian smiled at Harmon. "Thanks for taking the notes. You're almost as good at keeping track of things as Mauri." Brian looked at Jeff. "And call her, will you?"

"I already did." Porter disappeared.

Harmon continued his review. "Okay, so Becca believed she was Wren Brigham Enderly based on the paperwork she found. She showed up in Cedar Point, rented a house as Terah Dixon, and trekked back and forth to the prison in Duluth to glean information about Mack Enderly and why he abandoned her. When Enderly didn't give her the answers she wanted, she decided to hurt him by killing his son or anyone connected to him. Right?" He put a hand on Brian's arm and squeezed before continuing. "Joyce recognized her at the prison, called her out by name, tried to stop her by creating a fender bender." He looked at Daniel.

"Her car barely had a scratch on it," Joyce said.

"When Becca took off, Joyce and her son borrowed my car due to the damage of hers. They followed her to Cedar Point. Becca, *once again*, killed her alter, Terah Dixon. Then she dressed as a police officer and held the chief's family at gunpoint. She waited for Brian to show up so she could kill him as punishment for the man she believed to be her father, Mack Enderly. However, the chief's stepsons outsmarted her. At present, Rebecca Ann Hulls is in the hospital recovering from her injuries and is handcuffed to a bed with a guard stationed outside."

Joyce said. "It's surreal."

"What happens now? To Becca?" Daniel asked.

Brian released a long breath. "Well, you know as well as I do, that's up to the judge. But I'll do everything I can to encourage them to place her in a facility where she can get help rather than put her in the prison system. I think that would just exacerbate her condition." He huffed.

Daniel nodded. "There's something else you should know."

Brian eyes him suspiciously. "There's more?"

"Becca visited Serenity Park Hospital in Alexandria multiple times in the past couple of weeks. When I found out, I thought she was seeing a therapist." He looked directly at Brian. "But she wasn't. She was visiting your wife's ex-husband, Sean."

Brian slowly raised his chin. "Jane was supposed to see him Saturday morning, but that's when everything fell apart. The doctor said he had asked to talk to her." He looked at Harmon. "You and I are going over to see Hart. I don't think this story's over."

Brian got up and uncuffed Joyce and her son. "For now, you're free to go."

"Thank you." Joyce rubbed her wrists. She looked at Harmon. "I'm assuming there will still be charges filed."

Brian glanced at Harmon. "It's definitely possible. Warden Harmon or Officer Dillard could press charges—which they have every right to do. And if they decide to, I won't stand in their way." His jaw tightened. "You should have come to us immediately rather than interfering with this case."

Harmon eyed Joyce. "I agree with the chief. You work at the prison. Did it ever occur to you that what you were doing could land you there as an inmate?"

Joyce closed her eyes. "I just wanted to save her."

"By losing yourself? Your morals?" The warden shook his head. "For now, you'll be placed on unpaid leave. I've got a lot of thinking to do." He pointed to Tony. "But you're done at the prison."

Tony nodded.

"If I get my car back, I'll drive you back to Duluth tomorrow morning."

Joyce's shoulders dropped forward. "Thank you, Bob."

"Now, where's my car?"

"In Becca's garage."

CHAPTER SIXTY-ONE

CHIEF BRIAN ENDERLY & WARDEN ROBERT HARMON

By the time Enderly and Harmon left the station, the afternoon had turned into evening. They had a six o'clock appointment with Dr. Evenson at Serenity Park Hospital in Alexandria. If all went well, they would be able to talk to Sean.

Porter was holding down the station. Except for the paperwork, the BCA had closed the case, and the random men in suit coats had packed it up and headed home. The press release still had not been released, but it was only a matter of time before the townsfolk would know the secret the police had been harboring.

By 6:03 p.m., the chief and Harmon were seated in Dr. Evenson's office. They exchanged names, but Brian wasn't there for small talk.

"We were told Sean Hart had several visits from a woman recently." Bob set his notebook on the table.

"Yes. His cousin, Terah Dixon, was here many times. She's the one who helped bring his memory back."

Brian and Harmon exchanged a look. "She's not his cousin."

"What? Of course, she is."

"No, she's not. And her name's not Terah either. It's

Rebecca Hulls." The doctor looked confused. "Without speaking to Hart, I don't know what she was after, but my guess is she was digging for dirt on me and my wife."

"But she seemed…"

"She's not well." Brian crossed his arms in front of his chest and sank back into the chair. "My guess is she'll be a patient here before long."

The doctor shook her head. "How could I have been so stupid? I took her at her word."

"I wouldn't blame yourself," Harmon said. "She had everyone fooled, including us."

"We need to talk to Hart," Brian stood and pushed his chair against the table.

"Of course, but according to Terah…" Her shoulders dropped. "She lied. He never called her Emily. It was all part of… What did you say her name was?"

"Rebecca Hulls."

"It was part of Rebecca's act."

Brian jerked his head toward the door. "Sean," he said. "Let's go." He didn't have time to pussyfoot around this doctor. He needed to know what Becca had told him.

Sean was sitting at a table in his room when the three entered. Three additional chairs were scattered nearby. Each of the visitors claimed one.

Brian nodded at him as he sat down. "Sean. This is Bob Harmon, warden…"

"I know who he is."

Brian tapped the tabletop. "I suppose you do."

Dr. Evenson looked at Sean, seemingly shocked by his deep voice. "Clearly, you've been playing me for a while now. Exactly how much do you remember?"

He raised one shoulder. "Everything. I remember it all."

"Wow." Dr. Evenson dropped her pen on her pad. "Did you call *Terah*…" she glanced at Brian, "that woman who visited you, did you call her *Emily?*"

"No." Sean huffed loudly. "I knew she'd do something to

make me look like I'd lost my marbles again when she didn't need me anymore."

"How long has it been since you started to remember?" Dr. Evenson asked.

"About six months. At first, it was flashbacks. I wasn't sure what was real and what wasn't."

"Why didn't you say something then?"

Sean shrugged. "I've never trusted anyone in my entire life."

Brian watched Sean for several seconds. "So, the woman who came to see you was Rebecca Hulls. She has multiple personalities. Terah Dixon is one of them. At times, she can control them; other times, not." He waited for the pieces to connect. "What did Becca want from you?"

Sean shifted in his chair. His jaw tightened. The hatred he felt for Enderly radiated across the room.

Brian held Sean's eyes. "I get it. It's hard to trust anyone after you've been hurt." He snorted. "I should know. But if you still care about Jane, you'll do the right thing."

His jaw moved in and out as Sean clenched and unclenched his teeth several times. Finally, he looked down. "You," he whispered. He released a long breath before aiming his gaze back at Brian. "I'm pretty sure she wanted you. She told me she had a plan that would make us both happy—we'd each get what we wanted."

"So, what exactly did you want?" Harmon scratched a note on his paper.

Sean's eyes were soft when he looked at Brian. "My job. My boys. Jane. I wanted my life back—the way it was without my rage." He raised his eyebrows. "I know none of that's possible, but in talking with Ter… this woman, she made it seem like it was."

"So, she convinced you if she killed me, you could have Jane back, and it would punish my father. Is that right?"

"She didn't say it in so many words, but I'm pretty sure that's what she was planning. The thing is, I went right along with it. I guess I'm not doing as well as I thought."

"Other than information, did she want anything else?"

"Yeah. She wanted me to keep my mouth shut." He shook his head. "I don't know how I could think Jane would ever want me back after everything I did to her."

Brian stared at him. "You saved her life, Sean. That goes a long way with me in forgiving you. And my guess is, it does with her too." Sean looked down. "But forgiveness and wanting to reunite are on opposite sides of the world. Jane's happy. Your boys are great kids. When you get out of here, they'll see you again—or not. But that's up to them. You can't force it. But even if they do, it may not be like before. You understand that, right?"

"Yeah." His eyes were glassy. "I loved Emily, and I loved Jane. I still do. But I know it takes more than love to repair things I broke years ago."

"You're right, Sean. But you're moving in the right direction," Dr. Evenson said.

"Besides, it takes time." Harmon smiled slightly. "In time, maybe you can rebuild pieces—a friendship, perhaps." Sean returned a watery smile.

"Is there anything else you can tell us about Becca?"

"No. I hope you find her."

"She's in custody. You don't have to worry about her anymore." Brian stood, pushed his chair in, and offered his hand to Sean.

Sean rose and accepted the peace offering. "We'll see you on the outside one of these days. And I'll let Jane know you'd still like to see her."

A single tear rolled down Sean's cheek. "I appreciate that."

"I'll be back in a few minutes, Sean," Dr. Evenson told him.

Once outside Sean's room, Brian nodded to the doctor before he and Harmon walked away.

EPILOGUE

ADMINISTRATIVE ASSISTANT MAURI LOCKE
& CHIEF BRIAN ENDERLY

"Mauri," Chief Enderly yelled. Before he got the last syllable out, she was standing at his desk with a Diet Coke.

Brian laughed. "God, I missed you."

"What?" Mauri pulled her neck back and squared her shoulders. "Were you just nice to me?"

The chief shrugged. "Hmm. I guess I was." He raised an eyebrow. "But if you ever tell anyone, I swear to God, I'll deny it."

"I wouldn't expect any less." Mauri grinned.

Brian looked at his computer screen and grumbled. "Now, get back to work before I dock your pay."

"And there's the boss I know." She raised an eyebrow. "Oh, I just remembered something." She laid a hand on the back of his laptop and pressed it closed. "You're an ass."

Brian rolled his eyes and pointed toward the door. "Get out."

Mauri had spent her first morning back scrubbing and sanitizing every inch of the office. Evidently, the revolving door of fill-ins had never used a vacuum or a dust rag in their entire life.

Finally, satisfied with the lack of germs in the office, she sat down and stared at her new computer screen. Her cell phone pinged, skyrocketing her almost out of her chair. She glanced at the text message from her sister. *Check your email. I'll be waiting for your call.*

Mauri pressed the email button on her phone. Since she started her cleaning frenzy, three new messages had come into her personal account. The middle one was from Meggie.

She clicked on it. The email had been copied and pasted into three distinct parts. When she got to the third, her jaw hit the floor.

"Gotta leave for a minute, Boss," she called in an airy voice. "I won't be long."

"Whatever," he mumbled.

Mauri went outside, walked to the back parking lot, and climbed into her car. She pressed her sister's number. It barely rang before Meggie picked up.

"Sooo…" was all her sister got out before Mauri started in.

"Are you kidding me? I'm kind of freaking out here."

"Babies are a beautiful thing, aren't they?" Meggie laughed.

"Babies?"

"I just mean in general."

Mauri nodded. "Right. Oh my god! Have you mentioned this to anyone else?"

"Not yet. I thought it was your news to tell."

"I. I. Aye-aye-aye!" Mauri mumbled.

"Go to the website. But right now, I have to go. I'm already late for a massage. But call me later. I would love to talk."

Mauri sat in the car for a few minutes before climbing out. Her legs felt like rubber, making crossing the lot back to the station nearly impossible.

"I'm back," she said when she stumbled in.

Brian mumbled something that barely registered.

Mauri sat in front of her computer and logged into the site Meggie had mentioned. For the next few minutes, she clicked on every button. Finally, she printed out an image of a single page. She snagged it from the printer and stared at it.

Slowly, she walked into Brian's office and fell into the chair opposite his desk.

Brian looked at her. "Are you okay? You look like hell."

"Thanks, Boss."

"What's going on?"

Mauri looked at the paper she held in her hand. She tried to lay it on Brian's desk but could not let go. Finally, he pulled it from her.

His eyes grew wide. "What? What the hell? Is this even…"

"Possible? It sure looks like it."

"Shit."

"No kidding. I never expected this to happen so…"

Brian shoved his chair back, moved to the front of his desk, and dropped onto the seat next to her. "This is too much. How did this even happen? I didn't even know you…"

She poked him in the ribs. "You don't know where babies come from?"

"Be serious. This is too frickin' weird."

Deputy Porter walked into Brian's office. He looked from one shocked face to the other. "What's going on in here?"

Brian handed him the sheet of paper. Porter scanned it and started laughing hysterically. "This is the best news I've heard—ever." He turned toward Mauri. "Congratulations. I know you've always…"

"Is it good news?" Mauri's face was white. "Really?"

Porter walked behind the desk and dropped into Brian's chair. "The best." He grinned at Mauri and then Brian. "Just tell me one thing. Do we have to start calling you *Wren* now?" He slapped his knee.

Mauri looked at Brian. "Boss…"

Porter laughed. "The best part is that you don't have to call him Boss anymore. You can call him *brother*."

"Why was your DNA even on a public site?" Mauri asked.

Brian rubbed his hands together. "Jane convinced me to put it out there in case Wren…" he pointed to her, "in case *you* were looking for me. Why was yours there?"

"My sister bought me the kit. Now that our mother is gone,

she thought I should know more about my…" She glanced at Brian, "family."

Brian frowned when he looked at Porter. "Wipe that damn grin off your face."

"This," he rotated his open hands, palms down, in front of them, "explains a whole lot."

"Like what?" Brian asked.

The smirk on Porter's face widened into a full grin. "Like why you two fight like siblings. It's because you *are*." He stood. "I can't wait to tell…"

"Get out," Brian and Mauri growled together.

When he left, Brian stood, pulled Mauri to her feet, and wrapped her in a bear hug. She felt his tears tumble down her face, intertwining with her own.

Finally, Brian planted his hands on Mauri's shoulders and held her at arm's length. "Don't think this means I'm going to be nice to you or put up with any of your crap."

Mauri swiped a hand across her face. "I didn't think you would."

"Good." He turned. "Now, get back to work."

She grinned. "You got it, Boss."

Sitting at her desk, she heard Brian talking to Jane on the phone.

"I'm inviting my *sister* for dinner tonight," he said. Mauri heard the smile in his voice.

She grabbed another Diet Coke and headed into his office. She circled behind him and wrapped her arms around his neck before returning to her desk.

What Brian was feeling had to be so much more than what she felt. Mauri had grown up with a sibling—adopted, yes—but they had always been close. Brian had been an only child.

Today, all that changed.

ACKNOWLEDGMENTS

Books are not created in a vacuum. They are brought to life by a team of people who believe in both the author and the story. I am forever grateful for my team.

My husband, Mitch—Without your encouragement and support—alpha-reading, cooking, scheduling, tracking events, and keeping me in chocolate and water, I would never have been able to fulfill this crazy dream of mine. You are the best!

My beta readers, Barb McMahon, Laura Chevalier, Bridget Christianson, DeeAnn Eickhoff, Cheryl Meld, Ruth Novack, and Linda O'Neil—I can put the words on the pages, but your thoughtful suggestions make the story so much better. Thank you for helping me create magic.

My go-to guys for this novel, Curt Graff and John Adler—You answered every question I threw at you about police work. I appreciate your help.

My editor, Beth—Where would I be without you? There are not enough words to thank you for all you do for me.

My cover designer, Terrie Carlson—Your painting for this book is nothing short of perfect. It was as if you were in my head painting what I saw. A thank you is just not enough.

My kids, Brandon and Taylor—Thanks for letting me be your mom. I got the best gig.

My 3.8-pound Garden Parti Yorkie, Harper—You always sit on my desk or in the window seat and keep me company while I write. You always let me know when I need a break—or when *you* need one. You also invent a lot of new words when you walk across my keyboard. But I love you!

Finally, to my readers—Your comments, messages, and reviews let me know I picked the perfect "second act". You bring me so much joy. Thank you! Keep reading.

This sequel would never have come to fruition without you. I never planned to write a sequel. I loved the cliffhanger. You did not. Your insistence pushed me to write this book. Thank you. Together, we created something amazing.

AUTHOR'S MESSAGE

I did not choose writing; it chose me. When I was four, my mom taught me to use my imagination—watch people and tell their story—*but make it bigger*. Essentially, she taught me to lie. Because of her, I knew I would become an author one day. This has been an amazing "second act" for me. Every day, I am grateful for this gift I have been given.

This book was never meant to come to life. The cliffhanger at the end of *The Lies They Told* was intentional. I wanted readers to imagine their own ending. But then, I was bombarded with messages begging to know Wren's story. So, after a great deal of internal turmoil, a lot of soul-searching, and an incredible trip to Vermont, where the storyline revealed itself to me, I changed my mind. And I am so glad I did.

Researching religious cults and Dissociative Identify Disorder (DID) sent me down a deep, deep rabbit hole. I spent months digging into both. And just when I thought I knew everything there was to know, a new question would pop into my head and take me in a whole different direction. That process was exhilarating and exhausting. But once the first words hit the page, I felt my heart race with excitement.

Terah, one of Becca's alters, found her peace in Cedar Point. Where is your peaceful place? Do you visit often? Whether you can or cannot, wherever you are, find your people. Take care of yourself—mentally, emotionally, and physically. Life gets better when you find your happy place.

And remember, you are not alone. You are *never* alone.

OTHER BOOKS BY MARY PERRINE

HIDDEN

For Mary Claire, hiding wasn't a game. Abused as a child, she learned to hide in a room full of people. All she had to do was stop existing and begin surviving. As an adult, Claire fears history may be repeating itself. Only this time, her daughter may be the victim.

"This is a story that needed to be told—one we all need to hear."

THE LIES THEY TOLD

Jane wasn't an "oops baby". She was a "dammit". As a young child, she was neither loved nor cherished. Forty-seven years later, she discovers her entire time had been a life—carefully orchestrated to protect everyone but her—"Plain Jane".

"So many twists and turns. Be sure to clear your calendar. You won't put this book down."

LIFE WITHOUT AIR

As Norah, Grace, and Colton grapple with the loss of their only child, eyes are watching. The game master toys with their emotions, tormenting and harassing the three unnerved players through cryptic and terrifying warnings and threats. Instead of looking forward, they begin watching over their shoulders.

"Spellbinding, heart-wrenching, and hopeful. It's a black hole of family secrets."

OUTSIDE THE LINES

Tilly Wilson, a flawed and crotchety 89-year-old, takes 23-year-old Bell Levitsky, an orphan with terminal cancer, under her wing. Together, the two support one another as they squeeze every ounce of life from their remaining days.

"The characters are perfectly broken and beautiful. This truly is a book about living—not dying."

THE STORMS OF EDDIE GREER

For generations, the Greer men have perfected the fine art of assholery. And Eddie Greer does not disappoint. When his life implodes after seamlessly stepping into his old man's role following his father's questionable death, he can't shake the feeling his story is more twisted than he knows.

"Unforgettable characters you will hate, empathize with, and root for."

DISCUSSION QUESTIONS

Discussion questions for all books can be found at
MaryPerrine.com

REVIEWS

If you loved the book, please write a review.
You are the reason books sell.